KALANAY

A Tale of the Mountains

First Published in 2025 by
First Nations Writers Festival International Limited
T/as First Nations Publishers

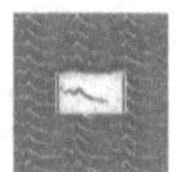

A Registered Charity (ABN 79 655 932 979)

2/53 Junction St, Nowra NSW 2540, Australia
Phone: +61 491 851 353

Email: firstnationswritersfestival@gmail.com
Web: www.firstnationswritersfestival.org
FB: www.facebook.com/firstnationswritersfestival.com

Cover Design: Busybird Publishing
Typeset: Busybird Publishing
Line Edited: Anna Borsi AM 2025
Printed and bound in Australia by IngramSpark

A catalogue record for this book is available from the National Library of Australia

KALANAY

A TALE OF THE MOUNTAINS

Chapter I

Daniel was in a jeepney on his way to work. As he looked around, he noticed the variety of passengers on board. In front of him, a grandmother was holding her grandson on her lap. Beside him, a man in a sharp suit and glasses was engrossed in a book. Four teenagers in school uniforms sat next to him, each with a book in hand. Adjacent to them, a woman with red hair and a daring outfit caught his eyes with a glimmer of desire. The jeepney hit a barrier that caught everybody off-guard causing the vehicle to spin.

The jeepney with its weak structure threw out the passengers with the windows at the back, and those at the front went through a now shattered windshield. The driver, and front seat passenger's face, were ravaged by impaled shards of glass that resembled a porcupine's back. The lady with the gorgeous dress was shredded into pieces. Guts all around and red stains of blood painted the interior of the vehicle. Distorted bodies with an eye popped from the socket and every other body part shuffled from its proper structure.

It was a disturbing scene that no one should have to witness. Even the first responders struggled to handle the situation. The bodies and accident scene were cleared after the investigation, but Daniel's body was never recovered.

A group of children were playing near a pile of garbage on the side of the road close to where the accident had occurred. They quickly scattered when one of them spotted Daniel's body among the debris. Emergency services were called, and rescuers initially believed he was deceased due to the time that had passed, a few hours later. However, they were amazed and considered it a miracle to discover signs of life as he was being transported in the ambulance to the hospital.

Daniel found himself in the darkness, surrounded by the strong scent of pine filling the air. Trying to stand and move forward, he felt a prickling sensation as if needles were piercing his skin. He had to rely on touch to navigate, grasping onto the rough surface of a tree trunk at times. Despite the discomfort, he persevered until he saw a faint light, which filled him with a glimmer of hope.

"Finally, some light. Maybe there's someone here who can help," he thought, gasping for breath.

The light revealed an empty grassy field with no one in sight. He noticed his white shirt was stained with blood and dirt, but his black leather shoes were still in good condition. His black slacks had tears in various places. He continued to walk, pushing himself to keep going. He arrived at a solitary house constructed from bamboo and a thatched roof made of dried grass and uneven pieces of wood. The house was empty and spacious.

He lay on the bamboo floor and fell asleep. His body was so beaten; he could hardly take another step. "What is going on? Where the hell am I?" he muttered. His lips quivering, his eyes were closing like a window in a stream and his system went into a resting phase.

He was awakened by the noise of a crowd of people. He went outside to find a group of men wearing loincloths and bearing weapons on their upper torsos, holding spears and knives as if they were prepared to harm him. He raised his hands to show that he meant no harm, saying, "I am not a bad guy."

Two men pushed him to the ground, tied his arms behind his back with a rough rope that caused bruises, and forced him to stand and move forward by kicking his back. They had perplexed faces because it was the first time they had seen a man fully clothed with footwear. They took off his shoes and tattered clothes, inspecting them closely, leaving him fully naked.

"Please, I have no ill intentions towards you. I am not your enemy," Daniel pleaded. One handed him his sash as a makeshift loincloth for Daniel.

They ascended a massive mountain that left him struggling to keep up against the men's impressive gait. At times, two of the men had to pull him along with his feet dragging on the ground, creating pain from the scraping.

They reached a cluster of 'kubo' houses similar to the one Daniel had slept in. Among them was a unique structure in the center, with more elaborate wooden walls, a grass roof, and intricate carvings on the panels with animal and human skulls displayed around the structure.

A man, larger than the others and adorned with what appeared to be golden beads and earrings, emerged from the structure.

Daniel was pushed to the ground, causing him to kneel before the large man whom everybody revered. "Who is this peasant before me?" he asked. "I am Daniel and please, don't hurt me. I have no idea how I got here. I mean you no harm," he pleaded with all his might almost depleting.

A tinier man, with long hair and a staff adorned with colourful feathers, observed Daniel closely. His eyes widened and trembled like an intense earthquake. He lit a cigarette rolled with some kind of a leaf using two crystals rubbed against each other that produced a spark. He gazed at the sky, chanting and raising his hand along with the staff.

The large man instructed some of his mistresses to accompany Daniel down the river to clean him with what they believed was water with healing properties. Six of the most beautiful mistresses assisted him in his ablutions, with two on each side wrapping his arms on the back of their necks, two in front, and two at the back carrying baskets of herbs.

They moved at a slow pace as they neared the bottom of the ravine, the sound of rushing water growing louder. The mistresses soaked him in the shallow part for a while, gently rubbing his skin with river moss to remove any dirt that lodged in his wounds. They then took him out of the water and applied the crushed herbs to his injuries.

Daniel, feeling rejuvenated, walked back without assistance from the mistresses, admiring their beauty and the perfect forms of their bodies especially the exposed flesh of their upper torso. He tried to conceal his sensual desire as his mouth watered and his body warmed up. It wasn't until later that he realised he was also naked with a strengthened manhood. The mistresses appeared unaffected and kept moving next to Daniel.

"Bring the stranger to me," were the words spoken by the large man as soon as Daniel and the mistresses arrived.

Daniel was brought forward by the mistresses. Another group, the older ladies, dressed him in a loincloth with red and black stripes and a cloth sash. He was then directed to the 'mambabatek,' who was in charge of giving tattoos. Daniel was initially very adamant, but he ultimately decided to comply with the leader's wishes to avoid causing a riot among the people.

The small man who had performed the prayer was revealed to be the 'mambunong,' the high priest and healer who, guided by nature and the gods, instructed the 'mambabatek' to mark Daniel with the tattoo of an eagle on his shoulder, symbolising something soaring high in the sky.

Daniel was unaware of what was being discussed and what he was about to undergo. The 'mambabatek' ground charcoal into a powder using a mortar and pestle made of coconut shell and wood, then mixed it with water from the river and herbal oils. Using a stick with a pomelo thorn, she started tapping on Daniel's shoulder, piercing the ink in his skin.

Five men had to hold him down as each tap of the thorn caused intense pain unlike anything he had ever felt before. He gritted his teeth and tried not to scream, not wanting to upset the community any further. The 'mambabatek' used her own homemade oil extracted from the 'diman kalumot' plant/five fingers plant/marijuana plant on the tattooed area, used to alleviate pain, prevent swelling of the newly etched tattoos and used to heal various illnesses.

"Behold the man marked by the majestic eagle," Ba-ay presented Daniel to the village after the tattoo was completed.

The community erupted in cheers once again and prepared for the celebratory ritual of "canao." The large man instructed the villagers to slaughter the finest boar in the pen.

Men struggled to hold the squirming boar in place. One of them used a sharp stick to pierce the animal's heart, causing it to squeal loudly, as if calling out to the gods believed to dwell on the nearby mountain, Mt. Pulag.

Daniel covered his ears and shut his eyes, unable to bear the gruesome sight. The boar was then dissected, and its entrails were examined by the Ba-ay, who interpreted it as a good omen. The animal's skin was then burned to remove its fur and cut into large pieces to be boiled in a communal pot without any seasoning. More boars were deemed unnecessary, as the animal butchered would suffice for everyone present.

Jars of rice wine fermented from 'kintoman' or red rice were presented, with an elder man assigned to scoop each serving using a coconut shell and transfer the juice to bamboo containers for everyone to enjoy.

Daniel, being the guest of honour, was given the privilege of taking the first sip before participating in the 'tayaw dance,' a celebratory dance. Two elders played the 'gangza,' a plate-shaped bronze instrument, using wooden sticks, while two others sat on wooden benches playing the 'sulibao,' a long drum-like instrument struck with the palms of their hands. Daniel's heartbeat got faster; his eyes were concentrated on the people performing before him hoping he could execute the movements the right way.

Ba-ay, handed him two heavy cloths and gestured for him to drape them over his shoulders and extend his arms. A female partner wrapped a cloth around her body and raised her hands opened, revealing her palms. Together, all participants moved in a circular motion until the music stopped, signaling the end of the 'tayaw' dance.

Loud outcries of "Oway! Oway! Whooo! Whooo!" was repeated twice during the dance believed to fend off evil spirits and bad luck.

The large man sat on a high wooden chair adorned with intricate carvings of an eagle on the backrest and idols on the sides, facing the celebration. A large snake coiled nearby. Ba-ay sat on his right side, with an empty chair on the left. "Come and join us," he commanded after Daniel finished the tayaw dance.

"You did well," the large man said, handing him some rice wine in a coconut shell.

"Thank you," Daniel replied followed by a deep breath.

"Thank you, your highness Kibara. That's what you should say," Ba-ay whispered into Daniel's ear.

"I officially welcome you to Dutab Kingdom," Kibara said as he smiled at both Daniel and Ba-ay.

Kibara expressed his love for the thrill of hunting and insisted that Daniel join him on a planned hunting trip during the festivities. Anticipating Ba-ay's prediction, Kibara arranged a hunting day with Daniel and a group of warriors in the Ahey Forest. They encountered a herd of wild boar grazing, which quickly scattered when they sensed the hunters.

Kibara chased after them on foot and successfully threw his spear, killing one by striking it in the skull. The warriors encouraged Daniel to take a shot, but his spear missed the mark and narrowly avoided hitting a fellow warrior after bouncing off a rock.

The warriors were laughing, imitating the failed attempt of Daniel with Kibara giving him a disappointed look.

"Your leadership. I apologise. I don't know what I'm doing," Daniel said. Kibara did not respond. He and his warriors were set to return to Dutab Kingdom. Daniel looked down, grabbed his spear and followed on.

Kibara went straight to Ba-ay's quarters where he was blending herbs.

"Who is this feeble person with a puny body that can barely hold a spear?" He asked Ba-ay with flaring nostrils so that Ba-ay could feel every breath he took.

"Your highness, he is significant. He is the individual I foresaw."

"May the gods curse him. Perhaps your vision is flawed?"

"No, your highness. Just give him some time."

Daniel ran quickly to his quarters near Kibara's, trying to avoid being seen by anyone. Using only the power of his mind, he was still trying to make sense of everything and figure out how to get back to his own world.

Sungkian, the warrior leader was skilled, adept in both combat and hunting. He was selected based on his lineage of renowned warriors, similar to how leaders and influential figures were chosen in society. He often visited a group of malevolent witches called 'mamantala' who lived on Ayungan hills to the west without being noticed by the Dutab villagers.

These seven elderly women were once beautiful in their youth, but illness had transformed this visage into beastly appearances. They lived in seclusion in a dark cave, and anyone who dared to enter would disappear in a mysterious manner. Sungkian would offer gold and make promises of granting them ruling power in exchange for their guidance and wisdom during his consultations.

"Great 'mamantalas' I seek your guidance. Accept this offering I present to you" Sungkian said as he handed the finest rice wine, the bulkiest meat and the sweetest honey to them.

"Who dare disturb me?" KopKopit, the 'mamantala' leader asked.

"It is me Sungkian of Dutab Kingdom. I wish to rid myself of this foreigner. This Daniel who was declared as the one. Whatever that means."

The 'mamantalas' would form a circle, with a large crystal at the center emitting various colours. They chanted prayers and placed their hands on the crystal, causing it to spark and create a powerful fire with smoke reaching the skies. Within the smoke, various shapes and sizes appeared, which only the 'mamantalas' could interpret. They provided Sungkian with instructions that he needed to follow upon his return to Dutab Kingdom.

For days after Daniel's discovery, there had been no rain in the world. Rivers and lakes had dried up, rice fields were parched, and the soil had cracked from the lack of moisture. The hunting pack struggled to find live animals, only encountering rotting flesh and bare bones emitting foul odours. The once green landscape had turned brown, and villagers were falling ill due to lack of nourishment.

In a desperate hunger-fueled rage, the villagers gathered at Kibara's frontage, pleading, "Our leader, we can't endure this any longer. Our children are getting sick, and we are falling ill."

Similar sentiments were echoed with loud cries filling the air. Daniel himself was uncertain about the situation. He had ideas to alleviate the suffering caused by the water shortage, but they were too advanced for this century to implement.

Kibara demanded Ba-ay's presence. "Quiet," Ba-ay commanded, waiting for the villagers to be calm before beginning the ritual. He recited a prayer in front of the gathered crowd, then tossed a handful of soil into the air. Instructing some men to bring a native chicken, he drew his dagger and with the swiftness of his hand, he slit its neck. The chicken was positioned on the ground, its wings flapping as it struggled, and its blood dripped onto the soil.

"Oh Kabigat, God of the granary and harvest, we seek your divine help. Accept this sacrifice as our offering," Ba-ay recited.

"Return to your homes, for the God Kabigat has heard our sorrows," he told the people.

A few of the villagers returned home with some still waiting for immediate result. Kibara had to interrupt and reiterate what Ba-ay had emphasised before they returned home. Yet days had passed and nothing changed, and this made everybody impatient. Ba-ay's rituals did not seem to work.

The opportunity was ideal for Sungkian to carry out his plan, but he was also impacted by the phenomenon, causing his mind to be preoccupied with the situation.

The villagers once more gathered together for another rebellion, but a heavy rainstorm came. There was an unusual occurrence where each raindrop was red in colour, but after a few drops, the colour changed to white, which was different from the usual colourless nature of rain.

The rice fields were flooded causing rivers and lakes to swell downstream. The ground became saturated as everyone basked in the gentle rain. It was later discovered that God Kabigat had sacrificed himself by cutting open his stomach, causing a mixture of blood and milk to drip onto the land, making it more fertile than ever before.

Celebrations filled the land. 'Canao' was done to signify thanks to the God Kabigat for the miraculous intervention. The first harvests and best hunts laid on top of a large rock in the east as an 'atang' or offering to Kabigat, accompanied by prayers recited by Ba-ay. The offerings were left there until they disappeared, indicating that the gods had accepted them.

Daniel participated in the festivities, but his mind was consumed by the cries of thinking. He continued to ponder how he had traveled back to the era of his ancestors and how he could find his way back to his own time.

Sungkian and his loyal followers joined in the festivities, pretending to take part. His loyal followers offered to help the elder in charge of preparing the 'tapuy.' When no one was looking, they secretly added powdered crystals obtained from the 'mamantala' to the drink. The villagers didn't notice the crystals at first, but after taking another sip, it was too late. They fell into a deep unconscious state, lying still on the ground, except for a few who remained awake, mostly women and children who hadn't consumed the tainted drink.

Daniel didn't feel like drinking, avoiding the crystal-laced rice wine. This allowed Sungkian and his followers to seize control of the Kingdom. Both the subdued villagers and the unconscious individuals were either confined in bamboo cages or had their arms tied behind their backs with vine ropes.

"I am now in charge. I have sovereignty over Dutab Kingdom," the self-proclaimed leader, Sungkian announced. His loyal followers bowed before him, ready to fulfill his every command.

A powerful wind swept through the Kingdom, destroying all the houses except for the leader's quarters. From the earth emerged the 'imbagyans,' complete human skeletons, wielding 'gamans' - axes used for headhunting with sharp edges on one side and hooks on the opposite. Sungkian, or Kanguy, and his followers were frozen in place, unable to move. The 'imbagyans' beheaded them with the sharp edges of their 'gamans.' As their dark spirits escaped from their bodies, the hooks of the 'gamans' pulled them down into the underworld below the earth alongside the 'imbagyans.'

Kanguy and his followers experienced the repercussions of their deeds, enduring torment in the red-abyss of hot lava of the underworld while Napuagan enjoyed their anguish. "We will follow your every command. Oh, God Napuagan. Just show us mercy," a voice pleaded, their cries reverberating through the eternal punishment of the underworld. The pleas fell on deaf ears. The cries of tortured souls were like music to Napuagan.

The wind ceased, and the sun illuminated the Kingdom once more. The inhabitants awoke, disoriented by the recent events. Kibara, using his exceptional strength, managed to break free from his restraints. He assisted others in freeing themselves from their cages and bindings. After surveying the damage, he instructed the people to begin repairs. Although they were still perplexed by what had transpired, Kibara and the others remained determined to rebuild the Kingdom.

Men gathered materials from the nearby forest, including bamboos, wood, and leaves. Women and children helped by weaving the leaves into strong sheets for roofs. The materials and foundations were not perfect, but they had to rush the repairs. Amidst their work, they found the decapitated bodies of several men, including Kanguy, identified by his tattoos. "These men made a deal with the wrong forces and suffered the consequences," Ba-ay explained.

Daniel observed all the supernatural events and tried to assist in his own way. "Here comes the one," a warrior remarked in a sarcastic manner. Daniel struggled to carry the smallest piece of wood back to the kingdom, while the others carried massive tree trunks with ease.

He then tried to dig a hole, but it was too shallow when he attempted to insert a tree trunk. "You should take a break and let us handle the rest," another warrior suggested. The group looked at him with disparagement, implying that he might not be the one due to his unsatisfactory efforts.

Chapter II

From the eastern part of the Balkek Mountains, the 'mamantalas' gathered at Bulalakaw lake in their natural beauty, ready to attract men for mating during their fertile periods coinciding with the blood moon's peak. They appeared revealing too much sweetness, emitting irresistible allures that enticed strong young men to saturate their tempting bodies.

After intimate encounters, the 'mamantalas' absorbed the men's life essence, turning them to dust. Nine blood moons later, they gave birth to 'mamantala' females or 'busol' males who would become headhunters. The infants resembled their mother if female and had large, muscular, dark features if male. The 'mamantalas' then returned to their original forms after.

The 'busols' in various regions established their own communities with the goal of eradicating those who were not like them and seizing control of villages. In contrast, the 'mamantalas' were dispersed among villages, living in seclusion either alone or with companions in caves and remote areas rarely visited by people, much like their mothers.

Kuchep, a mamantala, stood out from her peers due to her unique qualities. Despite being a member of her kind, she possessed the rare ability to appear as a regular maiden, captivating all who beheld her with her grace and beauty. Born in the Dutab Kingdom, her mother had made the mistake of falling in love with a mortal man, a simple hunter-gatherer without any special status. Their relationship was kept hidden, known only to a select few close relatives of her father. Kuchep's exceptional skill in transforming ordinary fibers from plants and animal furs into intricate cloths made her one of the most talented weavers in the Kingdom.

Despite the allure of Kuchep, Kibara held the most influence. He frequently sought out Kuchep's company, occasionally using his position as the Kingdom's leader to do so. He admired her ability to maintain eye contact during their discussions, a trait uncommon among women who were usually shorter than men. Her dark hair carried a pleasant herbal aroma, evoking natural scents rather than the artificial fragrances favored by Ba-ay in his ceremonies.

"What are your desires in life? I could fulfill them for you. You can command my men to do whatever you wish," Kibara said with a smile during one of Kuchep's visits. Without uttering a word, Kuchep responded with her typical seductive smile.

"I must depart now," she said after a moment and quickly returned to her home. She found more fulfillment in staying occupied with her duties than in being waited on at Kibara's.

Daniel was motivated to succeed in his endeavors, a change from his usual lackluster self. He hoped to prevent any possible resentment from Kibara for not fulfilling his responsibilities in the kingdom, especially since Kibara was also interested in Kuchep. He willingly took on tasks like hunting and carrying heavy logs or boulders for construction, despite his own doubts about his abilities. During a hunting trip, a group member sarcastically called him "oh wise Daniel," while another jokingly bowed down. As they trekked through a field of lanky grass, a herd of native deer approached. The group members chased after them without waiting for instructions, leaving Daniel behind. Disoriented by the thick vegetation, Daniel ran in the opposite direction.

He continued running, hoping that his speed would eventually catch up with others, but he soon realised that he was alone. His mind was commanding him with clashing information forcing him to slow down and he collapsed, unconscious.

The lanky grass concealed him from passing travelers, until an old man with long gray hair and a beard detected his presence. The old man found Daniel lying on the ground and, despite his age, managed to carry him to the top of the 7th mountain. He laid Daniel on a wooden floor covered with preserved animal skin.

Daniel woke staring at an unfamiliar ceiling. The room was filled with various sticks and blades of different shapes and sizes. As he stepped outside, he noticed an elderly man with a grey beard and long hair sitting cross-legged with his eyes closed under a pine tree. The man seemed to emit a powerful energy that manifested as waves of rainbow-coloured air.

Daniel approached the man, but the man's agility caught his hand as he tried to touch him. Opening his eyes, the man greeted Daniel and invited him to join him. Daniel sat beside the old man for a while, but grew tired and uncomfortable. He decided to lay down on the ground and fell asleep.

Daniel was jolted awake by a sudden splash of water on his face. The elderly man stood before him, holding a bucket. "Come inside and have a drink," he offered. Using a delicate teapot adorned with colourful designs, he poured a steaming liquid into two matching cups. Taking one cup for himself, he took a sip and motioned for Daniel to do the same. Daniel was taken and thrown off guard by the scalding heat of the drink and its unappealing taste. Despite accidentally dropping the cup on the wooden floor, it remained intact. The old man simply smiled at him.

Embarrassed by his actions, Daniel leaned over to pick up the cup and wiped the spilled tea with his bare hands. Glancing at the old man, who appeared unfazed, he marveled at the man's composure. The old man poured another cup of hot tea and handed it to Daniel, who made sure to hold it steady this time, determined not to spill a single drop.

"Your name is Daniel, isn't it?" the old man asked after taking a sip.

Surprised, Daniel asked, "How did you know my name?"

"The stars foretold me that a stranger would come someday," the old man explained. Daniel was speechless.

"Finish your tea and get prepared. We don't want to waste any more time."

"Prepared for what?"

They finished their tea and the old man went outside, gesturing for Daniel to follow.

"Do you see the rocks down there?"

"Oh, the rocks by the river?"

"Go down there and gather some rocks, then return and do it again. I will tell you when to stop," the old man instructed Daniel, who hesitated before considering the distance he would need to cover. The old man hit him with the staff in his hand, encouraging him to begin.

As he descended, a protruding root snagged one of his feet, causing him to roll. He was slow to get up and tried to climb as fast as possible, but the pain from the accident slowed him down. The old man grabbed his arm as he neared his destination. With a swift motion, the old man stretched Daniel's arm, causing him to scream in pain. He then examined the rest of Daniel's body and instructed him to sit.

Taking hold of Daniel's ankles, he manipulated them, causing Daniel to scream once more. The echoes of his screams disturbed the birds in the trees, causing them to fly away, and the wild animals to roar.

"This is enough for now. Go and rest. You'll need it tomorrow," the old man said.

Later that evening, two bowls made of the same material as the teapot were placed on the floor with two pairs of wooden sticks in each bowl. The old man served soup, rice, and meat. "Eat for your nourishment."

Daniel noticed the sticks and observed the old man use them to pick up the meat. He struggled to do the same and ended up eating with his hands, similar to the people of Dutab Kingdom. The old man then showed him how to use the sticks properly.

Daniel wanted to ask the old man's name, where he was from, and why he lived alone, but the old man was not one for many words. As Daniel observed the old man in silence, he finally mustered the courage to start a conversation.

"What's your name?"

"I'm Li Men," the old man replied, still gazing into space.

"Have you always lived alone?"

"I come from a land called Formosa. We arrived here years ago for trade, but our ship sank in a storm," Li Men explained, now looking directly at Daniel.

"You are not from this era. You are from the centuries ahead of us," he added.

Daniel gazed directly at Li Men with keen eyes, utterly incredulous at the words escaping the old man's lips. "He's so incredibly wise, it's almost otherworldly," his thoughts marveled.

The beginning of Daniel's true training began as Li Men woke up before sunrise, washing his face and rinsing his mouth with the cold, invigorating spring water flowing from a split bamboo near his home.

"Wake up. Wake up your senses for the day." Li Men exclaimed.

Daniel looked over the same landscape he had seen the day before while Li Men stretched his arms and legs. Determined not to make the same mistake again, Daniel took a careful step forward. Although he briefly lost his balance, he quickly regained it thanks to his pre-walk stretching. With the keen eyesight of an owl, he followed Li Men's movements until told to halt. Despite the challenging workout, he only felt a slight hint of fatigue in his body.

Li Men was preparing a tonic using a recipe from his homeland, adapting it to the ingredients available in their current location. "Drink this tonic. It will boost your strength, activated by your body heat."

Daniel hesitated to drink the tonic again because of its unpleasant smell and found it extremely bitter upon tasting.

"Drink it all at once."

Daniel was ready to chase the tonic drink with water, but Li Men cautioned him against it. Daniel grimaced in distaste. Li Men directed Daniel to retrieve a log from the yard, place it on his own set of shoulders. And then, to utilise its weight to bend the knees in order to develop strength.

Daniel felt a newfound sense of strength that he had never before experienced. Li Men was pleased with Daniel's progress. As time went on and Daniel's training intensified, Li Men believed that the young man was prepared to learn the ancestral fighting style from his homeland.

Daniel's once frail and lanky body evolved into a muscular form capable of handling heavy loads. Every part of his body became a tool for self-defense against potential dangers. Daniel punched a wooden plank in succession until his fists bled, strengthening his lower body with powerful kicks against the sturdy surface. He mastered the use of blades and blunt sticks, honing his agility by climbing trees like a monkey. His abdomen became as solid as a boulder, transforming him into a formidable version of himself.

Daniel ventured into the forest and encountered a group of wild boars with sharp teeth, two of which protruded like tusks. The animals perceived him as a threat, and the mothers with their piglets stuck together and started to flee.

The larger boars with the sharp tusks charged with heightened aggression aiming to harm him. He grabbed a rock and managed to knock one down. The remaining boars continued to pursue him, but upon realising the danger they were facing, they fled from his presence, leaving behind the lifeless body of their fallen companion. He carried the dead animal on the back of his neck, securing it by holding both legs.

"Master Li Men, I got us a boar," he said in excitement.

He unloaded the animal in front of the house, calling out for Master Li Men again, but received no response. After searching the house and the lot, he found the old man unconscious in the ravine where he trained. He rushed to rescue him and brought him back to the house, but it was too late. There was no sign of life. His cries echoed through the area, with birds flying in all directions and beasts howling from the forest.

He pondered why Master Li Men, as he referred to the old man, had passed away despite his strength and resilience, even at his advanced age. There were no signs of animal attacks or puncture wounds from weapons. Master Li Men simply lay lifeless, indicating that his life had ended suddenly.

He spent his days inactive, staying indoors and allowing his body to revert to its previous state, gradually shrinking. While sleeping in the darkness under the moon's glow, he felt a connection to his old mentor, who seemed to be calling out to him. The old man's voice conveyed concern and urged him not to squander the skills he had been taught, reminding him of his purpose on earth. Waking to the warmth of the sun on his face, he contemplated the message he may have received from his late master.

After the morning meal of edible fruits he found in the forest, he continued the training he had received from his mentor.

He entered the storage room, which was separated from the main house, and was immediately hit with the stench of the old man's decaying flesh mixed with the preserved herbs in jars. He felt a duty to give his master a respectful burial. However, he couldn't help but think of the customs of his master's home country when it came to the dead. Seeing the state of the old man's body, he decided to start a fire in the storage room not considering the consequences for the main house, which soon became engulfed in flames due to his reckless action.

Everything was destroyed except for a single sword. He strapped the sword to his back and watched as the flames consumed everything around him. With a heavy heart, he knew he had to leave in search of the purpose his master had implanted in his mind, unable to hold onto the memories they had shared as master and student.

He started his journey from the training ground, filling a container made from a carabao's hide with water from the river. The strong waves and current made crossing the waters a challenge, but he decided to swim across despite the difficult conditions.

The rising water level and powerful current pushed him towards the east side of the river, and he tried to navigate to avoid hitting any large rocks, but the force of the water determined his direction. Just as he was about to collide with a large rock in his path, a beautiful fair-skinned lady with long blonde hair and a fish tail appeared.

She was Angban, the spirit of the waters, and she flicked her tail at Daniel, causing him to steer clear of the rock. The water became calmer, and she guided him for the remainder of his swim.

He rose to his feet as he arrived at the shallow part of the river. He proceeded towards the mountainside, thanking Angban for her help. With a flick of her tail, she disappeared.

Continuing on, he found a large tree with ample leaves for shade. As night fell, he settled down to sleep under the tree.

Master Li Men, his upper body fully formed, floated gracefully with his tail of clouds in the sky. Daniel lay on a grassy plain, observing his master as he approached. Suddenly, his master stumbled and collided with a tall tree, falling onto a bed of thorns that pierced his cheek first. Despite Daniel's desire to help, he found himself rooted to the grassy ground, unable to move from the spot.

Daniel felt a pricking sensation on his right cheek and woke up to find a spear tip near his face. He saw a group of dark-skinned men in white loincloths, kinky dark hair and short stature, were standing around him, with one man holding the spear and another had his sword.

"Who are you and why are you here?" the man with the spear demanded.

"I am Daniel, just a traveler passing through."

One man forced him to kneel while another held his arms behind his back with a sturdy vine. After making him stand up, they kept a spear pointed at his back and instructed him to move forward. Daniel ended up leading the group, with others following closely behind him.

They arrived at a cluster of houses perched on the uneven terrain of a mountain. Some were built on trees, some on rocks, and some on flat ground. Daniel was shoved into a bamboo cage with another man. The cage was suspended in the air by a rope anchored to a tree, with a large carnivorous beast below in a dug-out pit.

It was a sight that Daniel had never witnessed before. The other captive, a bald man with a long black beard, was trembling in fear. The men surrounding the pit were shouting and making loud noises. To the right, a heavily seated man with white face paint and a shell necklace sat on a sturdy chair with Daniel's sword at his side, signaled thumbs down, prompting the other men to untie the rope. The cage fell, cracking open and exposing Daniel and his companion to the beast.

"Don't worry. Stay behind me," Daniel reassured him.

The beast lashed out with its sharp claws, and Daniel showcased his skill by dodging the attacks with high jumps and twisting motions of his body. He signaled for his companion to run and duck the beast's attacks. The man behind him ran to the opposite side and attempted to climb the rocky wall of the pit, diverting the beast's attention. Seizing the opportunity, Daniel climbed the edge and leapt onto the beast's back, delivering a series of powerful punches. The beast toppled forward, attempting to bite Daniel, but he managed to lift it and hurl it towards the men.

The men scattered, some of them falling victim to the beast.

"This is our chance. Let's go," Daniel urged his companion. They scrambled out of the pit. Daniel punched the heavily seated man and took his sword before they sprinted in one direction without looking back.

"I can't... I can't make it. Just leave me," Daniel's companion pleaded. "No, we have to keep moving. We can't be sure if we're safe here," Daniel insisted, helping his companion along.

They remained flat and hidden in the tall bushes as some men searched for them, gripping some spears, 'hinlung', and 'gaman' ready to strike. Daniel covered his companion's mouth to muffle his heavy breathing, which sounded like the howls of wild dogs. He only removed his hand when they no longer sensed the men's presence.

After a moment of silence, Daniel spoke up. "Why were you in such a dangerous place?"

"My... fellow villagers and I... were fishing when we spotted the men in the... distance. They... ran away, but before I... could do anything, they captured me. Those... despicable 'illios.' Yes, they... are 'illios.' They... capture anyone who is not one of them for their... own pleasure, just like... they did to us! Sorry... sorry you might be annoyed by my repetition... repetition. I don't know... know. I... I am just like this... this from my childhood.

"Don't worry about it and same here. They appeared out of nowhere and captured me. I'm Daniel, by the way from faraway place and time."

"I'm Betot from the Bokodian Village in the west and what... what do you mean faraway... time and place?"

"Never mind. I'm actually from Dutab Kingdom."

Chapter III

Betot became Daniel's faithful companion during their journey. While traveling, they noticed a shrill noise emanating from a rocky section of the mountain. They meticulously combed through every rock, bush, and tree in the vicinity in search of the source of the sound. Suddenly, a sizable wild dog, visibly in distress, limped towards Betot. The animal collapsed at his feet, prompting Betot to offer it water from his container. Betot's immediate nurturing instinct shone through, reminiscent of a mother tending to her offspring.

"That dog is too big for us to carry, especially since it can barely walk," Daniel remarked upon closer inspection of the animal.

"Perhaps the dog just needs some rest. It's… it's getting dark anyway. Let's rest here and share some of our food… food," Betot suggested.

Although Daniel was hesitant, they decided to rest under a tree with the dog. He made a fire with twigs and leaves while Betot tended to the animal. He roasted some mushrooms he had gathered, providing a meal for all of them.

Betot was woken up by the dog licking his face. The dog then went over to Daniel, who was sleeping with his mouth wide open, and pissed on it. "Curses! No! Stop it!" Daniel yelled while spitting out the urine. He rose to his feet and tried to kick the dog in the face, but the animal anticipated the movement of his foot enough to dodge it, showcasing its impressive agility.

Betot chuckled from the sidelines as he watched the scene unfold. He stretched and pulled Daniel by the head. "Just remember, you're the one who insisted on keeping the dog," Daniel said in irritation.

Betot mumbled incoherent high-pitched female-like words as Daniel restrained him.

"Have you finished? Can I let you go now?" Daniel asked, his expression stern.

The dog sat, tongue hanging out, panting and watching them.

Daniel went downstream to wash himself and remove the smell of dog urine.

They proceeded towards the northern side of the mountain, as Daniel was confident it was the right path to Dutab Kingdom. He kept walking without looking back at Betot and the dog trailing behind him. Betot's legs started to feel tired from the continuous walking, and he eventually had to stop and take a break when they reached a forest.

"Daniel, can we please rest for a bit?" Betot asked. The dog stayed silent but went over to Betot and laid its head on his lap. Meanwhile, Daniel stayed composed and showed no signs of exhaustion.

"Okay, stay put and wait for me here," Daniel instructed Betot, who was sitting with the dog under a pine tree.

Daniel walked over to the sparkling objects on a tree at a distance that had caught his attention. Upon closer inspection, he found red, round fruit the size of a wild boar's eye balls that he hadn't seen before. Without hesitation, he picked some and took a bite, savoring the sweet, juicy and enjoyable taste. He returned to Betot and shared the fruits with him. To their astonishment, the dog also enjoyed some.

They ate all the fruit until they were too full to eat more. While resting, they were surprised by loud hissing noises. The air was filled with the smell of rotting flesh. They immediately became alert and searched for the source of the disturbance. The bushes moved, uncovering green beings that looked like skeletal humans with ferns for hair. The creatures attacked them suddenly. Betot's dog courageously protected him by biting any creature that approached. Daniel unsheathed his sword and swiftly dealt with the creatures that attacked him. They ran away together from the threatening creatures.

"Head towards the cliff! The cliff" Betot yelled.

One of the creatures leapt onto Betot's shoulder and bit him. He fought back, rolling on the ground and delivering punches to the creature's head until it released its grip, leaving a small piece of flesh behind.

"Towards the… the cliff!" Betot shouted again.

"They… they will keep on leaping, even risking falling… falling off the edge," he added.

They discovered a cliff with jutting rocks on the side. Both of them leapt and clung to the rocks as the creatures continued to plummet to their demise. Daniel hoisted himself up using his own strength. Betot, however, had weakened strength and let out screams resembling those of a woman.

Daniel was puzzled as he only had Betot as his human companion. Peering down, he spotted Betot teetering on the edge of falling. Acting swiftly, he grabbed onto whatever he could and managed to pull Betot up with a firm grip on his arm. With rapid breaths, he successfully rescued Betot, both of them lying down, exhausted.

The Dog had a mouth filled with a yellow substance from attacking the creatures. Daniel quickly searched for plants with healing properties he had been taught by Li Men. He let Betot take a break while he used a rock to crush the leaves of the plant on a solid surface. After using up their remaining water to clean the wound, he applied the crushed plants directly to the injury.

"Ayayay!" Betot exclaimed. Daniel recognised the sounds coming from Betot once more, resembling a woman's cry. Daniel paid no attention to the cry and squeezed the plant's juices directly to the wound, instructing, "Remain still and endure the pain. These plants will aid in healing your wound."

The dog fell to the ground. Daniel approached the animal and observed that it was not breathing. After inspecting its body, he found a significant gash on the belly with the guts exposed. Betot shed a tear upon seeing the dog's condition.

Daniel glanced at Betot and shook his head. He urged him to get up. "We should leave now and abandon the dog. It's not safe here," Daniel said, supporting Betot with his uninjured arm around Daniel's shoulders and neck. Betot attempted to look back at the dog, but his injuries prevented him from turning his head. "I've known about the kutuktins that attacked us in the forest, those man-eating monsters but this is my first encounter with them," he remarked.

On a distant mountain peak, was a silhouette that resembled a man's head with pure black hair. As they drew closer, they found wild chickens with entirely black features - black feathers, beaks, comb, and feet. Betot preferred not to disturb them in their natural habitat, but Daniel had a different plan. He ran towards the chickens and grabbed two in each hand. Betot, though injured and wanting to stop Daniel, couldn't intervene. They believed the birds were the dangerous black 'balkaks' that could cause incurable illness if consumed. To avoid any potential consequences, they quickly left the area.

"Please… please release the birds," Betot pleaded.

Daniel continued walking, seemingly disregarding Betot's plea. Betot hesitated to approach him once more, worried about his possible reaction. The chickens were flapping and wriggling on Daniel's waist as they proceeded on their journey. Betot chose not to press the matter any further and allowed Daniel to be, in order to prevent any potential conflict. Suddenly, Daniel stopped at a sizable rock and forcefully struck the chickens against it, startling Betot.

The chickens were hanging with blood dripping from their beaks, a disturbing sight for Betot. On the left side, there were large pine trees and fruit-bearing trees arranged in a circular formation, blocking the view of what was at the center. Intrigued by some smoke and their curiosity, they turned away from their original path. As they went closer, they realised it was a village, guarded by men with spears and shields at the entrance.

One of the guards questioned, "Who are you and why are you here?"

"We are just travelers passing through," Daniel replied.

A man adorned in a loincloth and a long-sleeved shirt embellished with gold and semi-precious stones, wearing headgear made of woven rattan and eagle feathers, emerged. His mouth appeared full with the gesture of spitting on the ground with a red-coloured substance. The guards and Betot bowed to him, while Daniel remained standing. Betot tugged on Daniel's arm and whispered, "Bow down. He must be the revered leader."

"Our leader, Sendong of the Kalahan nation," a guard announced.

Sendong scrutinised Daniel and Betot from head to foot. He was particularly interested in the dead black chickens and instructed his guard to take them without any questions.

"Come, it's okay. You may enter," Sendong said.

They were escorted by guards who kept spitting something red from their mouths. The houses were taller than what Daniel and Betot were accustomed to seeing. Each house had four pillars made of large bamboo with a long ladder that connected to the house, almost reaching the sky but shorter than the trees. Sendong invited them into one of those houses.

The chickens were burned and cooked into a soup dish. While they waited, they were served rice wine.

"Where did you get the black chickens from?" Sendong asked after taking the first sip.

"I'm not exactly sure of the place's name, but about two mountains over, at the westside from here, we found a group of them and the two are what we obtained," Daniel replied.

"I see. Do you know that those chickens are precious? They are a rare commodity," Sendong said. "Perhaps the Gods are on your side because these are very illusive and difficult to catch."

Suddenly, they served the black chicken, its flesh and bones completely black, a true representation of rareness.

"Try some. It's practically meant for you," Sendong offered.

Daniel took a bite, while Betot, learning that it was not the bird he thought, took a nibble out of fear of Sendong.

Daniel was discreet about his interest in the woman who brought out the chicken. He was curious to know her name, which he discovered was Kitan. She had a fair complexion, long dark hair, a slim physique, and a mole on her forehead that was believed to represent intelligence and wisdom. Yet, it was her smile that truly captivated him.

There was something about the way her facial muscles moved, wrinkling her nose, that made Daniel desire her even more. Betot noticed the way he glanced at her.

"Please… please don't ruin this," Betot warned.

"Ruin what?" Daniel asked.

"They have welcomed us here, but by pursuing Kitan, Sendong's primary servant, you might get us into trouble. They could execute us." Betot said with some concern on his face.

"I appreciate your warning and sure, I agree," Daniel said with a smile.

Later that day, the women headed to the nearby spring to collect water using their clay containers balanced on their heads with cloth padding. Kitan was part of the group.

Daniel trailed behind, taking care to conceal himself behind bushes, rocks, and trees as he observed Kitan. He scaled a tree with a view of the spring to keep an eye on them. As Kitan finished filling her container, Daniel lost his footing and tumbled to the ground, drawing her attention. Worried, she hurried over to see if he was okay.

"Are you hurt?" she asked.

"I'm fine," Daniel replied.

Looking around to ensure no one was around, Kitan warned him, "You shouldn't have followed us. You know that what you're doing is not allowed."

"Don't worry, no one can see us," Daniel reassured her.

He led her away from the spring to a pine tree surrounded by bushes. Attempting to kiss her, Kitan turned her face away. Daniel then pinned her down on the ground, trying to kiss her again. Despite her resistance, he continued to touch her in inappropriate places, ripping her clothes off and fondling her. Kitan did not resist, staring at the sky without emotion as he took advantage of her.

Daniel returned to the village as if nothing wicked had occurred. Kitan was left alone, lying there. She crawled, trembling like a powerful earthquake, until she managed to stand and clean herself at the spring. She washed away the negative and pitiful feelings with as much water as she could. She put on her dress with the bright red, black, and white stripes, just like the way she used to wear it. Tears threatened to fall, but she held back and tried not to dwell on what Daniel had done.

Kitan walked into the leader's quarters with the container of spring water balanced on her head. She saw that Daniel and Betot were still there, but they were soon bidding their farewells as they got ready to depart.

Betot asked, "Where… where have you been?"

Daniel replied, "I was here the whole time, just exploring the village."

Betot nodded as they walked back along the route they had come.

Kitan's inability to complete her chores worsened as time went on. She would become exhausted just after a few movements of physical activity. Eating became difficult due to frequent vomiting. The women noticed the changes but were too afraid to inform their leader about it.

Sendong, concerned about her well-being as they were betrothed, insisted that a 'mumbaki,' their equivalent of a 'mambunong,' examine her. The 'mumbaki's' examination revealed Kitan's pregnancy. She had kept silent about her encounter with Daniel, but upon the 'mumbaki's' discovery, she had no choice but to confess.

Kitan's mother was disappointed and questioned Kitan's lack of shame for interacting with a stranger. Other women criticised her, accusing her of not meeting the moral and dignified standards expected of their leader's future partner. Kitan kept the truth of what happened to herself, crying silently.

In response, Sendong instructed his guards to escort Kitan to Mt. Tinakchi, a secluded area in the untouched forest filled with dangerous wildlife and toxic plants, leaving her to fend for herself.

The guards were on their way back to Kalahan when Kitan heard human screams and low-pitched roars not far away. She decided to venture deeper into a cave, hoping it would be a safer place.

A massive creature, the Sappao, with sharp claws, teeth, long horns, and thick fur resembling a wild animal, halted the warriors who escorted Kitan. Despite its ability to walk upright like a human, the monster attacked one of the warriors in a vicious scenario. The remaining three warriors attempted to defend themselves by throwing spears. However, the monster remained unaffected. With a swift motion, the monster struck the warriors with the back of its hand, sending them flying above the trees before crashing onto the rocky ground killing them instantly.

Kitan went to the entrance to observe the surroundings as they became peaceful. She noticed friendly creatures hopping, strolling, flying, and swinging from tree to tree. A feeling of calm and peace cleansed her feelings as she sat at the mouth of the cave, enjoying the beauty of the natural world. The Sappao's face appeared so close to her that she hadn't even noticed. When she looked to her right, she saw the monster. She tried to retreat further into the cave, but she was frozen in place, unable to move, and thousands of droplets sweat were falling from her body while sitting down.

The monster observed her without intervening. It left briefly and came back with a cluster of bananas, placing them near the cave's entrance. It patiently waited for Kitan to appear. When she finally emerged, she hesitated and shook with fear upon seeing the monster. The creature kept its gaze on the cave, waiting for Kitan to take some of the fruit. Its patience paid off when she began eating several pieces. Emboldened, she stood up and faced the monster.

The monster's eyes sparkled, contrasting with the horror in its smile. Kitan struggled to hide her fear as she observed the creature. It settled down next to the cave and drifted off to sleep.

Kitan cautiously entered the cave to rest. Inside, she found the rocky surface uncomfortable and uneven. The monster, sensing her discomfort, gathered some leaves and tossed them into the cave. Despite her exhaustion, Kitan found it difficult to sleep on the rough surface. She collected the large leaves to create a softer, more comfortable sleeping area.

Kitan slept peacefully, feeling content for herself and her unborn son. As she delved deeper into her subconscious, she found herself surrounded by mist. A tall green mountain devoid of trees emerged at a gradual pace as the mist dissipated. It was Mt. Pulag; the home of the Gods. In front of her stood a man with long gray hair and a beard, a muscular physique adorned in a loincloth with red and black colours accented with golden linings. She reached out to touch the man but encountered an invisible barrier separating them. "I am Kabunian, the God of all men" the man spoke, "and I tell you, Kina, do not be weary. You will give birth to a son who will establish a community of skilled woodworkers."

She awoke to find her body drenched in her own sweat, the stench of decay filling the air. Glancing towards the entrance, she saw the monster still asleep. Careful with her movements to avoid making any noise that might disturb it, she wandered around, losing her sense of direction, unsure of her destination.

Following the sound of rushing water, she pushed through bushes and grass until she reached a vibrant stream teeming with life. Clear water flowed into a small pond filled with colourful fishes, surrounded by creatures she had never seen before - from animals emitting high-pitched cries to those making guttural sounds, as well as tiny flying insects. Stripping off her clothes, she immersed herself in the water, turning the once-clear stream murky as it passed through the various creatures. Some succumbed to the pollution, while others managed to survive. It was at that moment that she realised she was a long distance away from where the monster was.

A bat-winged, fierce wild dog creature known as the gatui was hovering above Kitan observing her for a long time, drawn to her by the scent of her pregnancy. Unaware of its presence, Kitan had her eyes closed, enjoying the refreshing water. The gatui crept closer, attempting to inhale near Kitan in order to absorb the soul of her unborn child.

A woman with long, dark, shiny hair, hazel eyes, and fair complexion adorned with tattoos materialised behind the gatui. This woman was Ba-e, the protector of expectant mothers. With a piercing scream that only irritated the gatui and other canines, Ba-e scared the creature away. The gatui flew frantically, colliding with trees, boulders, and mountains, crashing to the ground unconscious. Ba-e vanished once more, leaving Kitan to rest undisturbed.

Kitan's experience of giving birth alone was both terrifying and empowering. As she laboured in the wilderness, she felt a mix of fear and determination. With no one by her side to offer guidance and protection from the elements, she had to rely solely on her own instincts and strength. Despite the intense pain and uncertainty, Kitan found a sense of empowerment in the experience. She pushed through each contraction with a fierce determination, knowing that she was capable of bringing new life into the world on her own.

As she held her newborn baby in her arms for the first time, she felt a surge of pride and accomplishment. Giving birth alone was not what Kitan had planned or expected, but it taught her a valuable lesson about her own resilience and inner strength. She emerged from the experience with a newfound sense of confidence and a deep appreciation for the power of the human body.

Chapter IV

The warriors believed that Daniel had strayed off course during the hunt. Some were worried that he had been lost and possibly eaten by wild animals. They were surprised when he eventually returned much later, looking stronger and healthier. "The gods must be on his side," one of them commented in amazement.

Tuliknek was a loyal warrior of Kibara, always ready to serve his leader, even at great personal risk. He was known for fearlessly confronting dangers. However, his loyalty was put to the test when he discovered the true identity of Daniel. While on guard duty, he observed Daniel leaving in a hurry. Intrigued, he followed with stealth through the grass and bushes. In the moonlight, he witnessed Daniel transform into a stunning woman with long dark hair, fair complexion, and cherry lips – the shape-shifter Babbawa.

Concealed in the bushes, he watched as Babbawa, with fiery red eyes and sharp fangs, sniff the air and scan her surroundings. He remained still, controlling his breathing, as she came close to his hiding spot still looking around. After she moved away, he returned to the Kingdom, seizing the opportunity to report what he had seen.

He acted as if nothing had happened the previous night. Besides, everything seemed to be going well. However, he remained vigilant, glancing at Daniel from time to time to ensure he wasn't causing any harm to others. Daniel continued to befriend Kuchep, often getting close to her and winning her favor. As darkness fell once again, Daniel hurried to the same spot where she was seen last. Daniel had been followed before, but that specific night was unique. It was the night when Napuagan presented himself to Babbawa as an elderly man with long silver hair and a beard holding on to a staff that was helping him stand.

He noticed them conversing, but he was not close enough to comprehend their discussion. He tried moving closer, but hesitated because he wasn't willing to take the risk of being discovered. A tree with numerous branches hanging above them, so he decided to climb the tree, providing him with a clear view of their conversation.

"…Yes, almighty Napuagan. Your wish is my command," Babbawa affirmed.

"Just ensure that it is executed with perfect accuracy," Napuagan instructed.

Babbawa bowed signifying worship to Napuagan. He missed the beginning of their exchange and attempted to retreat from his perch on the branch. However, the branch snapped, causing him to fall in front of the pair. Babbawa prepared to take action against him, but Napuagan intervened, casting a spell on his mind and emphasising his potential usefulness to them.

He was instructed to return to Dutab. The hypnotic effects of the curse wore off, causing him to forget all the spying he had done. He was truly deceived into believing that Daniel was the genuine article.

Babbawa transformed into Daniel's appearance following Napuagan's command after discovering Daniel's whereabouts. She observed him from a distance, noticing the noble eagle mark on his side as he ran alongside the river. From her vantage point in the forest, she realised the significance of impersonating Daniel to the Dutab King, as it would lead the people to believe that Daniel had returned safely without suspecting her true identity.

Daniel's presence had no impact on Kibara's fascination with Kuchep. The details of how Kuchep and Daniel grew closer, or what Babbawa symbolised, remained unknown to Kibara and most Dutab people. Daniel requested the elder council to arrange their marriage, known as the 'kalon.' The elders called for a meeting with Kibara and Kuchep, in the presence of Ba-ay, to discuss the marriage. Kuchep, being a woman, had no authority to object and was expected to follow tradition. Kibara presented animals and gold to Kuchep and her guardians, sealing the marriage with a toast of tapey shared by all participants.

Kuchep remained silent throughout the 'kalon' process, pretending to be a happy young lady eagerly anticipating marriage while feeling a strong sense of negativity. She had always known that the day would come and had her own plan in mind. She found a gap in the log fences behind the houses, the same secret passage Tuliknek had used. One night, she tried to escape but was stopped by a large number of guards. As the wedding approached, she made another attempt to escape, sneaking out of Kibara's quarters like a stealthy wild cat. She crawled through the dirt, stones, and grass, pausing whenever a guard passed by. Slowly but surely, she made her way out of the kingdom, continuing to crawl until she was certain she was safe from discovery.

She ran into the darkness without using a 'saleng' or wooden torch for light. There were various sounds around her, including sweet music in the air and flapping noises, but what really caught her attention was the roaring sound of what seemed to be predatory beasts. Unfortunately, she was one of the rare 'mamantala' who had inherited more of the mortal qualities rather than the power of witchcraft. She sprinted, even falling on uneven ground, then crawled and ran again without paying attention to the injuries she sustained.

She continued to push forward even as the noise faded away. As exhaustion set in, her injuries began to ache more intensely, causing unbearable pain. Despite her best efforts, she couldn't ignore the pain. Slowed by her injuries, she noticed a faint glimmer of light in the distance. As she drew nearer, the source of the light became clearer - a bonfire with Daniel and Betot. She squinted to get a better look and recognised Daniel.

"Is that really Daniel, or am I just seeing things?" she pondered. With a burst of energy, she hurried towards the bonfire, but collapsed unconscious just a few steps away.

Daniel lifted her with his gentle hands and then placed her on the animal hide he had spread on the ground for himself to sleep on.

"Is this? Is this? This is Kuchep! Yes, Kuchep!" he exclaimed with wonder.

"Who is she?" Betot asked.

"She is one of the maidens from Dutab Kingdom," Daniel said as he gazed on her unconscious beauty.

Daniel requested some of his medicinal plants to treat Kuchep's injuries. Despite their initial plan to resume their journey after a brief rest, Daniel and Betot decided to stay longer to tend to Kuchep. Her recovery took longer than anticipated, so Daniel and Betot took turns caring for her and foraging for food and water. Kuchep also went to a nearby spring for her personal hygiene needs, a discovery that surprised Betot.

"Why are you doing this to us?" Betot asked Kuchep whist she was taking a bath.

"Hey, why are you here? I'm naked," Kuchep responded.

"Don't avoid the question. You know what you did. Playing games with us, me and Daniel," Betot accused.

Kuchep remained silent and eventually apologised, nodding her head.

When Daniel returned with some skewered fish, he noticed the two arguing at the spring. He dropped the fish and approached them.

"What's going on here? And Betot, you. You... Kuchep, please go and get dressed," Daniel instructed.

"I know she's an attractive woman, but come on," he added.

Daniel and Betot were in disagreement, as Daniel suspected Betot of having feelings for Kuchep. Despite their differences, they all kept walking together. Kuchep was impressed by how quickly Daniel had dodged Dutab and found Betot.

Daniel was captivated by Kuchep's graceful demeanor as she strolled next to him. Betot's adorable yet determined look, with his lip caught between his teeth, also caught his attention. The trio proceeded in silence, prompting Daniel to wonder about Kuchep's decision to leave Dutab Kingdom and venture out on her own. The answer to this question remained elusive due to their current predicament.

One after another, they grew drowsy and collapsed on the ground. Daniel and Kuchep lay on their backs, while Betot fell face-first. The air was filled with the sound of musical instruments, reminiscent of a tayaw performance. Munduntug, the malevolent spirit of the nearby Kungaban Forest, materialised. Daniel found himself in a dreamlike forest, surrounded by gigantic bat-like creatures swooping down to attack him. Despite welding a sword, he struggled to defend himself.

Meanwhile, Betot was fleeing from angalos, towering giants determined to crush him with their heavy steps. Running in desperation, he tripped and clung to a rock at the cliff's edge. As for Kuchep, she was being tormented by pandek, small creatures with sharp teeth and a menacing demeanor, who ripped her clothes and took advantage of her in a disturbing manner.

They enacted their dreams in reality while Munduntug laughed a menacing echo. He took pleasure in their every move. Daniel swung his sword, but was tripped by Munduntug's roots, causing him to fall face-first to the ground. He regained consciousness in reality before slipping back into the dream realm. Seizing the opportunity during the interval of reality, he swung his sword cutting Munduntug's roots. The music faded, prompting Munduntug to retreat back to Kungaban forest.

"Are you alright?" Daniel asked Kuchep.

Kuchep stood and sat on the grass, asking, "What just happened?" as Betot called out for help. Daniel hurried to the edge of the mountain and attempted to reach Betot, who was far below.

"Hang on, I'll find something for you to hold onto." He discovered a long twig and offered it to Betot, who grasped it. Daniel strained to pull Betot up, but the twig started to break. Eventually, it snapped in two, and Betot began sliding down the cliff once more. Daniel was able to pull him just in time. He instructed the two to cover their ears with the leaves he folded in a specific manner to be fitted in the earholes that prevented sounds to slip in. Other attempts of munduntug did not take effect and were ignored.

The three resumed moving without taking a breather and only communicated with signaling. They only took a break when they determined that it was safe to do so.

The Kalingan territories were remote, and the trio traveled through them without realising they were far from other settlements or civilisations.

Unlike the 'mamantalas' who could blend in with the general population, the Busols of Kalingan remained a tightly-knit group. Their main objective was to increase their power and status by conquering territories and decapitating their enemies.

The group's members were nearly indistinguishable from one another, as they all shared a tall, muscular stature and were adorned with tattoos commemorating their triumphs in combat. The only way to differentiate them was by the intricate designs on their loincloths. The more elaborate the design, featuring the prominent colours of red, black, and white, the higher the individual's status within the group. Mayma, the group's leader, wore a particularly ornate loincloth, distinguished by dangling sea shells and gold string decorations, setting him apart from the other esteemed members of the group.

They cleverly outwit every animal they encounter during their hunts. Using their spears, they surround the animals and skillfully pierce their flesh with precision, targeting vital organs to inflict lethal wounds.

"This catch could easily feed a whole village," remarked one of the hunters.

Upon returning to Kalingan, the hunting party feasted on their catch with a sense of excitement, devouring the still-moving organs in a tradition known as 'kinigtot' satisfying their hunger.

Once, a lost stranger stumbled upon the village shrouded in darkness and reeking of a foul aura. The stone walls were adorned with a gruesome display of human heads, from fresh to skeletal. As he was cautious in his exploration, a warrior ended his life by slashing his neck with a 'gaman' faster than a blink of an eye. The head was then offered to their leader, Mayma. The group engaged in a ritualistic dance of 'bindiyan,' impaling the head on a spear and encircling it with blazing footsteps and jubilant cries. The blood dripping from the victim's head was mixed with 'tapuy' for a morbid toast.

"I… I am very sorry about Kuchep. I just thought she was deceiving you. By the looks… looks of it, she is recovering faster than expected," Beto explained.

"Forget about it and move on," Daniel suggested.

Kuchep woke up and saw Daniel with Betot next to him, both wearing sheepish smiles. "I'm sorry. I just needed some help and I really appreciated your company."

Daniel's temper flared up, but he was calmed in an instant by Kuchep's persuasive words. "Let's put it behind us and focus on moving forward," Daniel said, feeling a sense of relief as his anger subsided.

Betot was tired of traveling, "Where… where are we heading? It seems like our steps are leading us nowhere?" Daniel was about to respond when he heard noises of people approaching. "Wait, somebody or something is coming. Climb that tree," he pointed to a nearby tree. Kuchep went up first, followed by Daniel, but Betot struggled to climb and ended up hiding behind the tree trunk.

The group passing was of the 'Busols,' a sight familiar to Betot and Kuchep but new to Daniel. "I smell someone nearby," one of the' Busols' noted. They fanned out in different directions in search of the scent that resonated with them.

Betot was visibly nervous with sweat trickling down his face, and hoped the Busols wouldn't pick up on his fear. With one 'Busol' on the other side of the tree trunk, Betot managed to move along the ground hidden by the weeds reaching for the skies. Daniel and Kuchep, perched on tree branches above, were poised to act if needed.

"Advance, no one is here! It's probably just a wild animal," their leader ordered. Betot, Daniel, and Kuchep breathed a collective sigh of relief as the 'Busols' moved on. "Let's not stay any longer. Time to go." Daniel urged.

They hiked cautiously, only stopping when they found food and water. Daniel tried to navigate in the right direction but realised he was lost. This led them to a warmer path that descended and led them to a unique body of water. The area had an abundance of water that seemed to stretch endlessly. "Don't drink the water," Daniel cautioned Betot and Kuchep, who spat the water upon tasting due to its excessive saltiness.

Betot stepped into the water while trying to take a drink by accident. As he attempted to return to dry land, he was met with powerful waves that pushed him further into deeper waters. An enormous fish with sharp teeth and its mouth wide open was ready to attack. He struggled to move away from the creature due to his lack of swimming skills. Instead, his efforts made him sink deeper into the waters. Daniel dived over to help him, but the strong current made it difficult for even Daniel to swim against it.

A group of men arrived at the scene and aimed their weapons at the creature. One had a weapon that shot rocks using an elastic rope attached to a tree branch-like structure. Another wielded a curved weapon with a rope that launched a spear-like object. Daniel wielded his sword at the creature as well. Daniel tried to grab Betot from drowning, but instead, they were pulled deeper into the water. A whirlpool emerged, swirling them around before leading them into a light at its center. They were fortunate enough that some men with water skills were able to pull them to safety.

The men surrounded Daniel and Betot, with Kuchep being held against her will.

"What are you all doing here?" The largest man asked.

"We are just travelers who have lost our way," Daniel replied.

Daniel and Betot were bound together on their backs, while Kuchep was bound separately. They were compelled to walk without a break following the recent peril they had encountered. They reached a village that resembled the ones they had passed, but with an abundance of tools and weapons in use. The women were covered from head to toe, while the men wore loincloths paired with jackets on their upper torsos.

One of the houses was constructed from stone with a thatched roof and no windows. The only natural light came from the wide door. A tall man, dressed in attire distinct from Daniel and Betot, heard the commotion. He emerged to find his warriors dragging the two while pushing Kuchep forward.

"Who are they?" The man inquired with a deep voice.

"Kamahalan (our king)! They are strangers we discovered at the beach!" The head of the warriors replied.

The leader ordered the warriors to throw Daniel and Betot in the same cage, while Kuchep was forced into a separate confinement. The cages were similar to the leader's quarters but smaller, with dirt floors instead of wood. They were fed leftover rice or sweet potatoes and given water. They were in darkness, only experiencing light every time the warriors checked on them.

Daniel listened to Kuchep's screams with a sense of horror, as if she was being subjected to some kind of exploitation. He clenched the ground tightly, his fingers digging into the dirt and staining his nails with blood. Meanwhile, Betot remained sound asleep on the ground, as if he was unaffected by the noise coming from the neighbouring cage. Daniel couldn't help but wonder what the men in the adjacent cage might have done to Kuchep, considering a range of possibilities.

Daniel vomited slightly onto the ground although it was barely noticeable. It wasn't due to illness or bad food, but rather the disturbing memories of his past as a sexually drunk person with Kitan. "This must be some kind of a punishment for my past actions. It's all coming back to haunt me," he reflected. "I can't believe I was capable of such behavior." He lay on the ground, eyes shut, with Betot watching over him. Betot didn't suspect anything other than Daniel simply sleeping.

Kuchep was taken to the communal shaded bathing area, where water was brought in from a nearby creek through bamboo pipes. "Clean yourself and put on the clothes that have been given to you!" ordered one of the warriors. She washed herself and applied a mixture of fragrant fruits and flowers with coconut milk to her long black hair. The refreshing water calmed her nerves, making her feel carefree as if she was not in any danger. The clothes provided suited her, as if the maker had known they were meant for her.

"My lady, are you finished?" inquired a voice. Kuchep remained silent but emerged outside fully dressed. All eyes were fixed on her, captivated by her radiant beauty. "Bring her to me!" commanded their leader. The warriors hesitated, transfixed by her presence. "I said, bring her to me!" the leader bellowed, brandishing Daniel's sword in a threatening manner. The warriors exchanged glances and escorted Kuchep to him with reluctance.

Kuchep experienced a feeling of familiarity when the leader declared, "I, your esteemed leader Sulpasyon, have selected Kuchep to be my life partner." Some cheered, but many others objected to the decision due to Kuchep not being one of them. The village became chaotic as people questioned the leader's choice. The warriors surrounded their leader and Kuchep, while dissenters continued to voice their disapproval. Loyalists of the village clashed with those who opposed the leader, heightening the tension, with the warriors' weapons looming.

The tension created an opportunity for the prisoners to flee. The opposition tried to assault their leader, while the loyalists worked to prevent them. The conflict between the two sides turned into a physical altercation in a flash.

"Help the children and the elderly escape," Daniel instructed.

"What… what about you?" Betot asked.

"Don't worry about me. I will return for Kuchep and my sword," Daniel replied.

"Follow me. Follow me. Be quick," Betot urged the other escapees.

Daniel went to Kuchep, who was trying to escape from Sulpasyon. They had the opportunity to run, but a warrior blocked their path with his jungle bolo aimed at Daniel. Daniel punched the warrior in the gut, causing him to fall to the ground.

"Go and find Betot with the others," Daniel directed.

"What about you?" Kuchep asked with concern on her face.

"I'll be fine. Don't worry about me," Daniel reassured.

Kuchep gave Daniel a kiss on the lips before departing. Daniel took hold of the jungle bolo and faced Sulpasyon, engaging in a fierce battle with their respective weapons. Daniel delivered two swift kicks to Sulpasyon's belly, forcing him to kneel. Daniel then grabbed his sword and made a quick escape. A warrior armed with a spear launcher targeted Daniel, but his swift sword movements deflected the arrowhead, averting any harm. It was like Li Men reborn in action.

In the midst of the crowd, a young man with a fit body and a striking gaze emerged as the leader among the resistance fighters. His skin was decorated with tattoos of geometric patterns, varying from simple lines to rectangles and zigzags. He noticed Daniel's tattoo on his right shoulder and sensed that it carried a deeper meaning. After the commotion settled down, Daniel made plans to depart. Some of the loyalists escaped, but a handful, including Sulpasyon, were apprehended and placed in custody.

"Go and search for the escaped prisoners," the new leader commanded.

He made himself available for Daniel to talk with. "I am Rustan, the leader of the resistance. We have been secretly getting ready for this moment," he said.

"Daniel here."

"I can see the tattoo on your right shoulder. Where did you get it?"

"I got it from Dutab Kingdom whatever it means."

"You must be someone special."

"Our leader, we cannot find the escaped prisoners," one of the warriors interrupted.

"Forget it. Tidy up the mess and let's have a celebration to honour our guests.

"Throw him in with Sulpasyon!" The crowd shouted.

"Hold up and lower your voices. He is our special guest," Rustan declared.

The crowd fell into silence and welcomed Daniel. They gathered their offerings for the celebration, which included corn, rice, and various dishes from the waters. The feast was unlike anything seen in the highlands, with grilled fish, boiled crabs, shellfish, and other unfamiliar dishes. The village socialised without the need for music or dancing, engaging in activities like men sparring in fights, women in rice pounding competitions, and other forms of entertainment.

Chapter V

Daniel politely declined Rustan's invitation to stay and decided to continue on his own, thinking about Betot and Kuchep's whereabouts. He was given water, salt, and a few fruits for his journey out of the villager's good hearts as he headed into the mountains behind the village to search for his friends.

Walking along a path that appeared to be wide enough for a large animal to pass through, he noticed a horse-drawn cart accompanied by men who looked similar to his master, Li Men. Feeling a sense of unease, Daniel ducked behind a bush to avoid being seen, but his hiding spot was soon discovered by the men.

"Stop! I thought I saw something move in those bushes!" one of the men exclaimed.

Daniel unsheathed his sword with the confidence of defeating the group with the guidance of Master Li's spirit. He leapt out from his hiding spot in an attempt to attack. However, he was blocked by two men who leapt from the back of the cart. A fierce battle ensued, with each move and countermove seeming almost choreographed as the men fought with kicks, punches, and expertly executed maneuvers. Despite his best efforts, Daniel found himself outnumbered and outmatched by the skilled fighters. Someone noticed Daniel's tattoo on his right shoulder, combined with the marking on his weapon and his movements during the battle.

"Stop, this guy possesses a sword of a master!" a fighter yelled.

The men halted their movements as Daniel continued with his actions, which they avoided. Daniel observed that the men were not retaliating. They scrutinised Daniel and his sword with much intention, leaving him confused about the situation.

A woman in flowing, silky garments that enveloped her entire body stepped out of the cart. Her presence seemed to radiate a vibrant rainbow of colours in Daniel's eyes, leaving him speechless.

"Your movements and weapon are quite impressive. I'm curious, where did you acquire your skills in swordsmanship?" she asked.

Daniel remained silent, until one of the men slapped him on the back with much force. "Hey! Our most esteemed leader Xi Yan is talking to you!"

She repeated her question, and Daniel responded without hesitation.

"Master Li Men, huh? Yeah, he used to be one of us. However, he was expelled because of his belief that women should only follow, not lead. He insisted that females are just lower-class citizens without the right to lead," she explained.

As he walked among the men at the back, they brought him along to test if he was truly the person some of her men had identified him to be. In their journey, they had to veer off the main road onto a narrower path that led to a village nestled in the heart of a forest.

They were approaching a loud hissing sound. It was a 'gawan,' a massive serpent with four legs, rampaging through the village as people fled in fear. Some of the men armed themselves with large farming tools such as pitch forks, hoes, pick mattocks and others, but the 'gawan' attacked and swallowed one of them whole.

Xi Yan tricked Daniel into confronting the giant creature. Armed with his sword, Daniel attempted to strike the creature's belly, but his height proved to be a hindrance. He leapt and made a stabbing motion, barely grazing the creature.

The other men rushed to assist which was against their leader's will. One climbed a tall tree and leaped onto the creature's back, delivering a flurry of kicks. Another grabbed the creature's tail, holding it in place with all his strength. Daniel made a second attempt, slashing the creature's belly open and exposing its innards, causing it to collapse with Daniel on top of it.

Covered in blood and the creature's internal organs, Daniel emerged victorious.

He always approached things in his life with scepticism, requiring concrete evidence to convince him. Even in the midst of his current experience, he couldn't shake the feeling that it was all just a dream. The village did not rejoice as he had seen in other villages; instead, they solemnly disposed of the creature's carcass and burned it to ashes. Those who had participated in the battle went to a nearby spring to cleanse themselves, not only the remnants of the creature from their body with flowing water, but also their auras by meditating with the relaxing flow of the spring water. They believed the creature slain did not only bring terror but some bad omen that also needed cleansing.

"Witnessing your actions has made me consider allowing you to stay," Xi Yan remarked as she and Daniel strolled through the village.

Daniel was cautious when he stepped into Xi Yan's home, unsure of what awaited him. The scent of burning candles and herbs filled the air, calming his nerves. A portrait of an elderly bald man hung on the wall, and a lone window let in a sliver of light to the left side of the room. Intricate paintings of shapes adorned the walls, accompanied by Chinese characters that reminded Daniel of his former world. In terms of its contemporary relevance.

In front of the picture wall were papers with characters that he couldn't understand. He was fascinated by the people's ability to communicate when they spoke. Xi Yan brought a delicate tea pot with a dragon design and a couple of fragile cups without handles.

An elderly man, reminiscent of the martial arts movies and TV shows he had watched before this time, was invited in. He led them in a prayer, instructing everyone to close their eyes and meditate. He signaled to Xi Yan that it was safe to drink the tea. Daniel observed them and took a small sip as well.

After conversing with the three, Daniel felt curious. He observed a blacksmith working in a shaded area without walls, shaping molten steel into a knife. The blacksmith stopped his work and looked at Daniel from head to toe without saying a word, making him self-conscious. Daniel then moved to the neighboring structure and watched an elderly woman creating noodle threads with the skill of an expert using only her fingers on kneaded flour. He felt relaxed and at ease, as if he were a content cat lounging in the sun.

He spent the night surrounded by the sound of peace. The sleeping area was not simply a floor covered with animal hide or woven cloth. Every household was filled with a sense of comfort. The village was as well-organised as always. The day arrived and the village was calm. He approached the stage to meet Lidum, the messenger of the Gods, who appeared in a white glow. Lidum, a dignified middle-aged man, exuded an air of authority that demanded respect. Without understanding why, he knelt before him. "The Gods have revealed to me that you are tasked with a mission, destined for a specific purpose. You will be informed of this purpose in time."

He gazed at Lidum until he vanished. He was about to ask a bunch of questions but wasn't able to.

He awoke with the sky still dark. There was a presence of smell unlike anything he had ever experienced. "What was that? Is it real?" he pondered.

He tried to revert back to sleep, but another message appeared in his mind. Lidum appeared in a white void again, saying, "The Gods sense your longing to return home. Until you complete your mission here, you will not return to your current reality."

When he next opened his eyes it was already morning. It was at that moment that he began to realise he was sent there with a purpose. People remained indoors as the might of thundering roared, dominating the skies. The sun's rays were obscured by dark, gloomy clouds that unleashed a heavy downpour. Instead of engaging in physical labour, Daniel chose to stay in bed. A young woman arrived with a modern umbrella to deliver a bowl of noodle soup to him. He became stuck staring at the rain protection the woman used. However, the sight and aroma of the steaming food made his stomach rumble with anticipation. It had been a long time since he had enjoyed a genuine noodle dish, and his taste buds were thrilled at the prospect.

He devoured the noodles in a manner that lacked refinement, causing the lady to giggle at his behavior. Upon noticing Xi Yan's presence, he adjusted his eating style, delicately picking up the noodles with chopsticks and chewing them with care. The lady's giggles only increased at his sudden change in manners. After his meal, his feet were eager to wander further.

"I am content with this life, I feel a sense of belonging," Daniel said, experiencing euphoria. The pouring rain had stopped and the golden rays of the sun emitted warm energy that dried the wet surroundings. He spotted a tree he hadn't noticed before, covered in worms with bristly armour on their skins. The tree had holes in its leaves, and the fruit had been eaten before fully developing its sweet potential.

"Don't disturb those worms. They might move to another tree," an elderly lady cautioned from behind, causing him to nearly slip on the dusty ground.

He smiled with a hint of embarrassment. He didn't want to acknowledge the fact that he was surprised by the elder woman's startling voice. The elder woman then just moved along, resuming her previous activity. He didn't get the opportunity to enquire about why the worms were allowed to flourish and harm the tree. As an elderly man passed by him, he casually mentioned, "Those are silkworms for the silk."

Xi Yan was walking alone, wearing a newly crafted blue shirt and pants that resembled a shiny pajama with a green dragon design. The dragon had red eyes and yellow fins, hugging her slender body. It was the first time Daniel saw her in a different light. Something inside him ignited a lion's desire.

"This is strange. What is happening to me?" he whispered to himself. She kicked and performed acrobatic moves similar to Master Li Men; moves he couldn't perfect himself.

"There you are, Daniel. Join the other men. We need all the muscle we can get," Xi Yan requested. Daniel remained silent, gazing at her with a look of admiration, as if he were smiling like an anchor.

She kicked with force but making sure to avoid hitting his face. He blinked in rapid succession, bringing him back to reality.

"Hey, are you still with us?" Xi Yan asked, her expression showing a hint of irritation.

"Did you say something?" He asked.

"Go with the group heading to the riverside near the forest to gather rocks and logs," she instructed.

Daniel felt embarrassed and obediently followed her command without uttering another word. He tried to push down his feelings for Xi Yan, as the memory of Kitan, his first encounter with a woman's essence, was hindering his ability to fully submit to his desires without a genuine connection to a woman.

In the time before the world existed, only darkness and water filled the void. Lumawig, The Creator God, sent forth a great bird and a colossal serpent, called to form the land and sky. The bird flew high, creating clouds in its wake, while the serpent dove into the water, bringing up mud that hardened into the earth.

Lumawig descended from the celestial realm of Mt. Pulag; the home of the gods and saw that the earth was bare. Without hesitation, he began shaping the mountains and soon trees covered the hills, making the land vibrant and alive with nature. However, there were no people to inhabit this beautiful land. So, Lumawig climbed to the highest mountain and shaped the first man from the fertile soil. Pleased with his creation, he then created the first woman from the man's rib. Together, they learned life's essentials and how to care for the land. Lumawig gave them wisdom and strength to survive the challenges of nature. The village believed in the story about how humans and creations came to be, which Daniel learned about.

"I feel like being happy with this lifestyle," Daniel said, experiencing euphoria. He spotted a tree he hadn't noticed before, covered in worms with bristly armour on their skins. The tree had holes in its leaves, and the fruit had been eaten before fully developing its fragrant potential. "Avoid disturbing those worms. They might move to another tree," an elderly lady cautioned from behind, causing him to nearly slip on the dusty ground.

He smiled with a hint of embarrassment. He didn't want to acknowledge the fact that he was surprised by the elder woman's loud voice. The elder woman simply walked away, resuming her previous activities. He didn't get the opportunity to inquire about why the worms were allowed to flourish and harm the tree. As an elderly man passed by him, he casually mentioned, "Those are silkworms for the silk." Daniel was even more confused by the lack of any comments from anyone about what he had witnessed.

Xi Yan was walking alone, wearing a newly crafted blue shirt and pants that resembled a shiny pajama with a green dragon design. The dragon had red eyes and yellow fins, hugging her slender body. It was the first time Daniel saw her in a different light, and something inside him ignited like a lion's desire. "This is strange. What is happening to me?" he whispered to himself. She kicked and performed acrobatic moves similar to Master Li Men, moves he couldn't perfect himself.

"There you are, Daniel. Join the other men. We need all the muscle we can get," Li Men requested. Daniel remained silent, gazing at her with a look of admiration, as if he were smiling like an anchor.

"Hey! Are you still paying attention here?" Xi Yan asked, her expression showing a hint of anger.

She kicked her feet towards Daniel's face, jolting him back to reality. He blinked rapidly. "Did you say something?" he asked.

"Go with the group heading to the riverside near the forest to gather rocks and logs!" she instructed.

Daniel was confused by the events unfolding, feeling as though time itself was in chaos. "I was suddenly transported to this time period, and now this? It's like a never-ending cycle of repetition," he mused, shaking his head. Glancing back at Xi Yan, who was watching him closely, he hurried to catch up with the men to prevent any further conflict that may arise.

The men went ahead, leaving Daniel to catch up. "Hi, it's me, Daniel again. You might recognise me," he called out as they stopped and glanced back at him. They didn't respond, just giving him a look that made him uncomfortable. They continued on their way, each carrying baskets on their sides, backs, or bellies. As they reached a downhill slope, they were skillful in navigating the wet surface, avoiding slipping. The men caught fish and edible shells with their skillful hands, placing them in their baskets. Daniel, without a basket, watched and observed.

Once their baskets were full, some of the men carried large rocks uphill with ease, while others went into the forest with axes and bolos to chop down trees and carry the logs back to the village. They didn't speak to Daniel, assuming he knew what to do. He picked up a large rock and followed them back to the village.

The work continued until they had gathered enough materials to reconstruct the stone wall that had been destroyed by the heavy rain prior to Daniel's arrival. The catch, which included fish, shellfish, mushrooms, and edible greens, was prepared in a more elaborate method. The fish was grilled with a variety of spices, the mushrooms were turned into a soup, and the shellfish content was stir-fried. Once again, Daniel savored the food as if it were the best meal he had ever experienced. The men did not engage in casual conversation while eating, only the elderly men, women, and some young ladies did.

Some elderly men played instruments that he had never seen before, resembling guitars but with unique tones and a slightly different structure. Large drums were suspended on wooden frames sturdy enough to support their weight, and were played. Both the elderly and young women danced, moving as smoothly as silk and as lightly as feathers. Their movements included elements of martial arts that appeared complex, yet the performers executed them with ease. Daniel was always the first to applaud at the end of each performance, holding his breath with eagerness of what was their next move.

In the beginning, there was nothing except for the Gods living on Mount Pulag, surrounded by floating clouds in the sky and a body of water. Kabunian, the Supreme God, rubbed his palms together to create heat and threw it into the empty sky to form the sun. He then took pieces of rocks and created the planets by throwing them in the same direction as the sun. Water was poured onto the planets, with the third planet receiving the most for being the closest to Mount Pulag. The air was blown onto the planets, with the third planet again receiving the most. The wind's motion created lands, bodies of water, and life.

Kabunian noticed the lack of variety among the creations. There was the absence of a specie created in the image of the Gods. He gathered reeds from the land and scattered them in pairs throughout the planet, instructing them to animate. The reeds transformed into people, establishing societies in various settings such as mountain tops, wide plains, near bodies of water, rocky terrains, and forests. Each village was blessed with unique talents. One community excelled at planting rice, another had strong leadership abilities, one was skilled at imitating nature through intricate carving, and others had their own special skills.

It was the Dutab Kingdom that was blessed with natural leaders and skilled weavers. The peaceful and advancing society was seen as a divine gift. Kibara's leadership was bolstered by his loyal Ayumes, who were just as authoritative as he was. She promoted the importance of women in society unlike anyone else. Thanks to his efforts, the women weavers gained strength and asserted their independence, no longer content to be mere supporters. Over time, a shift occurred as some embraced a more progressive mindset, overshadowing tradition. Ba-ay, the current leader, inherited the throne as the grandson of Kibara, without possessing the same wisdom. Unlike Kibara, Ba-ay was weak and often relied on others for advice and guidance when making important decisions for the Kingdom.

Kibara and Ayumes had been together for many years, but they had not been able to have a son to inherit the throne despite their efforts. As they became older, the need to have a child became more urgent. They sought the advice of the mambunong, who instructed them to journey to the 7th mountain in search of a rare plant known as gipah. This plant was believed to have been planted by the gods themselves and had the power to cure major illnesses, including fertility issues.

"Travel to the 7th mountain and find the gipah plant," Kibara commanded.

"How will we know what we are looking for?" one of the warriors asked.

"It is the only green plant that grows on top of a large rock," the mambunong explained.

"Do not uproot it. Take only a few leaves and leave the plant to thrive," he added.

The warrior chief, Tampulak, was a tall, muscular man who led a group of battle-hardened men. Half of them were assigned to guard Dutab Kingdom, while the others set out on a search, particularly those skilled in tracking. Their journey began with a ritual where the mambunong required them to slaughter a native black pig and read its liver to determine if it had a sign of good luck for the day's journey. Once the liver was deemed favorable, they were ready to set out.

Before taking their first step, they were blessed by having some of the pig's blood sprinkled on their cowlicks individually, accompanied by a prayer chant. The entire Kingdom shared the meat, with each family receiving a portion of which every member was required to partake. Some of the meat, along with sweet potatoes, was given to the warriors to consume on their journey.

They headed east, counting the 7th mountain as the location where they would discover their mission. They fought through wild beasts, flying birds of prey, and mythical creatures that threatened them. One warrior was hit by a rock so powerful that it threw him against the cliff, while many other rocks were hurled at them. Among the trees, they saw the kulkulibuts, large mushroom-like creatures with red umbrellas, brown stems, white spots, and tails that flung rocks at them. The group scattered and took cover behind boulders, bushes, and trees.

"Formation!" Tampulak commanded. The warriors reorganised with their wooden shields in front and their bolos or spears at the ready. They advanced cautiously, attempting to chop or stab the creatures, but their efforts were in vain. One warrior had two crystal stones in his animal hide pouch and struck them together, creating flames that not only burned the creatures but also engulfed the entire mountain top.

"We need to get out of this scorching place!" one of the warriors yelled.

They hurried downhill in a chaotic manner. Their haste caused some of them to trip and sustain injuries. One of them became ensnared in vines that the others couldn't free him from, causing him to suffer burns from the heat. They didn't have time to mourn their fallen comrades and continued on towards their ultimate goal.

Their feet were planted firmly on the base of the 7th mountain. With no obstacles from the 6th mountain, they assumed the rest of their journey would be smooth sailing. As they ascended, a putrid smell filled the air, so foul that they struggled to breathe. It was even worse than the rotting etag, the preserved meat. The plants seemed to be moving as if someone was shaking them without the help of a wind.

The eldest member sniffed the air and felt the movement, "It's halupit! Halupit! Cover your ears!" he warned. A piercing high-pitched sound echoed around the mountain.

One of the warriors, unable to cover his ears, panicked and ran in a frenzy, forgetting their purpose. The others quickly caught him, held him, and carried him forward. Humanoid figures, almost fluid-like, began to materialise from invisibility.

"Don't worry, just keep moving. They may try to harm us, but their bodies won't allow it," the eldest man reassured them.

The warriors successfully reached their destination, but they encountered another challenge. A young man, eager to impress the experienced members, was the first to find the gipah plant. He hastily pulled the plant out of the ground with his bare hands and placed it in his pasiking or ratan backpack.

"I found it! We can head back now!" he declared confidently. The group gathered around him, and the eldest member inspected the plant with a hint of concern. He noticed the reckless way the young man had uprooted the plant but chose not to say anything. The priority was to deliver the plant to their leaders, Kibara and Ayumes.

Upon their arrival, the eldest warrior took the gipah and removed the leaves from its stem before heading to the mambunong's kubo. The mambunong then boiled the leaves in a clay pot over an open flame in his cooking area. After allowing the tea to cool, he brought it to their leader's quarters.

"Drink a portion of this tea three times a day until the height of the new moon. Then try to procreate. I assure you that you will have a son," the mambunong advised.

Kibara and Ayumes followed the mambunong's instructions diligently. However, a few days into Ayumes' tea regimen, the mambunong noticed a drop of the cooled tea had turned red, indicating a bad omen. He wanted to warn their leaders, but it was too late as the tea had already taken effect.

Ayumes' belly was swelling like a mountain, causing her great discomfort in her later stages of child-bearing. The moon was not bright and full, but instead a deep, blood-red colour reminiscent of slaughter. As the night progressed, flashes of lightning and the rumble of thunder filled the air, creating an ominous atmosphere for the impending birth. Despite the unfavorable conditions, Ayumes cried out in pain. "Fetch the mambunong!" Kibara commanded one of his servants, who hurried off in the rain to deliver the message. The mambunong quickly arrived at the leader's quarters, carrying a bark of a tree, herbs, and a piece of cloth.

"Support Ayume's head on your lap and hold her shoulder gently. Bring some hot water," the mambunong directed. He prepared a mixture of the herbs and bark on the cloth, using it to cleanse the birth canal. "Push hard, my lady," he encouraged Ayumes. The baby's head was moving in and out of the birth canal, which was a concerning sign. The mambunong encouraged Ayumes to give it her all and push one final time, leading to the baby's release.

He was named Ba-ey, which means "home," because he was born in the leader's abode. The mambunong noticed a red mark on the right cheek of the baby's bottom, indicating that the baby might grow up to be an ineffective leader or lack wisdom. The mambunong did not mention his observation and proceeded to wipe the baby with a clean cloth soaked with the rest of the hot water infused with the bark and herbs before handing him to Ayumes. The placenta, known as 'Nuhai ni nga-nga,' was washed and then given to Ayumes to consume raw, in the belief that it would quickly restore her strength.

Ba-ey's upbringing was marked by unfortunate events for his parents and the community. Instead of being viewed as a potential future leader, he was often seen as a troublemaker. His actions were not seen as positive contributions, but rather as bringing misfortune to those around him.

For his own amusement, Ba-ey hurled a spear, fatally striking one of the warriors stationed near the entrance gate. "Dispose of his body and let the wild beasts feast on it!" he commanded. This gruesome act instilled fear in the hearts of all who witnessed it. Mothers were quick to usher their children indoors, forbidding them from playing outside. The other warriors became hyper-aware of their surroundings, constantly checking behind them.

Ba-ey also harboured a lasting grudge against Kuchep, the one desire he had been unable to fulfill in his otherwise charmed life.

Chapter VI

Further downstream in the river's deeper section, a trial was taking place. Two men, accused of stealing Ba-ey's valuable necklace, were competing to see who could hold their breath the longest. A group of elders and the mambunong watched from the side, waiting to see who would come up first. The mambunong began reciting an intense chant, hoping the Gods would hear. One of the competitors emerged from the water, followed by the other. They were then given bolos to fight with, and everyone watched to see who would draw blood first. The man who surfaced later tried to stab his opponent, who managed to block the attack with his bolo. The first man tried again, and this time the second man's defense was not as successful, resulting in a wound.

The defeated accused was found guilty, and the victor was granted freedom from the accusation. Immediately after, a council of elders' member threw a gaman, beheading the loser and allowing his body to drift down the river. River creatures consumed the flesh until only bones remained. The head was collected and added to a pile of decapitated heads in a cave.

In addition to the determined penalty, the family of the guilty individual had the option to pay for the estimated value of the stolen item through animals or land, or a close female relative was required to serve their leader until the leader deemed that she had paid for her relative's guilt.

It was the rule that the winner must be free, however Ba-ey was dissatisfied with the decision. The victor was walking back to the village when Ba-ey took a warrior spear and threw it at the victor's back, impaling him. The victor came tumbling down into the water, with blood staining the clear water and his impaled body floating downstream with the river's waves, the spear still attached.

One warrior after another had been dispatched to the outside world beyond Dutab Kingdom in search of Kuchep. While there were other attractive women, it was Kuchep who had captured the leader's heart inexplicably. Those who returned empty-handed were executed, their heads severed on the chopping block.

"I am concerned about your well-being, Your Highness. The Kingdom is suffering from neglect, and the people are beginning to resent you," the mambunong expressed.

Ba-ey gazed at the mambunong for a brief moment. Though he remained silent, his eyes conveyed a wealth of meaning. Seated on his throne, he carried on with his duties and the quest to find the woman he adored. The council of elders, tasked with overseeing the kingdom's leadership, asserted that Ba-ey had ascended to power by the will of a higher divine authority.

Kitan lived on the other side of the mountain near the river base but continued to lead a self-sufficient life. Despite her poor fate and isolation, she demonstrated remarkable resilience by constructing a simple kubo house to provide shelter for herself and her son with Daniel. Drawing on her experience as a servant, she raised chickens she had captured from the woods, making them lay eggs and reproduce. She collected rainwater in split bamboo containers and cultivated root crops such as sweet potatoes and cassava. Kitan's pregnancy resulted in a son named Paklit, who, despite his young age was willing to help his mother with the physically demanding tasks without complaint.

"Mother, why is it that we are the only ones in this place?" Paklit's curiosity prompted him to ask.

"Just because..." Kitan struggled to provide a direct answer to her son's question, offering various explanations each time he inquired.

Betot and Kuchep, along with the other escapees, were covered in sweat as they scattered in various directions. Seeking shelter, they found a small hut where they could rest. Upon entering, they discovered a distinct cooking area with chicken meat hanging above the fireplace, still dripping with fat, suggesting recent use. Betot cut off a piece and began roasting it over the fire, while Kuchep took a break inside the main house.

"Hey… Hey wake up! I found some chicken and roasted it," Betot called out.

Kuchep smiled, but her eyes held a hint of concern. "The owner of this house might be upset."

"No one's here, and… and I'm hungry. If… if you don't want any, I'll… I'll eat it all," Betot teased, trying to reclaim the piece he had offered.

Kuchep took the piece back and took a bite, savoring it like a hungry predator.

Kitan and Paklit were coming down from the mountain slope with various fish skewered on sticks.

"Mother, did you forget to put out the fire?" Paklit asked.

"No, why do you ask?" Kitan replied.

"Look, there is still some smoke and it looks like a fire was recently burning. It seems like someone was cooking here," Paklit pointed out to his mother.

Kuchep dropped the fishes and hurried to the main house to check if there were any intruders.

"What are you doing in my house?" she asked with concern on her face.

Paklit followed her, "Son, stay back. These people might be dangerous," she warned with concern.

Kuchep was taken aback and looked at Kitan with wide eyes, "I'm sorry, we just escaped from the lowlands and don't know where to go. We mean no harm, I promise."

Betot woke up to see a familiar face but couldn't remember where he knew the angry lady from. Kuchep couldn't recognise the woman either. They stared at each other for a moment, "Please… please don't worry, we mean no harm. We will leave now," Betot finally said.

Betot and Kuchep departed with their belongings. Kitan embraced her son tightly, causing him to protest, "Mother! Please let go! I can't breathe!"

Kitan identified Betot as Daniel's companion during the traumatic sexual assault. She remembered that Paklit came about because of the bitter incident. Overwhelmed with emotions, she ran back to the forest, leaving Paklit in tears and haunted by the memory. She sought solace in the fresh air, allowing herself to release her tears in private.

After composing herself, she returned home, unconcerned about the welfare of Betot and his female companion who were there earlier. Frantically searching every corner of her house, she panicked when she couldn't find Paklit. "Why is this happening? Why is Paklit missing now?" she muttered to herself, feeling frustrated.

Just as she was about to search by the river, she saw Paklit returning. "Why did you leave the house alone? I was so worried about you!" she scolded, embracing him with relief.

"I'm sorry, mother. I was worried about you too, that's why I followed you," Paklit apologised. They went inside, promising never to leave each other's side again.

"I've seen… seen that lady before! I've seen that… that lady before!" Betot kept repeating to himself as they walked through a grassland.

"What are you mumbling about? Do you really know the lady?" Kuchep asked.

"Yes… yes, but I can't remember where… where or how," Betot replied.

As they pushed through, they came across a pile of dirt stacked like miniature mountains. Kuchep almost stepped on one, but Betot stopped her, grabbing her chest in an accidental movement of precaution.

Kuchep's face reddened and tried to push Betot away, "Hey! What are you doing?"

Betot, still concentrated at the pile of dirt with his hands still cupped on Kuchep's chest from behind.

"Hey! Let go!" Kuchep screamed, struggling to remove Betot's hands.

"I'm… I'm sorry! You almost stepped on one of these piles, which… which would have been disastrous," Betot explained finally removing his hands.

"What do you mean disastrous?" Kuchep asked.

Betot warned that disturbing the pile would result in bad luck and the culprit would suffer from a serious illness. Out of nowhere, a multitude of tiny beings materialised in front of them. The males sported pointed hats and green trousers, while the females were clad in long-sleeved dresses with flowing skirts and dark hair, lacking the pointed hats.

"Those… those are ampasit. They are small, annoying creatures that… that manipulate humans like toys. Be… be cautious," Betot whispered to Kuchep's left ear.

"Let's… let's leave this place," he suggested.

Kuchep was focused on the ampasit, who were playing like children. Her wide smile encouraged the ampasit to continue playing and showcasing their abilities. One performed a backflip, another did a handstand, and the others joined in. Betot attempted to pull her away, but she was captivated by the little ones and her feet remained firmly planted on the ground. He observed some of the ampasit blowing colourful dust at her face. They also tried to blow dust towards him, but he moved to the side to avoid it touching his body. Feeling a surge of determination, he lifted her motionless body with all his strength and headed in the opposite direction.

Kitan was gathering fruits and edible fungi just a few stone-throws away from their humble abode when her legs brushed against the fine thorn of a poisonous plant. She didn't think much of the redness that formed, but when she arrived home, her temperature suddenly spiked. Her young son tending to the chickens, noticed her condition and asked, "Mother, what happened to you?"

"I have no idea, Paklit. I must have gotten it from the woods while gathering food," she replied.

Paklit, unsure of what to do, carried out his mother's instructions to wash the affected area of her legs with lukewarm water. In his haste, he splashed hot water on his arms but continued with the task. He then fetched cold water from the spring, mixed it with the hot water, and poured it over the affected area. The swelling and redness subsided temporarily but worsened later on.

Meanwhile, Kabunyan, observing from a vantage point near Mt. Pulag, felt a deep sense of concern for the mother and child. He called upon Amba-hit, the healing spirit, to go to the human realm and aid Kitan in her recovery, showing Amba-hit the dire situation of the mother and child.

Amba-hit appeared behind Kitan, who was lying on the floor, out of nowhere. Paklit wiped away his tears and took a second look at the thin man with colourful loincloth, a protruding belly, fiery hair, and headgear made of plants. He was about to scream, but before he could, Amba-hit reassured him, "Don't be afraid. I am Amba-hit, and I am here to help heal your mother." With that, he vanished, leaving behind a smoke-like substance that moved towards the affected area. A voice then instructed Paklit, "Don't intervene. Just feed your mother and give her something to drink. Trust that she will heal."

That night, there was no improvement with his mother's condition which made Paklit doubt whether he should believe Amba-hit. He stayed up all night, watching over his mother. As the first rays of the sun appeared, the affected area started to peel like a fish scale, and the new skin returned to its previous state. Kitan woke up and exclaimed, "My Paklit. My Paklit." as she embraced him.

Paklit matured into a strong man, both in the physical and mental sense, due to the relationship he had with his mother.

A blood moon night that brought bad luck, appeared in the sky. While his mother rested inside, Paklit gazed at the stars, contemplating their mysteries. A foul smell filled the air, leading him to a decaying man who had intruded into their home. With his fast reflex, he scared the creature away with his spear, protecting his mother. Throughout the night, he kept a vigilant watch over her, only to find her lifeless the next morning, her skin became shriveled and dry. Overwhelmed with grief, Paklit did not realise that the decaying man he encountered was Bingil, the ghoul with a deadly touch.

Paklit cried non-stop throughout the entire day. The smell of death permeated the surroundings. He left his mother's body inside the house without taking any action. His emotions were overwhelming, and he felt like they would never end.

Uncertain of what to do next, he questioned his ability to carry on without her. Exhausted from his constant weeping, he collapsed into a deep slumber on the ground. Unmoving, he ignored the discomfort of red ant bites leaving red, swollen marks on his skin.

The intense heat from the sun worsened his condition, causing his skin to sweat profusely, then that evaporated, leaving it dry and red. He felt almost lifeless, struggling to breathe under the scorching heat. He found himself in a cold rainforest, where he saw an elderly man with a balding head and a heavy build standing to his left.

The man introduced himself as Semanget, his grandfather, and urged him to return to the human world. Startled, he woke with his skin still irritated and painful from the sunburn. Seeking relief, he sought shade and then cooled off in a nearby creek. After regaining his composure, he returned home and buried his mother Kitan in the backyard in a solemn lonely atmosphere.

He coped with the absent mother's passing by tending to his crops and fruit trees. He gazed at the starry sky every night, but instead of pondering its nature, he thought of his mother. One night, the sky was devoid of stars, prompting him to question their absence. The following nights were the same.

The 'adagots,' winged beings known as fairies, flew above the humans, including Paklit. They hesitated to reveal themselves to humans, fearing their violent nature due to past sufferings and conflict they witnessed. However, a daring 'adagot' named Bintang, meaning star, ventured closer to the land. She observed Paklit working in his fields near his small 'kubo' house, filling her heart with joy. She returned to the clouds with the other adagots to rest.

She disregarded her fellow' adagot's' advice and continued to explore the human world. She once more approached Paklit's house and landed at the front door. Paklit, concerned about her identity, hurried towards her.

"Who are you and what do you want from me?"

"I can sense your worry. Please don't be, for I am Bintag, one of the 'adagots,' here as your guardian."

He examined Bintag closely again, and her radiant smile that highlighted her beauty caused his body to heat up and his heart to race.

He invited her inside and prepared a meal of eggs, leftover 'pinikpikan' chicken, and 'tapuy' for her to try. Bintang, unfamiliar with human food, tasted and took a sip that made her fall asleep.

Seizing the opportunity, Paklit removed her detachable wings and concealed them under a stack of hay in the nearby storage room.

Bintag woke without her wings and recalled some of the events from the day before.

"Why am I here and where are my wings?" she asked.

"I'm not sure. I discovered you passed out on my front step, so I brought you inside."

She didn't understand at first, but they lived together and had two daughters and a son. While Paklit tended to his vegetable garden, Bintag looked after their children. While searching in the storage room for some cleaning tools, she discovered her wings. Realising what had happened, she attached her wings at her back and flew away, leaving Paklit to care for the children. Paklit raised their three children on his own until his passing.

Betot rested his exhausted body under a pine tree, leaning against the rigid Kuchep. As Betot fell into a deep sleep, Kuchep's body reverted to its normal state as the effects of the 'ampasits' dust wore off. A group of men dressed in full attire and riding horses discovered the two. One of the men nudged Betot's feet with the tip of his shoe to wake him, saying, "Wake up. Wake up." Betot, frightened by the men on horseback, attempted to climb the tree to escape, leaving Kuchep behind. However, they held him down, preventing him to do so.

"Please… please don't hurt me! Please!" Betot begged.

Daniel was standing behind the men, his laughter concealed. "I know them," he stated. The men remained silent but released Betot. "Daniel, you're… you're really enjoying this, aren't you? You knew all along but you let me embarrass myself before saying anything."

"It's your call, let's go," one of the warriors said, showing no emotion.

One of the men unsheathed his sword in shock and struck down a feral dog. Betot and Kuchep, who had just woken up, were startled by the sudden attack. Another warrior took the dead animal and the group proceeded on their journey without waiting for the friends to catch up.

As they walked, they came across a colony of beehives hanging from a tree. Betot and Kuchep ran to avoid getting stung by bees. In contrast, Daniel and the rest of the group moved closer to the hive.

"What… what are you doing?" Betot shouted from a distance.

Kuchep ran in concurrence with Betot. Daniel got closer to being stung. The warriors took the beehive and shook off the bees. They didn't retreat as if their skin appeared to be impenetrable. None of them reacted and simply brushed the insects off their bodies. They placed the beehive in a basket and carried it along. Kuchep and Betot assisted Daniel in removing the bees from his skin, causing him to scream in agony. The warriors noticed what was happening wearing smirks on their faces, deeming Daniel as a weakling.

They returned to the village with a wild dog, a wild chicken, and honey, which Betot and Kuchep had never seen before. The dog and chicken were cooked in various dishes to feed the entire village, much to the surprise of Betot and Kuchep, who had expected the hunt to yield less food. The honey was extracted from the hive, with some bees left and the larvae were saved for another dish. The sweet honey was squeezed from the honeycomb, and only a select few, including the elders and adults, were allowed to savor the liquid. The intense sweetness caused some to experience throat pains and dizziness, leading them to see things that weren't really present.

Early the next day, Daniel hurried to where Kuchep and Betot were sleeping. "Hey, wake up. We need to go," he whispered.

"What's going on?" Kuchep asked.

"No time to explain. Just come with me. We have to leave before anyone wakes up," Daniel urged.

They quietly made their way to the gate, and a young boy caught sight of their departure as he stirred from his sleep, then drifted back to sleep once they were out of the village.

Chapter VII

As time went by, Beyei noticed that she had gained weight and became preoccupied with her belly. She had been feeling unwell. The women in the village were aware of her situation - she was pregnant. The main question on everyone's mind was, "Who is the father?" It was clear that they suspected Daniel. The villagers gossiped about her behind her back, but they were too scared to confront her directly.

Upon hearing about the pregnancy, the advisors, the feng shui expert in particular, made sure to take measures to ensure that their leader stayed calm and rested in bed. He directed the servants to help her with most activities, as it was believed in their culture that lifting heavy objects or making sudden movements could pose a risk to the pregnancy.

One night, eerie spirits could be heard making faint sounds, keeping people awake despite their need for rest. An elderly woman was in Beyei's room assisting with the childbirth, with some servants by her side.

"I have a bad feeling about this," the elderly woman thought to herself.

She was in unbearable pain; worse than any childbirth she had ever seen. She cried out in agony, her words incomprehensible as she endured the labor. The older woman helping her had to forcefully deliver the baby and clear its airway in an attempt to save its life. Despite their efforts, the baby did not survive.

To spare Li Men from grief, the baby was quickly buried, and a servant's newborn was substituted in its place. The servant was bound, placed on a horse, and sent away to a distant land, fearing the truth would be revealed, never to return.

Ming, known as Beyei's son, was an average young man without any exceptional talents. He had grown up in his mother's household, surrounded by servants and a mentor in life. The number of aging warriors was on the rise. Ming required young men from each family to be honed as future warriors. Training sessions were held regularly.

The first group of pupils were torn away from their families; mothers pleaded for their sons to be exempt fearing for their safety due to the perceived extreme training. Fathers, however, urged their sons to undergo the training to toughen them up and bring honour to their families.

"Formations!" a warrior called out.

The young men were confused and unsure of what to do. The command was repeated with a hint of frustration. Other warriors gestured for them to form a straight line from front to back, facing their leader's quarters.

"Introducing the pupils to our esteemed leader!" the warrior announced loudly.

Beyei emerged and meticulously assessed each pupil. Satisfied with the group, she signaled to Cheng, the warrior chief, that the training was ready to commence. The pupils were then instructed to head to the 5th mountain, where they could put their hunting skills to the test on the abundant wildlife in the area, which was deemed safe for the young trainees to handle.

A herd of wild boars with sharp curved tusks detected the pupil warrior group's presence. The warriors were aware of the danger, but the pupils, being inexperienced, ventured into the woods first. Some of the pupils who entered the woods retreated in an instant upon encountering the wild boars.

"Wild... Wild boars! There are so many wild boars!" one pupil exclaimed, trying to capture his breath. However, a pupil named Xiaoxan remained in the woods. He climbed a tree and observed the animals below. One boar had strayed from the group and was feeding alone. Xiaoxan picked some fruits from the tree and threw them in different directions, causing the animals to scatter. The lone boar continued to eat, unaware of the danger. Xiaoxan leapt onto its back, swiftly stabbing it with his dagger. He then grabbed the dead boar and fled from the aggressive pack.

He stumbled once during his run but it didn't slow him down enough for the wild boars to catch up to him. "Help him!" a warrior commanded the pupils. They drew their weapons and swung at the animals, causing them to back off.

"I'm impressed. How did you manage to catch one and escape?" a warrior asked.

"I honestly have no idea. Maybe it's pure instinct," Xiaoxan replied.

"Return to the woods and do not come back until you have caught something! Xiaoxan, perhaps you can show how it's done!" the leader commanded.

The pupils went on with a single goal in mind: to catch as much game as possible. Boars were displayed in one corner, wild chickens in another, and some deer as well. Some pupils, eager to impress, rushed in without a plan. They hurled their weapons at any animal they could find first, causing them to scatter, making the hunt more difficult.

Xiaoxan called out, trying to stop them, but no one listened. Only a few of the pupils stood by Xiaoxan, watching their colleagues make a spectacle of themselves. Among the animals was a massive creature that stood upright, hairy with sharp teeth and claws. It let out a deafening roar that sent everything in its path retreating. The trainee warriors fled without catching anything.

"You have disappointed the forest guardian Sanadan with your actions!" the leader scolded.

"Try again until each of you has something to present to me," he demanded.

Despite objections, Xiaoxan assumed leadership of the group. They followed his plan, with some members climbing the tree and others positioned at the base, prepared to strike. The plan proved effective, as they successfully speared a deer. Two members carried the animal whilst the others hurried away to avoid being seen.

One member struggled to keep up despite his best efforts to run. When he glanced back, he spotted Sanadan. He made a desperate attempt to flee, but the creature caught him and dragged him in the opposite direction, towards its den. The pupil became the substitute for the animal they had hunted.

They departed from the woods with their two hunted animals. "Count off!" Cheng commanded. It was then discovered that they were short one pupil, a detail that the group had overlooked until they were on their way back.

Their return was not met with celebration. The hunted animals were prepared and served primarily to Xi Yan.

"How did my son Ming do?"

"Your son did well, he actually caught one of the two animals," Cheng replied.

In reality, Ming had done nothing to help. He had hidden behind a large rock and was one of the first to leave the forest. He was the weakest among the pupils and always needed help during the journey. The horses that were used to pull Xi Yan's carriage had two offspring. One of them was discovered to be in poor health with no hope of improvement. It was left in the wilderness to die naturally. It could not be consumed as food for it was believed to bring misfortune. Nearby, fierce predators with sharp claws, teeth, and voracious appetites surrounded the ailing horse as it fought to remain standing.

A group of nomad hunters found themselves witnessing what unfolded. "Look at what the beasts are doing!" they exclaimed. They then threw their spears at the beasts, hitting one and causing them to run away.

"What kind of creature is this?" one of them asked.

Intrigued, they brought the animal back to their temporary camp, offering it water to drink and food to eat as they observed it closely. They cleaned the animal as they crossed a river on their way to the settlement, eager to learn more about it for future encounters.

The animal developed into a magnificent running creature. It was harnessed to a cart and became the primary mode of transportation for their leader Talawa. Unlike the previous beast, the carabao, which required shade and constant water to stay cool, this animal could move with minimal water needs.

During one of their travels, they were ambushed by the Kumad tribe, a mixed group of highland and lowland people due to intermarriage. The Kumad tribe utilised a distinctive weapon, the rapid-firing bow and arrow, which was uncommon among mountain inhabitants. The nomads were under attack by the arrow weapons, leading to the deaths of many, with only a handful able to flee, including a creature that disappeared into the woods. A warrior protected Talawa by shielding him with his body, absorbing the spears' impact, but tragically, Talawa succumbed to subsequent spear strikes.

The creature sprinted past the original Busol community, located above Salaghayan, the underworld Kingdom of Napuagan, which had control over the majority of Busol's residents. In their quest to create a formidable race of warriors, they would launch raids on other kingdoms and villages to capture the most exceptional women, who would then give birth to superior men. With the guidance of the powerful Napuagan through visions, Dutab Kingdom was singled out as a target. Dutab was renowned for its exceptional women, believed to possess qualities that, when combined with the Busols, would produce extraordinary offspring as envisioned by Napuagan.

The night was calm, with everyone in slumber. The guards at the entrance gate had also drifted off to sleep. Unbeknownst to them, Busols had surrounded the Kingdom. Some were perched on trees, others hidden behind bushes, and some positioned behind rocks. They waited patiently for the opportune moment. One of them approached the entrance and peered through a gap in the log fence, noticing that two of the three guards were sound asleep. Equipped with makeshift ladders, they climbed the fortress walls. The startled guards were taken by surprise and attacked with daggers, spears, and bolos, or beheaded with gamans.

The commotion roused everyone from their slumber. The cries of numerous women echoed through the night. The warriors found themselves outnumbered as they tried to rescue the young ladies who were being abducted from their homes. The parents who attempted to defend their daughters were either killed or incapacitated.

Ba-ey ventured outside to investigate but did not intervene to halt the assault. Instead, he suffered a fatal blow when a spear pierced his chest. The Kingdom fell to the Busol, led by Mayangao, the largest and most formidable member of the group. Standing over Ba-ay, who struggled for breath, Mayangao seized him by the hair. With a swift motion, he raised Ba-ay and swiftly beheaded him using a gaman.

Mayangao confidently strode into the leader's quarters and settled into the ornate throne, made of sturdy wood and embellished with detailed carvings of an eagle, gecko, and warrior. His body adorned with the blood of the Dutab people, he radiated strength.

"I am the most formidable conqueror in the world!" he declared boldly. The surviving Dutab warriors were imprisoned in bamboo cages, while the chosen women became Busol partners, as many as they pleased.

In the western direction, Betot took the lead with confidence, stating that he knew the area well. Daniel and Kuchep exchanged confused glances and questioned inquisitively, "What… what are you referring to?" Betot clarified with a grin, "This path leads to my hometown: Ibohotak."

As they neared the village, Betot hurried towards the entrance, while Daniel and Kuchep followed behind at a casual pace. A young guard at the gate stopped Betot, brandishing a dagger at his throat. Betot promptly identified himself, saying, "I am Betot…, and… and I am a native of this village!"

An older guard arrived, and recognised Betot with a greeting of welcome. He reassured the young guard that Betot and his friends were allies. "It's okay, I can vouch for them," he said, smiling.

The young guard once again gestured with aggression towards Betot, pulling his dagger from Betot's neck. The older guard stepped in and moved Betot away from the young guard, advising him to calm down and relax. The young guard complied with the older guard's instructions, showing respect for his elder.

"Don't stress about him. He's just another one of those young warriors who always believe they have all the answers."

"These are my friends, Daniel and Kuchep."

Kuchep smiled at the guard while Daniel bowed. Before the guard could react Betot spoke again.

"This is my childhood friend Bekdas. We practically grew up together."

"Never mind bowing. A simple recognition gesture will suffice," Bekdas said.

They headed straight to Bekdas' house, where they enjoyed some fruit and tonic drinks.

"This drink is so refreshing. It goes down smoothly and really revitalises the body," Kuchep remarked.

"Ah, it's a blend of herbs, tree leaves, and forest fruits that have a cooling effect and can help the body recover from fatigue," Bekdas explained.

They strolled through the village, attracting attention from everybody. Kuchep tidied up the house and prepared dinner for the four of them. She made a dish of mushrooms with peanuts and sweet potatoes she found in the kitchen.

"Are you planning to stay here?" Bekdas asked.

"I'm… I'm not sure yet," Betot replied.

"I haven't seen… seen my nanang around here," Betot mentioned.

Bekdas looked at him with concern. "She passed away shortly after hearing the news that you were missing or possibly dead."

Betot took a bite of the food and tears welled up in his eyes as he lowered his head in grief. He refrained from crying out loud to avoid revealing his true identity. Daniel and Kuchep observed him with sympathy. "We're sorry for your loss, my friend," Daniel said, attempting to console Betot. He gently pushed away Daniel's hand and continued to cry in silence.

Bekdas resumed his position, while Daniel and Kuchep encouraged Betot to take a walk in the woods to clear his mind. Betot was still being tough on himself, so they had to push him to go.

At the entrance, the same young guard who had been on duty asked, "Where are you off to? Are you finally leaving?" with a mocking expression. He then made a kissing gesture towards Kuchep before letting them through. Kuchep was repulsed by the gesture, but Daniel comforted her, saying, "Just ignore it. The important thing is that he didn't touch you or anything."

Betot sat at the edge of a cliff, staring out at the horizon, which made his friends worry about him.

"Don't dwell on your mother's passing. There is nothing we can do but go on with our lives." Kuchep urged.

Betot looked at her incredulously, "How… do you know what I'm feeling? Do you have some kind of power?"

"As a matter of fact, I can sense it to some extent. You're considering jumping, but you lack the courage," Kuchep replied.

"Both of you, just be quiet! Betot, move away from the edge!" Daniel ordered.

Betot moved reluctantly, and they settled on a grassy area in the forest where the trees didn't block the view of the sky. Daniel directed them to find a comfortable position, and they complied. Betot sat cross-legged, while Daniel and Kuchep laid down. They were told to take deep breaths and remain quiet. As they concentrated on their breathing, Betot began to snore. Daniel and Kuchep allowed him to sleep and carried on with their relaxation exercise.

The sky was growing darker, and the yellow twinkling dots filled the air. Bekdas ventured out to find them. "There you are! Come inside. It's getting dark!" His shout startled the three back to the present moment.

They returned to the village, with only a single torch lighting their way. They assumed Kuchep was following behind them, but realised she was missing when they reached the village. Daniel and Betot went back outside to search for her.

"I wish I could join you in the search for your friend, but I have responsibilities here in the Bokodians," Bekdas said, handing them food and drinks.

"I… I understand, but this time I… I have to go with Daniel," Betot replied.

The two thanked Bekdas and continued their search.

"Where… where do you think she… she could have gone?" Betot inquired.

"It's hard to believe she could have disappeared so suddenly," Daniel replied.

Equipped with stronger torches, they pressed on with their search, remaining vigilant to any activity in their surroundings. They came across a small creature in the undergrowth, then a larger one. Tired, they eventually drifted off to sleep under a tree as the sun started to peek over the horizon.

Betot woke to an odour very familiar to him. He sought the source and saw blood droplets on the ground a few steps from his position. A piece of torn cloth from Kuchep's clothing was on top of a bush next to it.

"Daniel, wake up! Daniel, wake up!" He rushed back towards Daniel.

"What is it?"

"I… I found blood on the ground and what… what looks like a torn piece of cloth from Kuchep's clothes."

They proceeded to investigate the things much closer. Daniel kneeled and saw the blood closer, then picked up the torn cloth to take a closer inspection.

"The… the Busols must have taken her. I'm sure of it. The… the odour of the blood is… is very familiar to me. I couldn't think of anything else."

Daniel was overwhelmed by his thoughts. He couldn't stop thinking about his actions towards women he couldn't control himself around. The image of Kuchep suffering at the hands of the Busols haunted him.

"Kuchep is more than just a friend to me, she's precious. I need to focus on getting back home from this ancient realm of monstrosity," he kept telling himself.

Chapter VIII

The Busol was pulling Kuchep along as she tried to free herself. In her struggle, Kuchep managed to disrupt one of the Busol's faces.

"She's quite the fighter," the injured Busol commented. Impressed by Kuchep's resilience, some of the Busols thought she was special and chose to offer her as a gift to their leader. The Busols cheered excitedly with high-pitched screams, a noise that Daniel and Betot could hear in the distance.

The people in cages gasped loudly and their eyes widened as they watched Kuchep being presented to Mayangao.

"Your mighty and ever powerful leader! We present you this fine specimen of a partner!" one of the Busol warriors said.

"Bring her closer to me and I will make a true lady of her!" Mayangao declared.

Kuchep kept fighting, making one of the warriors trip as she attempted to flee. Despite her efforts, the warriors were able to subdue her. Filled with rage, Mayangao grabbed his spear and threw it at the warrior who had almost allowed Kuchep to get away, resulting in his immediate death. He then ordered the other warriors to take the body outside and get rid of it.

She was confined in an empty room within Mayangao's residence, the door shut for darkness. Despite her attempts, she succumbed to fatigue and hunger. Mayangao eventually opened the door, letting in a beam of light.

"If you promise to behave, I will set you free and you can serve as one of my servants," he declared, as a servant placed sweet potatoes and water on the floor. Kuchep looked at Mayangao without uttering a single word and eagerly devoured the food as if it were her first meal ever.

Mayangao stepped outside and gazed at the sun shining down on the natural world, feeling its warmth for the first time in what seemed like ages.

"I proved them wrong. Those who underestimated me, thinking I'm weak and foolish," he whispered to himself with a devilish smile.

Kuchep felt compelled to comply with every request from Mayangao out of concern for her own safety. She noticed that she received preferential treatment compared to the other servants. She wore luxurious woven garments and was treated as if she were the leader's equal. She was saddened to witness Mayangao mistreating the other servants, as he would grab one of them and lock them in a room together, causing female screams to be heard from outside. She noticed that the other servants had stopped their tasks and huddled together on one side, covering their ears, crying, and shaking as if there was a severe earthquake. Kuchep felt a strong desire to comfort them, but she was powerless to do so.

After the occurrence in the room, Mayangao emerged covered in sweat that nearly obscured the tattoos all over his body. The woman remained on the floor with tousled hair, staring off into space. Mayangao poured tapuy from a vase into a bamboo container and downed a large serving in one gulp. He then went outside to air dry in the cool breeze.

"This Mayangao is truly wicked. I detest him to the core of my being. I wish for him to be cursed or meet a gruesome end one day," Kuchep thought to herself. She tended to the woman, helping her get dressed. "No! Stay by my side! Let them do what they are here for!" Mayangao yelled in frustration.

Both Daniel and Betot had contrasting strong feelings about the events that unfolded as they delved into their purpose.

"To be honest, I'm not from around here. I come from another world and I need to find a way back home," Daniel explained.

"But… Kuchep is our friend, our sister, and… and she needs us, especially during this difficult time," Betot pleaded.

Betot stood still, arms crossed, indicating his refusal to accompany Daniel on his journey.

"Fine! Fine! I'll have to go on with or… or without you!" Daniel said, pausing briefly to look at Betot.

Betot went in the opposite direction towards the Busol territory, a path he knew well. Meanwhile, Daniel kept looking for a way back home.

Daniel's stubborn and selfish behavior gave Napuagan the chance to carry out his hidden plan. While walking through the Esimeng Forest, a vast and endless expanse of forest, Daniel paused at a guava tree to gather some fruit. After a brief break to savour the fruit, he resumed his trek, determined to find his way home. Despite his efforts, exhaustion set in as he walked for what felt like hours, only to discover he had unknowingly circled back to the very same guava tree where he began.

"What the…..? This must be the same guava tree I started from!" he exclaimed in frustration.

He was resolute in his determination to find a way back to the modern world he knew. He recognised parts of the forest he had passed before and made a conscious effort to avoid them, seeking out alternative routes. He left a trail by placing broken twigs with pierced leaves on the ground as markers of his route and also made slashes on trees to monitor his movement. He was confident that he would eventually find his way out, whether on the second attempt or the third, thanks to the methodical approach he had adopted.

"Damn it! I'm right back where I started!" Daniel in a strained quality of voice. He pounded his fist against a tree trunk.

Climbing up to a thick branch, he thought he was safe, but his snoring interrupted his breathing. Suddenly, he felt a heavy weight on his chest and saw an overweight man with dark skin and a pot belly, his dark shiny hair swaying. The man appeared and disappeared quickly, saying "Hi! Hi! Hi!" in a high-pitched voice. Daniel tried to scream but couldn't, losing his breath. Waking up in pain, he saw the man staring at him. "What do you want from me?" Daniel cried out.

His cries fell on deaf ears as he was left alone on the largest branch of the tree he had climbed. He tried to move a muscle, but his body was so stiff it felt like part of the tree. His feet were tangled in the branches, making it impossible to escape. He screamed until his throat was raw, eventually losing consciousness and drifting in and out of awareness. His mind was consumed with questions: "Why am I here in this situation? What have I done to deserve this?"

A drop of water landed on his forehead, followed by gentle droplets that soon turned into a heavy rain. He was suspended, his body drenched and supported by a branch. Despite feeling the cold from the dropping temperature, he remained still without shivering.

"If this is the end for me, so be it," he thought to himself. A loud crack of lightning filled the air, momentarily blinding him, but he couldn't react. A powerful thunderclap split the tree in half, causing him to fall. Luckily, he escaped injury as the tree trunk fell just a few feet away. It was Bagilat, the God of lightning and thunder, with his thunderous hair and strong physique, riding a moving cloud and wielding a thunderbolt, who had targeted the tree. Bagilat glanced at Daniel, smiled, and then floated away into the sky. The rain ceased, and the sun reappeared.

His body had dried and he had regained the ability to move, much to the anger of Napuagan, who was observing him from the underworld through the river of lava. He watched from a large rock where he stood, muttering, "Curses! Curses! The gods are somehow protecting him, thwarting my every move."

Daniel lost his parents at an early age to a bus accident, when it fell into a ravine. He was raised mainly by his grandmother with some relatives pitching in from time to time. He was a skinny overgrown kid who got picked on by almost everybody. Because of his situation, he did not have any friends and he thought that his intellect was off-putting to others. The school children always laughed at him whenever he arrived chanting "Four eyes post!" which he ignored. The important thing was they did not get physical with him nor hurt him.

"What is this happening to me again, that I could not comprehend?" Daniel asked getting in and out of consciousness.

A plump child stood at the school entrance, waiting for Daniel. "Hey, four eyes! What do you have there?" he said in a threatening tone. Daniel tried to ignore him and kept walking, but the plump child persisted. "Are you ignoring me?" he shouted, pointing to himself. Daniel continued to ignore him and walked on. The plump child then grabbed Daniel's backpack, causing him to fall to the concrete floor unconscious.

A passing teacher quickly called for a student to run to the nearby public clinic for help. The teacher then alerted her colleagues, who performed chest compressions and mouth-to-mouth resuscitation on Daniel. The plump child left the scene without checking on Daniel and went to his class. The other students who witnessed the incident also remained silent.

Daniel was transported to the clinic on a stretcher by two health workers and several teachers on foot. Students in the classroom looked out the windows to watch as he was taken away, with some fearing the worst. An X-ray was ordered, revealing no serious injuries. His grandmother arrived in a panic, asking, "What happened to my grandson?" Her cries filled the clinic with sorrow.

A health worker reassured her, "Don't worry, mam. He's okay. Just a minor injury." The grandmother continued to cry out, "No! No! My grandson!" as the health worker tried to comfort her.

The next look on her face appeared as if she was gazing into emptiness. However, she received information about the person who had been bullying her grandson. She identified the bully and understood how it had affected her grandson. In addition, she obtained the bully's family address. She calmly instructed, "Young lady, please keep an eye on my grandson as I need to step out for a bit." The entire clinic observed her departure with curiosity. She walked a short distance from the clinic to the bully's residence, which was practically a mansion. Upon knocking on the door, which was as large as a gate, the bully answered.

"Are your parents' home?"

"No, why do you ask? And who are you?"

She began chanting and pointing at the bully, causing the wind to pick up and even blow off the bully's cap. His curly hair became disheveled, and his skin hair stood on end, indicating a sense of unease. The bully quickly locked the door and retreated to his room. Daniel's grandmother returned to the clinic, appearing like a regular elderly woman taking a leisurely stroll.

After an hour or two, the bully's hands began to disappear, followed by his arms and then his head until he vanished completely. He hurried downstairs upon hearing his parents' voices. "Mom! Dad!" he shouted, but they couldn't hear or see him. A younger version of himself entered and handed over his report card.

"We are so proud of you and we love you, our dear Robert," his parents said in excitement as they embraced and kissed the child. It was a different name, as his real name was Albert, not Robert. A gust of wind swept him away, turning him into dust and erasing him from everyone's memories.

Daniel had left the clinic and was now at school, fully conscious without ill effects and attending his class. His grandmother waited outside the school gate, watching him through it with a smile on her face. She then headed home to make lunch for her grandson, as it was already 11 o'clock in the morning.

Daniel returned home as usual. To his surprise, his grandmother had prepared chicken adobo with rice and a Coca-Cola, a departure from their usual meals of green leafy vegetables or wild edible plants.

"Wow, Grandma, what's the occasion?" Daniel asked eagerly, digging into the adobo with his hands.

"Just a special treat for my special grandson," his grandmother replied with a smile, joining him for lunch.

Four years later, his grandmother suffered a massive stroke. Although she recovered from the first attack, her heart stopped beating a few months later. Relatives and friends from various towns and cities gathered at their old house, constructed from lumber and galvanised iron with some rusting parts. An aunt, who was Daniel's mother's first cousin and rarely seen, appeared.

Despite the traditional mountain wake and funeral customs, a simpler service was held due to the costly rituals. The town learned that they were not an original settler, only known by a few. Modest food and refreshments were provided, and eulogies were delivered during the Christian funeral at the public cemetery. The family sold the old property to settle debts accumulated over the years, including the funeral expenses. Contributions from relatives, friends, and attendees, known as "abuloy" in Filipino tradition, were collected to cover the remaining costs.

Daniel, at the age of 16, resided with his aunt and her family. His aunt took care of him, ensuring he attended school and providing for his needs. However, he felt overwhelmed with work and was not allowed to socialise and make friends. He attended a public school known for its poor quality of education, chosen mainly for its proximity to his aunt's large four-story apartment building, in which she rented out some units.

Even his cousins, a boy and a girl, were not particularly close to him, and he lacked a strong emotional bond with them. This situation felt like a form of mistreatment. Feeling disconnected from his family, Daniel decided to leave their care when he turned eighteen and lived all by himself. It made him independent and caused him to lose contact with his family.

"Seriously! What was that? Is it only the figment of my mind or reality playing on me?" Daniel in confusion.

Betot, as stealthy as an eagle, used his spear to infiltrate the Dutab Kingdom one night. Unfamiliar with the area, he silently approached a house. He encountered Mayangao's imposing guard, whom he quickly subdued. However, the guard retaliated by grabbing Betot's hair and effortlessly throwing him into a cage.

"A new victim," one of the captives commented.

Betot stared at them without any reactions, feeling discomfort on his scalp.

"Hey, are you with us?" the captive asked, waving his hand near Betot's face to get his attention.

Betot blinked several times and turned to the captive speaking. "I am alone, trying to rescue Kuchep. Have any of you seen her?"

"First, who are you and where do you come from?" a female captive inquired.

"I… I am Betot, originally from Bokodian."

Everybody in the cage chuckled as if Betot was delivering a joke.

"I… I am just like this… this when I talk," Betot explained.

"I'm Mauchi, and I have no idea of who you're referring to. And everybody must stop! All of us are captives here!" she said in a loud voice as she turned her sight to everybody

"We are not familiar with Kuchep," the male captive stated.

"Does… does anyone here know Kuchep?" Betot asked the group.

No one recognised the name Kuchep until one mentioned a woman taken to Mayangao's quarters. He also explained that Mayangao was the Busol leader.

As darkness fell, the servants served yams and water without meat. "Hey… hey, have you heard from Kuchep? Do… do you know her?" Betot whispered. They continued to provide food and drinks without answering, their furrowed brows showing their concern. Then they left as if their interaction with Betot had never happened.

A light drizzle came, causing the ground to become muddy. The bamboo cages were not water resistant, allowing water to seep in and wet the captives inside. Some of them, particularly the elders, were shivering uncontrollably. Meanwhile, everyone who was in their warm and dry houses ignored the captives and showed no concern for their well-being. Given that the captives were in locations visible to the public.

"Hey! Hey! There's an old man here… here who is sick and needs help!" Betot shouted in a panic.

When no one responded, he shouted again.

"Don't bother. No one here cares about us. We're just nothing," one of the captives remarked.

Betot disregarded the comment and kept making noise. Mayangao, annoyed by the screams, instructed a group of warriors to remove the old man from the cage and silence Betot.

"Be quiet! You are causing a disturbance to our leader!" one warrior scolded as the rest of them carried the old man into Mayangao's quarters.

Betot complied, unaware that the old man was left to deteriorate until his eventual death.

Kabunian was keeping a close watch over Daniel, his heart filled with concern.

Fully grown mushrooms had sprouted where the lightning had struck. Daniel gathered them and used the remaining embers from the tree to start a fire. The mushrooms provided him with much-needed sustenance after his ordeal.

In the distance, a bright light caught his attention, drawing him closer. As he approached, he found an open door leading to a room where a stunning woman stood, her skin glowing and hair shining. She also had the perfect curvature of a real woman. Beside her lay a beautifully woven blanket. The woman laid down, and as Daniel moved closer, his lips could not resist touching her supple cherry lips, experiencing a pleasure like never before.

However, as they went on enjoying each other, memories of Kuchep flashed through his mind. Eventually, the woman's true form was revealed - an old, hunched woman named Kapkapo, a shape-shifting deity with evil intent. Daniel quickly donned his loincloth, leaped over Kapkapo, grabbed his sword on the floor, and repeatedly stabbed her until she finally stopped moving.

He quickly went outside and found himself in the woods again. He kept walking until he came to a body of water, where he drank until he was no longer thirsty. The body of Kapkapo was on the ground, covered in blood, and a human infant emerged from it, leaving behind two dead siblings that crawled out of the woods. The infant stopped and cried in distress while lying on its back. Out of curiosity, a wild boar approached, and the infant's mouth extended a long, snake-like tongue that coiled around the animal's neck, cutting off its air supply, causing it to squeal and die. The infant then swallowed the boar whole. It was the birth of the toyong, a result of Kapkapo's deceitful ways and Daniel's uncontrolled desire for physical pleasure.

Daniel heard the cries of the infant and the squealing of the pig, but he chose to ignore them and ran away in fear. He kept moving, feeling like the forest was the only place on earth. Eventually, he reached the edge of the mountain overlooking a river below. However, every time he tried to approach the river, an unexplained force prevented him from doing so. He even considered jumping into the waters, but an invisible force hindered him.

He heard a thumping sound that he first mistook for a wild animal in the forest. He observed a group of men carrying spears and shields, leading women, children, and elders on horses and cows. He got closer and screamed out for help, but they continued on as if they couldn't hear him as if they were deaf or nobody screamed at them. Despite his repeated cries for help, they paid no attention until they had passed through the forest. Daniel then collapsed against a boulder and wept himself to sleep.

He remained in a specific part of the forest, contemplating his next move. "How can I get out of this endless forest?" he wondered. He noticed a group of birds flying overhead, but none of them landed in the forest. He typically didn't spend much time pondering, preferring to take action as situations arose, but recent events had given him the opportunity to reflect.

"Maybe this is a punishment on me for being so damn horny and couldn't stop my lust?" He thought to himself, thinking of the Christian God that he kept on ignoring from his reality.

He did not attempt to flee the forest any further and accepted his fate.

He may have been foolish in that moment because he never tried to use the power of his sword to cut through the forest and what was preventing him to reach his freedom. Using his strong sword, he collected wood and gathered fine needles from the ground, placing them in one spot. He also collected vines to make rope, dug the ground, and constructed four walls using the wood. The roof took longer to complete due to the short and fine nature of the materials. He discovered clay during his hike and used it to fill the gaps between the wooden walls.

There was no nearby body of water or water source available. He created a watering basin by digging up the ground and placing stones around the edges and an opening to catch rainwater, strong enough to penetrate from above. The humble dwelling evolved into a more intricate structure as he dedicated more effort to his ideas over time, ultimately thriving as a result.

He hiked along the edge of the cliff where wild edible root crops grew. He noticed a small patch of pine needles moving, so he carefully removed the surface layer to reveal a tiny creature. The creature was pinkish in colour with a black snout and emitted a faint squeal. He gently picked it up, noticing that it was only half the size of his hand, and brought it back to his house. He mashed mushrooms and mixed them with the root crops, boiling them together before dipping a piece of cloth into the mixture and placing it near the creature's delicate mouth.

Initially, the creature did not respond, but Daniel persisted, and eventually, it began to suck on the cloth. He placed the creature in a clay bowl with pine needles on top, tending to it with care and attention. Sometimes, he would even leave it inside the house while he went out to gather food. Over time, the creature's teeth grew sharper, its legs became more muscular, and its colour darkened, resembling that of a wild dog. It grew playful and would often run around the house, joining Daniel on his food-gathering trips.

Daniel's dog was no ordinary pet; it was a pili, a guardian of his property with special abilities. Some nights, unseen spirits, known as adi-kaila, would try to disturb and harm Daniel at the command of Napuagan. The pili could see these spirits, unlike humans, and would bark loudly to irritate and drive them away. It could also bite the spirit form of the adi-kaila, instilling fear in them. The pili was named Bertha despite being male. It was dedicated to Daniel's grandmother, who had been his protector when she was alive. Bertha's presence helped to alleviate his loneliness.

A stranger showed up at Daniel's doorstep. His pet Bertha behaved surprisingly well and didn't show any signs of aggression towards the stranger. The visitor was an elderly woman with pale skin, and everything appeared normal as she knocked on the door.

"Please, can someone have mercy and let me in?" she pleaded.

The house was empty, and she waited until Daniel arrived with a few herbs.

"Hmmm!" He noticed the old lady. "Who might she be?" He asked himself.

"What are you doing here?" He asked the old lady as he approached her.

"I am Kopkoppatti, and I have been here for a long time. I believe we can help each other thrive."

"Okay, I am Daniel. How can I help you?"

"As you can see, I am old and can't do heavy work. I can help you with food production. We can support each other."

Daniel didn't respond but allowed the old woman to live with him, thinking they were the only people in the forest.

Chapter IX

The Adagot descendants, the siblings Bantas and Sultana, were married and had a young son named Nugal. Unfortunately, their other sibling remained single. Nugal was not satisfied with staying in Batan forever; he craved adventure. When his parents and aunt were away at work, he would daydream about the world beyond. He would imagine himself riding a majestic beast and using a stick as a sword, pretending to battle imaginary foes. "I am a powerful warrior! Surrender now, defeated enemy!" he would exclaim.

Aunt Kuling arrived from the slope plantation of chayote and taro. "Wow, Hero!" she exclaimed to Nugal with a smile. "Yes, Auntie! I am a strong warrior!"

They entered the house, and Nugal enjoyed some leftover taros and water while his aunt prepared lunch.

Nugal was drawn outside by the sound of marching, leaving his snack unfinished and without his aunt's knowledge. He followed the sound to find warriors with fierce faces, adorned with tattoos, wielding spears and shields. He was so close to them that he could almost touch their heads. Meanwhile, Sultana asked Kuling about Nugal's whereabouts, prompting a frantic search for him. Bantas saw his son dangerously close to the warriors and quickly pulled him back inside the house.

"Where have you been? We've been so worried about you!" Kuling exclaimed.

"He was trying to approach the marching warriors, but I stopped him and brought him here," Bantas explained.

"Please, don't do that ever again. Those men can be dangerous," Sultana cautioned.

Nugal appeared to comprehend everything, but he continued to act in his own childish ways. He ventured into the woods a short distance west of their home. He spotted a butterfly tainted with colourful red, yellow and brown. He decided to follow it until it settled on a sunflower. Unfortunately, he failed to notice a colony of wild bees near the cluster of sunflowers. As he approached the flowers, his shoulder accidentally brushed against the hive hanging from a nearby tree, causing it to swing. The bees swarmed out and began to attack him. Nugal quickly ran back home, but not before the stings had caused his head to swell up like an inflated frog's mouth.

"Nugal! Nugal!" Sultana yelled as she removed the stings with her bare hands.

Nugal wailed in agony, the sound reverberating across the mountain top and reaching the nearest village. Banta and Kuling hurried back home to assist Sultana in extracting the stings. They applied herbs with powerful marijuana oil to the affected areas. Later, they submerged Nugal in the icy mountain stream, which helped numb the pain, reduce the swelling and helped his hot sweaty body.

"Nugal! Why did you do this? You need to behave, or you could have seriously hurt yourself this time!" Bantas exclaimed in frustration.

Nugal couldn't eat and slept the entire afternoon until the sunset. As he woke up, he saw a tan-skinned lady with long, silky dark hair and blue eyes walking in front of him. Her aura was shining brightly, as if rays of the sun were emanating from her. He was mesmerised by her presence and found himself drawn towards her. Even floating on her way. He noticed that his hands looked bigger and saw a more mature version of himself reflected in her eyes. Just as their lips were about to touch, he realised that the lady was as mature as he was. A large, overweight woman with unkempt hair and a strong odour, surrounded by flies, grabbed the lady and sat on his chest, making it difficult for him to breathe. He struggled for an inhale as he was jolted awake from his sleep.

"Nugal! Nugal! Are you alright?" a voice called out.

"Huh! What's going on?" Nugal asked as he woke up.

"You've been asleep since you were stung until this morning. You were tossing and turning and screaming," his aunt Kuling explained.

He described the sequence of events in his dream, which included the fat lady.

"The fat lady you mentioned is likely Bitebit, the spirit of an overweight woman responsible for your current experiences. Her heavy spirit would sit on the chest of anyone who is asleep. It appears that you may have disturbed her dwelling also when you shook the beehive," Kuling clarified.

"Thank the gods, my son, for they must have favoured you, as many who go through similar experiences are not as fortunate," Bantas said.

The near-death experience did not deter Nugal from his adventurous spirit. Instead, it fueled his curiosity about the woman in his dream.

Once again, a group was passing by on the forest passageway near them, as expected. Nugal got older but his curiosity was still as strong as ever. It prompted him to observe the passersby, who were tattooed muscular men riding with a skinny man and a lady tied with ropes being dragged on foot. Nugal made some noises that startled the horses, causing them to run and pull the captives while the men fell and chased after the animals. The captives were on the verge of falling off the cliff, and one of the muscular men met his demise. The rope was caught on a dead tree's root, but it wouldn't hold for long under the weight of the captives. Nugal acted quickly, pulling the man closer to safety before assisting the lady.

Nugal and the woman sought refuge in a cave on the adjacent mountain. He remained by her side for an extended period, hoping that any remaining men had moved on. The woman was so weak that she could barely stand. Nugal offered her some water and instructed her to stay put while he went back home to fetch food, assuring her that he would return. The woman trembled uncontrollably, her head shaking in an unusual manner. Nugal couldn't tell if she was nodding in understanding or due to her weakened state, but he had no choice but to leave her.

"Why are you taking our food?" Kuling asked, catching Nugal in the act.

"I'm just hungry, I'll explain later," Nugal replied, rushing outside with his aunt in pursuit, but she couldn't catch him.

The young lady quickly devoured the sweet potatoes and meat, indicating that she had not eaten in a long time. Nugal remained silent as he watched her.

"I'm sorry. I haven't eaten in a long time," she apologised.

"It's okay. That's why I gave you the food," Nugal replied with a smile.

"What's your name, by the way?"

"I'm Shadimeg from the Kalahan Village. We were attacked by the Busols, and some of us were taken captive."

"I've heard stories about the Busols from my parents and aunt, but I had no idea how ruthless they are."

Nugal could no longer explain why he frequented the outdoors with food and drinks; despite the reasons he had previously given to his parents and aunt. He eventually disclosed the presence of Shadimeg in the cave. His parents accompanied him to meet her in person. She shared her story with them, detailing what had happened to her and her village, leading them to invite her to stay with them in their home.

"We are willing to have you stay with us, but you will need to contribute by helping out with some tasks," Bantas instructed.

"Yes, I am more than willing to do my part," Shadimeg replied.

Nugal's face lit up as if he had just received a stroke of luck or a blessing from the gods.

Shadimeg went to the nearby spring to get water, sticking to her regular routine. Nugal was tending to the goat and its young. Shadimeg handed him a container of water, which he drank without acknowledging her. She felt a little let down but kept fetching water, stealing glances at him as she went by. He never appeared to notice her.

Sultana and Kuling observed Shadimeg's subtle signs of affection towards Nugal, which he seemed unaware of. At dinner, Shadimeg gave Nugal special attention, looking at him with admiration, and even preparing his food with extra sweet potatoes and meat. Nugal, however, seemed indifferent to her gestures and ate his meal without acknowledging the special treatment.

They went to bed with Kuling still awake. "Are you blind?" she asked Nugal.

"What do you mean?"

"I mean, can't you see that Shadimeg likes you?"

"I have noticed it at times, but I thought she was just being nice not just to me, but to all of us for letting her stay here."

"No, you should be mature enough to recognise when a lady is interested in you."

Mayangao and the other Busols were eagerly awaiting the arrival of their comrade, hoping for captives to serve as fighters and servants. As time went on with no sign of their comrade, their impatience increased.

"Why hasn't anyone arrived yet? What could be the delay?" Mayangao demanded, his face showing his frustration.

The Busol warriors, clearly disturbed, struggled to answer their leader. "I don't know, my leader," one said, preparing for any consequences.

There was complete silence, with no indication of anger from Mayangao, no sounds of concern from the Busols or the captives.

Mayangao then directed another group to search populated areas for captives.

"Nangdod! Lead the group!" Mayangao commanded.

"Yes, your leadership?" Nangdod responded as he knelt before Mayangao.

"I name you the leader of this group. Do not return without captives!" Mayangao ordered.

"Yes, your leadership."

The group gathered weapons of all sizes. Their mambunong chanted a prayer and selected a captive, the weakest among them, and beheaded it, letting the blood gush onto the group. He ensured that the blood touched all the members. The captives struggled, some shook, some screamed, and others watched in silence as if they were not witnessing some gruesome scene. The Busol warrior group's screams were so loud that they could disturb the spirits of the afterlife.

This older generation group traveled on foot, unlike the previous one. They always traveled and attacked without transportation and with few weapons. Every step they took and every breath they made instilled fear in every creature they encountered. Birds flew away as their bodies brushed against the bushes. After some time, the group came across a cow grazing in the abundant grassland. A Busol warrior raised his spear, pointing it towards the beast. With a swift throw, he killed the animal instantly. The spear hit the cow diagonally on its side, a remarkable sight to behold.

They efficiently gutted and skinned the cow. The meat was roasted over an open flame. They had strong stomachs, able to digest the still-moving entrails in a dish known as kinigtot. After resting at the spot where the animal was killed and butchered, they waited for the skin to dry so they could use it for clothing before resuming their journey. The flesh provided them with additional energy, causing their movements to be faster than before. They quickly made their way through the trees and bushes, eventually arriving at a village which turned out to be the Bokodian village.

The village was surrounded by a stone wall. They waited until nightfall, chewing a mixture of betel nut, gawed leaves, and lime powder to stay alert. Nangdod made an owl-like sound to signal the attack. The larger Busols broke through the walls while the others entered through the opening. They silently stabbed or slashed the guards. The second attack was successful, capturing several young men and women. The Bokodian guards were unable to defend their village, resulting in a tragic outcome for the Bokodians.

"Why do we keep getting attacked? It's like our village is cursed by the gods," one of the captives remarked. The others exchanged glances filled with sorrow, silently hoping that the Busols didn't overhear her. They tramped along with their captors; their hands bound together in a long, taut rope. They were prodded, kicked, or dragged whenever they displayed signs of exhaustion until they reached the Dutab kingdom.

"Your leadership! We have these three attractive young ladies and two fine young men here!" one of the warriors announced.

"Put them with the other prisoners!" Mayangao commanded.

The Busols were enjoying their successful catch with tapuy, a traditional alcoholic beverage, and a broth made from animal meat. The tapuy had a potent and spicy flavor, enhanced by the fiery chilies that intensified the drink. Laughter filled the air, creating a lively and festive ambiance similar to a celebration in the underworld. It seemed as though their merriment resonated in the underworld, leading Napuagan to direct some adi-kaila to visit the human world and join the Busols in their revelry by granting them extra warrior prowess.

"Get the captives out!" Mayangao commanded.

Betot and the other captives in cages observed the situation. "Why are they coming? What will they do to us?" one of the new captives asked, trembling in fear.

"Be prepared. They will choose two of us to fight each other for their amusement," another captive explained.

"He's right. We need to be prepared," Betot said to the new captive.

They swiftly discussed the strategies they would use during the fight.

"Hey! Two of you need to come out!" a Busol warrior demanded.

When no one replied, the warrior became furious. He forcefully grabbed two individuals with his large hands. One original captive and a new one. Without giving them a moment to catch their breath, he tossed them into a muddy pit encircled by Busol spectators. The crowd cheered "Till death" as they consumed tapuys and boiled meat seasoned with a mixture of salt and chili sauce.

A spear was thrown at the new captive, almost hitting him, while a bolo was thrown at the other.

"Get the spear and throw it at me like you mean it," the original captive said.

The new captive threw the spear but missed his target. The original captive swung his bolo, almost decapitating the new one by a hair and missing. They hugged each other tight. "Hey, if you want to survive, we have to give them a great show as we agreed," the original one said. The new one picked up the spear from the ground and attempted to stab his opponent, but he was punched in the face and knocked unconscious. A spear came flying from the outside and hit the fighter on the ground. The one standing ran to the far edge of the pit and tried to climb out, but he too was hit by a spear. Both met their ends.

The captives in the cage watched with fear and concern as the events unfolded.

The cheers died down and the Busols turned to their leader. "This is the consequence of disobeying my orders," Mayangao said, pointing at the captive with a fierce expression.

Betot witnessed the incident, causing his hair to stand on end and his emotions to weigh heavily on him. He repeatedly scanned the visible area, but Kuchep was nowhere to be found, intensifying his worries.

In Bokodians, luck does not appear to be on their side. They collected many logs and hollowed them out to serve as coffins for each deceased individual. The bodies were placed inside these makeshift coffins and then placed in the cave graveyard. The leader and some elders who died during the invasion were seated on bamboo chairs with spaces between them, and they were positioned under a kubo house with a similar floor pattern as the chairs. Herbs and salt were used on the bodies, and a fire was lit to create smoke that entered the kubo through the floor gaps, without causing harm to the structure. This process continued from days to weeks until the bodies were dried in this mummification process.

The mambunong recounted the stories of the deceased, which were sung by elder women in a ba-dew chant. Special pigs were chosen based on the mambunong's divination. If the mambunong deemed the pigs to be favourable, they were consumed by the entire village. If the divination was negative and indicated bad luck, the pigs were burned as a sacrifice to the gods, and other pigs were slaughtered for consumption by the community.

The village had a somber and melancholic atmosphere. The mambunong collected fingers from the deceased and scattered them on the ground while chanting prayers to seek divine intervention from the gods in healing and protecting the village from invasion. The fingers were then distributed to the family heads for safekeeping, believed to bring good fortune to their families and the entire community.

Mayangao's interest in the Bokodians stemmed from a past incident where they had rejected and exiled him due to his rivalry with Saropa, his beloved. Saropa was taken by Baldano, the leader at the time, who disapproved of their relationship. When Baldano discovered their secret love, he planned to execute Mayangao by beheading him in front of everyone, claiming that Mayangao, a peasant, was unworthy of Saropa. In a desperate attempt to save Mayangao, Saropa agreed to marry Baldano against her will. Mayangao was instead exiled and lived as a nomad in the forest and crossed paths with the Busol tribe during a hunting trip.

Impressed by his skills, the mambunong took him as his slave at first but later recognised his talents. During a festival, Mayangao persuaded the mambunong to let him join a contest where men fought to the death to decide the next leader. In front of the old and frail leader, all the participants were thrown into a pit with different weapons. Despite facing opposition, Mayangao emerged victorious by killing four out of the eleven participants.

Daniel was initially unsure about Kopkoppatti's friendship, but he decided to give her a chance. She became his closest companion in the forest. Upon returning from gathering food, he found Kopkoppatti in front of his house, examining a large log covered in grass. She suggested transforming it into a functional mortar and pestle, sparking Daniel's interest.

After bringing his foraged items inside, he returned to the log and contemplated how to relocate it closer to his house. Despite its bulk, he managed to secure a vine rope around it and effortlessly pulled it, impressed by Kopkoppatti's suggestion.

"Thank you for the help. I can see that you must be exhausted from gathering food and carrying the log. Let me prepare some soup for you and your pet as a token of my gratitude."

Daniel lay on his back indoors with his pet by his side while Kopkoppatti made the soup using ingredients from his foraging and some special additions of her own.

Not long after, Daniel caught a whiff of the enticing aroma that filled the air. He woke up from his slumber and checked on the soup. His body couldn't wait to savour the dish with his mouth watering. Kopkoppatti served him a bowl, one for his pet and another for himself to enjoy.

"That was fantastic! It really woke me up and energised me right away!"

"I'm glad you enjoyed it."

The pili appeared content as he laid there, gazing at Kopkoppatti and making a grateful noise like a happy mut that he was.

The master and pet eventually fell back asleep after a while. Kopkoppatti gently touched the ground near the house and quietly recited a chant, focusing on the plants. She envisioned edible mushrooms and mushrooms began to sprout from the ground. Then, she thought of a fruit-bearing tree and it quickly grew before their eyes. The plants grew rapidly, reaching maturity in just a few moments.

Daniel and his pet were once again disturbed by heavy footsteps. They ventured outside to discover a group of strong, tattooed men carrying coffins containing the mummified remains of their leader.

"Who are they?" Daniel inquired with interest.

"They are members of the Bokodian tribe, transporting their leader's mummified body to its final resting place in a nearby cave," explained his companion.

"Hey! Hey!" He screamed.

"They are oblivious to your calls, much like those who came before them."

"Wait, did you say they are from Bokodian?"

"Yes, they are the Bokodian tribe from Bokodian village."

"My dear friend Betot is also from the Bokodian tribe."

Daniel sat on the ground, lost in contemplation, unaware of the changes around him. His mind was consumed with thoughts of the potential tragedy that may have befallen the Bokodian village.

Chapter X

A new day dawned on the Kapangan village as Xi Yan welcomed a baby boy into the world. In a society where both the Formosa and the adapted mountain culture frowned upon such situations involving women, Xi Yan stood out. Not only was she a woman, but she was also the village leader, a role typically reserved for men. Despite the norms, no one dared to protest against her, fearing her command over the warriors and the belief in her ability to manifest her desires into reality.

Instead of criticism, the village rejoiced in the birth of the baby boy. Festivities ensued, with pigs being prepared in various dishes with the main dish being the traditional wat-wat, some cooked with vegetables, others with sauces, and the broth mixed with noodles to create a unique dish. The celebration included the traditional tayaw dance and acrobatic shows, accompanied by drinks of tapuy and fermented mountain fruits. The majority of the attendees were men, all partaking in the joyous occasion.

The feng shui expert was celebrating with the village, but he was strongly opposed to the birth of a fatherless infant, regardless of who the mother was. "Congratulations on your new baby, the next in line for leadership," he told Xi Yan to her face, feigning sincerity. Xi Yan believed every word her trusted right-hand man said.

Everything seemed normal in the village, with life flowing smoothly and no apparent problems. Despite the peaceful facade, there was an underlying tension building. The feng shui expert, with his keen intuition, sensed the energy of Xi Yan's aura, as he always did. His exceptional insight urged him to bide his time and wait for the opportune moment to address his growing resentment towards his leader.

Yichen, as he was known, grew into a healthy boy. He was always active in the village, often disrupting everyone's activities, but no one seemed to mind. Many of the villagers who had initially opposed their leader's situation had a change of heart after witnessing Yichen in their daily lives, melting their hearts with care. He had one distinctive feature that set him apart from the other boys; a perfect circular mark on the sole of his right foot.

The feng shui expert showed special care for him, which the public noticed. One day, Yichen ran towards his quarters while he was writing with charcoal, and processed wood pulp. Yichen's sudden appearance surprised him, causing him to make an error in his writing. Yichen's screams as he ran also disrupted feng shui expert's concentration, almost causing him to lose his temper. However, he managed to control himself and refrain from lashing out at the boy. "Someday, I'll find a way to use that kid to my advantage," he thought to himself.

Under the moon's glow, the feng shui expert mounted a horse and rode silently towards the Kadasan mountain, home of the revered Patobog. The Patobog, a large man with bronze skin and a bald head that housed his wisdom, sat cross-legged on a boulder in deep meditation. As the feng shui expert approached, the scene was serene and mystical.

"Who dares disturb me?"

"It is I, the feng shui expert. I apologise for interrupting, but I am in need of your wisdom."

"What do you want from me?"

"Your great Patobog. I am seeking guidance on how to eliminate a malevolent force."

"What do you really want me to do?"

The feng shui expert gave more details about his task, and Patobog gave him precise directions. He was told to travel to the scalding pits of Badekbek, where a special tree bearing round red fruit grew. The feng shui expert was instructed to pick one of the fruits, dip it into the boiling pit, and present it to the individual he wished to eliminate. Consuming the dipped fruit would cause the person to be influenced by the giver and driven to carry out the giver's wishes.

He came back to the village while everyone was still asleep and the sky was dark. It was surprising that the guards didn't notice him.

"I couldn't sleep last night and I needed your help. But you weren't there," Xi Yan said the next day, the first thing she said when she saw the feng shui expert.

"Your highness, maybe you came when I was in the bathroom," the feng shui expert replied, with rapid breathing, his temperature rising and his clothes damp.

"Perhaps," Xi Yan said as she walked away, while the feng shui expert bowed to her.

"She must have known something. I must execute my plan soonest. No more with the timing," the feng shui expert whispered to himself.

The following night, he made his way to Badekbek despite not being the right time for the proper harvest. For the fruit must be harvested in the peak of the first moon beaming at the boiling pit. Once again, he managed to leave the village without being noticed.

He bypassed the Patobog to perform the necessary ritual before embarking on his mission. His horse reared with its front legs high, throwing off the feng shui expert. The horse sensed the presence of three serpents. The feng shui expert got up, dusted himself off, and grabbed the rope on the horse's back. He also spotted the serpents and swiftly threw his daggers, killing two of them. He then stomped on the third serpent. He attempted to lead the horse, but it refused to move forward. Trying to push the animal onto its back only resulted in it almost kicking him. He held onto the rope and gave the horse a kick, prompting it to run like the wind. He held onto the rope and struggled to mount the horse until he finally succeeded.

"Halt! Stop!" He shouted, attempting to rein in the horse as he caught sight of smoke and detected the foul odor of rotten eggs. It matched the description given by Patobog perfectly. There lay a pool of bubbling mud, with a lone, surviving tree bearing the coveted red fruit beside it. Eagerly, he plucked the fruit, filling his basket to the brim until the tree was nearly stripped bare. He dipped the fruits into the pit and quickly removed them along with the basket. As he turned to leave, his attempt at stealth was thwarted by a guard who had observed his entry into the village unnoticed.

As the first light of dawn appeared, the servants were getting ready to prepare breakfast for their leader. The feng shui expert unexpectedly took charge of the cooking that morning, much to the surprise of the servants. He peeled and sliced the red fruit before mixing it into the soup bones.

"Your highness, I have prepared a special meal for you to give you strength for the whole day."

"This is something new," Xi Yan with an unexplainable look towards the feng shui expert.

"Yes, your highness, it's a special dish just for you," with a smile that emitted fakeness on his face.

"Why are you serving my food today? You don't usually do this."

"I thought today was a special day and the right time for me to serve you, your highness."

Xi Yan accepted the meal. The feng shui expert stayed nearby, watching closely to see if his leader would take the first bite.

"Why are you still here? You should know of all the people that it's considered disrespectful to watch someone eat unless you're joining in."

"I apologise, your highness. I will leave now."

Xi Yan instructed her servants to discreetly dispose of the food and return the container unwashed. Later, she expressed gratitude to the feng shui expert for the delicious breakfast. The expert smiled and bowed in response. Secretly, the expert planned to continue this tactic until all the fruit was eaten and Xi Yan would be affected by the mind-altering food.

All he needed to do now was wait for the fruit to take effect.

"Your highness!"

"Yes?"

"Nothing."

The feng shui expert tried to assess his leader, but things were not going as planned.

"What's going on? The fruit isn't working. I'll have to find a way to mix it into her food again," he pondered.

His failed attempts left him feeling disappointed. He began to question the Patobog's instruction on how effective it was or if he was just lying straight at him.

He returned to the Patobog's lair to confront him, finding him standing on the boulder with his wooden cane, as though he had been expecting someone to come.

"Ah, there you are!" the Patobog said with a thundering voice.

"You were expecting me?"

"Yes."

"How did you know?"

"It doesn't matter and you should know that you didn't follow my instructions exactly as I have told you. Those impatient such as yourself always find their way back."

The feng shui expert recognised his error, remained silent, and left. What kind of expert was he? It's as if he was completely clueless about the process. One could even claim that he was a fool for making such a grave mistake.

The Patobog determined that the feng shui expert had a sinister nature, because he was harsh towards those with malicious intentions. The feng shui expert journeyed on foot without the aid of a horse. Everything seemed normal until halfway through the journey when his leg suddenly became rigid and immovable. Despite his efforts to move, his legs crumbled beneath him. The same fate befell his other leg, causing him to collapse and shatter into dust-like particles. A gust of wind scattered his remains, causing him to disappear into the air.

Daniel faced the passageway that he could not cross. He had no idea what happened the night before. The demise of the feng shui expert. At the stop right beside where he stood.

"I'm exhausted with my situation! Can't you see that I've been trying to escape this forest prison?" Daniel asked Kopkoppatti, feeling frustrated.

"Patience, young man. You will leave at the right time."

Daniel sat on a leveled rock a few steps from his house and finally noticed the mushrooms and greenery in the front yard.

"When? How?"

"My way of saying thank you."

Daniel was amazed by the richness of the soil. His eyes lit up as he gazed at the plants and mushrooms. He didn't say another word, with his back to Kopkoppatti standing at the door, watching over him.

"Remember, take only what you need for the moment."

Daniel returned to his current reality and decided to prepare a meal using mushrooms and green vegetables. It was his time to take charge in the kitchen, and Kopkoppatti observed from the sidelines. The house was filled with the enticing smell of fresh ingredients as Daniel prepared a soup with a root vegetable. He followed Kopkoppatti's instructions, using just the right amount of ingredients, with only a few leftover scraps that were not necessary for the dish.

"Let me try some." Kopkoppatti said licking her lips.

They both enjoyed the meal together, with Bertha having its own bowl on the floor. Kopkoppatti savoured the broth and took a few bites, her face lit up with joy. They were amazed to see Bertha finish its meal, even though it didn't have any meat in it.

Daniel no longer had to scavenge for food, but he remained determined to find a way to escape. His conversation with Kopkoppatti was unproductive, as she considered the forest her home. Despite this, he continued to explore and eventually discovered a hidden cave. The entrance, covered in vines and vegetation, was revealed when a gust of wind moved a hanging vine aside. A wooden barrier resembling a modern door sealed the entrance. Daniel tried to open it by pulling on the handle, but it remained firmly shut. He exerted all his strength in a second attempt, but the door remained unyielding.

He hurried back home to inform Kopkoppatti about the discovery, hoping she could assist in some way. As he left Makiubaya, the spirit guard of the gateway kept a close watch on him, curious about his next move.

"Hey! I stumbled upon a cave entrance that I couldn't open on my own!" he exclaimed, trying to catch his breath.

Kopkoppatti, who was still inside, came out to speak with him, her expression filled with concern as if anticipating something dreadful.

"Why are you looking at me like that?" Bertha came outside barking, as if agreeing with Kopkoppatti. He approached him and patted his head, causing him to squeal like a sick puppy.

Kopkoppatti then remarked, "Look, Bertha even has concerns for you. She can sense a bad omen approaching."

Kopkoppatti revealed that the cave he found could either be the gateway to the underworld controlled by the malevolent Napuagan or the path to liberation. The reason for the closed door was attributed to the spirit guardian known as Makiubaya. In the past, the cave entrance was open, and numerous individuals ventured inside only to meet their end by mistakenly choosing the route to the underworld.

Daniel was hanging on every word Kopkoppatti spoke, eager for a solution. "Are there ways to successfully enter the passageway? Do you have any abilities that can help?"

"In order to get to know you better, I will share something I have never mentioned before. During the dark night sky, you can see the stars. There is a particular star called Mi'lalabi that can guide you in the right direction even inside the cave."

"How can I recognise the Mi'lalabi?"

"The Mi'lalabi is the brightest star in the north, almost within reach. You will know it when you see it."

Daniel was diligent in looking at the sky during nightfall, to the point of not sleeping. Frustrated, he again confronted Kopkoppatti.

"What are you trying to do? Are you playing with my desires?"

"Be patient. It will come in time. The more patient and calm you are, the better the chances the Mi'lalabi will manifest."

Daniel's frustrations continued to mount as he waited in the darkness, unaware that he was gradually becoming more relaxed. One night, he fell asleep earlier than usual and was awoken by a bright triangular light in the sky. The light approached him, illuminating the cave entrance. At the entrance, he found pieces of etag in a coconut shell and a jar of tapuy that were offered. The light transformed into a small man with a protruding belly and a mustache, who pointed towards a door that Daniel opened in one pull. The man then led him down two pathways, one to the left and the other to the right. The left path was adorned with beautiful flowers, enticing sounds, and a sweet fragrance, while the right path was a plain rocky entrance. The man illuminated the right path.

He woke up to Bertha licking his face as the morning had already arrived.

"You had a good sleep," Kopkoppatti said.

"Yes, I had a dream that showed me the right path and what I need to do," he replied. "It breaks me to leave you, but I appreciate everything you've done for me," he told Kopkoppatti.

"I understand. Just focus on your mission here," Kopkoppatti replied.

He bid farewell to Kopkoppatti, hugged Bertha, and patted its head. As he took his first steps, Bertha followed him. "No! Stay! I have to go alone on this mission," he said to Bertha, who looked at him with a sad expression. Daniel, not one to show much emotion, hugged Bertha one last time before waving goodbye to Kopkoppatti. "Come here!" Kopkoppatti called, and Bertha went to her.

He first went to a remote part of the forest where people wouldn't think to look for stored food and drinks. He collected the etag and rice wine substitute, which were actually wild grains he had fermented. Carrying them with some calculated steps, he headed towards the cave entrance. Feeling the powerful wind and watching the leaves swirling around him, he set down the rice wine and etag. Unsure of what to do next, he knelt on the ground and began to pray.

"Dear Makiubaya, spirit guardian of the cave, I humbly ask for your acceptance of my offering and for the door to be opened!" he called out, hoping his plea would be heard.

After the wind passed, there was no immediate change. He continued to pray and beg for Makiubaya to listen to him. Only when he grew weary of his efforts did he attempt to open the door. To his surprise, it had been unlocked all along, as he had felt the wind against his body. Lighting a piece of wood with fire, he entered the doorway and pushed forward until he reached the intersection. It was just as he had envisioned in his dreams. He chose the correct path and proceeded through it, not realising he had reached the exit until he felt the plants brushing against him. The next thing he knew, he was standing on the dusty road.

He wandered on foot aimlessly, as if he was unfamiliar with the path. He continued on, taking breaks when needed and foraging for food and water whenever possible. His hair had grown to a great length, and his face was covered in fur from the upper lip down. He was constantly sweating, with his body hair always damp.

"I've been traveling for a while now, looking forward to seeing my friends and hoping to return home. But this time, nothing seems to be going as planned," he pondered.

He sat on a grassy area that seemed familiar to him, although he couldn't recall why. The rocks were arranged in a circle around him, and he gathered dried leaves and twigs to the center of the circle to start a fire for cooking. He had collected mushrooms on his way and carried thinly sliced kiniing (a type of preserved meat), which he skewered on sticks and cooked over the fire. He drank some young fermented rice wine called imbaya from his container. As it started to get dark, he heard a howling sound but continued cooking. After eating his meal, he drank more imbaya before going to sleep.

The sun was shining brightly, but he had lost all hope and chose to keep sleeping. He had no motivation to seek out his friends. "I'm trapped in this unfamiliar world!" he whispered to himself. From Mt. Pulag, Kabunian watched him from the seven lakes that encircled the sacred mountain. Kabigat also gazed at Daniel.

"Are you not going to use your powers to help him?" Kabigat asked.

"I wish I could, but he needs to learn how to control himself in order to fulfill his destiny."

Chapter XI

Daniel continued on his journey away from his starting point. Whilst attending to his needs in the bushes, a wild boar suddenly appeared and began consuming his waste. Surprised, he quickly stood up and cleaned himself before moving away from the animal. As he retreated, a spear flew through the air and killed the boar instantly.

Seeking safety, Daniel climbed a nearby tree to hide from the unknown hunters. A tall, fair-skinned man approached the dead boar and retrieved the spear, accompanied by a group of men who shared similar physical characteristics. Though some were shorter, they were all taller than the average mountain dwellers.

Daniel's attempt to hide was unsuccessful because of his height, as they spotted him when one of them looked up.

"There's someone here," one told his companions.

"Hey! Who are you?" one of them asked.

"I'm Daniel, and just looking for fruits to eat."

"Do you think we are that stupid? This is a non-bearing fruit tree," the same person said.

Daniel was swallowing repeatedly, trembling and sweating as he gazed at the men with fear in his eyes.

"Let's take care of him," one of them suggested.

"Yes, let's remove his head from his body. His lower jaw could make a great handle for my gangza," another added.

"Please spare me, I mean no harm," Daniel pleaded.

The man, who wore headgear and was held in high regard by the others, directed them to escort Daniel back to their village. He clarified that it was not their decision to decide what would happen to Daniel. They tied his hands and had him walk, with some of them on horseback, including the leader and the elderly, while the others walked behind.

They were traveling along the dusty road. Napuagan watched them from the flowing hot red lava of the underworld. He exhaled, creating two large boulders with limbs and faces. The two figures carried massive clubs. He ordered them to disrupt the earth, causing a powerful tremor. Yogyog was responsible for the Northern region, while Alyog oversaw the Southern area. They emerged in the human world, causing a major earthquake. They pounded the ground, creating aftershocks. Daniel and his captors stopped and quickly retreated to avoid being swallowed by the splitting road. An elder and a horse fell into the crevice, along with some of the men on foot.

"Untie me please!" Daniel pleaded. One, among the men, heard him. He only stared at him without doing a thing. "Come and untie me please! I promise, you won't regret it!"

He took Daniel's sword from the ground and was about to cut the vine tied on his wrist but another tried to take the sword from his hands. The one holding the sword gave his companion a kick and finally cut the vine.

"Follow me," Daniel instructed.

"Everybody! Follow him!" The man shouted to his companions.

The group ascended the nearest mountain like lizards slithering in a lightning mode, while others hesitated and ended up being too late, meeting a tragic fate as they were engulfed by the cracks on the road. Daniel directed everyone to the mountain's topmost center, where there were no trees or rocks.

"Get down on the ground!" he instructed.

Kabunian was observing the situation and commanded Umalgo, the sun deity, to use his heat to approach Yogyog and Alyog. Umalgo first went to the North and melted Yogyog, causing the melted substance to flow into the cracks leading back to the underworld. He then repeated the process in the South. After completing his task, Umalgo returned to the sky, and the earthquake came to a halt.

Everyone was in a hurry to get up, but Daniel shouted at them to stay down and assess the situation for safety first. He indicated that they could stand up after a few moments.

Dulagan, the leader, came up to Daniel and expressed gratitude for his help. Daniel introduced himself and mentioned that he was a solo traveler looking for his lost companions. Dulagan gave back Daniel's sword and directed his men to get food ready for a camp on the mountain. He stressed the importance of pausing their journey for the time being until they could confirm if there were any other possible threats.

When they reached Batan, a somber mood hung in the air. The residents were visibly upset. Dulagan hurried to their home to investigate the situation. There, he found his father's lifeless body on a chair surrounded by mourners.

"No! This can't be true!" Dulagan cried out as his Aunt Kuling got close to him to offer comfort.

"My dear nephew Dulagan, I understand your pain. The passing of your father is a great loss for all of us in the Kingdom, but we must come to terms with it."

"I didn't even get to tell him how much he meant to me," Dulagan responded with tears started pouring from his sorrowful eyes.

"You must stay strong. You must not give in to tears or despair. You are next in line for leadership, and you must be prepared for that responsibility."

The remainder of the group brought their hunted animals to their leader's house, a long kubo house with the grounds serving as a preparation area for the Kingdom's special occasions. Daniel, who witnessed what was happening, decided to join in and help with the food preparation.

"Who are you? I haven't seen you here before," Kuling asked Daniel.

"Aunt, that's Daniel. He helped us during the earthquake," Dulagan explained.

"Yes, I'm Daniel and I want to help with the preparation," Daniel replied.

"Stay with us as our guest," Kuling said, noticing the tattoo on Daniel's right shoulder.

At the center part of the kingdom, a bonfire burned brightly, surrounded by stone benches. Elderly ladies sat on the benches chanting, while an elderly man led the group in reciting the lyrics.

The body underwent the mummification ritual and the funeral concluded with the sacrifice of a horse. The spiritual leader recited a prayer asking for the horse's spirit to be the leader's spirit vessel to Mt. Pulag, where the spirits would find the final resting home.

Daniel felt out of place and wanted to continue his journey, but Kuling stopped him.

"Daniel, you're welcome to stay. You don't have to leave," Kuling said.

"I have to find my friends. They could be in trouble," Daniel replied.

"I get that, but you need to be ready for anything. Do you even know where they are?" Kuling asked.

"I have a rough idea, but I'm not certain," Daniel admitted.

Dulagan overheard the conversation between Daniel and his aunt. He kindly offered a vacant room in his quarters, which Daniel accepted as a gesture of respect. Daniel was a hard worker and assisted with various tasks in the Kingdom. While he was carrying firewood, Kuling was busy preparing ingredients for lunch. It was at that moment that he noticed the sparkle in her face, which highlighted her beauty in a way he hadn't noticed before. Despite being older, Kuling was still very attractive.

"Sorry," Daniel apologised as he dropped the firewood, causing Kuling to jump a little. She responded with a sweet smile, saying, "It's okay."

The next day, Daniel and a few other men were fishing by the river. A tree was growing on the riverbank, with some of its roots reaching into the water. Daniel managed to catch a big fish with his hands, but it slipped away and swam under the tree. When he tried to grab it again, he instead found a shiny yellow stone the size of a fist. The other men gathered around him, fascinated by the stone's glowing appearance.

Daniel didn't consider anything about it at first, not even its true value, but then recalled the tales of gold prospectors and concluded that it must be real gold.

"I've discovered gold," he announced to the group.

"What's gold?" one of them inquired.

"It's a valuable stone. A precious commodity that can be traded for other goods, food, and anything else we might need," Daniel clarified.

"Oohhh! Gold!" they simultaneously exclaimed.

The group informed Dulagan about the gold, and Daniel explained how to extract it according to his limited knowledge. Dulagan ordered a group with digging tools to explore for this so-called gold with Daniel's guidance.

The group was let down because they were expecting a result like what happened to Daniel. However, Daniel explained that this wasn't always the outcome, which he had forgotten to mention. He requested that the rocks be crushed with their large sledgehammers until they became powder. The powder was then heated over an open flame. Impurities were separated out, and some of the substance became a liquid. The liquid was poured into a bamboo container to cool. After solidifying, the bamboo was split to extract the solid material.

Daniel presented the gold to Dulagan, but the leader was disappointed with the amount.

"What? Is this all you found? After all that digging, just a finger's length worth?"

"Your leadership, we did our best. Isn't it better than finding nothing?"

"No, we need more. Our allies from the lowlands expect a larger haul in exchange for salt."

Daniel was distracted by a massive, muscular man with a long beard without hair on his head, wielding a sledgehammer on the left mountain peak, creating a hole.

"Did anyone else see that giant on the left mountain?" Daniel asked.

"No, what are you talking about?" a warrior responded.

The kingdom was in a state of shock when they discovered a couple of holes on the side of the mountain upon closer inspection. They turned to Daniel for guidance, as he was considered an expert despite his limited knowledge. Daniel asked the leader to assemble a group to explore the area after the giant man he had seen had completed his task. It was later revealed that the giant was Bal-litoc, the gold deity sent by Kabunian to lead the people to the location of gold.

The group of men, armed with digging tools and led by Daniel, went to the mountain to inspect. They entered the first hole they came across and discovered gold on the sides and top of the hole. The men were quick to extract the mineral, but Daniel warned them not to disturb the site. Despite his warning, they ignored him and began removing the gold with their tools. As a result, the hole collapsed, and the men came running out. Some of them, particularly those at the deeper part, were buried in the collapse, while the others who managed to escape were covered in dirt.

"Is anyone injured?" Daniel inquired with raised eyebrows.

"Some of our comrades were trapped under the rubble," one replied.

"Clean yourselves up and gather some tree stumps. We need to reinforce the hole to prevent another collapse."

He directed the men on how to use the wood for support, with some digging, others placing the support, and a few at the entrance handing over the materials.

They discovered several of the buried men, but unfortunately, they were already deceased. Despite this, they continued their task and successfully filled two baskets.

"What should we do with the bodies?" one of them inquired.

"We will leave them here, but they must be buried in that empty area with markers for identification later. The gold is already weighing us down enough; we don't need any additional burdens," another replied.

They proceeded to the mountains with the baskets of gold, with everyone pitching in to carry the load. They took breaks along the way until they finally reached the kingdom.

"Where are the others?" Dulagan asked as the men brought the baskets of gold into the common cooking area.

"Your leadership. They died when they were buried in the hole," Daniel replied.

"So, where are the bodies?"

"We buried them next to the tunnel because we couldn't take them with us. The baskets of gold were already heavy enough."

The gold extract was processed according to Daniel's instructions. The crushing method was upgraded from manually pounding the stones on a hard surface to using a crushing wheel powered by animals such as cows, carabaos, or horses. The receptacle was swapped with a metal bowl bought from the lowlands, along with other metal materials needed for other purposes. A massive load of firewood was also gathered to accommodate the quantity and melting point of the mineral.

Dulagan instructed a team to barter the gold with the lowland dwellers in exchange for salt, seafood, and metal items like knives, jewelry, and kitchen tools. The excess gold was crafted into jewelry for the chief and the affluent individuals who owned vast lands and numerous animals to set them apart from the ordinary folks. As a result, they acquired the skill of metalworking and jewelry-making to create intricate ornaments and practical tools, reducing their dependence on the lowland traders.

While the group from Batan engaged in trade with the lowland residents, they were unaware that foreigners from a distant continent were observing the transaction. A Spanish monk, in particular, was intrigued by the valuable materials that the highlanders brought for trade. He hurried to the Catholic church where his fellow monks lived and shared with them all he had seen.

The group came back with the goods obtained from the trade. The monks sent a young soldier to track the mountain dwellers and gather information. The spy skillfully stayed hidden while observing the group. The group appeared to be tough and resilient, causing the spy to struggle with the steep terrain and high altitude that his body was not accustomed to.

The trading group returned to a celebration as gangzas and solibaos were played by the skilled elders. The council of elders orchestrated the marriage of Daniel and Kuling, with the mambunong giving his approval to the union.

"I wish you both a lifetime of happiness," a man from the group remarked.

Daniel and Kuling sat together on a special chair made of sturdy apitong wood, decorated with intricate carvings of men, women, and patterns reminiscent of warrior tattoos.

Wild boars were pierced with sharp wooden sticks, causing their cries to echo loudly, reaching the mountains in the distance. The spy, observing the butchering process up close, struggled to remain composed but kept silent to avoid revealing his presence to the people. He remained motionless in the tree until the festivities concluded. Only then did he descend and return to the lowlands to report his observations.

The news about the presence of the gold deposit in the mountains reached Governor-General Agapito, the leader of the Spanish-speaking conquerors of the entire archipelago. He was made aware of the news when the Catholic monks sent him a letter stating the details of what a member of the monks had witnessed and the result of the spy's operation they sent to the mountains.

"Is there really gold in the mountains?" The Governor-General asked his men after reading the letter.

He penned a reply to the monks, asking for the spy to join an exploration group he was organising.

"Deliver this letter to the monks and have Lt. De Guzman come to my chambers immediately," he ordered one of his men.

He directed the Lieutenant to ready some of his troops for the mountain expedition once he obtained the monks' approval and with the assistance of the spy under the monks' authority. The Lieutenant saluted the Governor-General in acknowledgment and exited the chamber.

Daniel pretended to be happy when he realised that he had developed genuine feelings for Kuchep. Despite being in a relationship with Kuling, he grappled with the choice of starting a family with her or pursuing his true feelings for Kuchep. He concealed the reality of his heart, particularly from Kuling, who appeared content whenever they were together. His apprehension of facing consequences from Dulagan also contributed to his internal struggle of keeping his love for Kuchep hidden.

"Are you really happy to be with me, or are you just complying with our "kalon" (arranged marriage) situation?" Daniel asked of Kuling as they lay on the floor.

"Why do you ask?" Kuling responded.

Daniel immediately regretted his question, feeling foolish for even bringing it up.

"It's nothing," he was quick to dismiss.

Kuling didn't dwell on Daniel's question, and they slept with peaceful dispositions through the night.

Chapter XII

The Batan kingdom was surprised by a visit from a group of warriors who wanted to meet with their leader. The guards at the entrance were ready to defend, holding their spears high and pointed at the visitors. Some had their hands on their bolos, ready to use them if needed.

"Please, we come in peace. We only wish to speak with your leader," one of the visitors implored.

"What's going on over there?" Dulagan inquired as he stepped out of the entrance.

"I'm Kildo, and these are my friends from the Bokodians village. We just need to discuss something important with whoever is in charge here."

"I'm the leader here. My name is Dulagan." "Don't worry, let them in," he ordered his warriors.

The Bokodian group was permitted to enter, with some warriors watching them closely, along with Dulagan. They were escorted straight to Dulagan's quarters.

Dulagan requested Daniel, to please come and join us.

They sat on chairs facing each other, observing and anticipating the next move of each group.

"What is your purpose here?" Dulagan asked.

"We are here to propose a peace pack amongst our territories. We must unite in these times because we observed a group of men with metal armour and shields heading this way to the mountains."

They further discussed their unity and concluded with a bloodletting ceremony. Each person at the meeting was required to contribute few drops of their blood to a receptacle, which was then mixed with a little bit of pure rice wine. They each took sips to solidify their new agreement and potential friendship.

Troops from the South unexpectedly joined the discussions but insisted on taking control of the new alliance, a demand that was vehemently rejected by the other groups. The leader of the South raised his voice in defiance when his demand was refused, leaving a sour taste in the air.

As they traveled back South with their horses, they realised that the armoured men were closer than expected. A member of the group was sent back to the Batan kingdom to warn the others, riding swiftly like the wind.

Upon receiving the warning, the allied group swiftly assembled near the location where the armoured men were sighted. They strategically placed traps, including pointed bamboos and concealed wooden obstacles along the slope where the approaching group was expected to traverse.

Utilising available materials like boulders and stones, they improvised weapons and hurled them at the enemy. By rolling boulders and logs down the cliff, they surprised the armoured men. The mountain dwellers' familiarity with the terrain proved advantageous as they engaged in a fierce battle.

The armoured men retaliated by shooting arrows, causing casualties among the mountain dwellers. However, with their determination and resourcefulness, the mountain dwellers managed to penetrate the armour of the invaders. Bones were crushed, metal armour was pierced, and the remaining armoured men were forced to retreat to the lowlands with less than half of their original numbers.

After the dust of the battle cleared, a blurry figure came into view. It was Hipag, the war spirit protector. Taking the shape of a wild boar standing upright like a human, he held a gaman in one hand and a bollo in the other. Hipag aided the mountain dwellers by ensuring that their weapons could pierce through the metal armour of their enemies. The mambunong of the Batan kingdom summoned him through prayer chants and a pig sacrifice.

"The gods are truly favoring us," Dulagan shouted triumphantly.

The remaining men echoed their battle cry with enthusiasms, shouting "to victory!" as they brandished their weapons.

They lined up the bodies of their fallen comrades. The enemies they had killed were beheaded, and they kept their heads as trophies and their armour for practical use such as remelting then into plates, knives, gamans and other weapons. The remaining bodies were left out in the open to decompose or be consumed by wild animals.

A joint victory celebration called 'canao' took place at Batan Kingdom, where the Bindiyan dance was performed. The heads of vanquished foes were mounted on spears and animals on the ground, usually pigs, for sacrificial purposes. Occasionally, wild dogs, wild cats, bats, monkeys and snakes were also included to provide additional sustenance. Men circled the display in a right circular formation, while women formed an inner circle and moved in the opposite direction. Allies shared rice wine as the mambunong chanted a prayer of gratitude.

The Batan casualties were respectfully laid to rest in wooden coffins that were placed in a nearby cave as their final resting place. The other allied casualties were allowed to be taken by their comrades for proper burial after the victory celebration. The most courageous warriors and noble men who participated in the battle were honoured with the opportunity to undergo the mummification process before being laid to rest.

Close by was the village of the Naapil, a group of men who had been rejected by society who also carried weapons. They arrived at the battlefield, but it was already too late. Their slow pace had cost them the opportunity to join the fight. Some of them had physical disabilities: one had only one leg, some couldn't speak, others couldn't stand straight, some had poor vision, and some were twins and homosexuals that were deemed to be curses from the gods.

"It appears that the enemies have already been defeated. All that remains are decaying flesh," remarked the man with one leg.

"We have traveled a long way without taking a break. We are already exhausted. We need to rest," a man with poor vision said.

They traveled to the nearest Kingdom, Batan, but were denied entry by the gate guards. Despite their appeals, the guards stood their ground, fearing that their entry would bring sickness and misfortune to the people. This belief was unfounded, yet the guards remained steadfast in their convictions.

They tried to push their way in and stand their ground, but their physical limitations held them back. The man who struggled to stand upright attempted to attack a guard with his spear, but his aim was so off that the spear hit the wall instead. The one with poor eyesight threw several daggers, but they all missed their mark. The guards took advantage of the situation and quickly punched and kicked them away.

The group had to trek a considerable distance before eventually pausing to rest in a forest.

"Those inconsiderate fools. I hope they will be cursed by the gods as they deserve," grumbled one of them, who had only one arm.

They set up a temporary camp under the trees. Some ventured out to scavenge for food while others drifted off to sleep. Their activities were abruptly halted by a sudden downpour.

"It feels like we're cursed. We always find ourselves in dire circumstances," one of them cried.

The trees offered minimal protection from the rain. They tried to seek a more solid shelter, like a cave, but their attempts were unsuccessful, resulting in them getting soaked. By the time the sun came out, they had already dried off. However, the scorching heat of the sun was unbearable, making it feel like their skin was being seared by the intense rays.

The Spanish-speaking group returned to the lowlands feeling the defeat they had experienced. Their leaders immediately sprung into action.

"What happened to the group I dispatched?" Governor-General Agapito inquired of his right-hand man.

"Your Excellency, they were defeated. Nearly half of them perished," the right-hand man reported.

"What? Are you telling me they were bested by barbarians? Savages?" said the Governor-General in a ravaging rage and rough voice.

"Your leadership. In fact, they were defeated by leaser numbers. They claimed that they felt like there was someone or something invisible helping them. Or maybe they had powers," the right-hand man said.

The Gobernador-Heneral urgently requested a meeting with the government's top officials and church leaders at his disposal. He emphasised the need for strict confidentiality regarding the incident, treating it as if it never occurred. In addition, they discussed plans for another exploration and ensuring better preparation for the next attempt.

They had their own ally in the form of Valeriano Aguinaldo, a woman from the mountains who was among the first to convert to Catholicism in the region. While she lived among her people, her beliefs shifted from traditional practices to the new Christian ways imposed by the Spanish-speaking colonisers, who sought to replace the old culture with what they deemed as the correct Christian way of life.

Behind the conflict, the trade between the mountain dwellers and foreigners was as strong as ever. A solitary elderly man was journeying with his cart filled with goods pulled by his faithful horse. He arrived at the Batan kingdom and tried to enter the fortified kingdom where guards were stationed at the entrance.

"What brings you here?" a guard inquired.

"I am simply a lonely old man conducting business wherever my feet and trusty horse take me," the old man replied.

The guards examined the cart concealed by a large cloth and discovered numerous items they had never seen before. Shiny vases adorned with intricate designs, bowls, plates, jewelry, and more. They were so impressed that they granted the old man permission to enter.

A guard informed Dulagan that an elderly man was present, claiming to be here on business, as the other allies departed for home.

"Let's hear what he has to offer," Dulagan said.

Dulagan and Daniel approached the old man outside. He displayed his products, captivating many. One item was a vase adorned with dragon art. The dragon transformed into a large silhouette, soaring into the sky, enveloping the sun, and breathing fire to light the old man's pipe.

"What kind of sorcery is this?" Dulagan inquired. Some of the warriors aimed their weapons at the old man.

"Your leadership, the old man is simply here to trade. He demonstrated only some harmless magic," Daniel explained.

"Magic? What kind of magic?" Dulagan questioned, curious about what Daniel was referring to.

"Just illusions, magic tricks for entertainment, right?" Daniel clarified, gesturing towards the old man.

"Ah, yes, just harmless tricks for entertainment," the old man confirmed.

The mysterious old man, completely cloaked from head to toe, intrigued the onlookers who had never seen him before. Dulagan ordered his servants to take the old man's finest products in exchange for gold. The old man grinned with excitement, his eyes shining and mouthwatering at the prospect of the trade. Despite witnessing the unfair exchange of cheap breakables for precious gold, Daniel could do nothing to intervene as Dulagan had already made up his mind without outside opinions.

The elderly man continued to visit Batan Kingdom and other areas where the mountain people lived, trading fragile and low-quality goods for valuable items, primarily gold.

"Hello, old man," he heard a whisper, though no one was visibly talking.

"Hello, old man," the whisper repeated.

"Is this real? Who is calling me?"

"It is me."

"Who? Show yourself."

The old man jumped from his cart on the trail and ran into the forest, with the voices still following him. Eventually, Napuagan appeared in front of him.

"How foolish of me. Why am I afraid of this illusion?" the old man said, catching his breath in front of the figure.

"I can offer you abundant wealth in exchange for your obedience to my commands."

"Then, who are you?"

"That doesn't matter. I am the one who can bring you lasting happiness."

Napuagan vanished without a sound once more. The old man was perplexed but chose not to dwell on the strange encounter. He convinced himself that it was all an illusion. He returned to where his cart was, which was still filled with the goods he was trading. He strained to hear any whispers on the wind, but no sound reached his ears. He climbed onto the cart and resumed his journey.

He arrived at a new village, the Bokodians, who had a reputation for being unwelcoming to strangers because of previous incidents involving deception, harm, and abduction. "No one visits here unless it's absolutely necessary," the guard told him. The elderly man clarified that he was only there for trading, but the guard stood his ground, stating, "You're very persistent. Our answer is still no."

Despite the elderly man's efforts to display his merchandise, the guards kicked his cart and tossed some of his goods, resulting in a dangerous situation with sharp fragments scattered on the ground.

Feeling embarrassed, the elderly man withdrew and sought comfort in the forest. He discovered a tree as ancient as himself and set up camp. His horse was spooked during the incident and fled with whatever remained of his cart and goods. He managed to gather a few edible mushrooms and greens. Fortunately, he still had his dagger and was able to cut some bamboo in half to collect water. He roasted everything he found, including the greens, and added a secret ingredient from the inside pocket of his cloak for extra flavor. Despite his frail body, he had no trouble sleeping on the uneven ground as he was accustomed to it.

He regained consciousness whilst observing his sleeping body. He was amazed at his ability to do so.

Napuagan appeared once more and informed him, "You are deceased and observing your own body." The old man begged Napuagan not to allow him to return to life, as he felt unprepared. Napuagan understood that he needed to accompany the old man to his death, as he had a special purpose for him and knew of the darkness within the old man. With the old man's pleas, Napuagan decided to grant him life once more.

The elderly man continued to live a solitary life. Despite his efforts to gain entry to various kingdoms and villages, he was always denied. Feeling desperate, as Napuagan had made him, he leapt from the edge of a mountain and fell into the river, meeting his demise. Napuagan escorted his spirit to the underworld. At the entrance, the old man's horse and cart were parked.

Napuagan pointed at it and proclaimed, "From now on, you will be called the Tuwong responsible for guiding the dark spirits to the underworld!"

Daniel was very observant of his surroundings. His wife was expecting their first child. In some communities, women in lower social classes continue to work manual labor while pregnant. Kuling was lucky to have a break during her pregnancy because she was related to Dulagan, the leader. Daniel took on all the household tasks and heavy lifting that Kuling would have done. He accepted his responsibilities without complaint, understanding the importance of this stage in her life.

One day, a surprising event occurred - the birth of his child. He felt a mix of excitement and nervousness. He was thrilled to finally see and care for his child, but also anxious about the added responsibility.

"Please call for the mambunong," he requested as his wife was in pain.

The mambunong arrived with herbs and a special cloth.

"Please, do not interfere. Let me handle everything. Just follow what I tell you to do," the mambunong instructed.

"Everyone, please leave the room. Only the husband and wife should remain, but stay nearby in case I need assistance," he added.

He tied a rope called bigkis around and above the swollen belly, believing it would aid in pushing out the baby. He then asked for hot water. The herbs were crushed and mixed with the hot water to cleanse the birth canal.

"Push!" he urged Kuling, with Daniel by her side. Another push was made, and the baby was delivered. The remaining herb and hot water mixture was used to bathe the newborn, revealing that they had a son. The baby was then wrapped in a special cloth. Breastfeeding was still not recommended, so water with edible herbs was given first.

Kuling held her son, tears streaming down her face. "I was afraid I would never have a child. Oh, my son. Thank the gods."

Daniel smiled at his wife and son, feeling nostalgic about his other children who could have been there with them. Seeing his family together triggered these thoughts.

Dulagan and the servants entered the room, all captivated by the precious baby. Dulagan felt a mix of happiness and concern, knowing that without a partner, his newborn cousin might inherit the throne when the time came.

A group from a distant place was heading towards the Batan Kingdom. The guards prepared themselves with their weapons, anticipating a potential battle. However, as the group approached, it became evident that they were not a threat but rather a peaceful gathering of men, women, children, and livestock. These individuals were villagers from Kalaliag, a semi-nomadic group constantly seeking better opportunities.

While they had a home village in Tinod, they were always on the move in search of greener pastures and would return to their village when they grew weary of their travels.

A young boy named Pati was chewing a buai mixture. In the group he was a kind child who always respected his elders. He was not particularly remarkable in appearance, just an average boy who was no different from the others. People often overlooked him and didn't pay much attention to what he had to say, even though he was usually right. Despite this, he didn't let it bother him and just went with the flow of life.

The mambunong of the semi-nomadic group observed something peculiar. He found himself constantly looking at Pati whenever he encountered him in the village. There was something about Pati that intrigued him, although he couldn't quite pinpoint what it was initially.

Returning to his quarters, he forcefully broke the head of a rooster with his bare hands, causing it to separate from its body. The rooster flapped its wings and struggled on the ground until it eventually died, leaving a pool of blood in one spot. Within the blood, a vision appeared, a powerful warrior wielding a spear and shield, leading other warriors to victory.

A sudden pinching feeling struck the mambunong in the chest. "Could this be? Could he be the one?" He whispered to himself. His expression was that of a frightened child, as if he had seen a bug, a stranger, or the sight of blood.

"Hey!" The leader called out.

He continued to wave his hands in front of the mambunong's face, but there was no response. Concluding that the mambunong was in a trance, he left him standing in front of his quarters, staring into nothingness.

He would glance at Pati whenever possible but remained silent. Pati, in turn, observed the mambunong's actions and feared that he was under a curse or some other threat. "What is it that the mambunong has learned about me?" he wondered anxiously.

The mambunong did not have a deep understanding of Pati as time passed. However, he was quietly observant, keeping track of any changes in Pati as he developed into a stronger and more skilled fighter. In fact, Pati was one of the top young boys being trained as warriors.

The group of young men gathered in a wooded area, with trainer Balkag directing them to form lines of six rows with eight men in each row. Due to the limited space, this was the best formation they could achieve. Balkag instructed them to observe the branches above and emulate the movements of monkeys by climbing the trees and jumping from branch to branch.

The young men assumed their positions and one by one, they climbed the trees and followed Balkag's orders. Some experienced warriors supervised their actions. Unfortunately, one of the young men fell from a tree, but fortunately, he landed on a soft patch of ground, sustaining only minor injuries.

"Take him to the mambunong!" Balkag commanded.

"Return to your formations!" He added.

He advised the young men to resume their usual activities and prepare for the upcoming journey the following day.

The mambunong predicted that the nearby mountain slope would give way due to the heavy rainfall. Furthermore, the mambunong administered a massage and herbal treatment to the injured young man's ankle, and performed manipulations on the rest of his body to enhance mobility.

"How are you, mother?" Pati asked as he arrived at his mother's temporary shelter.

"I am fine, my son."

"Here, have some of the tonic drink I have made for you."

Pati's mother was not feeling ill, but her advancing age was leading to a decline in her strength. Pati made every effort to be with her, even with his responsibilities as a warrior-in-training.

That evening, the mambunong alerted them to potential danger. They gathered their belongings and set out on their journey, using wooden torches to light their path.

Pati helped with the packing and carried most of their belongings, while his mother rode a horse, together with a nursing mother on her back. The horse was familiar with the route and stayed on track. After traveling a few miles, a light rain started to fall. The campsite they chose eventually became muddy due to the nearby pile of colossal dirt still considered as a mountain.

Chapter XIII

The light rain gently fell over Batan Kingdom, providing a welcome blessing from the gods. The rain nourished their crops, which had been suffering due to the lack of water during the extended dry period.

Daniel was inside their home with his wife, in a residence provided by the leader. He was carrying their baby in an "eban," a cloth wrapped diagonally around his body to keep the baby safe. Meanwhile, his wife was resting on the floor.

The strong smell coming from the baby filled the room, causing Daniel to nudge his wife, Kuling, for assistance. "Kuling, our baby smells really bad. What should we do?"

Kuling took their baby straightaway, opened the window to freshen the room, and changed the cloth protecting their son's crotch area. She bathed him in the spring water guided from the mountains through a bamboo pipe and then handed him to Daniel to dry off. After washing the cloth, she advised Daniel to let their son soak up some sunlight.

"Wow! You really need to spend more time with your son because you don't know anything. Hehehe," Kuling said in a joking, giggly manner.

Daniel chuckled along with his wife as they sat on a wooden bench near their house, enjoying the warmth of the sun.

"Do you enjoy the life that we have?" Daniel asked.

"Yes, I do. Why do you ask?" Kuling replied, looking puzzled.

"I was just thinking, if we weren't 'calon' and you were still young... then..."

"Stop thinking about that. I love our life together."

They exchanged smiles as their son sat on Daniel's lap.

Several mountains away, the Dutab Kingdom continued to be in turmoil under the oppressive rule of the Busol. Betot remained locked up, awaiting his unknown destiny. Many male prisoners were perishing in the savage battles that amused the invaders. Mayangao had a daughter, a rarity among Busols, and Kuchep was the companion. Despite putting on a facade of contentment with Mayangao's presence, she held deep-seated animosity towards him. Mayangao never permitted her to be seen in public; she remained secluded in her chambers, tended to by servants who fulfilled her every requirement.

"Someday, I will have my revenge. Mayangao will feel my wrath," Kuchep declared as she lay on the floor.

Just then, a servant entered the room. "Your lady, dinner is ready and his leadership demands your presence."

The servant bowed before her and left. Kuchep indicated that she would come later. "I hope she didn't hear what I was saying."

The warrior's return was heralded by the arrival of new captives from distant mountains, a journey that had taken seven moons. Kuling noticed a young man with a powerful physique that could rival any beast as she peered out the window. She returned to her seat on the floor, deep in thought about the familiar face she had just seen. She gazed at him again, trying to place where she had seen him before. Suddenly, her forgotten powers surged within her, igniting a fire in her eyes like two crystals striking a spark together. In that moment, she saw a vision of Daniel. "Why Daniel?" she pondered.

The captives were placed in their cages, with the young man placed in the same cage where Betot was held. The young man kept to himself and didn't interact much. Betot observed him from a distance and noticed a strong resemblance to Daniel. Knowing Daniel well, Betot suspected that the young man could be one of his offspring. Despite this, he chose not to approach or engage with the young man, assuming that he was simply adjusting to his unfamiliar surroundings.

Betot was expecting that he would be the next one to go since they hadn't thrown him into the fighting pit. "Why… why am I still here?" he thought to himself. Another day went by and two men were killed in a battle for amusement.

The young man approached Betot and expressed his concerns about their fate. He asked, "What will happen to all of us?" Betot explained that the men would be pitted against each other for entertainment, while the women would be forced to serve them. Betot didn't ask for the young man's name as he had already heard him introduce himself to others, so he introduced himself to the young man instead.

Balkeg, as his name was called, gazed at Betot and the other prisoners. He tried to project an image of bravery, but his expression and huddled position in the corner betrayed his true feelings.

"What a coward!" someone taunted.

Many of the prisoners viewed him as a useless brute and didn't hesitate to express their opinions.

"Stop… stop the taunting! We… we need to act appropriately and… and stay united! It's our only chance!" Betot shouted.

"It's easy for you to talk like that! We don't know how you manage it, but it seems like luck is always on your side! You're the only one who hasn't been in danger here!" someone said with a loud angry demeanor.

Even the prisoners were divided into two factions, one in favor of Betot and the other against him.

Napuagan watched with a mouth filled with hot red lava, unaffected by the heat. He appeared in Kuchep's dream, offering assistance in escaping her unwanted life. He then visited Balkeg, manifesting through his consciousness. Balkeg felt a sensation of heat, as if something was about to burn his skin, when he thought he saw a being outside the cage.

In Kuchep's dream, Daniel's face was in the sky with clouds in the background. A large bird of prey, capable of capturing and carrying off a large animal with its claws, appeared and focused its peck on the eyes, then the rest of the face. The face then vanished, leaving only blood dripping from a man fallen. Kuchep hurried to the man and realised it was the young man seen earlier. The bird let out a piercing cry and flew off, creating a powerful wind that stirred up dust and obscured the sky. Once the air cleared, the bird was nowhere to be seen.

Balkeg encountered Napuagan once more, and he crumpled like a piece of paper for the second time. He was momentarily frozen in place. Mayangao approached to inspect the prisoners and noticed Balkeg's ideal physique for the upcoming fight.

"This new prisoner. Take him out of the cage. He's up next," he commanded his warriors who were guarding them.

Balkeg was then dragged out of the cage and thrown into the fighting pit. The impact of his landing brought him back to reality. He observed the Busols screeching and making noise around the hole where he was situated. As he stood up, he scanned his surroundings, unsure of what would happen next. A dog-like creature, much larger in size, bared its sharp teeth and displayed its long, pointed claws. Balkeg's heart raced as he attempted to escape by moving to the opposite side and climbing out of the hole, but the Busols pushed him back.

"Throw him a dagger!" Mayangao commanded.

The dagger was thrown and landed near the animal. Balkeg, still attempting to escape the fighting pit, spotted the dagger and lunged for it despite his injuries. The animal clawed at him, wounding his right ribs. Balkeg swung the dagger wildly, inflicting wounds all over the animal's body. As the animal lunged at him again, Balkeg bent his knees and raised the dagger, slicing open the animal's belly. Its internal organs and blood spilled onto Balkeg's face. A spear was shot towards him.

"Do not kill him. Release him from the pit and return him to the cage," Mayangao ordered. "Bring the mambunong and let him see the young man," he also ordered.

The mambunong inspected the young man in the cage and then instructed for him to be taken out and placed in an open area. Eventually, they moved him to the mambunong's living quarters. The mambunong cleaned the young man's wounds, applied herbal ointment, and gave him herbal tea to drink. Finally, the mambunong recited a prayer.

Mayangao visited the mambunong's quarters to see how the young man was doing.

"How is he?" he inquired of the mambunong.

"Yes, he is fine, your leadership."

"Please give us some privacy."

The mambunong left, curious about the situation.

"Who are you?" Mayangao asked.

"I am Balkeg of Bokodians. The one you and your men invaded."

Mayangao looked at him from head to toe as if he was inspecting a prize animal. "Balkeg, take some rest. You will need your strength in the days ahead."

He advised the mambunong to utilise all of his skills to help Balkeg recover and improve his condition. Balkeg was instructed to rest for several days and consume the internal organs and broth of native chicken, which were believed to provide additional strength. He received special care and received additional training in combat skills from the Busol warriors.

A disturbance arose in the community as a warrior carried a servant with her right arm appearing to be dislocated. Suddenly, thunder rumbled and a bolt of lightning flashed across the sky.

"What happened?" Mayangao asked of the warrior.

"She was struck by lightning. I saw the sky, and I am certain that Kidol aimed the lightning at her," the warrior explained.

Mayangao gave permission to the mambunong to set up his sacred space by offering prayers to the gods. He almost overlooked Balkeg's presence but instructed some warriors to assist Balkeg in moving to the next kubo for rest. He wrapped the servant's injured arm with cloths to immobilise it in a delicate and comfortable manner. While the servant remained motionless, Mayangao sprinkled water infused with herbs that had been blessed through his chants and proceeded with the ritual.

A red image appeared on her back, connected to her affected arm. It looked like a tree with roots and branches, but no leaves. It was believed to be a message from the gods.

The next day, the servant seemed fine as if nothing had happened to her. She continued with her chores, and her affected arm was functioning normally. While cooking for her master, she suddenly felt a sharp pain in her right eye and had trouble seeing clearly. She put out the fire and sat down, holding her eye and blinking rapidly.

"What's wrong?" The other servant asked.

"I don't know. It feels like something is poking my eye, and I can't stop blinking so fast," she replied.

"Go rest in your room. I'll take care of the cooking."

She lay in her room, trying to sleep, but her eye kept on blinking rapidly. Memories from her past flashed before her eyes, followed by unfamiliar events. "What's happening to me?" she whispered.

The mambunong quickly realised what was happening to her. He hurried to her room, bringing saleng with him to create incense that filled the entire room with smoke. He also burned herbal leaves alongside the saleng to purify her with the power of darkness.

She entered with a twitching body, foam around her mouth and her eyes rolling back to reveal only the whites. She moved around the room, bumping into walls and causing animal skulls and containers of potions and healing materials to fall. A servant tried to enter to check on her, but the mambunong stopped her, reassuring her, "Do not come in or let fresh air in. This is a normal part of the process, do not worry."

Mayangao was unable to tolerate the situation, not out of concern for the servant, but due to the fear that her misfortune would bring harm to his kingdom. Despite the mambunong's reassurance that the kingdom would not suffer any consequences because of her, Mayangao still instructed his warriors to kill her and dispose of her body in a distant location.

Daniel suddenly felt a discomfort in his chest while holding his son. "Please take our son," he said, handing Kuling their son in their room. He collapsed on the floor and began to jerk, as if something invisible was shaking him around.

"Daniel! Daniel!" Kuling shouted as she rushed to the mambunong's quarters holding their son. Dulagan, who was in the adjacent room, heard the commotion and called for nearby servants and warriors to help him restrain Daniel. Kuling and the mambunong arrived, but Daniel had stopped moving. A servant took their son to another room, where he cried and screamed upon hearing the noise.

Daniel woke up as if nothing had happened. "Why are you all here?" he asked, his face filled with wonder.

"You fell and were jerking around on the floor. I was afraid you were dying," Kuchep said, tears streaming down her face."

"Yes, she's right," Dulagan agreed.

"I don't know about all of you, but there's a hunt this afternoon, and I want to be a part of it," Daniel said.

"No, it could be dangerous for you," the mambunong warned. "Clear the room and let me examine you," he added.

Everyone exited the room, leaving only the mambunong and Daniel, who had been coerced into staying. The mambunong lit dried leaves and insisted that all exits be sealed. When Daniel attempted to open the door, he found it locked. The mambunong noticed his efforts and moved the burning leaves closer to Daniel, causing him to collapse. The mambunong then departed, leaving Daniel to be overcome by the smoke and lose consciousness.

He found himself in a hospital room with tubes attached to his mouth and an IV on his left arm. Bandages covered his head, shoulder, legs, and various other parts of his body, indicating the severity of his condition. Despite being conscious and able to see his own body, he felt disconnected from his physical self.

The mambunong decided when it was appropriate to release the smoke from the room. He instructed the servants to open the door and windows. Once the smoke had dissipated with the help of the outside air, Daniel sat down on the floor.

"What is this happening to me?" he asked the mambunong with so much confusion.

Daniel looked into the mambunong's eyes and then requested some space to clear his head before the mambunong could respond. Everyone respected his wish, and Kuling was in the other room taking care of their son.

No one knew that a similar incident had occurred before he married Kuling. Long before their marriage, he had experienced an unexplained injury to his ribs, as if he had been wounded by a sharp object. He didn't dwell on it much at the time, but it resurfaced when the mambunong made predictions. This made him think about the well-being of the mothers of his children, wondering if they were doing well or facing difficult circumstances.

"Who am I truly? What have I done?" echoed in his thoughts.

Chapter XIV

Napuagan saw Daniel's situation as an opportunity to manipulate him and create disorder in the community. He wanted to prove that Kabunian couldn't just dominate him because he was the God of the underground. He constantly felt underestimated, according to his own perspective.

He called upon the dark butatos, the ancestral spirits who had committed evil deeds in their previous lives. Butatos were supposed to be yellowish spirits if they had done good in their past lives.

Napuagan revealed to Daniel a glimpse of his dire situation. "That's Daniel and those who can further worsen his already miserable life? I offer a substantial reward, perhaps even your freedom."

Daniel's thoughts were scattered, filled with random memories. The most prominent among them was the painful recollection of being deceived by women who pretended to be interested in him, only to cruelly reject him later. These memories haunted him, especially the ones where he was ridiculed at parties for his thin frame and nerdy demeanor. It felt like a cruel cycle of rejection and humiliation.

Marissa was the love of Daniel's life, or so he believed. They met in one of his college classes, where she was the only girl who talked to him and would go for snacks or meals with him. They also spent time hanging out at the park when they had free time.

"Roses for you," Daniel said as he presented her with a dozen flowers, he had saved up for over a couple of weeks, right outside the college where everyone could see. Marissa hurried off to class without accepting the flowers, leaving Daniel feeling embarrassed as their classmates passed by.

From then on, Marissa avoided speaking to him whenever they crossed paths. She would even look away or take a different route if they accidentally ran into each other in public. Daniel often pondered what caused her strong dislike towards him. What had soured her feelings so much that their friendship could not be salvaged, not even a trace of their former companionship remained.

"Daniel! Daniel! Daniel!" Kuling knocked on the door.

Daniel snapped back to reality. Without saying a word, he opened the door. Kuling embraced him, clearly worried. Her tears soaked his shoulder as Daniel held her tightly. He wiped away Kuling's tears with his hands. Looking into his eyes, she said, "Let's go, our meal is ready."

"Are you feeling alright? Would you like to take a break and rest a bit longer?" Dulagan asked.

"I'm perfectly fine," Daniel replied, rising as if he was joining them for a meal for the first time.

"Please, come and sit with us."

Daniel joined the others on the floor, sitting cross-legged, and enjoyed some meat and sweet potatoes with his hands. He drank some rice wine and poured himself a second serving. He tried to pour more, but Dulagan stopped him by holding his hand as he reached for the bamboo container. The spilled wine mixed with the food on the floor.

"Please stop," Kuling said.

Daniel remained silent and returned to their room.

"Let him be. Maybe he hasn't had enough rest," Dulagan said.

An invisible presence entered the room. A dagger lay on the floor in plain sight. Daniel picked up the dagger.

"Daniel, this is the end. Daniel, this is the solution," the unseen butato whispered.

Daniel was startled to hear such a command without anyone visible in the room. He looked around, even opening the window, but found no one inside or outside.

"Daniel, cut yourself. It is the only way," the butato whispered again.

Kabunian made himself felt by the mambunong while he was napping. The mambunong listened to everything Kabunian had to say. He hurried to their leader's house and warned everyone. The mambunong grasped Daniel's right hand as he prepared to stab his belly. There was already blood dripping from Daniel's cheek, but it was not fatal. The mambunong instructed the servants to bring vine ropes to tie Daniel to a post. He then applied healing potion and recited prayers. Daniel regained consciousness.

"We need to perform a complete cleansing of Daniel. The evil spirits are playing him," the mambunong said.

The village followed the guidance of the mambunong and performed the ritual of Daw-es, sacrificing primarily pigs, sometimes with dogs and chickens. The mambunong continuously chanted prayers to Kabunian while the village continued with the butchering process until Daniel was purified.

Daniel went back to his old ways for a few days. Sadly, the voices in his head came back stronger than before. He stayed alone in his room, which he was supposed to share with his wife Kuling and their son. Eating and taking care of himself became infrequent. When villagers tried to reach out to him, he would make threats of self-harm or harm towards them.

"There is no hope for him. We have to get rid of him because if he stays any longer, he will bring bad luck and devastation to our village," the mambunong said.

"No, please! Give him another chance! There must be something you can do to help him," Kuling pleaded on her knees.

"We have done all we can. Your son must grow up without a father. That is the sacrifice that must be made for the greater good."

Dulagan, with a heavy heart, ordered for Daniel to be banished to the wilderness, as far away from the village as possible. His immense strength in his current state made it difficult for the warriors to carry him. They eventually tied his arms and ankles and used a bamboo pole to transport him, similar to how they would carry a hunt.

Half of the warriors had to escort Daniel because of his misbehavior, making the task more challenging. Three warriors on each side carried him while the others guided and observed. They crossed the river, with Daniel briefly submerged underwater. The warriors prioritised completing the task efficiently ever ensuring Daniel's safety.

He was freed from his restraints, and the warriors departed from the location where they had left him to prevent him from following or tracing them back to the village. Their worry was unnecessary as he was not in a state of mind to do so in the first place.

He roamed without any good direction, eventually collapsing on a grassy area where danger lurked nearby. A serpent slithered towards him, hissing loudly. It approached him, crawling over his legs and up to his neck, coiling around it. The sudden pressure brought him back to reality, and he attempted to grab the snake with both hands, but it only tightened its grip with each struggle.

A group of unusual creatures were gathering herbs and fruits when they noticed the serpent coiled around its prey. "Look at the serpent attacking its prey," one of them remarked.

The others turned their attention to the scene.

"I believe that is a man?" one of them asked.

"Yes! We must check it out," another one said.

A huge man wielded a dagger larger than a jungle bolo rose up and sliced the serpent into pieces without harming Daniel. The remains were not left behind; a man the size of a child staggered over, gathered the pieces, and placed them in a basket he carried. A slender man, as thin as a twig, retrieved some herbs from his animal hide pouch. He crushed them with a stone on a solid surface and had Daniel inhale the scent. The fragrance brought him back from unconsciousness to full awareness of his surroundings.

"Where? What is all of this?" Daniel asked, gesturing with his hands in a circular motion at the surroundings.

"You were in danger. A snake almost killed you," the thin man explained.

"We are Anina by the way," the towering man said.

Daniel couldn't help but notice how thin the man was as he spoke.

"Where is my wife? Where is my son?" Daniel asked.

"We found you alone here. That's all," a lady with one arm replied.

"Stop wasting our time. Let's continue with what we are supposed to do," an impatient lady stated.

The group stopped talking to Daniel and got ready to leave, but Daniel begged to come along, and they allowed him to join. They entered a dense bamboo forest where it was hard to see any signs of a community, with bamboo covering the ground along with a few trees and animals. The entrance to the community was so well-concealed that they had to navigate through a complicated pathway.

Daniel's eyes were wide with wonder at the sights before him. He found himself in an underground space with a natural bamboo ceiling that had been intricately woven over time. The inhabitants were a diverse group, ranging from giants to dwarfs, hairy ladies to bedridden individuals, and everything in between. There were also twins and people that seemed to be homosexuals. The bamboo ceiling was not tightly packed, allowing for air to flow in and out.

"Welcome to Angdil, which means to bamboo," one of the residents explained.

At the community center, a long bamboo table was set up with benches on each side, filled with a variety of food. The dishes included roasted snake; the same snake that was about to kill Daniel was seasoned with salt, roasted wild dog heads with eyes, ears, and snout intact, "Pinikpikan" soup, and various types of insects. Side dishes included ferns and fruits, with the staple being a wild root crop called 'tugi.' Everyone sat down and ate using their hands, and the person next to him offered a bamboo cup of imbaya, their version of rice wine.

A man on the right end of the table stood and motioned for Daniel to do the same. "What's your name and where are you from?"

"I'm Daniel. Honestly, I come from a different time, but I remember being from Batan with my wife and son."

"I'm Kidip, the leader of this community, Angdil. As you've seen, we all have special abilities." He raised his cup and took a sip, with everyone following suit. "We don't judge as long as someone doesn't have bad intentions or a want to hurt us."

"Thank you for the kind reception. I just want to make it clear that I am not a valuable asset in your community."

The feast carried on, and it became clear from their discussions that they were all individuals who had been cast out from different locations and left behind.

"You two. I can't help but notice something unique about you," Daniel remarked to the women across from him.

"As you can see, we are identical twins. We were abandoned in the wilderness; twins are considered to bring bad luck. We don't even remember where that village is. All we know is this place is our home, where we have grown up."

The dinner concluded with a performance of the 'tayaw' dance and some impressive tricks involving men jumping high and balancing on top of each other. Daniel participated in the 'tayaw' dance with a cheerful attitude, applauding and smiling throughout each performance.

Daniel drank too much 'imbaya' and laughed until he lost consciousness. He woke up lying on a bamboo bed covered with cowhide. He stood immediately but went back to bed because of dizziness and a headache. A young man with only one functioning eye entered. "Here, have some of this tonic drink. I know you had too much 'imbaya' yesterday." Daniel took the drink and tasted it, his face showing displeasure.

"Drink the entire thing. It will help with your dizziness. Believe me," the young man gestured at Daniel.

"What is this awful thing?" Daniel asked.

"It is a tonic drink made from wild herbs."

"Where is everybody? And why are you still here?" Daniel asked, taking the last swallow.

"Well, the men are out hunting and the women went foraging."

"And you?"

"They let me stay as always with a few others because I am more helpful here, and I accepted it," he paused for a moment. "Anyway, I am Ital, the one-eyed man, as you can see," he smiled and jerked a bit.

"I am..."

"I know who you are, as you introduced yourself at dinner last night."

He departed without saying another word. Daniel felt even worse, his stomach twisting in agony. The pain escalated until he was vomiting a dark liquid. After a while, he started to feel brand new. He grabbed some water and quickly poured on the dirt floor to mask the presence of his own vomit.

He decided to explore the village on his own, eager to see what he had missed before. As he walked around, he was greeted warmly by the villagers, who nodded and smiled at him indicating their hospitable nature. The bamboo houses and long table from the day before were still there, but there was one house that stood out. It was built from piled stone that formed the walls and he could hear the sound of dripping water coming from inside. Curious, he approached the house, but was stopped by a very fair lady with a complexion as white as salt. So white that there was barely any darkness in her eyes.

She explained that the house was reserved for healing purposes only, as it was the healing spring.

"You mean to say, this spring has healing properties?" Daniel asked.

"Yes," she answered.

"Then, why don't the village take advantage of it to heal everybody's inflections?" he was curious. "I am sorry, I am Daniel by the way," he added.

"Oh, you are the Daniel. The one that they say. I can't see that much. And also, I am Bawikan," she said.

"Yes, I am," Daniel said, followed by an awkward silence. Bawikan left without answering Daniel's question, and Daniel decided not to pursue the healing spring, returning to the house he came from.

Suddenly, a baby started crawling towards him. He was surprised and picked it up since there was no one else around. A snake, similar to the one coiled around his neck, emerged from a hole in the wall. Startled, he tried to leave the house to alert someone about the snake's presence.

"Oh no! Where did the baby go? I just had him, but now he's gone!" he exclaimed in a panic.

He then noticed the baby getting closer to the snake. "No!" he shouted. The baby grabbed the snake and flung it against the stone wall of the spring area, causing it to slither away fast from the bamboo community.

The baby was giggling as he held onto Daniel's bicep. A woman with a limp was in a hurry. Without hesitation, he gave the baby to her, not questioning her identity. The woman exclaimed, "My baby! My baby!" Worried about the baby's well-being, as if the baby needed protection from the snake or anything based on how the animal was handled.

"Thank you so much. Oh, you're Daniel, right?"

"Yes, that's me."

"I'm Teng," she said with a smile.

She noticed the eagle tattoo on his shoulder, understanding its significance to Daniel, but chose not to delve into it.

"See you around," she said instead.

Napuagan observed Daniel's situation from above the lava. "Curses!" he shouted, reprimanding his unsuccessful henchmen. He zapped them with lightning from his finger, transforming them into rats, cockroaches, or similar creatures. He chuckled with satisfaction as he squashed a cockroach that couldn't evade his anger.

"No one can be trusted to do the job correctly. I have no choice but to take care of everything myself," Napuagan vented, feeling frustrated and disappointed.

Dust swirled up from the ground, forming the recognisable figure of Napuagan, this time with fiery eyes. Right before Daniel. He remained silent, yet his imposing presence instilled fear in anyone who laid eyes on him, causing their hearts to tremble and their bodies to weaken.

Daniel, initially afraid and considering fleeing, found himself puzzled by a sense of familiarity with Napuagan, unsure if he had encountered him before or if he was a stranger. This uncertainty prevented him from feeling any specific emotion.

It may have been a reflex, but he attempted to retrieve something from his back, only to find nothing there - neither the sword nor the scabbard. He even tried to pick something up from the ground, but all he gathered was dirt under his nails. When he tried to punch Napuagan, his fist passed through, capturing only a cloud of dust. The same result occurred with his kicks - they simply passed through Napuagan.

Many of the bamboo people witnessed the event. Bawikan rushed to the spring and fetched some of the healing water. She spattered it on Napuagan, causing the dust to transform into mud that dropped to the ground. Napuagan disappeared but his voice continued to whisper in the air. The infant who had tossed the snake burst into laughter so loud that it drowned out the whisper until it faded away.

Chapter XV

In the lowland region, the conquistadors exploited nearly all of the territory's offerings, including natural resources, species, and the local population. They also forced the submission of manpower and beautiful maidens. Comandante Hernan Cortez eventually emerged as the leader of the colonisers, succeeding the initial attempt in the highlands.

A young man named Liston was walking through the market center. He appeared dirty and unkempt, with clothes stained with mud and dirt. His long, brown hair showed signs of not being washed for many days, with a foul odour of rotten animal carcass. As he passed by the bread seller's booth made of wood and woven rattan, he caught the attention of the vendors. On the other side, the vegetable seller displayed a variety of produce like okra, eggplant, and onions.

The vendors looked at him with expressions of disgust, and one even shouted, "Get out of here, you peasant!"

Suddenly, a guy running on the opposite side grabbed a bunch of mansanas from a nearby booth. The guards, wearing metal armour and carrying swords, quickly approached the scene. Despite his protests of innocence, the guards dragged Liston away, accusing him of stealing the mansanas. The vendors joined in, pointing fingers and accusing him of the theft to distance him from their business.

"No! Please! It was a different guy who stole the mansanas!" Liston cried, his legs blistered in pain from the dragging along the ground.

"Stop it! Keep quiet!" one of the guards at his back shouted.

A group of men armed with bolos and makeshift spears made from pointed bamboo attacked the guards. Onlookers scattered in various directions to avoid getting caught in the conflict. One of the attackers hurled a bamboo spear at a guard, but the guard's metal armour deflected the blow, causing the spear to bounce off the stone pavement. Additional guards stationed in the castle tower noticed the disturbance and fired their boom stick towards the assailants. Several of them were injured or killed on the spot, while a few survivors managed to rescue Liston and retreat back to the hills from where they had come.

"Don't stop until I say so," one of the men said as they continued running up the hill.

"Thanks for saving me back there."

"Don't mention it. The main thing is that you're safe."

"Who... who are you and your group?"

"We're the rebolusonaryos. We're fighting against the oppressive conquistadors, fighting for our freedom. We are against the oppression by the conquistadors against our countrymen like you."

As they talked, they walked into a village of kubos surrounded by bamboo and wooden fences on the hilltop, far from any immediate danger.

"I am Bula-es. I became the leader of the revolutionary group because I witnessed my mother being raped by the conquistador soldados while my father was executed by firing squad."

Liston remained silent, his eyes wide in shock, before finally speaking. "Many have suffered and sacrificed for my sake."

"Yes, they understand the risks involved, as do I. We are willing to take those risks to put an end to their oppression."

Liston shook his head in disbelief. Bula-es said nothing more, instead leaving briefly and returning with corn and pork fat.

"Thank you very much," Liston expressed his gratitude with his mouth full.

One day, a group of travelers, both on foot and on horses, found themselves lost in the mountains, unknowingly passing through Busol territory. The Busol, positioned strategically on the mountain top and along the ravine, attacked the travelers from all sides like spiders descending on their prey. The Busol's ferocious gaman caused blood to spatter as they beheaded most of the men. Despite the travelers' attempts to fight back, they were unprepared and unable to drive off the attackers.

In the chaos, Batajao, a Busol, stabbed an elderly man who had tried to protect a woman. After the attack, Batajao stood still, covered in blood, and locked eyes with the woman, both of them stained red. Without hesitation, he grabbed the woman and ran away from the ongoing fight.

"Why did you save me?" the lady asked.

"I'm not sure. It just felt right," Batajao replied.

They continued running without any objections from the lady until they reached a forested area filled with ripe fruits. The lady hesitated and was reluctant to share her true name with Batajao.

"Who are you?" he asked. She was standing on the opposite side of Batajao under a tree full of green rounded fruit. "Ay! Ay! Ay!" she cried. Batajao approached with a concerned expression, his demeanor shifting from barbaric to caring. He noticed red ants from the tree causing red rashes on the lady's skin. Her face formed red spots visible against her milky white skin, but she quickly regained her composure.

Batajao observed that her facial features were unlike any other women he had seen before. Her nose resembled a bird of prey's beak, her eyes were as green as the grass, and her white skin had a clay-like texture.

"I apologise," Batajao said as he pulled the lady away from the group of ants.

He carefully removed the remaining ants from her skin. "Please don't touch me!" she exclaimed.

"I'm just trying to help by removing the ants that were causing you pain," Batajao clarified.

They settled on the grassy area of the forest as night fell. The lady's long dress provided some protection against the cold mountain air, but she still felt a chill. She had come to Batajao with the intention of seeking warmth through skin-to-skin contact.

"What?" Batajao startled from his sleep.

The lady simply held him tighter, shivering from the cold. Batajao initially was okay without malice, but his warm, muscular body soon began to feel an effect. His body heat helped to alleviate the lady's discomfort. In response, she planted a kiss on the back of his head. This gesture sparked a surge of passion between them. Their embrace deepened as they shared a passionate kiss, and Batajao's hands explored her body, eliciting joyful tickles from the lady. They became entwined on the grassy ground, lost in the moment.

Liston, the half-Busol and half-conquistador child, faced challenges due to his mixed heritage, which was not accepted during that time. His mother passed away during childbirth, and his father convinced the Busol community to take him in. Liston lived a nomadic life until he eventually settled in the lowlands, finding it easier to live there compared to the harsh mountain landscape.

The resistance group was discovered by a passing friar. The location of their hideout became risky due to the colonisers creating a shortcut for the friars, priests, and church workers to reach the Santa Maria Iglesia Catholica, the main place for the activities of the church devotees.

The friar hurried to his destination and reported his observations to the archbishop, who had strong ties to the government of the conquistadors. Arzobispo Miguel Juan Sagredo of the Santa Maria

Church congregation personally visited Teniente General Brigido Guzman, the appointed officer of Demasiada Sal, the town near the mountains.

The Arzobispo unexpectedly entered the office of the Teniente General.

"Teniente General, we have learned that the group of resistance fighters who attacked the market center is based in the hills we use as a shortcut."

"Thank you for bringing this information. We must plan a surprise attack to eliminate any resistance against us as soon as possible."

The Teniente General wrote a letter to inform different headquarters about the resistance group and requested reinforcements for the planned attack. A messenger escorted by two guards departed on horseback to deliver the message. The Arzobispo remained smiling with anticipation in the Teniente General's office after the messengers left, prompting the Teniente General to offer a bag of Lima gold coins.

"Here, this is what you were waiting for, isn't it?"

"Yes, Teniente General, and I can assure you that the information is accurate."

A cold mist enveloped the cage where Betot was imprisoned, causing him to shiver. The sensation of the mist entering his breathing filled him with agony, and he soon fell into a deep sleep. When he awoke the next morning, the sun was rising as if nothing had happened.

That night, Mayangao woke up screaming in fear, his eyes red and wet with tears. A servant rushed to his side to see what had happened.

"What's wrong, your leadership?" the servant asked.

"I had a vision, a very real vision that felt like I was living in the moment," Mayangao replied, his voice trembling. "What does this mean?" Mayangao inquired, receiving a clueless look from his servant.

In the group, there was a rebel and a nearby group trying to kill

Mayangao. However, their weapons couldn't pierce his thick skin, which acted as his natural armour. He broke through their defenses with ease using only his fists. Suddenly, a fully clothed man, unlike the others in loincloths, appeared and quickly beheaded him with an unknown weapon. The man then carried his head by the hair as he pleaded for mercy. They both disappeared, just as it was described in his dream, believed to be a vision.

Mayangao called for the mambunong to make sense of his vision. The mambunong stood before him, who instructed the servants to bring the clearest water in the widest container available. After chanting a prayer, the mambunong tried to peer into the water but saw nothing. This happened two more times without success.

Betot flew into a rage that caused his cellmates to move away from him.

"I…I need to get out! I…I need to get out!" He screamed.

"Quiet down or I'll silence you!" a guard yelled back.

"I… I understand what your leader is experiencing! I… I know the meaning," Betot pressed his face against the bamboo bars.

"What do you know? What is the meaning?"

"Release me. I understand the meaning of your leader's vision."

A guard, fresh from their leader, released Betot under strict supervision. He was brought before their leader.

"Your Excellency, one of the prisoners. He claims to comprehend the meaning of your vision," the guard announced.

"That's impossible! I can't even decipher the signs, let alone interpret the vision," the mambunong said incredulously.

Betot knelt and then stood, explaining to all present the interpretation of their leader's vision. He spoke of "the one" who was not a native of the mountain tribe, who would defeat their leader and save the people. It is "the one" who will behead him and carry his head by his hair.

"You profess to be the mambunong with unparalleled power and ability, yet you cannot even interpret my vision," Mayangao said, looking at the mambunong with disappointment.

"Your leadership, Betot must be lying. He must be doing it for freedom," the mambunong pleaded.

Unknown to everyone, Kuchep was listening closer than ever, feeling excited when she heard about Betot's presence.

"Yes, why all of a sudden do you claim to have the ability to interpret visions, especially mine?" Mayangao asked, staring at Betot with a doubtful expression.

Before Betot could respond, Kuchep emerged from the back of the leader's quarters. "I know him. I can vouch for his ability. His interpretations are accurate."

It turned into a battle of words between the mambunong and Kuchep, with Mayangao ultimately siding with Kuchep. He ordered the mambunong to be imprisoned for his perceived incompetence in the matter. The mambunong was being dragged away by two guards when Mayangao assigned Betot on the spot as his replacement. Betot was surprised by Mayangao's decision but he gladly accepted the position as it gave him the chance to fulfill his mission of rescuing Kuchep.

Kuchep pulled Betot to a secluded spot when everybody's attention was elsewhere.

"Why are you here?"

"I...I tried to save you, but I was captured and imprisoned."

The two had to end their discussion abruptly as the kingdom was preparing for a celebration.

"This calls for a celebration!" Mayangao declared.

"We need to be visible to avoid arousing suspicion," Kuchep advised.

They took part in the festivities, where a range of dishes, including insects like ants and bugs, as well as snake, were served. Wild boars were hunted and their meat was cooked into the customary dish known as kinigtot. Betot experienced a feeling of revulsion as the food being served did not appeal to his appetite. However, he reluctantly consumed some as it was better than the food offered in the cage, and he was quite hungry.

Mayangao always made sure that Betot stayed nearby as time went on. Betot eventually became Mayangao's most trusted Busol. Mayangao's choice was never questioned because of Betot's fierceness in battle and the respect he commanded from those around him.

Mayangao was determined to take action after his dreams and visions consistently featured a man from a distant land. Concerned about the mention of 'the one' in his visions, he assembled a team of warriors and skilled individuals to search for the man described. They raided villages near the mountain slopes, bordering rivers and lowlands, killing and decapitating every young man who fit the description. The remaining villagers were treated as collateral victims, with women becoming servants and men forced into entertainment fights. The same ruthless tactics were employed in other villages to ensure that they did not miss "the one." However, the secretive location of the bamboo village, unknown to the Busol, saved Daniel from being killed.

Daniel received a message about the events unfolding when a small man overheard Mayangao's instructions. The messenger, Dedan, had traveled through three mountains and crossed two rivers, surprising Daniel and the bamboo villagers. Dedan, used to reside in Angdil Village but had a thirst for adventure that took him beyond the usual boundaries of a regular bamboo villager.

The Angdil village was not led by a single individual, but rather by a council of wise men, not necessarily elders. The majority of the villagers agreed that the council of wise men should offer advice to help protect the village from potential disaster. They gathered around a long table, with each villager contributing to their meal.

They said to Daniel "You are always welcome here, but we have made a sudden decision to ask you to leave our village with a heavy heart on our part. I hope you understand. For the sake of the villagers, we must ask you to leave. However, remember that you are always welcome to return once the threat has passed," announced a wise man, as the villagers listened attentively.

Daniel, despite his heartbreak, remained stoic as he packed his belongings and prepared to leave. Some villagers provided him with food and water for his journey.

As Daniel was leaving, Dedan approached him and asked, "Can I join you on your journey? I need to leave this village as well."

Daniel simply shrugged in agreement, and the two set off together. They were unsure of which direction to take - should they go east, west, or through the 7th mountain? With no clear guidance, they decided to head north. Daniel continued to forge ahead, following a trail that led to an unknown destination.

Daniel seemed to have endless energy, never showing signs of fatigue. Despite Dedan enjoying traveling, he couldn't keep up with Daniel's pace. Eventually, Daniel ended up carrying Dedan on his back for the remainder of their journey. When they arrived at a body of water, Dedan asked to stop for the night. They rested under a solitary tree. Dedan observed Daniel, who appeared unfazed by the physical exertion. Daniel went to fetch water from what he assumed was the cleanest part of the river, filled their container, took several sips directly from the river, and then offered Dedan the container full of water.

They chatted briefly. Daniel succumbed to sleep. It was still bright, and Dedan went fishing for their meal. Despite his short stature, he was not deterred. He stacked numerous stones in a section of the river to create a barrier that slowed the water flow. He waited patiently as fish of all sizes gathered. Using only his hands, he skillfully caught the fish, as if he were picking up twigs. He used a large leaf even larger than himself as a makeshift container. Dedan then prepared and roasted the fish over an open flame.

"Thank you for the meal," Daniel expressed as the cheerful ambiance clashed with the encroaching darkness of the night.

"No problem," Dedan replied with a smile, enjoying a bite of the fish skewer.

Chapter XVI

Kuling ignored her son and isolated herself in her room for a while. Concerned about her mental health and not wanting her to end up like Daniel, Dulagan was resolute in intervening. When he saw Kuling's state, he acted quickly. He broke into her locked room and dragged her out, seeking the mambunong's assistance for her surface-level problems.

No!" Kuling screamed, making sure that everyone in the village would witness her outburst with dramatic actions. Although the villagers did see her, they paid little attention and continued with their daily routines. The mambunong was afraid that her situation would bring misfortune to the village, so she was banished. However, as the sister of their leader, Dulagan arranged for her to be placed in a remote area with a kubo house, a servant, and a guard. Despite living a relatively comfortable life with all her needs met, she passed away shortly after due to illness brought on by old age.

No funeral rituals were conducted for her. Instead, a wooden coffin was prepared and she was positioned on the side of a rocky mountain, secured with sturdy wood to prevent any accidents. This setup was arranged to aid her spirit's journey to Mt. Pulag and for the gods to easily welcome her spirit. Only the mambunong and the servants involved in placing her in her final resting place were allowed in her vicinity.

Dulagan and her son, as the leaders, were forbidden from touching her, her coffin, or anything associated with her to prevent any misfortune from befalling their village. The mambunong and the servants who handled her were cleansed with water that had been blessed and prayed over by the mambunong. This water was poured over their entire bodies, ensuring thorough purification, especially of the areas that had contact with the deceased.

Without Daniel's knowledge of the situation, they continued their journey with only water. They traveled east as recommended by Dedan, as it was the terrain he was familiar with since they didn't have a clear direction.

"What are we doing? I may be adventurous, but at least I have a sense of direction," Daniel commented.

Daniel looked at Dedan with a blank expression and shrugged.

Dedan reacted with wide eyes and raised and lowered his eyebrows.

Nothing more, they simply walked on, following the paths and leaving their footprints.

"Let's stop here by the rocks. I saw some mushrooms. We haven't eaten anything this morning," Dedan suggested.

"Fine, whatever you say," Daniel replied.

Dedan gathered some mushrooms from beneath a red tree, assuming they were all edible by the way they appeared. He returned to find Daniel sitting on the edge of a cliff, gazing at the clear blue sky. In silence, Daniel sparked a fire with twigs he had collected. Dedan tossed the mushrooms into the flames, some turning black and others bubbling and turning golden brown.

Daniel took most of the golden-brown mushrooms, leaving the burnt ones for Dedan. He quickly stuffed the mushrooms into his mouth. Dedan used his dagger to scrape off the burnt parts before reluctantly eating the mushrooms, trying to ignore the unpleasant burnt taste. Daniel savoured the sweetness of the mushrooms but suddenly collapsed to the ground, muttering incoherent words.

Dedan sat beside him, observing the strange turn of events. Daniel felt his body becoming weightless as he floated. He saw beautiful women seated on floating clouds, some of whom seemed familiar to him. Some servant women blew kisses to him, while others, like Kuchep shedding a tear and Kuling looking on expressionlessly, caught his attention. A group of young women with stunning bodies approached him, dancing as they removed his loincloth. One of them revealed sharp teeth and a snake-like tongue, poised to bite his private parts. Panicking, Daniel screamed, "No! No! No!"

"Daniel! Daniel! Wake up, Daniel!" Dedan shook him and slapped his face, bringing him back to reality.

"What? They were attempting to bite off my private parts," Daniel exclaimed.

"Haha! Haha! Haha!" Dedan chuckled.

"What's so amusing?"

"It must be your imagination because you ate the brown mushrooms that I was going to throw away. Those mushrooms can make you feel intoxicated and cause you to experience things that aren't real."

"Is that so? It felt incredibly real."

"Here, have some of this tonic. It will help counteract the effects of the mushrooms."

Daniel and Dedan slept side by side. Upon waking, they continued their journey and stumbled upon a peculiar structure that piqued their interest. It was hill-shaped with triangular sides and a pointed peak. Intrigued, they paused to inspect it. Dedan could enter through the entrance, but Daniel could not.

Daniel urged Dedan to enter and explore, but Dedan hesitated out of concern for potential danger. Eventually, Daniel convinced Dedan to go inside by suggesting there might be something valuable to find inside wishing he could fit through the entrance himself. The interior was so dark that Dedan could barely see, and they decided against lighting a torch in case the passage was narrow. Dedan spotted a shining object and quickly retrieved it, ignoring the eerie darkness that his senses couldn't explain. He grabbed the object, which had some weight to it, and brought it back to the entrance with much care. Daniel's eyes sparkled with joy at the discovery of the golden earring.

"Balitok!" Dedan exclaimed loudly.

"Keep it. We might need it in the future."

As they journeyed further, they spotted different items placed on the structure, including leftover fruits, vegetables, and animal ones. They took note of these as they progressed. Over the next mountain, they encountered what looked like a village in the distance, surrounded by wooden fences with an open gate. Upon closer inspection, they found burnt kubo houses and bodies in different stages of decay. The sight of skeletons and rotting flesh emitting a foul smell filled them with fear. They hurriedly left the area, their expressions showing terror and disgust.

"That must have been the Busol's doing, searching for me. I hope the Angdil village did not suffer the same fate," Daniel said, his expression filled with deep sorrow.

"Let's pray to the gods that such a thing does not happen," Dedan said, his eyes showing concern.

They traveled a great distance to steer clear of any possible run-in with the Busol, with Dedan expertly guiding their way. Daniel was resolute in his decision to avoid the Busol after witnessing the devastation inflicted upon one village. Dedan stood by Daniel's side throughout their travels. They discovered peace in a meadow of wildflowers, finding comfort in the serene natural beauty that calmed their spirits.

A half-man, half-bird of prey creature hovered over Daniel and Dedan as they closed their eyes and breathed in the freshness of their surroundings. Their peaceful moment was abruptly interrupted by large chunks of fecal matter dropping on them with great force. The foul smell was so strong that it caused the flowers to wither into dried, fragile petals. Daniel and Dedan quickly stood up and ran to avoid the next unpleasant surprise. After hiking several paces, they finally stopped to catch their breath.

"What was that? Was that a man with bird wings and talons dropping feces on us?" Daniel asked.

"That was Kabunian's messenger, Makalun. I'm not sure why that happened," Dedan replied.

The area where they were having a relaxing time became infested with Danag, a blood-sucking creature after they left. It looked like dead trees with sharp teeth and powerful claws used to pierce human skin and suck blood. These were some of Napuagan's loyal followers who were instructed to eliminate the two using their expertise. In order to thwart Napuagan's scheme, Kabunian dispatched Makalun, who took drastic measures by destroying the lovely flower-filled area to ensure the safety of the two.

Daniel and Dedan descended a slope in search of a body of water, as their own bodies were sticky and fowl-smelling to the point that even their own sweat could not eliminate the unpleasant feelings it brought. Their quick movements caused them to tumble down with minor injuries that they paid little attention to. They were thrilled to find rushing water, and without regard for their safety, they dove in. The once clear water became murky with dead fish floating in it. They soaked their bodies for an extended period, ensuring that any fecal matter and its properties were thoroughly washed away.

Once more, they took a break by the riverbank, unconcerned about potential discovery. Daniel was the first to awaken and noticed a gleaming object in the water once it had cleared.

"Gold once more?" he murmured.

Intrigued, he approached for a closer look. The object became increasingly recognisable as he neared it. It turned out to be his sword, missing its scabbard.

"How did my sword end up here?" he pondered.

The Busol launched an attack on the Batan village, beheading every young man who resembled Daniel. The villagers were caught off guard by the Busol's strength and many were killed, although some managed to escape. In the midst of the chaos, Dulagan wielded Daniel's sword and successfully killed several Busol warriors. However, he lost his grip on the sword and it fell to the ground. One of the Busol warriors, intrigued by the weapon, picked it up and ran off with his comrades after completing their mission. They crossed the river in search of another village to raid. The Busol who had taken the sword was careless and dropped it in the water, where Daniel would later find it.

Daniel gripped the sword with a sense of determination, lifting it into the air and then wiping off the excess water. "That was quite a moment," he reflected. He roused Dedan from his slumber to discuss the peculiar route to the Dutab Kingdom from where they rested, fully aware of the perils that lay ahead.

They had been walking for a long time, with blisters forming on their feet. They were hoping for softer ground, but were surprised to only encounter sand, rock, and dirt.

"Yes! He! He! He! They are experiencing the discomfort of the heat! The harshness!" Napuagan watched them from the underworld.

They also began to experience a burning sensation on their skin, which caused a deep, painful ache. They were unaware of the lowland terrain they had passed due to their lack of proper direction.

"I can't take it anymore," Daniel complained.

Dedan's mouth was so dry, he couldn't say a word. Dedan was surprised when water spouted from the dry land right there on the spot where they have stood. He tried to touch the spot again making sure his eyes were not deceiving him, and water continued to flow, leaving them both in awe. Daniel swatted Dedan and told him he would drink first. "Let me have some water too!" Dedan pleaded, trying to reach the water. Daniel pushed him away and drank until his thirst was quenched. Dedan then crawled over and finally got the water he had been longing for.

Napuagan knew about the help provided by Kabunian, but he was not pleased. "Curse that Kabunian, always interfering with my plans!" He would not be satisfied until "the one" faced his wrath.

Dedan was disappointed to realise that Daniel had manipulated him for his own gain, making him feel insignificant and not a true friend. Daniel fell asleep, following his usual routine to help his body recover. The sound of his breathing was a blend of a howling dog and the chirping of insects after a rainstorm on the sand. Dedan, moving stealthily like the night, was able to escape without Daniel's awareness.

"Dedan, where should we go next?" Daniel asked as he wiped off the sand and dirt on his face with his bare hands.

He looked around the vast sand. Looking beyond the endless sand on the South and the way towards the mountains on the North.

"Where are you, Dedan?" he screamed looking at the South and North and vice versa, blanking on what to do next.

He examined his next move, scanning the area for any clues to Dedan's whereabouts and the direction he might have gone. Unfortunately, the weather and winds had made it difficult to track Dedan's movements. Despite the uncertainty, he decided to head North, unsure of what challenges that awaited him. He worried that the Busol might catch up to him and expose his identity, leading to his execution.

Daniel effortlessly climbed the steep mountain slope, enjoying the sight of the pine trees around him. Suddenly, an arrow whizzed past him, narrowly missing him and striking a tree. Realising he was in the middle of a battlefield, he saw the Busol warriors retreating from their fierce enemies, the Kumad. The Kumad used their advanced weapons, such as flying arrows, long blades, and powerful physical attacks, to overpower the Busol with their larger size and strength.

Daniel hesitated before joining the battle on the Kumad's side. As he attempted to advance, a swiftly flying arrow narrowly missed him again, embedding itself in the tree behind him. A Busol warrior observed this and hurled his dagger towards him, striking his shoulder. Despite his injury, Daniel managed to draw his sword from his waist and, with a swift motion, severed the Busol's head from his body.

Daniel persisted in his fight against the Busol, making every effort to avoid being identified. "I hope the Busol didn't recognise me," he whispered, after the battle subsided.

The Kumad warriors buried their deceased to avoid bad luck, as they believed it was necessary to bury those who died in accidents or battles immediately. On the contrary, their enemies were left in the open for wild animals to consume, but their heads were decapitated first to be taken as trophies.

"Who are you?" a warrior asked, holding a spear threateningly close to Daniel's face.

Daniel, pressed against the mountain side, felt the rough terrain digging into his back, causing discomfort. It was the rocky surface, not the warrior's assumption, that elicited his grimace.

Another warrior intervened, taking the spear from his comrade. "Leave him be. I witnessed him battling a Busol."

The spear-wielding warrior hesitated, then relented. "Identify yourself and state your origin."

"I am Daniel, hailing from the Dutab Kingdom."

"An unfamiliar name to me. Why are you here alone?"

"I became lost while trying to fulfill my duty."

The warrior noticed the eagle tattoo on Daniel's arm, blood seeping from a wound sustained in combat. He applied a pre-pounded herb to Daniel's wound and wiped the blood around it with the same herb. The unbearable sting made Daniel scream in pain. After giving Daniel some water to drink, Daniel consumed it in one gulp and thanked the warrior.

As they continued on their way to the village, the warrior mentioned recognising the tattoo but couldn't quite place where he had seen it before. Daniel was about to explain, making it through the pain, but the warrior already understood the significance of the tattoo and the danger Daniel was in.

The travel was shorter than the usual mountain trek. They arrived in an area clumped with kubo houses. The similarities were uncanny with the villages and group of community within the mountains except there were skills and tools the village used that was not influenced by foreign bodies. The bow and arrow, the usage of wooden spoons and carved plates. Other simple tools were transformed into a more advance tools like the usage of spade and pitch fork for agriculture.

"This is puzzling. Despite being in a mountainous region, the temperature here is extremely hot," Daniel thought to himself.

The warriors then presented Daniel to their leader, who introduced himself as Bastian. Daniel also shared his own name and was surprised by the fact that many of them had names that were reminiscent of his original modern era names. They conversed in a mix of native mountain dialect and some lowland dialects that made Daniel more amazed.

Food was prepared for Daniel, but he was reluctant to try anything other than the steamed white rice cooked and served in a clay pot. The dish seemed to be a mix of vegetables, but it had a bitter and slippery taste that didn't appeal to his palate. While he had tried bitter and fatty soup in the past, this vegetable dish presented a unique flavor for him. He only took a small bite and mixed it with plenty of rice. The villagers didn't bother him and didn't join him, including Bastian.

A woman with blonde hair, hazel eyes, smooth bronze skin, and a stunning figure caught Daniel's attention as it seemed always to be the case. She would steal glances in his direction while going about her daily tasks. Whether fetching water at the communal spring or helping her mother with weaving, she would sneak a look at him. Daniel felt a rush of heat and strong pounding heartbeat every time, momentarily forgetting everything else, but in haste, he would remember his purpose and refrain from indulging in thoughts of her youthful allure.

While Daniel was helping the men set up a pole, an elderly woman watched him. She walked over to Daniel and said, "That young woman is the daughter of a prayle from the lowlands. The prayle was said to have raped her mother, who sadly died during childbirth. It's a tragic situation." Daniel listened to the woman's words, thinking about his past behavior, his treatment with women, and whether he had children that he neglected.

One of the workers interrupted the old woman's talking, by asking Daniel, "Hey, could you please help me carry a log from the forest?"

Daniel remained silent, his thoughts consumed by the fate of his possible children and their mothers.

"I'm asking you to come with me and help carry the log from the forest," the warrior said again, growing frustrated.

"Sorry, okay," Daniel finally responded, snapping back to reality.

While hiking in the mountain forest, he learned that the warrior's name was Pitong. Despite introducing himself, Pitong was already familiar with him as a newcomer to the village. As they trekked up the steep mountain with a heavy log, Pitong made a misstep, causing them to stumble. The log crashed to the ground and began sliding downhill. Both men hurried after it, with Pitong attempting to grab it, resulting in scrapes on his arms from the log's bark. Although the wounds were not severe, they were painful.

Daniel also tried to halt the log's progress by acting as a barrier, but it continued to slide and even rolled once it reached level ground. They retrieved the log and carried it back up the mountain, enduring the discomfort until they finally returned to the village.

"That was quite a moment," Daniel said with a slight smile.

"I apologise. I didn't mean it to happen. I didn't realise the rock was weak."

"I get it. You should take care of those scrapes on your arm."

Pitong's arm became plump as boar's belly accompanied by a

burning sensation that even the toughest creature could not tolerate, so they had to reach out to the "Mangagas," their healer, for treatment. He was required to proceed to the healer's place for treatment. Meanwhile, Daniel carried on with the task at hand without needing any treatment.

Pitong stayed the night in the Mangagas' quarters to continue recovering. In the village center, a bonfire burned brightly, casting endless flames and shadows. Mothers scolded their children, urging them to sleep. Unable to rest, Daniel wandered to the bonfire to relax and gaze at the stars. Feeling a light tap on his thigh, he turned to find a little girl by his side. Seating her on a log near the fire, more children approached, followed by concerned mothers trying to retrieve them.

"I understand you want your children to sleep, but let me share a short story with them," Daniel said to the mothers. After some persuasion, they allowed him to proceed, acknowledging that his tale might help the children drift off.

The children eagerly awaited every word that Daniel spoke, their eyes filled with anticipation. Daniel noticed their excitement and started incorporating gestures into his storytelling. Some of the mothers were impressed by his cleverness and playful actions.

He recounted a tale of a witch who abducted a handsome prince from the castle and took him to her cave. The witch flew on a broomstick into the princess's room while she was sleeping and kidnapped her, tying her to a wooden pole to prevent her from escaping. Despite treating her well and offering food and drink, the princess refused to accept her captivity. A brave knight happened to pass by the cave and managed to break through the sealed entrance with his sword. Daniel embellished the story as he went on. Just as the knight was about to help the princess escape, the witch returned on her broomstick. The knight swung his sword at the witch, who unleashed a lightning-like power from her hands that the knight narrowly avoided. Undeterred, he swung his sword again, this time leaping to make the witch fall to the ground. The witch unleashed her power once more, but the knight raised his sword, deflecting the lightning-like energy back at the witch, shattering her into pieces.

Daniel was so engrossed in his storytelling and actions that he found himself standing with his sword raised in his right hand. However, the children didn't seem to grasp the story, and most of them fell asleep. Some of the mothers had also dozed off.

The mothers then carried their sleeping children back to their huts. Daniel sat for a moment, watching the mothers, before returning to his room. The wound was almost forgotten by him. He didn't even feel it while working, but the pain and fatigue returned during the storytelling, especially after he wielded his sword.

Chapter XVII

Dedan reached the summit of a peculiar mountain that had caught his eye. Unlike typical mountains, this one lacked vegetation and wildlife. The surface was a mix of soft and hard areas but he could not explain why. As he was about to continue his journey, he felt the ground tremble beneath him. To his surprise, because only the mountain was shaking. With his next step, he found himself on the adjacent mountain, unable to move or even blink as he witnessed the mountain shifting to reveal Angalo, a mighty giant that leaves massive footprint everywhere he stepped. Dedan clung on tightly as Angalo's long hair and beard brushed against him as the giant walked.

Angalo's wide and sturdy feet flattened every path he walked, making the forest leveled to the ground, the trees, rocks, and all. He moved forward continuously without any opposition, slumping his bottom at the center of the lake.

Dedan, perched on Angalo's head, lost his balance and slipped into Angalo's ear. "Hey! Hey!" Dedan shouted as loudly as he could inside Angalo's ear.

Startled, Angalo looked around, trying to figure out what was happening. Dedan screamed again, causing discomfort in Angalo's ear. Angalo attempted to clear his ear by putting his finger in it, but Dedan successfully hid in the crevasses of his ear. Despite Dedan's continued loud screams, Angalo's attempts to remove him from his ear were unsuccessful.

In a bold move, Dedan leaped onto Angalo's hair, swinging himself in four attempts before landing on the giant's left eyelid. The giant's neck stiffened as he blinked many times, causing Dedan to be incorporated with the tears but still able to hang on to the eyelid. The giant's eye became irritated, and he rubbed it with his hand. Miraculously, Dedan survived the ordeal with only minor scratches, encapsulated in a tear that flowed onto the giant's palm. From this vantage point, Dedan saw that the giant was a fascinating creature, especially considering Dedan's size. The giant then gently scraped his hands at the side of the lake to save Dedan.

Green water animals with monstrous teeth and rough leathery skin were lurking on the side of the lake, waiting for Dedan to approach. However, Angalo's presence caused some of them to retreat to their individual holes on the side of the lake. Some individuals who did not fit into the holes seamlessly blended in with the moss. An aggressive one tried to bite off Dedan's feet, but Angalo swiftly noticed it and tossed it aside with its tail.

Angalo held Dedan gently in his fist, allowing him to breathe. As they walked, Angalo left imprints along the path. He then opened his palm and examined Dedan closely. He reverted to a lying position creating a mountain-like structure with Dedan left on the top of his belly.

Angalo rarely spoke about the quiet realm of mystics and humanity. His imposing presence seemed to unsettle the world, causing it to struggle to adapt to his existence. With each of his actions, he disrupted the natural order, shifting the positions ordained by the revered gods worshipped by the indigenous populations. However, their devotion was being challenged by the intrusion of conquistadors.

Catholic churches were proliferating like mushrooms in the wild throughout the entire archipelago, replacing many cultural traditions and beliefs of the people. The worship of native mythical gods, goddesses, and creatures was supplanted by devotion to the Christian God, Mary, and the saints, as evidenced by the statues displayed in the church altars. Practices such as headhunting and tattoos, which were integral to the culture, were prohibited. The indigenous people had fewer rights than the conquistadors, who could act with impunity, despite this going against the teachings of the church.

The people silently observed everything that was happening, with only a few groups opposing the negative events. The rebolusyonaryos were unaware that their command post also served as their community center. Bakaso, a dedicated rebolusyonaryo soldier for the past few years, was a close friend of Bula-es and was privy to all the secrets of the revolution. A meeting was held to nominate a new leader, following their tradition of giving potential leaders a chance.

Bula-es and Bakaso were the choices, and their loyal followers made pacts to support them. Ballots were created from paper during the meeting, allowing participants to freely write their preferred leader. Many pledged their votes to Bakaso, leading him to believe he would win, but ultimately, Bula-es was elected as the new leader. Despite his disappointment, Bakaso accepted the outcome but harboured resentment towards Bakaso.

Bakaso headed towards the town center with the intention of engaging in negotiations with the friars at the church compound, as he believed it was a more diplomatic approach to dealing with the conquistadors. He was aware that going directly to the government could lead to severe consequences such as imprisonment, torture, or even execution.

Before the church would inform the government officials, Bakaso revealed the rebolusyonaryo's plan to attack the town's government building in order to free their comrades. The attack was scheduled to coincide with the celebration of the feast of Sta. Maria Katolika. In exchange for his information, Bakaso anticipated receiving gold rewards from either the church and the government, as well as political favors from them.

The reinforcement group, under the command of Comandante Alberto Dela Cruz, arrived at the munisipyo equipped with metal armour and advanced weapons including boom sticks, heavy cannon blasters, and sharp swords made from modern metal alloys. Bakaso guided them through a hidden passageway to avoid detection and emerged at the gathering without anyone noticing.

The horses were making a lot of noise as they dragged the cannon blasters up the steep mountainside. Unfortunately, two of the horses had mishaps - one slipped and fell down the slope towards the river, while the other became so tired that it stopped breathing once they reached the mountain peak. They were forced to leave the heavy weapon behind as it was impeding their progress.

Bakaso joined in the celebration of Bula-es' victory, enjoying a feast of roasted pig, rice, noodles, vegetable stew, and other dishes prepared by contributing families. The main alcoholic beverage was tuba, or sugar cane wine. Bakaso pretended to be part of the festivities until the people were drunk.

The colonisers, who were hiding in nearby trees and bushes, attacked suddenly as Bakaso raised his container saying "A congratulatory toast for my dear friend Bula-es here" in loud resounding voice. They ran out and began slashing their swords at the men, while others fired their boom sticks with deadly accuracy. Many men were killed in the initial attack. Bula-es and several mothers with their children were conscious enough to have witnessed the horrifying events.

Women and children were not the prime target, but some of them became collateral victims. The remaining men who survived were also captured and imprisoned in a dungeon at the base of a castle-like structure in the town center. Among the prisoners was Liston. Bakaso received his reward in gold from Arzobispo Miguel and promised a high government position.

"Here is your reward, 20 gold coins in the bag," the Arzobispo said, tossing it to Bakaso.

"What about my own army?" Bakaso asked, catching the bag.

" ¡Fuera de mi cara, tonto! Before I change my mind!"

With a cold sweat, he accepted his reward, knelt at the wooden crucifix, made the sign of the cross, and departed from the church, never to be seen again. It was assumed that he had fled to an unknown destination.

Unbeknownst to him, several of the conqueror's soldiers were lurking near a stone building, and as he turned a corner, he was suddenly attacked with a dagger. He collapsed onto the stone pavement, his blood staining the ground red. Despite the presence of two witnesses, they simply walked past him as if it was an ordinary day. Later, feral dogs discovered his decaying body and devoured it, leaving no trace of his existence.

"Ahhh! Ahhh!" Liston cried out as the spiked horse whip pierced his exposed back. The conqueror soldier, with his swift reflexes, intensified the pain. Liston and others like him were chained by their arms and ankles, facing the stone brick wall.

"Please! Stop! Please! Stop!" the woman beside him begged, her cries filled with sorrow. A soldier was exploiting her feminine beauty. Liston couldn't bear to witness the soldier's satisfaction with each thrust.

At that time, Teniente Juan Martines, the designated officer, went into the dungeon to inspect the prisoners. He observed that Liston's arms were adorned with tattoos that were unlike those of the natives he had encountered before.

"What are those markings on your arms? Where did you get them?" he inquired with an imposing voice.

"Uh... um..." Liston responded in full agony.

"Release him and give him something to drink!" ordered the teniente.

A soldier removed Liston's shackles and then he collapsed to the ground, experiencing tremors. He drank from a copper goblet without pausing until he had finished all its contents, then took deep breaths to recover.

"I'll ask you again! Where did you get those tattoos and what do they mean?"

"I received these tattoos when I was young to signify that I am part of the Busol tribe in the mountains. My father gave them to me."

"Take him to the river for a bath and dress him with a new robe!"

Liston was subsequently invited to the teniente's dinner to discuss an agreement that the teniente wanted, promising to spare Liston's life and stop harming his fellow captives from the revolution. Liston did not provide any response, leaving the teniente feeling disrespected. The tension between the two parties in the discussion could be altered by the sound of a metal object falling.

"What did you decide about my proposal? Make sure to choose the right one!" the teniente said with a rugged and roaring tone.

In the midst of the ongoing events, the mountains retained their mysterious characteristics, closely tied to the traditional beliefs of the indigenous people.

The clouds multiplied, taking the form of a man complete with loincloth and headgear. Rain cascaded down like waterfalls from all directions, creating whirlpools on Bulalakaw lake. The powerful creation destroyed everything in its path.

The nearby village of Dinaki, with one of the largest populations, was peaceful as villagers went about their daily tasks. Kitan was weaving a loincloth while her son helped plow the fields with a carabao using a wooden contraption called an 'aracho' to till the ground for rice or corn.

"I heard a loud thunder nearby. The sky must be getting ready for rain," an elder remarked.

The mountain right next to the village was experiencing heavy rainfall, causing rocks and loose soil to tumble down. The unprepared village was flooded by the rushing water and rocks, destroying structures one after another. Many people lost their lives, and even the nipa huts were swept away by the disaster.

Kitan clung to a log wedged between rocks in a stone wall. The force of the water was so strong that it caused the structure to shake. Her son attempted to swim to her side and pull her to safety, but the rushing water was relentless, like an overflowing waterfall. Kitan, along with others and debris, was swept into the ravine, sealing their fate.

"No! Mother!" Kitan's son cried out, desperate to be with the rushing water. Despite his protests, several villagers pulled him through the mud to safety on higher ground. The survivors watched helpless from a safe vantage point as the rest of the village was engulfed and destroyed by the water.

The group of survivors was drenched from the rain, with no one spared from the downpour - adults, children, and elderly alike. Despite waiting for the rain to stop, it showed no signs of letting up.

"It's getting dark and the rain isn't stopping! We need to find shelter!" one person exclaimed.

They climbed to higher ground and eventually stumbled upon a cave.

"No, we can't go in there. It's the sacred resting place of the mummies. Disturbing it will bring us bad luck," an elder warned in a fearful tone.

Ignoring the elder's warning, the group entered the cave, seeking refuge from the cold and wet conditions. The elder, trembling not from the cold but from fear of the supposed bad luck, decided to separate from the group in search of another place to stay.

The heavy rain persisted until nightfall and finally ceased the following morning. Some of the elderly and children were unable to get up, still feeling exhausted and sore. An elderly woman remained motionless with her eyes closed. Kitan's son placed his arm near her nose and realised she was not breathing.

"She must be dead!" he exclaimed.

They didn't care as they were too fatigued and hungry to do anything about the old woman's body. Kitan's son and another volunteer ventured outside to search for food and water. Despite their physical condition, they walked a long distance and came across a wild banana tree. They gathered all the fruit, including the unripe ones, consumed some, took a brief rest, and then returned to the cave. The survivors were writhing in pain, worsened by their hunger. They ate the bananas voraciously, disregarding the bitter taste of the unripe ones. Their sole focus was to alleviate their hunger.

Kitan's son lit a wooden torch to explore further into the cave. The torch illuminated a few steps into the darkness, revealing numerous coffins scattered around. He nearly stepped on one, noticing that some of the wooden coffins were decayed, exposing the preserved bodies inside. The tattoos on their skin were still visible, and some had gold accessories adorning their bodies. He felt a temptation to take the gold, his hand wavering near the coffins. However, he remembered the old man's warning and thought better of it.

Buran, one of the elders who had survived, took charge and organised the men. "I have decided that we need to find a new place to live. It is dangerous to return in our village," he declared. They fashioned sturdy twigs into spears, carved staffs from hard wood for weapons, and crafted wooden shields for protection. They journeyed for miles, crossing rivers and mountains until they reached a forest with abundant trees and fewer predators, ideal for the safety of the villagers.

Half of the group remained to initiate the development of the area by clearing trees from the forest and constructing nipa hut houses. The other half went back to fetch the remaining villagers. They were reassured to find that the old man's prediction did not materialise. During their journey, they encountered human bones along the way.

Initially, they did not give much thought to it, but upon discovering remnants of the old man's loincloth and pendant, they recognised it as someone from their group. They briefly stopped in remembrance but proceeded on their way, unable to offer a proper tribute to their deceased companion.

A new day brought a new community. Although their initial move was challenging, they evolved into a cohesive village where everyone worked together to meet each other's needs. The village operated without a single leader, instead following the guidance of a council of elders or wise men. Kitan's son was responsible for overseeing the defense sector.

While pounding rice for supper, a village mother's little girl approached her, crying. The mother advised her to wait for supper instead of eating uncooked rice. The girl persisted, prompting the mother to scold her for talking too much. After finishing the rice pounding, the mother winnowed the rice, removed the chaff, and covered the rice in a basket. She then carried a jar on her head to fetch water from the spring.

The little girl usually accompanied her to play in the water, but this time she stayed behind. When the mother left, the girl tried to take rice from the basket but accidentally covered herself with it. Upon returning, the mother heard a bird's cry coming from the basket. She uncovered it to find a brown rice bird, 'beshing' that flew away, bidding her goodbye and mentioning that she didn't give it any rice to eat.

The rice fields were overrun by numerous 'beshing' birds that consumed rice plants and disrupted the irrigation with their landings. A farmer used 'sampalit,' a rope made from banana bark fibers, to create a loud noise by hitting large rocks. Meanwhile, other villagers enjoyed playing the 'kelchang,' a bamboo string instrument for their own amusement. The loud noise from the 'sampalit' blessed by the 'mambunong' startled the 'beshing' birds, causing them to freeze. The villagers left the birds alone as they were believed to be the spirit of the little girl and her descendants until the birds returned to their natural state after the next harvest.

The rice planters sensed the presence of Angtan, the plantation spirit as they listened to the enchanting female voice harmonising with the music of the 'kelchang' carried by the wind. This indicated a bountiful harvest approaching, much awaited by the village.

An elder expressed optimism, "We are destined for a prosperous harvest this season."

Napuagan was once again observing from the underworld as Kabunian bestowed blessings upon the people. The community was joyfully celebrating a plentiful harvest with the Canao ceremony, under the watchful eye of Binudbud, the spirit of the feast.

"Curses! The people are filled with happiness once more!" Napuagan exclaimed.

He called upon Bumigi, the deity of worm control. Bumigi, residing in the underground realm close to Napuagan's domain, heard his call but chose to ignore his words.

"What does Napuagan want now?" Bumigi asked, with a hint of annoyance.

Refusing to respond to Napuagan, Bumigi harboured resentment towards him and his destructive ways. Napuagan had caused harm to everything, even the worms that Bumigi protected, which had nearly become extinct due to Napuagan's actions.

"You dare defy me! You are nothing!" Napuagan exclaimed, frustrated with Bumigi's disregard for his orders. In a moment of anger, he banished the earthworms to the underworld and began to engulf them in molten lava until Bumigi finally agreed to comply.

"I will do as you wish. Please spare the earthworms, as they hold great value to me," Bumigi pleaded.

The earthworms were essential in maintaining the rice fields near the mountain's edge, ensuring the soil remained soft and preventing the stone structures from collapsing. Without them, the soil dried up and cracked, making it impossible for rice or other crops to grow. As a result, the rice fields on the mountainside were abandoned.

Despite the villagers' attempts to solve the agricultural problem, they faced continuous setbacks. The council of elders suggested transitioning to alternative crops such as sweet potatoes and corn, which required less water and could sustain the community.

Chapter XVIII

The conquistadors attempted to act justly on this occasion. A courageous friar stepped forward to mediate, believing he could facilitate understanding between the conquerors and the mountain natives. The mountain natives watched as the friar and his sole companion approached. They traversed the dense forest, tackling steep inclines and facing wild creatures and dense foliage that hindered their journey. The friar and his companion bore red marks on their skin, and their breath labored to match their movements.

With confidence, the friar attempted to communicate with the mountain natives through actions and the limited language he understood. However, the natives did not believe him and reacted with that disbelief. Despite the friar and his assistant's efforts to share the message of Christianity and God's love for all people, a warrior wielding a 'gaman' swiftly decapitated the friar, while the other mountain natives cheered.

The assistant, fearing for his life, tried to escape but was impaled by a spear and then decapitated. The heads of the foreigners were celebrated, and the 'bindeyan' dance was performed, accompanied by animal sacrifices blessed by the 'mambunong.' The heads of high society and a foreigner not native to the mountains are held in higher esteem than the heads of the ordinary mountain people.

Napuagan once resided on Mt. Pulag before being banished to the underworld by Kabunian. From his new vantage point, he continued to observe the creatures on Earth, particularly drawn to Alukoy, the enchantress spirit. Napuagan never failed to admire her radiant red hair and captivating smile whenever she lit up her surroundings.

Napuagan decided to go down to earth to see Alukoy up close. Their first meeting was not without failure. Alukoy did not like Napuagan's pushy and boastful approached. Dismayed, Napuagan returned to Mt. Pulag among the gods. His second attempt was right-on the success rate but it was done with deceit. He cast a spell at Alukoy blowing the kiss of love that the air directed straight to her lips from above Mt. Pulag.

"Alukoy, your beauty is incomparable," Napuagan confessed as he descended from the realm of Mt Pulag.

She smiled back, showing her appreciation and admiration for Napuagan. Unbeknownst to them, Kabunian was watching them from the water of life spring, closely monitoring their actions. Just as Napuagan and Alukoy's lips were about to feel each other's sweet taste, Kabunian intervened. He pointed at Alukoy, breaking her free from Napuagan's spell. Kabunian banished Napuagan to the underworld, where he would reign for eternity. It was within Kabunian's power that one day his son Kadaklan would fall in love with Alukoy when the time was right.

Kadaklan, a kind spirit and one of Kabunian's children, possessed an undeniable charm. He was a handsome demi-god with powerful muscles capable of carrying heavy loads. Despite his divine lineage, he remained concealed from both humans and the gods. Living a nomadic existence in the untamed forests alongside the nimble monkeys called 'aki,' he seemed to inhabit a sacred realm, born from the darkness and had affection of Alukoy.

The two instantly fell in love with each other. They vanished mysteriously, leaving the gods perplexed about their fate.

Daniel had been residing in the village for some time before he decided to join the hunting team. "I have no fear! The Busol cannot do me any harm. The gods are on my side," he affirmed to his spirit, feeling assured of his invulnerability.

The Ki-bungan Mountain was the nearest forested mountain with plenty of bush meat to sustain the entire village. Moreover, it was teeming with the most aromatic vegetation.

"Halt! I can hear some noises," Subagan, the leader of the crew with heightened auditory abilities, warned. "Proceed with caution. Keep your movements discreet," he whispered. A kitten was spotted nearby, but the crew remained unfazed. "Stay quiet and don't alert the little creature to our presence," Subagan advised. Next, a small puppy appeared, different from the previous dog they had encountered. The tough demeanor of the previous canine was replaced by soft, round eyes that exuded charm and a sense of tranquility, which the crew was in need of. "Let's continue on," Subagan whispered, this time with a tinge of annoyance.

A headless mouse hopped by, followed by its floating head. The hunting crew recognised it as Manputol, the headless shape-shifter. "Be ready for anything, even battle," Subagan warned. The crew, including Daniel, armed themselves and advanced into the dense forest, prepared for whatever may come their way.

"Is there a way to the forest?" Daniel inquired of Subagan as they took a break.

"If I recall correctly, there is a narrow entrance on the side that is so small one must crawl to enter," Subagan replied.

"Excellent. If you're on board with my plan, most of us will go through the main entrance while a few of us will use the side entrance. You'll lead the way."

Subagan looked up at the clear blue sky, the sun shining brightly. He then nodded at Daniel. The crew entered quietly; their footsteps barely audible. Subagan guided Daniel and the others to the side entrance, moving through the bushes with precision.

Suddenly, the Manputol appeared, creating a disturbance in the forest. Monkeys chattered loudly from the treetops, while wild boars and other unfamiliar creatures charged towards them. The crew quickly threw their spears, taking down some of the animals. The monkeys descended, attacking the crew from behind, causing chaos. Despite some escaping, Subagan and his strongest crew members fought back, driving the monkeys to retreat back into the trees.

In the midst of the commotion, Daniel noticed a person-like figure amidst the monkeys. It was like staring at his own reflection, as the figure moved in a manner that closely mimicked the monkeys. Surprised, he quickly joined the group. A lone chicken roamed freely, catching Subagan's attention. He swiftly grabbed the chicken and tossed it a great distance.

The team returned to the village with the deceased animals. Those who were injured received treatment with herbs and were secured with vine ropes. The able-bodied members transported the captured animals, while the injured were carefully carried to avoid worsening their condition.

The celebration featured the 'takik' dance, which was similar to the 'tayaw' dance with slight difference, but the cooking process was more complex. Additional spices like garlic, onions, and ginger were used, along with herbs and wild vegetables mixed in with the catch. 'Wat-wat' was served, but only to villagers of higher status. Coconut milk was included in both savoury and sweet dishes. Daniel thoroughly enjoyed the variety of flavors and food items at the celebration.

Daniel savoured the food with delight, relishing its familiar and appealing flavours. Subagan gave him a knowing look as he washed down his meal with 'basi,' a sweet alcoholic drink made from fermented sugar cane juice that he favoured.

"I heard you saw a man among the monkeys," Subagan asked.

"Yes, he even resembled me," Daniel confirmed.

"Truly?"

"Yes."

Daniel thought Subagan was intrigued by his revelation, but the leader quickly dismissed his observation. Subagan wasn't too keen on hearing stories from a stranger.

A woman named Gemmelayan was well-known for her large stature, muscular physique, and strength that rivaled that of men. Daniel was always intrigued by her, but he never expressed it. "What an unusual person. I wonder if LGBTQ is even a concept in their world," he thought to himself.

"Hey, Daniel. How are you doing?" Gemmelayan asked, coupled with a smile.

"I'm fine. I'm doing well," Daniel replied.

Men were lifting rocks with their strength at the top of the stone wall construction. Gemmelayan, on the other hand, used planks of wood to help support the weight of the rocks and a rope to secure them in place temporarily. The men didn't seem to notice her method and continued to work in their own way, flexing their muscles as they lifted rocks. Gemmelayan was unfazed by their display of strength.

"Don't bother with her. Plenty have tried to win her over and ended up unsuccessful," a woman remarked as she noticed Daniel gazing at Gammelayan.

"No, I am not interested in her. I am just curious about how she became a large woman," Daniel said with a clear expression of curiosity on his flushed face.

"Hey, could you please help me lift this rock on my shoulder," one of the male workers interrupted, Daniel never had a response to his question from there on.

That night, the moon shone brightly and everyone was expected to be asleep. However, in the nearby woods, the sound of flapping wings and hooting was disturbing the village. No one dared to confront the source of the loud noise. Daniel, feeling impatient, drew his sword and prepared to wave it to scare away the bird. As he approached, he noticed that the creature looked like an owl but with longer legs than usual.

A man spotted him and hurried over, urging him to stop. "Please don't disturb the Akop, as it could bring a curse to the village. If left undisturbed, it may bring good luck," the man explained. Daniel, with his sword raised, looked at the man with wide eyes, listening intently.

"How do you manage to sleep with that noise?" Daniel asked, lowering his arm and relaxing.

"We have no choice but to become accustomed to the sounds throughout the night," the man replied.

An elderly woman emerged and cautioned, "Do not disturb the Akop."

"I have already been warned, and we are returning to bed," Daniel assured.

"Very well, but please refrain from doing so in the future," the woman requested.

Daniel nodded, and they all went back to sleep.

The somber atmosphere in the Dutab Kingdom, coupled with the Busol's relentless pursuit of pleasure, led the people to seek food and resources in far-off lands. The once abundant forested mountains were now depleted, causing a struggle for survival. Many were suffering the consequences of this man-made disaster, including Mayangao, who wanted to eliminate the captives, like Betot, but was also affected by the crisis.

The Busol pack stumbled upon a dense forested mountain filled with wildlife and vibrant vegetation. They helped themselves to the colourful fruits hanging from the trees and bushes, despite not knowing if they were safe to eat. Their hunger drove them to devour the fruits eagerly, causing chaos among the plants and animals. Still not satisfied, they decided to hunt the local wildlife. Some of the Busol were so engrossed in eating that they tripped over an unusual black twig. As they tried to remove the twig, it moved revealing a massive spider known as the pad-padi emerged from the shadows.

With its hairy black body, sharp fangs, and powerful legs, the pad-padi attacked the Busol with ferocity. They were unable to defend themselves against the massive spider, despite throwing their spears and wielding their bolos, and ultimately fell victim to the flesh-eating creature due to its overwhelming size. The pad-padi devoured the Busol mercilessly, leaving no survivors.

The creatures of the forest were aware that the pad-padi's lair were not to be disturbed, with only a few falling victim to the monster who consumed it for food. It was the fatal mistake of the Busol that eradicated them, leaving no survivors in hand.

The Busol continued to wait, chanting prayers to Napuagan in the hope of being saved, but their pleas went unanswered. The Busol did not obey every command of Napuagan as he wanted. They were faithful in the beginning but fell on their own desires.

Betot secretly stored food such as 'etag' and fermented root crops that could last a long time, without the knowledge of Mayangao and the rest of the Kingdom. He and Kuchep consumed the food discreetly, exhibiting symptoms of hunger in a subtle manner. They controlled their intake to avoid constantly feeling hungry and moved slowly, showing signs of malnutrition.

The night was silent, with everyone in slumber. There was no one in sight, not even the guards were on duty. Betot stealthily approached Kuchep's room, where she and her son, along with Mayangao, were gathered.

"Be quiet, this is our chance to escape," Betot whispered, covering Kuchep's mouth to prevent any noise.

They made their way through a hidden tunnel in the bushes that Betot had found, leading them to the outside world. Running as fast as they could, they didn't stop until they were certain they had left the Busol territory behind. The heavy rain made it challenging, but they persevered. Despite the tough conditions, they kept moving until the sun emerged and dried the ground.

A guard was patrolling his designated area when he noticed some bushes near a kubo that were growing close to the fences, with branches freshly twisted and plenty of leaves on the ground. He also observed a section where the entrance of a tunnel was recently made visible. Curious, he decided to investigate and discovered that the tunnel led to the outside.

"Your leadership, I found a tunnel covered by bushes that leads outside," the warrior informed, bowing before the leader.

Mayangao's son cried out for his mother, but she was nowhere to be found in the room or the cooking area. The absence of Betot in his quarters was also noted by the other warriors.

The Dutab Kingdom was in turmoil, not only because of their predicament but also because Kuchep and Betot were nowhere to be seen. Mayangao ordered their search, but they remained elusive. After a long trek, the warriors grew weary and disheartened due to their dwindling food and water supplies, prompting them to abandon the search. Their morale improved upon reaching a river abundant with fish and fruit trees along its banks. They redirected their focus to satisfying their hunger instead of continuing the hunt for Kuchep and Betot.

Betot and Kuchep set out on a journey into the heart of the vast and forbidding Kagubatan forest, where a village was nestled. The village was well protected by natural barriers of trees, boulders, and untouched landscapes, with guards stationed at the entrances of a high wooden barricade. Despite the challenging terrain, they did not waver in their determination and maintained their courage.

The village had unusual features, as the people with their fair skin, slanted eyes and golden coffee-tinged hair. They were covered not only in their most sensitive areas but in every possible part of their bodies to shield themselves from the elements. Their attire was not ordinary, consisting of refined animal hides, flowing silk garments for the women, and sturdy footwear. The enticing scent of the air beckoned outsiders to revel in the sensory pleasures of the village.

"We haven't seen you around here before," remarked one of the guards.

"We… we seek refuge. We managed to escape from… from the Busol who have taken over the Dutab Kingdom," Betot explained.

The guard granted them permission to enter the village but made sure to accompany them to meet their leader, Xi Yan. She welcomed them warmly, understanding the challenges they had faced.

"I heard that you both escaped from the Busols?" she inquired, her gaze intense as if trying to extract information forcefully.

"Yes, we were held captive for a long time. It was only recently that we found an opportunity to break free," Kuchep confirmed.

A servant brought them bowls of noodles and cups of tea. The intricate designs on the utensils captivated them, with Betot struggling to use the two sticks provided for eating. Kuchep observed Betot's attempts and exchanged glances with Xi Yan.

Xi Yan smiled and said, "These are chopsticks. Let me show you how to use them." The two paid close attention as she demonstrated the proper technique, but they struggled to master the hand technique. Despite her frustration, Xi Yan remained patient and instead allowed them to eat using the bowl like a cup and slurp the noodles like slimy worms, which satisfied their hunger.

The two were pleased with the new experience and expressed their gratitude for the delicious food and drinks. Xi Yan then instructed a servant to show them to their respective bedrooms, with Kuchep sharing a room with the servants and Betot having a room for men. The servants glanced at Kuchep but remained silent, as it was already late and everyone needed rest for the activities of the following day.

Kuchep was awakened from her slumber by a servant urging her to rise and start the day. Despite her initial attempt to get up, she collapsed back onto her soft mattress, grateful for its comforting layers of cloth. Although her mind was willing, her body was still fatigued from their journey. After stretching to alleviate some of the discomfort, she regained her strength and joined Betot and the villagers for breakfast. Xi Yan instructed a servant to take her to the spring for a refreshing wash, and with some effort, Betot managed to use the chopsticks.

Kuchep washed her face and hands with the servant by her side.

"Relax, there's no one else around. What's your name?" she asked.

"I am Ming Dao," he replied, hesitant to engage in conversation.

"Don't worry, it's just us," Kuchep reassured with a smile.

Later, they came back and Kuchep joined the rest for breakfast. They chatted a bit during and after the meal. Betot worked with the men in the fields, while Kuchep helped the servants with their duties.

A tragedy struck the village as children were found dead in the morning, their bodies pale and lifeless. Night after night, one, two, three children perished, leaving the villagers in shock. Xi Yan called for a gathering to honour the deceased children and investigate the cause of these tragic deaths.

"This is the third time we have lost children. We must all remain vigilant and uncover the source of this disaster," Xi Yan declared.

The day's brightness and the night's darkness were in a constant battle for dominance, casting a yellow-orange hue in the sky. A group of black birds, resembling crows or owaks, circled above the village. The villagers didn't pay much attention to the birds, assuming they were ordinary creatures. The birds blended into the dark surroundings, almost invisible. As the villagers went to sleep, the birds quietly entered through the crevices of the huts, making minimal noise to avoid detection. Their hunger for young blood made them move cautiously, avoiding any actions that might attract attention.

The next morning, two more children were found dead in their sleep. The feng shui expert who was also the medicine man decided to intervene. He took some human finger bones, placed them in a container, and shook them. After throwing the bones on the ground, five out of ten were scattered on the ground while the rest remained in the container. The expert interpreted the bones and then addressed the gathered villagers. "Have any of you noticed black birds in the sky as darkness approached?" Some villagers confirmed the expert's suspicions. "I fear that the bekeks are behind these attacks. They are black birds similar to owaks, but a bit larger with fangs that suck the blood of children!" The village was shocked, their faces reflecting disbelief and fear.

As darkness fell once more, the feng shui expert called for a bonfire to be lit in the center of the village. As expected, a flock of bekeks began circling the skies. The fire burned steadily, but its magic would not take effect until the night was fully upon them. Servants tended to the fire, while the villagers waited in anticipation. The feng shui expert reached into his animal hide pouch and sprinkled white powder onto the flames, making them burn brighter. He then added red, blue, and yellow powders, each time strengthening the fire. Soon, a massive fire bird emerged from the flames and soared towards the bekeks, engulfing them in its fiery embrace until they were no more. The fire bird kept on flying around and above the village. The feng shui expert extinguished the fire with water and dust making the fire bird disappear to ensure it could not cause any harm.

The entire village was filled with a sense of celebration, but there was still an undercurrent of fear as they were unsure if all the bekek were eliminated. Despite the reassurances of the feng shui expert, the children remained hidden at night and did not venture out until the day arrived. Thankfully, no children were harmed on that miraculous day, thanks to the feng shui expert's intervention in preventing further tragedies.

In a surprising turn of events, every household brought dish after dish. Xi Yan, observing the situation, instructed her servants to prepare food for a celebration. This wide variety of dishes were served, including various styles of noodles, dumplings, roasted pig, wat-wat, rice, and fermented drinks. Betot and Kuchep were amazed by the festivities and were invited to join in. The feng shui expert assessed the situation and deemed it to be auspicious. The preparation of the food, the combination of hot and cold dishes, and other factors all contributed to the positive outcome. Betot watched from the audience, while Kuchep was encouraged to participate in a graceful dance with the women. Despite her limited preparation time, Kuchep demonstrated expert dancing skills, seemingly floating through jumps and slides, unaware but highlighting her natural talent as a part-mamantala.

Chapter XVIX

A group of Busol warriors in formation was approaching. Paklit noticed the direction the group was heading and became alert.

"What? Are they really going to attack me? What have I done to provoke them?" he wondered.

Preparing himself, he grabbed a 'paseking' filled with food and drinks, his bulo at his side, and a dagger strapped to his arm. Without waiting to find out their intentions, he decided to leave before they reached him. He crossed the river and ventured into the nearby woods, determined to keep moving forward without looking back. His heart raced, sweat dripped down his face, and his breathing grew heavy from the continuous hiking.

He sat on a grassy area in the forest, feeling the coolness against his backside. Taking his spear, he struck a white stone he had found, creating sparks. Initially intending to sharpen his spear tip, he accidentally discovered a way to start a fire.

Walking aimlessly through the forest, he kept an eye out for potential prey. Spotting a young deer grazing alone, he hid behind a tree nearby. With trembling arms and a heavy spear, he struggled to maintain his aim. Despite his shaky stance, he threw the spear in an attempt to hunt the deer. The animal bolted, causing a commotion that scared off other nearby creatures.

All of a sudden, a cry of pain caught his attention. Upon further investigation, he discovered a woman bleeding on her left side with his spear standing upright in the ground a small distance from her. Carefully, he moved her to a more open area where the sunlight could reach. He treated her wound with medicinal herbs and tree sap to aid in healing. To protect her from potential threats, he covered her with leaves and twigs. With renewed vigour, he descended the mountain to gather water and perhaps some river creatures for sustenance.

While fetching water, he noticed some fish swimming against the current. He planned to catch a few when he suddenly felt a powerful vibration in the water. A wave was approaching his location from the deep part of the water. As it drew nearer, a 'gaki' appeared. This giant crab had pincers capable of shattering even the toughest rock. He sprinted at lightning speed, but the pincers managed to grab hold of him and pull him closer to the face. He raised his spear and tried to stab the creature, but noticed a flicker of movement in its expression. The creature paused, allowing him to notice a spear lodged in one of its eyes, clearly bothered by the creature's behavior. The creature's hold weakened as he leaped to the spear. He pulled the spear, causing him to fall. The creature then grabbed him by his claw and placed him on the riverside. It took some fish and placed them beside him, as if thanking him, before disappearing into the deep part of the river from whence it had originally emerged.

He was breathing heavily with immense relief, almost unable to stand. He took some of the fish and water, pushing through the pain with the lady's well-being on his mind. He was halfway up the mountain when he slipped on the loose soil, but with his quick reflexes he was able to get back up and continued, being more cautious thereafter. He followed the markers and arrived at the correct location, taking note of the bent or broken branches he had seen on his way to the river. In a frantic scream, "What happened? No! No! No!" he searched for the lady. Taking a few steps eastward, he found her leaning against a tree.

"Don't attempt to stand. Let me help you lay down," Paklit said.

"Ah! Thank you for the help. "

"Here, have some water," he dribbled water onto her lips. He grasped her shoulder as she lay near the pile of wood and twigs, he had gathered earlier. Once again, he struck the white stone against his spear tip to create a fire. Using his dagger, he cleaned the fish and placed it haphazardly on the fire. The woman reclined on the grass, appearing as though she was as comfortable as if she were floating on clouds, and soon drifted off to sleep.

"Wake up and have some fish to help you regain your strength," Paklit lightly tapped her cheek.

They both ate the fish. Paklit, tired from the difficult task, lay down next to the woman to rest, and they both drifted off to sleep. In Paklit's half-conscious state, he heard several women giggling floating without legs in every direction. He screamed in a sudden drenching of sweat. To his right, he saw the absence of the woman he expected to be there. Looking around, he spotted her floating without legs, giggling like the women in his dreams. He woke up again, feeling damp all over as if he had been swimming. The woman was there when he looked beside him, but the giggling continued. These female spirits, known as Buta-tew, caused confusion for those who heard their laughter.

"What is happening?" Paklit exclaimed, standing up with his hands on his head, feeling like he was spinning along with the sleeping woman.

The woman regained consciousness and presented the buta-tew some fish and water as offerings. Feeling unsure of what to do next, she recited a prayer to show that they meant no harm which happened that one of the spirits was actually her grandmother, who was among the group of ancestor spirits. Paklit stopped complaining suddenly and lay down on the grass. He passed out briefly but soon came to and became aware of his surroundings.

"What happened?" he asked, still confused.

"You were a victim of the Buta-tew, a group of women spirits that caused your consciousness to spin into confusion," the lady replied.

"Is that so? Then why are the fishes scattered around us?"

"Let them be. I offered them as a gesture of hope to alleviate your suffering."

They both leaned against a tree and took sips of water. "We should leave. Perhaps this place is cursed," the lady suggested.

They began their journey towards the southern part of the mountain where the river flowed. Paklit continued to gaze at the lady as they walked slowly, still processing the events that had transpired. The lady noticed his gaze as they walked side by side.

He smiled and said, "I never got the chance to ask your name."

"Ah, I am Biklay of Bokodians. I consider myself fortunate to have survived the attack of the Busol."

"Nice to meet you, Biklay. I am Paklit. I also fled my home when I saw the Busol approaching. I was with my mother, but she died."

Their journey continued in silence until they reached a barren rock devoid of trees, with only a few miniature versions of trees, grass, and plants.

They were about to rest when Biklay began to tear up, gazing at the blue sky and the passing clouds.

"What's wrong?" Paklit asked, with his curled eyebrows.

"It's just... I'm reminded of what happened to my village. I can still see the women and old ladies, bloodied and some with decapitated heads on the ground. My husband and I managed to escape the chaos, but he saved me... he shielded me with his body when a Busol was about to kill me with his bulo," her tears continued to flow.

Paklit wasn't certain, but he allowed Biklay's tears to flow like a river. He stayed close to her, ensuring her safety. Suddenly, they heard a noise coming from behind a nearby rock. A bald, bearded and muscular man adorned with tattoos appeared. Paklit instructed Biklay to hide behind a tree as he approached the man with caution, brandishing his dagger.

"What are you doing here? And how many others are with you?" Paklit asked.

"I am by myself. Trust me," the man replied.

"I know you are a Busol. Where are the rest of your group?" Paklit pressed.

"I swear to you, I am alone," the man insisted.

"Take the vines and bind him," Paklit instructed Biklay. Without the stranger having the opportunity to reach for his weapon, Biklay secured the stranger to the tree stump with Paklit's arrow aimed at him.

Biklay was left holding Paklit's dagger, with instructions to watch over the stranger while he searched for food. He emphasised that she should not even blink if necessary.

The barren surroundings offered little in terms of edible options. Paklit managed to find some mushrooms growing in the cracks of the hard rock. Although he was not an expert, he gathered them with hope that they were safe to eat and would not cause sickness or poisoning.

Paklit came back to find both Biklay and the stranger asleep. "Hey! Wake up!" he exclaimed, startling Biklay back to awareness.

"Sorry, I must have drifted off," Biklay apologised, noticing Paklit's annoyed expression.

"Alright, forget it. The main thing is that he didn't escape. Get these mushrooms ready for our next meal," he said, the hint of irritation disappearing from his expression.

Biklay washed and cleaned the mushrooms, then roasted them over an open flame while Paklit kept an eye on the stranger.

Despite the numerous distractions around him, Daniel once again struggled to maintain focus on his tasks. He was thoroughly enjoying his time in the welcoming new village, with thoughts of the Prayle's daughter occupying his mind and igniting desires within him. "Here we go again," he thought, acknowledging the powerful longing he felt.

Daniel suddenly felt a cool breeze and asked one of the guards, "Do you feel a cold wind or something?" Despite being near the bonfire, the guard simply looked at him and did not acknowledge the question.

Another guard asked, "What are you saying? You should know, we are in the mountains."

"No, I just felt an unusual cold breeze, like it's not something common," Daniel replied.

"What are you talking about? You must be out of your mind," then the guards laughed.

Daniel gazed at them with a worried expression on his face. "Daniel," followed by a whooshing sound and then the chilling sensation once more. This sequence repeated three times. "Waaahhh!" Daniel let out a scream.

"What's the matter with you today?" one of the guards commented.

Daniel fled from the bonfire, the whispers still echoing in his ears and the cold breeze chilling him. A guard hurried to the mangagas' kubo as Daniel caused a commotion in the village. The mangagas instructed for Daniel to be taken inside his kubo. Multiple guards seized Daniel and pushed him into the mangagas' dwelling, securing him on the bamboo floor with an abaca rope.

Dried herbs were burned, and the smoke was contained inside the room by securing the doors, windows, and other possible exits. This ritual was intended to cleanse Daniel of his illness. A container of cold water was prepared, and beeswax was burned and dripped into the water which created the shape of a lady. The smoke caused the room to become colder than the outside temperature. Everyone present felt the cold breeze and heard whispers, unlike when Daniel first experienced the sensations alone. The mangagas stated that Daniel is being played upon by the goddess Angtan.

A wild boar had to be sacrificed by burning it until the smoke's aroma reached the heavens. The mangagas insisted on this ritual. The guards took the animal, stabbed it until blood flowed onto the bonfire, and then burned the carcass. The mangagas recited a prayer to Apo Langit, asking for intervention to lift the curse from Daniel. After the animal turned to ashes, the mangagas instructed the guards to release Daniel, who emerged from the kubo as if nothing had occurred.

"Why are you all here?" he asked, curious.

"You're not aware of what happened?" one of the villagers inquired.

Daniel examined his arms and the rest of his body, noticing they were covered in soot as if he had been burned and roasted. "I don't understand what's going on."

"Son, your mind had been played by the goddess Angtan, who has clouded your perception," the mangagas explained.

"What? She must have wiped my memories of what just happened because I don't recall," Daniel said in a panic. "I recognise you... and you... and you..." he added, pointing to each person.

"No worries, you're purified now. You're back to your old self."

Everyone scattered as if they didn't care. The mangagas did not instruct Daniel to return to his kubo.

"Stay here for a while. I just want to make sure Angtan doesn't return, or if she does, we'll be prepared," he said, patting Daniel on the shoulder. Daniel took a sip of the ginger tea and nodded in agreement.

"I want you to sleep in the center of my house, in the living room," the mangagas said, placing an animal hide where Daniel would sleep. He then directed Daniel to lie on his back until he fell asleep, surrounding him with salt. A whole pinikpikan chicken in a container and its raw blood in a coconut shell were placed at the entrance as an offering to appease Angtan. The mangagas sat near the entrance, doing his best not to doze off.

The mangagas continued to recite a prayer while holding burning herbs in his hand. After a few moments, a high-pitched sound known as a bulintang, believed to be from Angtan playing a copper instrument, filled the air. The mangagas' chant grew more intense. A vague figure of a woman with an exposed chest, long dark hair, and a fit body materialised. Her face was radiant, making it difficult to fully see her beauty. She listened to the mangagas' plea as he chanted. The pinikpikan and blood vanished. She tried to enter, but the salt barrier prevented her from doing so, as it was one of her weaknesses. This was why the pinikpikan offering was made without salt.

Angtan emerged in the underworld, much to Napuagan's disappointment. "Curses! Why do you allow humans to manipulate you instead of manipulating them?"

"I am not your slave! You should stop trying to control me!"

"Your dare defy me! We had a deal!"

"I'm telling you! No one can dictate my actions! Nobody can order me around!"

They engaged in a fierce battle, with Napuagan hurling a stream of scorching lava from his hands at Angtan. In response, Angtan used her powers to manipulate Napuagan's mind, reciting spells and locking eyes with him. As she dodged the molten lava, Napuagan's own hands turned against him, sending the fiery projectiles back towards him. Despite the searing heat, Napuagan's immunity protected him from harm. Angtan insisted that Napuagan fulfill his promise to grant her the freedom to explore beyond her current boundaries. Napuagan, who was stronger, teleported Angtan back to the world of people, where she continued to bewilder humanity whenever they crossed her territory.

The village became familiar with metalworking as blacksmiths became integrated into their community. The blacksmiths crafted advanced gardening tools like hoes, picks, mattocks, spades, and more, making planting easier and more efficient. They grew vegetables like tomatoes, eggplants, okra, corn, and tobacco introduced by the colonisers. The villagers celebrated their prosperity, but the mangagas, responsible for the spiritual aspects of life, often forgot to thank the gods.

Kabunian, observing this, was unsure of what to do. "I fear that people are beginning to neglect the gods," he said. His wife, Bangan, shared his concern. She despised the idea of people disregarding the gods and goddesses.

"Kabunian, my dear it is unjust for the people to neglect your praise. They have forgotten that they are dependent on you," she said earnestly.

Kabunian commanded Puwok, the god of storms, to bring rain and flood the village, including the farms and houses.

The village was in chaos as the typhoon water caused it to dissolve. The villagers sought refuge on higher ground, watching helplessly as their homes were destroyed. Kabunian observed the devastation, his wife Bangan nowhere to be seen. He expected her to play a vital role on the event that was happening. He sent a warning sign through a single rotting guava tree at the village, which the mangagas interpreted as a message of impending disaster. The reason the villagers were able to evacuate to higher ground without any casualties.

Kabunian signaled for Puwok to cease the intense rain and wind. In-Init, the sun god then took over with Kabunian's implied signal, swiftly drying the village and its vegetation. Busila, the spirit of assuring successful harvest helped the villagers rebuild their lives through successful farming. He ensured that the crops would not be disturbed. All of this occurred without Bangan's awareness.

The village chief called a meeting with the villagers. "I encourage all of us to show appreciation to the gods for the blessings we receive. This is important for all of us, not just for me," he reminded the villagers. Another festival began, and everyone remembered to thank the gods for all they had.

The typhoon came to an end near the lake where the mamantala's thrived, close to the spot where Angalo regularly bathed. This lake was one of the four mythical lakes. In Lagud, one of these lakes, resided Iyu, a colossal creature with an eel-like body and a dragon's head. Iyu was roused from its long slumber, causing powerful waves and deafening howls. The festivities were abruptly halted by Iyu emerging from the lake and making its way towards the village. Daniel's sword started to emit a bright glow as the howling intensified. Iyu slowly advanced, leaving a trail of destruction in its path. Its eyes glowed red as it spewed out flood water, causing chaos in the village where Daniel was standing.

The village was once more drenched in what appeared to be a downpour. The village warriors tried to halt the monster by hurling their spears and striking it with their bolos and daggers, but its immense size and floating quality thwarted their efforts. The monster didn't even flinch at the projectiles being thrown at it.

The gleam of the sword showed on the monster's eyes catching its attention, causing it to focus on Daniel instead of attacking the villagers. As the monster attacked Daniel with its jaws wide open and sharp teeth exposed, Daniel quickly dodged each bite, causing his face to collide with a large rock. When the monster tried to attack again, Daniel swiftly stabbed it between the mouth and nose. The monster recoiled slightly, shaking its head in irritation. Meanwhile, the warriors targeted the monster's tail, diverting its attention. Seizing the opportunity, Daniel leaped forward and repeatedly stabbed the monster at the back of its head while it was distracted. The monster spurted out a stream of blue blood, some of which splattered on Daniel, soaking him.

It then retreated back into Lagud Lake, turning the water blue. Unbeknownst to everyone, the Iyu was not the only one present, as others were hibernating in different parts of Lagud Lake and various other lakes.

Chapter XX

"You have been incredibly supportive and welcoming to me. I truly appreciate how you have treated me like family. However, I have come to the realisation that I must carry on with the duties and responsibilities that have been entrusted to me," Daniel shared during a gathering.

Everyone expressed their gratitude for his contributions to the village. They spoke as though they were saying goodbye to a beloved member of their community, as he was the first outsider to live among them. The council of elders performed a ritual, praying to the gods for guidance for Daniel on his journey. He was offered a horse to ride and a lady as a companion, as well as a shield made of the strongest wood, but he declined all. He chose to continue on foot, understanding that he needed to complete the mission independently and without any distractions that could impede his progress.

He postponed his trip to await the nightfall when the star controlled by the star maiden, Taraw, would appear. He followed the star's western direction, gazing at the golden twinkling of the celestial body with each step. Despite walking for a considerable time, it felt like he was progressing along an endless path. Nevertheless, he continued with faith in the guiding light of the star.

The next few steps were so familiar to him. His eyes focused on the bamboo plants, which seemed to have transformed from pine trees. "If my memory serves me right, this is the way to the Angdil village," he thought to himself. As he continued deeper into the bamboo forest, he noticed a few differences such as denser bamboo growth, but he was confident it was the correct path. Upon reaching the arching entrance, he expected to find himself inside the dome, but it appeared more fortified than before. Knocking on the door and calling out his identity yielded no response. Trying another smaller entrance, he found it sealed as well. Sensing someone following him, he hid behind a bamboo plant and saw Bawikan approaching.

"Surprise!" Daniel exclaimed, startling Bawikan. Expecting Bawikan to be happy to see him, Daniel was taken aback by Bawikan's negative reaction, as if he was a threat.

"Why are you here? Go away!" Bawikan said firmly.

Confused, Daniel insisted, "It's me, Daniel!"

Bawikan's response was unwelcoming, stating that they had decided not to welcome him back and didn't want any trouble because of him. The other villagers inside also expressed their dislike for Daniel, allowing only Bawikan to enter before attempting to close the door on him. Despite his efforts to explain himself, Daniel was overpowered by the villagers and prevented from entering. Daniel attempted to plead once more, but it seemed as though everyone was deaf to his pleas.

He pondered at the entrance, wondering why the Angdil village harboured such animosity towards him. When the entrance remained closed for an extended period, he decided to leave. While walking on a hill, he heard shouts, cries, and the sound of clashes. Though he was at a distance, he could see smoke rising from the Angdil village. He hurried back, and as he approached, the flames grew more intense. Despite slashing at the entrance with his sword, he arrived too late. The entire village was engulfed in flames.

"No! This can't be happening! They are good people!" Daniel screamed, despite their recent mistreatment of him. He watched helplessly as the fire continued to spread, devouring everything in its path. His frustration and anger intensified as he surveyed the ashes before him. Desperate to find survivors, he began clearing away the debris, hoping against hope. His efforts paid off when he discovered a young woman who had miraculously survived, albeit with injuries. As he tended to her, he noticed movement nearby and found an elderly man who had been severely burned. Despite his best efforts, the man did not survive.

He carried the woman to the river, where he washed her burned skin and applied herbs to the injured area. The ordeal had left Daniel exhausted, and he needed to rest in order to regain his strength.

"What's your name?" Daniel inquired of the lady.

"I am... I am Stumbalik," the lady replied, her head bearing patches of burn scars and half of her face affected as well.

"I'm Daniel. Way back when, I was at the village, but I don't recall meeting you."

"Oh, I see now. I was just a young girl when you were in our village."

"Really?"

"Yes, I knew of a man from outside who stayed but I was too young to remember everything that happened."

Daniel ignited a fire that made Stumbalik cry when she saw the sparks flying.

"What's the matter?" Daniel inquired.

"Fire! No! Fire!" Stumbalik exclaimed as she tried to move away from the fire until she passed out. Daniel laid her down on the soft grass, her face turned towards the sky. He continued to eat the mushrooms and vegetables that had been cooked over the open flame. "How am I supposed to keep my promise and make it back home when obstacles keep getting in the way," he pondered silently while chewing on the charred mushroom.

Upon waking up, she had a hazy memory of the events from that afternoon. Daniel provided her with some leftover food and water to help regain her strength.

"How's your recovery going?" Daniel asked.

"I'm improving, thank you for asking," she said.

"Good. We need to keep moving, and I have to leave you at the next village we come across."

Stumbalik's expression showed a mix of sadness and hopelessness as she gazed at Daniel.

"I'm sorry, but it's necessary for your safety."

They packed up what little they had left early that morning. Some food and drinks were left behind. As they started to move, Stumbalik remembered something.

"I almost forgot. We should pray to the gods for a safe journey," she suggested. Daniel remained silent as Stumbalik recited a prayer without any animal sacrifices or offerings.

They were not far when they spotted three men riding a cart pulled by a horse in the distance. "Let's hide behind this rock," Daniel suggested. They waited until the cart came to a stop and the men disembarked. These men were clearly not locals, as they were dressed in vests, loose pants, and footwear. After a while, when the men stopped talking, Daniel cautiously emerged from their hiding spot to ensure the coast was clear.

However, the men had not gone far and quickly noticed Daniel. Ready to defend himself, Daniel drew his sword from his waist. "Hold on! We mean you no harm. We are simply traders looking to exchange our goods for something of value. We just need some directions," the bearded man explained.

"It's fine! Come out! They are not dangerous!" he called out.

Stumbalik emerged from her hiding spot. "I overheard what you said. You're heading in the wrong direction. There's a village nearby where we're headed."

The three men offered them a ride. The cart they were pulling had extra cargo in addition to their merchandise.

"Why are you two traveling alone?" the bearded man asked.

"We're also searching for a village," Stumbalik replied.

The skinniest of the two introduced themselves. "I'm Aarv, this is Kabir, and the one driving is Sacdep."

"Those are unique names for this place," Daniel remarked.

"Yes, we are from a distant land called Aryavata," Aarv stated.

"Interesting. What brought you here?"

"We were brought here as slaves by the colonisers, but some of us were able to escape. Sacdep and others came here as free men, looking to trade and do business," Kabir explained.

Stumbalik quietly listened to the conversation without joining in. They were approaching a cluster of kubo houses that resembled a village. Daniel and his companions were unfamiliar with the area. As they neared the entrance, Daniel noticed several guards who appeared to be Busols.

"Keep moving! Don't stop!" Daniel urged, his face flushing with heat.

The others spotted the guards soon after, and Stumbalik also identified them as Busols.

"What? Who are the Busols and why are you so afraid of them?" Aarv inquired.

"They are dangerous individuals. They are willing to murder and decapitate anyone who stands in the way of their goals," Daniel explained.

As they journeyed on, Daniel remained hidden at the rear of the cart. Stumbalik dozed off while the other three kept watch ahead. Daniel seized the opportunity to sneak away and return to the territory controlled by the Busols. He jumped onto the curb and hid behind a pile of bushes at the side of the rocky road.

He remained quiet and still for a long time, ensuring that no one was nearby. As he made his way towards the Busol territory, the darkness was setting in. He crawled on his stomach, made a calculated move forward to avoid being seen. The moon rose in the sky as the sun disappeared.

He lunged at the shadowy figure of a man bathed in moonlight, slashing at him. The loud clash of metal against wood reverberated through the village, drawing the attention of a guard carrying a torch. With the guard's help, Daniel was quickly subdued and restrained on the ground. He was then taken to a secure cave, barricaded with bamboo and wooden gates, where he was locked away.

The next morning, a man with the most tattoos visited him. "Who in curses are you? And what is your purpose here?"

Daniel gazed up at a bald man with a long beard, who was highly respected and referred to as "our master" by the people. The man awaited Daniel's response, but he remained silent. He then ordered for Daniel to be brought before the crowd. Daniel was bound and dragged across the rocky ground, causing bruises on his feet. Four men held him up, facing the ground with his arms and feet elevated. A large, tattooed brute with long hair and a beard emerged, holding a rope-like material in his right hand. He began beating Daniel on the back with it.

A familiar figure, Napuagan, appeared before Daniel with a smirk on his face. He screamed in terror as the crowd cheered for his execution and demanded more punishment. Eventually, he was taken back to the cave, much to the crowd's disappointment. The leader understood the crowd's desire for his death but insisted on extracting information from him first, suspecting there was more to the situation. As the crowd dispersed, Napuagan approached Daniel again and offered to help him escape in exchange for completing a task. Daniel, overwhelmed by pain and unable to hear clearly, fell unconscious.

"Daniel! Daniel!" He heard a familiar voice filled with love and care. It was his grandmother, offering him his favorite meal of chicken adobo with the sauce mixed in with the rice. The aroma and taste of the dish were unmatched, making him feel like he was back home. His grandmother sat at the dining table, smiling as she served him the adobo meat with potatoes and pineapple chunks on top of his rice. With each bite, he felt his grandmother's presence fading until she disappeared, repeating his name.

A guard was splashing water on him. "Wake up, you lazy bum! You're so weak!" His mind snapped back to reality. He couldn't stop wondering, "What was that all about?" Confused as usual, he eventually realised that it couldn't have been real. It all seemed too impossible.

The leader, as Daniel had suspected, instructed his men to bring him before him. "Are you the one we once hunted? Are you the one?" the leader asked, gazing at Daniel's blood-soaked face with dried blood streaks diluted by water.

"I am not even certain myself," Daniel replied.

"Let him clean himself in the river and give him a fresh loincloth and food. I may receive a clearer response with those," the leader commanded.

Every time the water washed away the dirt and blood from his body, he felt a renewed sense of purity within himself. He joyfully splashed and stomped in the water like a child, while two guards observed from a distance. They kept a close eye on him, ready to intervene if he tried to escape. They had no other motive but to eliminate the intruder and stranger in their midst, nothing more, nothing less.

"Hey! Come and join in! You probably never wash yourselves!" Daniel screamed.

"Can you please answer my question with some sense?" the leader asked.

Daniel, who had just finished bathing, stuffed his mouth in no time without paying any attention to the leader. The leader left Daniel to finish his meal before addressing him once again.

"I don't know," Daniel replied with a clueless expression.

"Drat! This is frustrating!" the leader exclaimed, convinced that Daniel was hiding something.

Stumbalik awoke to discover that Daniel was missing. "Where is Daniel?" she inquired of the others.

The three simply shrugged and halted the cart. They all disembarked and began searching for him. Stumbalik retraced their steps, while Sacdep called out, and the rest scoured the area, checking the trees, bushes, and even the ravine in case he had fallen.

She kept retreating and calling out for Daniel, but her voice couldn't carry far enough. As the sky darkened, she realised she had gone too deep. "I must have gone too far," she thought. She tried to run back to the cart, but it was already gone. Her heart raced and her breath visible in the cold darkness. She was alone, with no choice but to venture by herself.

Her feet started to ache. She could barely take another step. She found a more secluded spot under a tree to rest, believing that her feet were simply exhausted. Leaning against the tree, she suddenly felt a sharp pain in her forehead, which spread to her entire head in an instant, causing an exploding pain. She let out a scream that made the leaves rustle towards the sky. However, no one appeared to hear her cries of agony. She slipped into unconsciousness and then regained consciousness. She faintly glimpsed the Abat; men and women suspended in the air, dressed in white garments that enveloped their entire bodies that caused the sore feet and headache.

Sporadic high-pitched cries could be heard whenever someone walked past the spot where Stumbalik had endured the intense agony before her untimely death from injuries inflicted by the Abat. These cries acted as a cautionary signal to passersby about the Abat, notorious for causing headaches and sore feet. Whoever disturbs their sinister spirits.

Not far from the river, Daniel continued to splash and enjoy the water like a child. The guards were distracted facing the opposite side, with one taking a piss and the other preparing the ingredients of his moma. Daniel dived to the deeper part of the river and disappeared, holding his breath until he sensed the guards were gone. He swam continuously until he needed to surface for air.

"Good, the guards are gone," he thought confidently.

Emerging from the river in the nude, he suddenly felt a sharp pain in his back. Whirling around, he found one guard holding a dagger to his skin. Attempting to flee, he was met with another guard poised to hurl a spear. A shiver ran through him, uncertain if it was from the icy water or the fear of being attacked. He realised he had no chance of escaping the guards' preparedness to strike.

"Okay, you two caught me. I'm just trying to get you to join in," Daniel said, looking back and forth between the two.

The guards' expressions hardened, their faces taking on a beast-like quality. They stood in position, silent and watchful, like predators stalking their prey. One guard pulled Daniel back while the other stood close by, keeping a watchful eye on him. They pointed to a fresh loincloth for Daniel to put on. "Go ahead," one of the guards said, pushing Daniel forward. They escorted him back to the village, with Daniel in the middle.

"Why did it take him so long to clean himself?" the leader asked, staring furiously at the guards.

"Your leadership, we are sorry, but this one tried to escape," the guard behind Daniel explained.

"I should have killed him so we wouldn't have any problems," the guard in front muttered without making eye contact with their leader.

"Hey! Are you questioning my decision?"

The two guards knelt. "Your leadership, we apologise. We never question you."

The leader instructed that Daniel be brought back to the prison cave and kept separate from the other captives. He was concerned that

Daniel might incite a rebellion if he was allowed to be with others.

"Let me out! I can't stay here! I need to be free!" Daniel yelled.

An annoyed guard entered Daniel's cell. "Cut it out!" He kicked Daniel in the stomach, causing him to collapse and spit out blood, staining the floor.

He rolled over the muddy ground due to the pain he suffered. 'Man! This one just won't quit!' remarked a guard.

Daniel struggled to remain upright in the darkness, surrounded by the sound of gongs and chants from outside. The villagers held a deep reverence for a particular 'dusong' tree, considering it sacred. The village elder instructed for a pig and some native chickens to be slaughtered at the base of the tree, allowing the blood to seep into the roots. He offered a prayer of gratitude known as sos-oa, thanking the gods for their blessings and seeking guidance on the meaning of Daniel's presence. A group of elders sang a traditional tune called liw-liwa, accompanied by the sound of 'ganza', while women joined in the 'canao' celebration dance.

The canao celebration continued for several days with multiple rituals performed under the 'dusong' tree. Additional offerings of rice, sweet potatoes, vegetables, and fruits were made. Despite not receiving any news about Daniel, the villagers were relieved that snakes, birds, and other animals were absent at the tree as it was considered a sign of good luck.

Daniel and the other prisoners were provided with water and meager rations to sustain themselves. The image of his grandmother persisted, and he continued to hear her voice calling out to him. Determined to decipher its significance, he pondered whether it was truly his grandmother or simply a figment of his imagination.

"What is the meaning of all this?" Daniel pondered to himself. He continued to live, feeling that it was all meaningless. He rubbed his face with his hands, trying to make sense of it all, but he couldn't come up with any answers. Despite his awareness of his own existence, he couldn't piece together a clear picture. Hidden in the leader's quarters was his sword, glowing brightly, yet no one, not even the leader, was aware of its radiance.

After a while, he was given a torch that burned every night. He could hear the sound of dripping water but couldn't pinpoint its source. The torch was not powerful enough to illuminate its precise location. Noticing that the next torch provided more light, he seized the chance to locate the water source. The dripping sound grew louder as he went further in the cave. Eventually, he discovered the source of the sound at a wall and found that the soil around it was soft and muddy. Using his bare hands, he started digging and creating a hole, doing so discreetly to avoid detection. Over time, he created digging tools from stones and bones he found in order to speed up the process. The hole grew larger until a grown man could fit through it. The dripping water turned into a flow, making the cave floor muddy. Daniel worried that the mud would attract attention and lead to the discovery of the hole. However, his fears turned out to be unfounded, which was a relief.

It was time for the escape. The markings on the wall guided him to the hole in the dark. He chose to go without a torch to avoid being detected. The hole was wide enough for him to pass through, but its sharp edges and wet nature caused some scratches and made him bleed. Despite the pain, he was determined to get out. The hole didn't lead directly outside the fence, so he had to crawl away from the village. He didn't even consider retrieving his sword, his only focus was on escaping the terrible place.

"Hey! Meal time!" The guard handed Daniel his food through the opening.

"Hey! I said! Here's your food!" The guard said with an angry tone.

"What the?" The guard unlocked the entrance only to discover that Daniel was missing.

He hurried to the leader's quarters. "Your leadership! Daniel has escaped!"

"Then what? Have you searched for him?" The leader asked, his face contorted in anger.

"Your leadership, we are currently looking for him. I thought you should be informed," the guard replied.

"Join the search, you fool!" the leader shouted.

The guard quickly returned to the search party. Meanwhile, Daniel continued to crawl through the muddy ground, enduring the discomfort of rocks, twigs, and debris scraping against his skin like potatoes being poked by a sharp knife. He remained still, hoping the mud would conceal his whereabouts. The sound of guards running around searching for him echoed in the distance.

The leader collapsed, struggling to breathe. A servant hurried to the shaman for assistance, but by the time they arrived, it was too late. The leader had lost consciousness and his skin had turned a bluish hue. Besides, the boni healing ritual, which required sacrificing a pig and examining its liver, could not be carried out due to a shortage of manpower and the unavailability of a pig.

"Please don't find me. Please don't find me," Daniel thought overwhelmingly as he struggled to breathe while lying face down in the mud, partially submerged. After the commotion had passed, he crawled further until he reached a body of water. He found himself underwater, surrounded by fish, moss, and the loud croaking of frogs. Slowly, he surfaced, trying to avoid drawing any attention. "Okay, nobody's around," he whispered.

Frogs jumped onto Daniel's back, their slick bodies making it difficult for him to shake them off. He managed to swat away the smaller frogs, but the larger ones clung on tightly. One frog, the size of a human, stood out from the rest. Daniel's eyes widened as it crawled towards him, never breaking eye contact. This was Pel-pel, the leader of the frogs. Pel-pel moved towards him in a way that resembled a human, causing Daniel to sprint away in fear as the creature approached.

A spear was hurled towards Daniel, who assumed it was Pel-pel and the frogs. Another spear followed, narrowly missing him. A group of young men scattered, attempting to attack him. Seeking refuge, he climbed a tree and peered down to see the men below. "Please, I am alone and unarmed!" he called out. The group surrounded the tree, demanding he come down. Descending with mud and moss clinging to him, some of the men aimed their weapons at him. "I mean no harm! Please, spare me!" he pleaded, his voice trembling.

He couldn't control it, he followed with heavy panting as his lungs were not as strong as before, despite his best efforts. This was especially difficult due to the recent events that led to his weakened state.

"Lower your spears and allow the man an opportunity to explain," someone interjected.

The person who interrupted Daniel gave him a critical look, scanning him from top to bottom. "Join us. You appear to be alone," he said. The group offered him food and drink, and he ate while they continued on their journey. The rest of the group watched him disapprovingly, as they were not accustomed to revealing their destination to strangers.

"Are you crazy?" was the question posed.

"I understand that this may seem reckless, but I am confident in my actions," replied the person who had invited Daniel.

"By the way, who are you?" he inquired.

"I am Daniel. I am trying to find my way back home."

"I am Ming Fei, and these young men are pupils in the art of war."

Chapter XXI

Daniel's mind was in disarray, struggling to remember important events. He gasped for breath as he hiked, feeling like he had been around for ages. "Who am I? I feel as old as a tree," he muttered with a dry mouth, worried about finding his way back home.

"What are you trying to say?" one of the pupils asked.

"Nothing. I'm just trying to catch my breath."

The pupil's ear grew warm, accompanied by a strange sensation inside him.

"Why are you by yourself? Don't you have a home to go to?" he asked Daniel, his gaze filled with curiosity.

The pupil doesn't resemble him exactly, but they share similarities not only in appearance but also in their mannerisms and speech. Daniel found himself unable to stop glancing at the pupil as they moved and talked with the group.

"What's your name?" Daniel asked as he approached the trainee once more.

"I am Yichin, why do you ask?" he responded with curiosity.

Daniel remained silent and instead fixed his gaze on Yichin for a moment. When Yichin received no response from Daniel, he joined the group in the middle, with Daniel being intrigued by the similarities between them.

Unaware that they had reached their destination, the final stop was a cave entrance. It appeared like any other ordinary cave from the outside. However, it was actually a long passage leading to a massive underground society. The houses were carved into the stone walls, complete with doors and windows, interconnected by passageways hidden within the walls. "Oh!" Daniel exclaimed, his eyes widening in awe as he took in the sight.

The center was a spacious dirt clearing with wooden human figures and large wooden blocks with targets. Human and animal skulls adorned each doorway. "Welcome to our training grounds," a warrior greeted. "We used to be in a forested location, but we had to relocate due to security concerns," the warrior added, fixing a piercing gaze on Daniel.

"Our glorious leader Chu Sun!" a warrior proclaimed. The leader appeared from the grandest stone buildings, with everyone bowing low to the ground as he passed by. Chu Sun approached Daniel and halted in front of him. "Bow down," the warrior behind Daniel whispered. Daniel complied, lowering himself from his standing position as Chu Sun continued on his way.

Daniel looked over the group and noticed their familiar characteristics. They bore a resemblance to individuals he was acquainted with, particularly those who were journeying on foot. While only a handful seemed to be indigenous to the mountains, a combination of native mannerisms and those from Formosa validated his assumptions. "Am I going crazy, or is my vision playing tricks on me?" he pondered, hoping for reassurance of his observations.

"Our leader requests your presence," a warrior hurriedly approached Daniel.

The warrior escorted Daniel to the leader's quarters. "Please, come in and speak with me," the leader said. Daniel entered, his heart pounding as loudly as the resonating sound of a gangza.

"Who are you?" the leader asked directly.

"I am Daniel."

"I can see the tattoo on your shoulder, which made me think you are the one my aunt used to speak of."

"Alright, I'll be honest. I am the one the Busol are searching for. The chosen one. Whatever that entails," Daniel said, a frown creasing his face.

Daniel was expecting a negative result, but he was pleasantly surprised when Chu Sun invited him to stay, have a meal with them, and participate in their training sessions. "Do I have any other option?" Daniel wondered. The meal included a substantial selection of meats, vegetables, and root crops, ideal for warriors gearing up for battle, with no fish or light dishes in sight.

Chu Sun had set the table, and they both sat on opposite sides. "You seem to have plenty of 'aba' taro root but no 'pesing' taro leaves and stems," Daniel remarked as he ate.

"It's just the two of us. Where are the others?" Daniel inquired.

"Don't worry about the others; they are also having their meals outside. You are my guest," Chu Sun replied as a servant poured rice wine into Daniel's bamboo cup.

"So, what's the plan?" Chu Sun asked, taking a bite of the meat with his hands.

"What do you mean?"

"Why are you here?"

"I'm not sure. I just want to go home."

Chu Sun took a moment to let Daniel savour his meal without interruption. He observed the tattoo on Daniel's shoulder but chose not to bring it up.

He welcomed Daniel into their home, helping with training and daily activities, without revealing much about their past or personal thoughts. Daniel's perception of them was based solely on their daily interactions.

Daniel emphasised the importance of building strength and endurance during his training session, noting that these aspects were often overlooked in favor of fighting techniques. He brought a large rock and a log into the center of the village.

"With your leader's approval, I encourage you to gather more rocks and logs and bring them here," Daniel instructed.

Many of the pupils followed the instructions. However, upon their return, they seemed to have a different energy compared to when they had left while following the instructions.

"What happened? Why do some of your fellow pupils appear so different?" Daniel inquired.

"I'm not sure. Some of them paused near the 'pising' plants and seemed to become more resilient and emotionless," a pupil responded, only noticing the transformation in his companions when questioned.

Unknown to the pupils, the vampire-like spirits called Danag, who planted the 'pising' plants, were also the cause of the pupils' changed behaviors. Their unseen influence enabled them to hypnotise and feed on the blood of unsuspecting passersby near the 'pising' plants, leading to loss of consciousness that could be reversed through intense activities or high-pitched sounds. The more they were infected by Danag, the more they became unstoppable. Some could leap as high as mountains, others were immune to pain, and some were as strong as beasts of burden.

"These young men are not novices, but seasoned warriors," Daniel remarked, his eyes widening as he observed their skills. None of them could be deemed as feeble. They were prepared and highly skilled in facing a true life-and-death struggle.

"You are being summoned by our leader Chun Sun," a warrior informed Daniel. He was then escorted to the leader's quarters. Upon entering, he found the leader seated with crossed legs, eyes closed, surrounded by the scent of herbs wafting through the smoky air.

"You are dismissed," Chun Sun told the warrior who accompanied Daniel.

The warrior bowed before departing.

"We must gather food and I expect you to join the hunting team," Chun Sun stated, locking eyes with Daniel to convey the sense of duty.

Daniel bowed respectfully and asked in a surprised voice, "Your leadership. Do you mean right now?"

"Please go right away. We need more food, especially for the warriors."

Daniel left and found the warriors prepared for the hunt. Chu Sun's trusted companion recited a prayer, striking the metal and passing it through each warrior. The vibrations made some contact with their auras, believed to bring good luck.

"Get off your horses and let's go on foot. It will hinder our mission more than help," Daniel suggested.

The warriors reluctantly got off their horses, giving disapproving looks to Daniel as they abandoned their mounts. They traveled south from their starting point, passing numerous guava trees that acted as landmarks. Mt. Kalugong, named for its shape resembling headgear, was a large rock covered in lush green vegetation and abundant plant and animal life, making it an ideal hunting ground.

As they approached the mountain, some of the guava trees, as tall as an average man, stood in their way. Daniel noticed that the warriors didn't mind getting scratched by the branches of the trees and chose not to clear them with their bolos.

"Why don't you use your bolos to clear the guava trees instead of struggling to pass through?" Daniel asked one of the warriors.

"We have respect for the guava trees because they mark the grave site of our ancestor who was betrayed by her husband. Legend has it that the husband buried her alive in a coffin so he could be with a younger woman, despite their long history together since the beginning of time," the warrior explained.

Daniel nodded in comprehension, and the warrior acknowledged him with a smile and a wink. They arrived at their destination and set up a temporary camp in a haste like never before, leaving their belongings and collecting firewood. They were preparing to go hunting when one of them had to stay behind to guard their possessions, but then it started to drizzle.

"Take our belongings under the trees," a warrior instructed, pointing to a higher area of the mountain.

"We should not proceed. We must wait until the drizzle subsides. It is a sign from the gods that something bad may happen if we push forward," the same warrior added.

Night descended with the drizzle; it cannot qualify as rain. It continued until the next morning when the sun finally appeared. The weather had improved enough to proceed with the plan to hunt for the animals. A hollowed bamboo with a woven bamboo string was placed among the bushes while they searched for larger animals to hunt and edible vegetation to gather. There were no obstacles that would prevent them from carrying out their activities. A wild boar appeared from the bushes and ran, setting off the traps with its movements. It narrowly avoided the traps but was struck by a flying arrow, leading to its doom. A skilled warrior hurled his spear, hitting the target with precision. The wild boar let out a squeal reminiscent of an uneven wooden floor. The animal met its end as the warrior finished it off by thrusting the spear deeper until there was no sign of life.

A group of mostly young men, led by Betot, visited the hidden village. They were fortunate to arrive just as Daniel was returning with the hunting group, who had successfully caught a wild boar and some rodents using bamboo traps. Betot was preoccupied giving instructions to new trainees and didn't notice Daniel's arrival with the hunting group.

"That… that man who just walked in seemed really familiar," Betot whispered as he observed the newcomer from afar. Intrigued, he approached for a closer look and confirmed that it was indeed Daniel. "Daniel! Daniel!" he exclaimed loudly. Daniel turned to him with a puzzled expression. "It's… it's me, Betot!" he said, beaming with joy and excitement.

"Betot? I can't believe it's really you!" Daniel exclaimed with excitement, embracing his friend in a rare display of affection for warriors. Betot tried to pull away from the hug, but deep down he felt a strange sensation, something he had kept hidden out of fear of being discriminated or even executed.

"Any… any clue?" Betot asked, testing Daniel's knowledge.

"What clue?" Daniel responded, scratching his head in confusion.

"Well… well?" Betot paused. "We are in Kapangan's training ground."

Daniel remained silent, his confusion growing as he nervously bit his nails. He shot Betot a look, silently urging him to stop talking. He then walked away, leaving Betot to his own devices. Unbeknownst to them, a nearby warrior observed their conversation.

"There is a secret that these two are keeping. I'm not sure what it is, but I will uncover it," the warrior muttered to himself.

Daniel helped in preparing the hunted animal for preservation and food. He cut the skin with fat into thick strips, seasoned them with salt and herbs, and hung them near the cooking area to be smoked for preservation. He and another person cleaned the intestines, filled them with blood, salt, and herbs to make blood sausage, and boiled it until it was tender. Some of the lean meat was ground by chopping it repeatedly until it was fine and mixed in with herbs and wild vegetables.

Banana leaves were spread out in the training area, located at the heart of the village. A variety of food was served, including meat and vegetables from the recent hunt, sweet potatoes, and preserved meat from previous hunts. Eating without utensils, everyone gathered around the serving area. Coconut shells and bamboos were used to hold soups and rice wines. The meal was enjoyed by all, with Chun Sun and the warrior chief being the first to sample the delicious food served on clay plates and bowls.

"Kuchep… Kuchep is here with me, I… I mean in Kapangan. We arrived together and were warmly welcomed. Just wanted to let you know," Betot informed.

Daniel calmly enjoyed a blood sausage, focusing on his meal and tuning out any distractions.

"Did you hear me? Kuchep is in Kapangan!" Betot exclaimed.

The entire table fell silent, turning their attention to Daniel and Betot.

"What's the matter? Why don't you just eat your food," Daniel said loud enough for everyone to hear.

The two young pupils, who bore a striking resemblance to Daniel, had come back to Kapangan to secretly listen in on Daniel and Betot's conversation. The warrior who had overheard their earlier conversation remembered Daniel from a previous encounter and their leader Li Men's belief that Daniel could be his son.

"I'm sorry. Let's carry on with our meal," Daniel said, addressing everyone.

"Let's save that conversation for later. We can discuss it in private," he whispered to Betot discreetly.

They exchanged glances and engaged in conversation on various topics in a quiet tone so as not to disrupt the others. Suddenly, a wild dog entered without warning. Some of the warriors stopped eating and prepared their weapons to kill the animal. Daniel intervened, saying, "Wait! This is a female and she appears to be pregnant." He approached the animal with the stealth of a silent night, and at first, it growled and tried to bite him. The warriors were ready to attack, gripping onto their weapons, but Daniel stopped them, insisting, "Let me handle this!" With determination in his voice, he offered the animal a piece of blood sausage with his hand, which it accepted and licked some of the remnants from his palm. He then placed a coconut shell filled with water on the ground for the animal to drink from.

The dog was accepted and became part of the community. Daniel named it Blacky, a name that others didn't quite understand but stuck with the animal. With its black fur and smaller size compared to some other dogs, Blacky was also fierce. It was a native breed well-suited to the wild environment, capable of surviving in various situations.

Blacky passed away while delivering her twelve puppies. Daniel stepped in to raise and train them as warrior companions. He educated the community on caring for dogs, a new experience for them as they had previously only encountered wild dogs in the forest. Daniel advocated for incorporating dogs into their hunting and battle strategies.

It was found that the dogs had a powerful sense of smell, allowing them to track the whereabouts of creatures. While their biting strength was not the greatest, their determination could scare off any predators, including formidable warriors. The twelve were paired with skilled warriors, including Daniel, who named his dog Mighty. The others didn't understand the significance of the name, but they didn't bother to question.

The dogs were not allowed to sleep and eat with the humans. They had their own cages and were brought out during trainings or when they were needed for their functions. Betot was allowed to stay and requested Daniel as his companion in the same house. As night fell and the sun set, they no longer needed to go out to check the darkness of the surroundings. The dogs' howls sent shivers down everyone's spine to indicate that it was night time.

"Hey… hey, Kuchep is in Kapangan and what… what are you going to do about it?" Betot exclaimed as they were getting ready to go to bed.

"What do you mean, do about it? Is she there against her will?" Daniel replied, sounding defensive.

"No… no, but aren't you going to… to visit her at least?" Betot pleaded, raising both hands in a gesture of please.

"Okay, if I have permission to leave. The people here have been so welcoming and kind to me, I don't want to disrespect their hospitality," Daniel emphasised, acknowledging the kindness of the locals.

"Let's rest and wait to see what happens when the sun rises. Whatever will be, will be," Daniel said, displaying his exhaustion.

In the days that followed, Betot and Daniel discussed their time apart and shared their experiences. Betot revealed that he had developed the ability to interpret dreams while imprisoned in Dutab Kingdom. Daniel talked about the people he had encountered and explained why Betot had not seen the sword he had before. They also talked about Kechup having a child with the Busol leader. The conversation was casual and there was no surprise on either side as they continued to help the village with their work and training.

Daniel made an unexpected visit to Chun Sun. "Your leadership, I come humbly to reveal my true identity. The eagle on my shoulder signifies that I am the son of the people, destined to help save them," Daniel said as he bowed before the leader.

"I had a sense that your words held truth, but I kept my thoughts to myself. I needed to hear it from you directly," Chu Sun said as he approached Daniel and stood facing him. As more information about Daniel and his situation emerged, Chu Sun called a meeting with the warriors, selecting Daniel to lead them to the Busol's main territory. Their mission was to seek retribution for the devastating raid on Kapangan, which had brought death and grief to the community.

They concocted a plan with other villages on how the Busol attacked each one when searching for Daniel. Chu Sun very much expected that victory was on their side with Daniel's presence. Daniel led the eager warriors, mostly young men, with only few tested men in years. Some move gradually without letting themselves be known as approaching, whilst some were hidden in the forest near the Busol village. "Attack!" the young ones murmured with themselves being out in the open. "Hide your stupid selves!" Daniel's voice cheeped as the others voiced out the same sentiments.

Several warriors launched an attack without warning. Daniel attempted to remind them of the instructions he had given earlier, but they ignored him. The warriors who followed the instructions stayed by his side. One of them questioned whether they should assist the first group, who were now being injured by the flying spears and rocks. However, he believed it was important for them to learn the consequences of not following instructions. He also feared that the second group of warriors might face a similar fate as the first.

"Please help us!" Some of the survivors cried out in pain.

Daniel directed those in hiding to stay put and quietly moved away from the approaching Busol. Some were brave enough to try and save the injured, but their heads were severed by the Busol with their blades. Those who adhered to Daniel's instructions managed to survive.

Chu Sun and the pupils witnessed the few remaining warriors returning, some of them injured, mostly on their upper torso. "What happened? And where are the others?" Chu Sun asked.

"Many of the warriors did not follow instructions," Daniel explained. "Euges, right? Explain to Chu Sun why we failed!" Daniel grabbed the warrior and pushed him in front of Chu Sun.

"Who are you?" Chu Sun demanded in an angry tone.

Euges bowed and explained what had happened, his body trembling and tears filling his eyes. His words were barely audible, but Chu Sun ordered him to speak up. As it became clearer, Chu Sun realised that the disobedient warriors were mostly from Bokodians.

"Those who are Bokodians! Step to the right!" commanded Chu Sun.

Nearly half of the Bokodians warriors were injured and barely surviving.

"Get out of here! I hesitated to welcome some of our supposed allies because they are too weak and too foolish, and what has it brought us?" Chu Sun ordered.

"Please, Your leadership! Please reconsider! At the very least, let us rest and give our injured warriors time for treatment," a warrior quickly bowed and pleaded. Unfortunately, his pleas fell on deaf ears, and those who resisted were forcefully removed.

Chapter XXII

The Bokodian warrior's journey was a harrowing ordeal. The able warriors had to carry their injured comrades, with one being carried on the back despite hearing a repeating popping sound. The warrior carrying his injured companion did not give up and continued on. They climbed a mountain and upon reaching a river, gently laid the injured soldier on the ground. The warrior fetched fresh water to drink and brought some to the injured soldier, who did not respond in an unfortunate occurrence. Another warrior tried to clean the wounds of their injured comrade with clean water, but there was no response. Despite attempts to apply medicinal herbs, there was no improvement. Sadly, other injured warriors also perished during the journey.

Betot left quietly, unnoticed by Daniel and the others. He was frustrated by Chu Sun's actions despite the mistakes made by the Bokodian warriors. The moonlight that night was shining so bright, illuminating his path as he walked alone in the dark. As he passed through a small grove of trees along the trail, he heard a piercing cry, capable of shattering delicate objects. He chose not to investigate the source of the sound and instead hurried on his way. However, as the cries grew more frequent and irritating, he sprinted away from them as fast as he could. Unaware that he was hearing the cries of Stombalik's spirit, Betot unknowingly avoided taking the wrong turn in his journey as he fled from the unsettling noise.

The unfortunate incident occurred when Betot's rushing feet accidentally swept over an Annai, a humanoid creature that resided near the trees. The Annai, who typically consumed fresh, animal flesh, were outraged by the accidental killing. As Betot slowed down, the Annai attacked his exposed feet, devouring them with their sharp fangs and long tongues. The scene was gruesome, with blood and flesh scattered on the ground, and Betot's screams of pain filled the night air. Overwhelmed by agony, Betot fell to his knees, leaving the rest of his body vulnerable to the hungry Annai.

"Noooooo!" Daniel screamed as he heard Betot's screams.

Others could barely make out what he clearly heard with trembles. All eyes were fixed on him. Tears welled up in his eyes; he was unable to speak as they inquired about what was troubling him. He retreated to his room without saying a word.

"Let him be," Chu Sun said as the others continued to stare in his direction.

At dawn, Daniel embarked on a quest to locate Betot. The other warriors disregarded the matter, assuming Betot had been dismissed along with the Bokodian warriors. Unlike Betot, Daniel did not come across Stombalik's spirit or the Annai during his journey. Despite his pounding heart and heavy breathing, he was triumphant on scaling a mountain and traversing a river. His only goal was to find Betot, and he was oblivious to the distance he had covered from his initial location. His orientation was off, and his mind was muddled with confusion.

He descended to the riverbank to drink some water when a gaki emerged from the depths. Armed only with his dagger, Daniel faced the monstrous creature. The gaki swiped its powerful claws as Daniel looked on in terror. He attempted to retreat, but the rough pebbles beneath his back made it difficult to move backward, causing pain as they scraped against his skin. The creature raised a claw, aiming it like a spear descending from above. Daniel trembled like the turbulent waves that disrupted the once-calm river. "Nooo!!!" he cried out in fear. The claw struck a couple of crocodiles with jaws open, poised to devour him.

He managed to escape the fray, running far from the battle. The gaki sliced one crocodile in half, while the other clamped down on its legs. The crocodile twisted, tearing off two of the gaki's legs. In retaliation, the gaki struck down more crocodiles before they retreated from the scene.

The gaki remained motionless by the riverside, its mouth foaming. Daniel took a moment to catch his breath before crossing to the other side. He gathered some freshwater fishes with his bare hands to feed to the creature. With a final push, he flipped the gaki over and applied algae to its body. It then crawled into the deeper waters as if nothing had occurred. Nearby, Daniel collected driftwood from the riverbank. He allowed the sun to dry the wood, which he used as fuel for cooking the fish he caught for himself. Over time, the gaki reappeared with numerous small crabs clinging to its injured legs, almost as if they were rebuilding its limbs.

Daniel's gaze remained fixed on the creature. As he regained his composure, he recognised it as the same creature he had helped before. The one he had rescued from potential blindness. The creature paused by his side for a brief moment before returning to the water with a graceful motion. Daniel simply smiled as he observed the creature going about its business.

The gaki returned to the deep water while Daniel took a break on the other side of the river, where there was grass under some trees. When he woke up, he found the creature lying next to him, surrounded by fish. Daniel ate his share of the food and attempted to leave, but the gaki trailed behind him. An idea struck him, and he gathered some fish, tying them to a vine attached to a stick. Climbing onto the gaki's back, he dangled the fish in front of the creature, guiding it in the direction he wanted it to go.

The creature climbed the mountain with Daniel, who fed it dangling fishes along the way. They reached a spring where Daniel fetched water and poured it on the creature to keep it wet. As they continued, Daniel still held a fish that became stinky and the creature refused to eat. They arrived at the Busol's village, where some Busol were crushed by the creature's size. Spears were thrown at them, and Daniel fought back by stabbing several Busol with his dagger. He headed towards the Busol leader's quarters to find his sword. The creature used its claws to attack the Busol, but they managed to injure it. Despite the attacks, the creature fought back, causing casualties. Daniel retrieved his glowing sword and struck down three Busol with one swing. He then leapt on the creature as they escaped the village, narrowly avoiding a flying spear.

The Busol warriors caught up with the strike of a chetah. "Hurry, my friend," Daniel urged. Despite Daniel's efforts with his sword, he couldn't fend off all the Busol. The creature was pinned down, oozing blue goo from its wounds. It continued to struggle but eventually succumbed. Daniel leapt to safety, hiding in a ravine where the Busol couldn't locate him. They focused on the creature instead, cutting it up and carrying the pieces back to their village for food.

Daniel, perched on the edge of the cliff, attempted to climb back up after a brief period of concealment. Something caught his eye. In the distance, he spotted a group of fully armoured men on horseback, accompanied by carriages. "Who could they be?" he wondered to himself. Seeking a better view, he moved to a different vantage point and confirmed that they were the advancing conquistadors nearing the mountains. Without hesitation, he hurried to the nearest village, regardless of whether they were friend or foe, determined to warn someone. Arriving at an unfamiliar village, he urgently called out, "I must speak with your leader!"

The guards, hostile at first meeting, brandished their weapons, but Daniel persisted in his plea. Despite a spear being thrown his way, he managed to evade it. Engaging in a physical altercation with the guards, he found himself outnumbered and under attack. However, someone inside the village witnessed the commotion and rushed to investigate what was going on. Noticing Daniel's glowing sword, the onlooker intervened to prevent further violence.

It was a woman, but not just any woman. She was the highly regarded wife of the village leader. "Let him come inside and listen to what he has to say," the woman said. The guards allowed Daniel to enter despite their animosity towards him. They only let him in out of respect for the leader's wife.

"It's fine. Please, come in," the lady gestured for Daniel to enter the village.

"There... Augh! There..." Daniel replied.

"Take a moment to relax before explaining yourself clearly," the lady advised.

Daniel sat down and asked for some water before proceeding with his warning. "There are groups coming from the lowlands heading this way. I believe their intentions may not be good."

The woman nodded and went to her husband's quarters to tell him about the situation. The leader was unsure, but Daniel insisted on following the trail where he had seen the group. The leader then sent some of his warriors to accompany Daniel and report back to him. It was at that moment that he realised the need to prepare for any possible conflict that could arise.

"Who are you?" the leader inquired as he observed the group.

"I am Daniel, at your service," Daniel replied.

"I am Kalag, by the way. How did you come across us and this situation?"

"Your leadership, Kalag, I spotted the group from the cliff of the mountain to the East," Daniel explained, pointing towards the mountain near the group.

Kalag was a kind leader who was well-liked by all. So, he had no problem mobilising everybody. He was also trusted by the neighbouring villages. He instructed his messengers to visit every accessible village to alert them to the imminent threat. "We can't be certain that the troops we've spotted are the only ones heading our way," he stressed.

He instructed women and children to seek safety in the underground bunker. He then directed for all weapons and available materials that can be used as weapons to be prepared for easy access. The warriors were to take turns guarding, with double shifts required, and young boys capable of fighting were to join the warriors in battle.

"You have the mark. We know who you are or at least us men and older folks," Kalag whispered to Daniel as the men were going to the formation.

The village was heavily fortified because Daniel recognised it as the Kafaguay village, known for their skill in building stone walls. The gate was well guarded with metal armour like that of the oncoming invaders, indicating they had faced similar attacks in the past.

The Mumbaki prepared the men for battle by spitting moma as the first signal. "Listen up!" he yelled, with everyone gathered around him at the village center. He recited a prayer with a melody that sent small ripples through the air, reaching even the women and children in the shelters. "May our powerful Chal-chal, the god of the warriors grant us the courage and ability to face our enemies," the mumbaki intoned, standing tall with his hands raised in reverence like branches reaching for the sky. The warriors felt a mysterious strength welling up inside them as the vibrations pulsed through their bodies.

Liston, at the forefront of the conquistador's journey, attempted to lead the group in the wrong direction. Comandante Luiz Sagrado Montano noticed this and spoke up as the group stopped at a spring for water. "Hey, we've been traveling for quite some time and still haven't reached a single community," he said abruptly.

"Don't worry, be patient. Trust me, we'll get there," Liston assured.

As darkness fell and the soldados grew weary, they decided to establish a temporary camp near the spring. This group's stomachs were not accustomed to all types of food, so they had brought along cheese, red wine, and other provisions stored in one of the carts for sustenance. Liston, in his own resourceful manner, foraged for mushrooms and small animals in the woods, which he then roasted over a fire he had built. "What on earth are these?" one of the soldados exclaimed, his face twisted in disgust.

"Be quiet and don't eat it if you don't want to! Nobody is forcing you to!" Liston exclaimed.

Liston picked up a roasted rodent and bit its head first. The soldados kept staring at him with revulsion, and some were even retching. He didn't care and grabbed a cup made of copper, taking some wine to wash the rodent down. They had no problem with the mushroom and even mixed it with their cheese. Liston was not a mushroom expert; one of the soldados vomited after swallowing the mushroom and cheese mixture, and soon after, the others followed. Many were vomiting and unconscious within moments. Fortunately, Liston had not consumed any of the mushrooms as the soldados had eaten it first and left the rodents for him.

Liston watched as the soldiers fell into unconsciousness and collapsed in their positions. He promptly rose from his seat, looking as if he was ready to sprint. One of the people, who he initially mistook for a soldier, turned out to be a young man driving one of the wine carriages. This young man stayed awake as he had not ingested the mushrooms. It was a mystery to him why he had steered clear of the mushrooms, even though he couldn't explain it to himself.

Liston sprinted without restraint as the carriage driver jumped onto him in an attempt to control him. However, Liston effortlessly shrugged him off, as the youth was so light that he was almost lifted off the ground as Liston ran. Struggling to navigate the uneven terrain, the young man eventually had to release Liston when he managed to pry the young man's arms away from his neck.

"He's gone! He's gone!" the young man repeated as he continued running until he was far away from the group. Soon, he had to stop and catch his breath, feeling the fear deep inside him growing stronger. His breathing became rapid, his heart pounded, and the veins in his body throbbed with intensity. Exhausted, he collapsed and began crawling towards the nearby village. The same village that Daniel had spotted.

"Who's this man crawling towards us?" a warrior called out as Liston approached the gate slowly.

"Please, help!" Liston cried out, his energy fading as he struggled to catch his breath.

"Let him in," Daniel insisted.

With some hesitation, two warriors helped Liston inside and placed him underground with the women and children.

On the other side of the mountains, another group sent by the conquistador consisted of soldados armed with big swords, long spears, mighty arrows, and skilled archers. There were no men of God among them, only soldados. They traveled on foot until they encountered a vast lake with a mysterious aura. The sound of beautiful humming filled the air, emanating from the alluring mamantalas. The soldados were captivated by the sight of the female figures and approached the lake, ignoring the potential danger. The mamantalas lured the soldados into the deep waters, leading them to their watery doom.

The village of Kafaguay waited patiently for many moons, but eventually grew restless. The once vigilant warriors began to relax their guard, though some still stood watch at the entrance and other key points along the stone walls. Liston received care from the Mumbaki for his injuries, resting in an underground chamber while healing tonics and herbs were applied to his wounds.

Kalag greeted Liston with a warm smile upon noticing the tattoo on his body, the mark of Busol that raised concerns about his character. They pondered whether they should be wary of him or allow him to stay. Liston shared his experiences with the villagers, detailing the challenges he had faced. Daniel proposed that they keep him around, as he could potentially be of help in the future.

There was often a miscommunication between the natives and the conquistadors due to a language barrier. However, this was not an issue with the mountain dwellers, as they were very protective of their villages and wary of outsiders. They were only welcoming to visitors who displayed certain civil characteristics or had reasons deemed true by the gods. The mixing of races led to tribal considerations of offspring in order to produce superior generations of people.

A soldado named Juan Stephano got lost from his fallen comrades and roamed in the mountains. He saw Liston being punished in the dungeon, getting cuts on his back that would leave lasting scars. Stephano, far from reaching Daniel at the end of the mountains, struggled to hike in the high altitude. Each breath he took drained his energy. Eventually, he collapsed unconscious in the thick pine forest. Monkeys and wild dogs closed in on him, poised to devour his motionless body. "Ay Dios Mio!" he cried out as two monkeys grabbed his feet, while a skirmish broke out between the wild dogs and the monkeys nearby.

He ran faster than the wind. The sight of the animals around him gave him a surge of energy. The thorns and rough bushes he had to navigate through didn't register as pain on his skin. All he could focus on was staying alive. Like a martial artist's kick against a solid rock, he tumbled into a shallow ravine.

"Help! Help!" he shouted, clinging to hope that someone might come to his rescue. There was complete silence, broken only by his piercing screams echoing through the sky. There was no one around, not a single animal or creature in sight. The heavy metal armour around his body only added to his immobility, weighing him down.

The gods were tainted by their fading memories of existence, their importance diminishing. With fewer native dwellers believing in them, Napuagan feared they would fade into nothingness if forgotten. It was his mission to punish those who didn't revere them.

"Death is approaching. Suffering is ever-present," was whispered in the air. Juan, lying on his back, tried to move along the contours of the uneven ground, but his efforts were futile. He remained as rigid as a log. Napuagan then appeared before Juan and declared, "Follow my demands or face the consequences!"

Juan stared back at Napuagan, unable to respond, his forehead damp with a mixture of sweat and blood with his body pulsating with fear. Juan's screams were incoherent, unable to form words as his condition deteriorated. Napuagan had placed a spell on Juan, causing his thoughts to be muddled and hindering his ability to communicate effectively. Despite Juan's resistance, Napuagan was able to control him easily, taking advantage of the fact that it was challenging for Kabunian to intervene with the non-native mountain dweller.

Kabunian appeared with a surprised expression on Napuagan's face. "Stop interfering in my affairs!"

"I could also tell you to stop causing suffering to humanity!" Kabunian retorted.

"I'm telling you! The people you care for are also the ones who will eventually forget about you! We need to instil fear to remind them that we are gods who deserve worship!" Napuagan exclaimed, surrounded by burning flames.

"I understand, but we must face the future! Humanity is not the one to blame for everything!" Kabunian declared, radiating with glory.

Napuagan felt threatened by Kabunian's gesture, as Kabunian was poised to transform Napuagan into dust, erasing him as if he had never existed. In response, Napuagan vanished, returning to the underworld and leaving Jose and Kabunian alone.

Jose got up and kept walking. "What happened to me?" he muttered to himself. His injuries were only minor, but it appeared as though he hadn't been injured at all.

He came across a large spring where several women were bathing and washing clothes and utensils. Concealed behind a bush, he observed with a mixture of longing and apprehension as the women's bodies shimmered in the sunlight. Without warning, he sensed the presence of men behind him, their spears directed towards him. Turning his head cautiously, he spotted the weapons aimed at him. In a state of panic, he reached for his sword, only to discover it was gone, misplaced during his travels.

"What are you doing here?" one of the men asked.

"Just passing through," Jose replied, trembling.

"You're a spy, aren't you?" another man in the group accused.

"No, I swear," Jose protested.

"Take off your clothes and clean yourself," one of them instructed.

Jose, feeling confused, followed their instructions and removed his clothes, as the others did the same. They guided him into the water, where the women used smooth rocks to massage his back. Some of the men then requested the same treatment from him, adding to his unease. Despite his discomfort, Jose didn't want to offend them and participated in the unconventional activity. The group appeared unconcerned about being naked, with both men and women bathing together as if it were routine. Although surrounded by unclothed men, Jose kept his feelings of discomfort to himself.

Chapter XXIII

The men and women have completed their task at the spring. Jose was also instructed to finish up. The women carried potable water in large clay jars on their heads, while the men carried hunted animals and fish. Jose was compelled to accompany them, with a dagger pointed at his back, as they made their way to the village. No one exchanged names or identities, as Jose was still seen as a possible threat.

Suddenly, Jose sensed danger from the group when a warrior nodded at the other that prompted him to smash one of the clay jars with his bare hand, causing water to spill out. Seizing the distraction, he sprinted away as fast as he could. Spears were hurled in his direction, one grazing his face and drawing blood. Climbing a tall tree like a monkey, he evaded his pursuers. With a drop of blood trickling down his wounded face, he whispered, "Please stay hidden," hoping to evade detection.

One of the men was right below Jose with his hand pressing against his wound. The rest were spread out around the area. "He went this way!" Someone yelled. Jose's fear intensified, still hoping to remain hidden. The men departed after they were unable to find him. "I'm so glad I got rid of my armour," he said with a sense of relief. He slid down when his wound stopped dripping his own blood. He was completely lost, not just in terms of directions, but also within himself.

"How did this happen to me?" he muttered, standing motionless under a tree. Unaware that he was heading south, he eventually arrived at the village of Kafaguay.

"Please, let me in! I need medical attention and I haven't eaten in days!" he pleaded with the guards at the gate. "What now?" one of the guards muttered. Liston rushed to the gate, recognising the man outside as one of those responsible for his scars.

"You two! Leave my village immediately or you will be forcibly removed!" Kalag shouted as Liston was about to attack Jose with a threatening body slam. Liston, with a disapproving expression on his face, stopped his actions and remained silent, staring at Jose intently like a predator eyeing its prey. Jose, on the other hand, stayed calm and did not react, demonstrating to the village that he had no ill intentions and was there with kindness. Daniel, who had been quietly observing, decided to speak up, saying, "I may not know the two of you or the situation between you, but we must respect the wishes of the village and show them gratitude for their hospitality. We are strangers here and should act accordingly." Liston and Jose then bowed before Kalag and offered their apologies.

"I understand that it has been difficult for you, especially recalling your past hardships. However, this is not the appropriate time or place to delve into such painful experiences," Daniel whispered to Liston, offering advice in a brotherly manner. He did not speak to Jose, who was seated on a rock beneath a cherry tree, gazing upwards as if eager to pick some fruit. Kalag noticed Jose's actions and instructed some servants to lead him to the dining area for a meal and some water. Liston returned to his task of assisting the men in constructing a pit for the farmed pigs.

The servants provided Jose with a lavish meal fit for a village. Later, Kalag observed Jose thoroughly enjoying the spread, which included wat-wat, pinuneg or blood sausage, various sweet potatoes, and copious amounts of their finest rice wine.

Curious, Kalag inquired about the feast.

"We are serving the foreigner, your excellency," a servant replied.

"Yes, but I never instructed you to treat him like the most important person here!" Kalag exclaimed, his demeanor fierce.

"We apologise, Your Leadership," the servants chorused, quickly clearing the table of all the food.

"I'm sorry!" Jose stammered, feeling overwhelmed by the situation.

"It's fine. I trust you had your meal," Kalag said.

"Thanks. I had a sufficient portion," Jose replied.

Kalag headed back to his quarters and summoned the three foreigners to join him. He was unsure whether to extend their stay and contemplated their behavior and movements carefully. He was concerned that they could be spies sent to gather information about their community.

"This is a rare situation for us. Explain why you are here. I'm warning you. We will either behead you or make the three of you our slaves, not even servants have that extent of freedom," Kalag declared in his powerful voice from an elevated platform in front of the three foreigners.

"I was tortured by this soldado of the conquistadors when I was captured!" Liston said, pointing at Jose with a stern expression. Jose knelt down in silence, unable to comprehend Liston's revelation. Daniel was excused, as Kalag recognised the significance of the tattoo on his shoulder.

Jose was led outside at night and abandoned. He was unaware of his surroundings. His cries for help went unheard by the village. Kalay was also on the verge of ordering the exile of Liston with the guards, but Daniel intervened, convincing Kalay to spare him by vouching for Liston's character. Daniel even offered to face the consequences if he was wrong, suggesting they both be executed if necessary.

"Alright, but I will remember your promise," Kalay agreed with the proposal.

Jose struggled to see in the darkness, feeling his way in a careful movement, whatever direction he was heading. His ears were attuned to the subtle sounds of the night, his foot path was shallow, sinking into the earth with each step. Unsure if it was mud or soft earth beneath him, he heard a faint whizzing sound with every movement. Unfamiliar to him, he was treading on the territory of Kalangit, a small insect-like creature with six legs and two large eyes. Ignoring the softness underfoot and the accompanying whizzing sound, he focused on the distant light ahead, determined to keep moving forward.

He arrived at the illuminated area on the other side of the mountain where the moon was shining so bright. Along the way, he wasn't paying attention to his lower body. However, upon reaching the light, he discovered several scratches, some of which were deep cuts that caused him pain. The wounds felt as if they were burning with a spicy sensation as if vast chillis were applied on his wounds, causing him to scream in agony. His face turned red with the intensity of the pain. He was so preoccupied with his injuries that he failed to notice the nearby village.

A young woman with bronze skin and long black hair, illuminated by the moonlight, caught Jose's attention. He was so focused on her that he momentarily forgot about the pain he was suffering from. He was curious about how she had appeared. When she looked at him for the first time, her face showed empathy. Her furrowed eyebrows, wrinkled forehead, and quick approach towards him conveyed concern. "You poor thing, suffering from wounded legs," she said in a soothing voice that turned shaky as she examined his injuries up close.

Jose remained silent as the men approached him, accompanied by a woman. He was trying to move back as they were approaching, but his injuries were too severe for him to escape. The woman reassured him, "Don't worry, we're here to help," as the men began to lift him up.

"Ay! Ay! Ay!" Jose screamed.

The men were puzzled by the situation and remained silent as they transported him to a kubo house. Inside, they found a medicine man surrounded by various herbs with different fragrance and stones of different purity. The walls were adorned with human and animal skulls, as well as feathers from different birds. The medicine man ground herbs and other substances in a small mortar and pestle, chanting prayers as he did so. Smoke filled the room, its source unknown. Jose felt the sting of the medicine until he eventually slipped into unconsciousness.

The medicine man used a native chicken feather dipped in an oily substance to splash on Jose's body. Jose felt the kalangit nibbling on his feet and lower torso, which the medicine man sensed.

"The kalangit is the cause of this. He must apologise for intruding on its territory once he is healed," the medicine man declared in a powerful, authoritative voice.

Jose was left alone with the medicine man, who checked on him from time to time. He remained unconscious for a while, but fortunate enough that his wounds were healing in an accelerated time, more than what was expected. When he became alert, he walked outside feeling rejuvenated, as if he was brand-new, like nothing wrong with him. The villagers he encountered regarded him with awe, as if he were a hero or someone remarkable.

"The outsider has left! Bring him to me! I must speak with him," a commanding voice exclaimed.

Jose was accompanied by two men with bulos on their belts to the 'tongtongan ti umili' area, a place surrounded by stones with a fireplace in the center, under a raised kubo where village issues were discussed by the leader and a council of elders.

The medicine man led a prayer chant, followed by the council of elders, as Jose was instructed to stand near a blazing fire. The heat was so intense that he longed to move away from the scorching flames. The smoke enveloped him, causing his eyes and nostrils to sting with irritation. The elders believed that the pain and difficulty of breathing caused by the smoke would reveal whether Jose brought a good or bad omen.

A native chicken was sacrificed, and its blood was allowed to soak into the fire. The medicine man then read the smoke, with the elders' approval, to determine the true nature of the omen brought by Jose. If it was determined that Jose brought a bad omen, he would face execution by beheading. However, if the omen was deemed good, he would be welcomed to live among them.

The village remained untouched by conquistador attackers and unfamiliar with outsiders. Jose stood out with his long blond hair, bright hazel eyes, and fair skin. He sought guidance from the divine ancestors on how to proceed in their presence, and the response was positive, welcoming him as one of their own. Bolay, the woman who discovered him, had the most tattoos among women, marking her as one of the most beautiful women in the village. Jose observed the mambabatek applying tattoos to a man's chest with a stick and a sharp thorn, wondering about the significance of this painful art form.

In the heat of the day, a larger group of conquistadors were hiking the steep mountain that Jose had spotted. He was conflicted about whether to warn the village or wait for the conquistadors to arrive and surprise them with an attack. In the Kafaguay village, they also sensed the approaching enemies and felt a sense of impending danger. These were not just a few individuals, but warriors from ten villages coming together. They had horses and large, imposing men among them. Jose was strong, but he was no match for the massive men in wave after wave in formation moving at the mountain slope.

"We have another group of armed men approaching. This time, they are just as numerous as before," Daniel cautioned.

The Kafaguay people were prepared for any situation, standing in formation. Warriors and able-bodied men armed themselves with various weapons such as machetes, spears, knives, bows, and even makeshift tools. Some rode on horses and other animals. Daniel and a warrior ventured outside the village to rally potential allies and warn them of the impending threat.

Although unfamiliar with the terrain at first, Daniel gradually recognised their surroundings as they journeyed. They first reached the Kapangan training ground, where they were headed due to their relationship with the villagers. Continuing on, they encountered the remaining Bokodians. "There's no time for doubt," Daniel reminded himself, understanding the urgency of their message.

A soft voice in the wind murmured, "Jose, these people trust you." Encouraged by the spirits, he made sure to inform the village leader promptly about the approaching conquistadors, a warning corroborated by other villagers who had also spotted the group advancing up the mountains.

The leader remained silent in response. After a moment of contemplation, he informed the group that a threat of invaders was rapidly approaching. The council of elders, along with the medicine man and the leader, gathered at the 'tongtongan ti umili' area. They formed a circle, raised their hands, closed their eyes, and chanted prayers in a language that was incomprehensible to the average person. In the center, a fire blazed, and an animal, typically a pig, was sacrificed and burned as an offering to the Afunijon or gods in the hopes that their prayers would be heard.

The warriors stood guard on the rock wall fences surrounding the village, armed with spears, large rocks, and pointed sticks. The strongest men were positioned outside the fences, ready to push boulders as the first line of defense. There was no time for conversation, only for following the leader's orders. A mist of fog suddenly enveloped the village, rendering it invisible from the outside but allowing those inside the fence to see out. The fog appeared right after the prayers had concluded.

The incoming group split up, with one heading west and the other heading east towards the village where Jose was located. The conquistador fighters were confident, holding their heads high and brandishing their weapons, including the powerful guns known as "boom sticks" by the mountain dwellers due to their superior firepower.

The Bokodians were fearful of the approaching threat they referred to as impending doom. They believed that powerful conquistadors armed with weapons were on their way to destroy them completely. This sentiment was shared by most of them, causing them to feel cowardly and physically tremble with fear, their faces showing a raggedy and expressionless appearance. However, only a few rare members of the village were considered brave enough to fight for their traditional way of life. They were ready because they were situated in the potential path of the invaders.

The conquistadors had not yet appeared. Some began to wonder if the information they had received was a ploy to assert dominance over the Kafaguay village. As time passed without any sign of an attack, the Bokodians and other villages lowered their guards. Life resumed its normal course, with a sense of relief replacing the fear that had gripped the Bokodians.

The group of conquistadors traveling west was resting by the riverside, with some sleeping while others stood guard. A group of tattooed, muscular men, skilled at remaining hidden, observed them from the bushes and trees. They were armed with rocks, spears, and improvised weapons. The guards on duty noticed the ambush too late and warned their comrades to wake up and run, but many were already under attack. Some managed to fight back and kill a few of the hidden warriors, the loud booming sound was executed from their boom sticks but others were struck by arrows and other weapons. The conquistadors, realising they were outnumbered, quickly retreated.

The fleeing conquistadors ran without stopping until they were too exhausted to continue. They slowed down but did not stop, fearing that the group who had attacked them might still be pursuing them. The five remaining conquistadors were not yet safe from danger, as they were nearing the invaded Dutab Kingdom. The keen eyes of the Busol warriors spotted their approach. One warrior prepared to throw his spear at them, but their leader intervened and instructed some of his warriors to track them down. The conquistadors' fate was sealed as the Busol warriors swiftly closed in on them, using their skilled hands to swiftly decapitate each conqueror with a single stroke of their gamans.

The group traveling east spotted a village from a hill across from their location. They dispersed and concealed themselves in dense vegetation and behind rocks. Instead of launching an immediate attack, they waited until nightfall. Under the cover of darkness, only two soldados approached the village to scout for guards or any signs of resistance. The village appeared to be going about its usual activities without any unusual activity. There were guards stationed around the stone wall fences, but they did not seem to be on high alert for a potential battle. They were simply carrying out their routine duties of protecting their home.

"I didn't see anything out of the ordinary in the village," one of the soldados reported back to the group.

"There were around seven or eight guards positioned near the stone wall fences," the other soldado added.

The other soldados provided similar assessments, concluding that there were no significant obstacles in their way. They waited until the spy soldados gave the signal to attack.

"We've been waiting here for a long time now. I'm tired of this hiding game," a soldado complained, echoing the feelings of the other soldados.

"Keep quiet and be patient. You will all give our position with your ranting," the group leader said.

Later on, the village became quiet and most of the people were in their houses with the warriors on guard who were the ones alert. Some of the soldados were becoming sleepy with a few who were already asleep. One of the spies soldados waved his arm signaling that it was a great time to attack.

"Get up and prepare," the leader murmured.

The soldados were vigilant, heeding their leader's instructions.

"Surround the village and arm yourselves," the leader directed.

They encircled the rock wall defenses and readied their ropes with hooks. Swinging the ropes until the hooks caught, they used them to scale the village walls. Once atop the walls, the guards spotted them, but it was too late. The guards were either stabbed by the leaping soldados or struck by rocks from above, resulting in their demise or incapacitation. The villagers scattered in fear as the soldados fired their guns at the huts. The sound of gunfire and smoke filled the air as the village burned. The men of Bokodian tried to fight back, but their fear and lack of focus resulted in only a few soldados being killed. The fire quickly spread through the village that made it visible to the vantage point of the Kafaguay village, and the warriors of Kafaguay rushed to help, but it was too late. The village was destroyed, with many dead and only a few survivors. The bestowed might from the gods and warriors of Kapangan helped the revenge on the soldados, and those who tried to escape were killed.

The dawn had broken the night, and the Kafaguay village prepared pigs for a thanksgiving to the gods for driving away the conquistadors. The Bokodian survivors who had taken refuge with the Kafaguay people were not in a celebratory mood. They wept amidst the festivities. The medicine man recited a prayer and placed his hands on the survivors, asking the gods to grant them strength to overcome their sorrow. He then interpreted the pig's entrails, which indicated good fortune for the days ahead.

The survivors initially remained sorrowful but gradually began to relax as the atmosphere filled with joy. The entire village participated in the canao ceremony. The pigs were cooked into wat-wat along with tapuy and kintoman, complemented by sweet potatoes and other root crops. Jose and Liston joined in the village celebration, setting aside any animosity or grudges, especially Liston towards Jose.

A warrior approached Kalag to share his thoughts. "Do we still have trust in the three outsiders under your leadership? It appears that trouble has followed them that has greatly harmed us" he said, bowing and gazing at Kalag with a worried expression.

"Let's give them an opportunity to prove themselves. I trust Daniel, but I have my doubts about Liston and Jose. They say they're not a threat, but just look at the troubles we've been through because of them. Let's wait and see! Let's focus on the celebration and put this issue aside for now," Kalag declared with a commanding tone.

The warriors continued their victory celebration, fueled by tapuy that left them in a state of impaired consciousness. Their excessive food consumption added to their fullness. The festivities lasted well into the night, with some of them becoming too drunk and falling asleep on the spot. Others, with stronger resistance, carried on until the break of dawn.

The loud noise of a large gangza startled everyone. Kalag instructed the women and older children to clean up the mess, while the men were told to go to the river to freshen up. This was to help them feel better after drinking too much. Many people were enjoying swimming instead of focusing on cleaning themselves up, causing them to stay in the water longer than Kalag had anticipated. He instructed a woman to go and bring them back.

The men hurried back to the village in response to Kalag's urgent request.

"Form a circle," Kalag instructed.

"Liston and Jose, step forward!"

"How are you?" Kalag inquired, facing them directly. The other men watched closely, waiting to see how the two would respond to their leader.

"I'm well, thank you for asking," Liston replied.

"I'm doing fine," Jose answered.

"Under the guidance of Bulan, we must test these two outsiders to determine their true character and trustworthiness!"

Daniel implored Kalag to reconsider the test and assured him of the outsiders' reliability, but Kalag stood firm. The men were then directed to proceed with their tasks. The community supported their leader's choice, with only a few individuals, including Daniel, expressing disagreement. Women were largely in the minority and had little influence on the decision-making process. Additionally, Daniel was cautioned that he would be included in the test if he persisted in his plea.

Daniel had a private conversation with Liston and Jose, keeping it confidential. He was cautious about being seen with them. He assured them that he would make an effort to help, but also cautioned them to be prepared for uncertainty. He inquired with people, particularly those close to Kalag, but none were willing to speak up, even those who shared his views. Despite his daily efforts leading up to the test, he faced rejection as others were weary of his persistent stubbornness.

The night had arrived, casting a glow over the village with the moon's brightness. Daniel thought to himself, "This must be the night."

"The night is here! Prepare for the test!" declared a warrior.

As the warrior spoke, Kalag stepped out of his quarters. "Our leader, Kalag! Bow before him!"

The fire was ignited, and the sound of a squealing pig echoed throughout the village. After the pig was burned, the mumbaki examined the remains with a prayer to the gods. Everyone watched eagerly as Jose and Liston were instructed to approach the fire after the cooking was completed. The fire was kept burning as the two men were told to walk through it. Liston went first, visibly frowning and taking deep breaths as he moved through the flames. "Walk through the fire!" Kalag impatiently ordered. Liston ran quickly and made it to the other side without incident, narrowly avoiding the food prepared in receptacles.

Jose, observing Liston's actions, felt his heart racing with nervousness as his turn approached. With armed warriors behind him, he closed his eyes and ran through the fire, reaching the other side unscathed. Both men crossed the fire without sustaining any major injuries.

Without allowing them any rest, a bamboo table was placed in the center of the village for all to see. A warrior directed the two individuals to the table. Their arms were instructed to cross. "This is a test of strength! The winner will be deemed trustworthy!" declared the warrior.

The sangkur or arm-wrestling match commenced. Jose struggled to get up due to the pain creeping into his body, while Liston only sustained minor injuries and had a higher pain tolerance due to his life experiences. "Prepare yourselves! Lock arms and begin!" announced the warrior.

Both contestants gave their all, but Liston emerged victorious with the stronger arm, causing Jose to cry in defeat. The warriors then took Jose and threw him into the dungeon, while the village enjoyed the roasted pig. It was decided that the punishment would be carried out the following day.

Liston enjoyed the food like everybody and consumed more tapuy than usual to help him endure the pain throughout the night. He figured that if he didn't show any signs of pain, he might be spared. Everyone had a good time and gradually went to sleep.

The next day, Jose was released outside the village and given a chance to run. Several warriors were instructed to chase after him with their gaman. Jose ran until he reached a forested area and climbed a pine tree, hoping they wouldn't find him there. However, the warriors searched the forest diligently and eventually discovered him due to his loud sneezing. They pulled him down from the tree, and the warrior who decapitated Jose was the same one who had complained to Kalag. Jose's head was brought back to the village and displayed in front of Kalag's quarters.

Chapter XXIV

In the lowlands controlled by the conquistadors, Comandante Joselito Romualdez, the highest-ranking official on the island, was filled with anger. "Why can't these mountain barbarians be vanquished?" he exclaimed in frustration. Despite their most sophisticated weapons, the conquistadors were unable to defeat the mountain dwellers. The conquistador officials concealed the defeats by the mountain people, and anyone caught discussing it faced execution. This was how the conquerors maintained their reign of terror.

They halted the mountain explorations to avoid further embarrassments. They concentrated their authority over the areas they could influence. Unexpectedly, they encountered a formidable opponent from a foreign land when their massive ships arrived at an island. Despite being outnumbered, the newcomers possessed superior weaponry. Their soldiers wore mushroom-shaped headgear and pointed boots. Their firearms had greater firepower, endurance, and capacity. Their blades were stronger and more sophisticated.

A soldado was hurrying towards the government palace. "Comandante! Foreigners have arrived by ships and landed!" The soldado said with a worried expression.

"Line up our men and prepare for battle!" The comandante ordered.

There was no time for the soldados to form a proper formation or receive a briefing. They immediately engaged the incoming foreigners. The conquistadors were met with large floating cannons and guns that could be loaded with multiple rounds of ammunition. Rapid fire decimated many soldados as the clash of swords rang out. The conquistadors' metal armour offered little protection against the onslaught.

The foreigners moved swiftly and lightly without heavy armour, relying on their weapons. The island's comandante, who usually did not participate in battles, was forced to join the reinforcements due to the dwindling numbers of soldados. The foreigners advanced while the conquerors retreated, eventually overtaking the government palace in victory.

Lieutenant Alfred Wright, the commanding officer of the island's new English-speaking conqueror, instructed his men to take all the prisoners to the dungeon. The news of capturing one of the conquistador's territories had reached the island's capital, signaling the rapid expansion of the new superpower. Concerned about potential defeat and further embarrassment, the conquistador leader sent a messenger with a proposal that they were willing to agree to, in hopes of avoiding conflict.

Lieutenant Wright and Comandante Romualdez, along with their high officials, were seated in the heart of the island's capital city. The forum took place within the walls of the Gobierno Centro Edifico, where individual chairs with tables faced a stage occupied by higher central officials, including church representatives for the conquistadors. The lower chairs with tables were reserved for representatives from towns and provinces. Initially chaotic, with each side expressing their thoughts and desires, a temporary peace treaty was eventually reached. The conquistadors ultimately agreed to sell the islands to the new conquerors, solidifying the agreement through another treaty held within continental Europe.

In the mountains, there had been years of peace, at least in terms of protection against foreign invaders. Daniel, along with several village leaders, successfully repelled Busol's treacherous invasion of the villages, including the freedom of Dutab Kingdom. Daniel believed that the gods had shown mercy by allowing him to return home. As he matured, both in his outlook on life and in age and physical strength, he felt grateful for the experiences that had shaped him.

Daniel and Kuchep had a slim chance of ending up together. Kuchep was so enamored with her life in Kapangan that she chose to stay there permanently. Similarly, Daniel appreciated the blend of simplicity and modernity in life. However, unlike Kuchep, Daniel felt burdened by what he perceived as a monumental responsibility, but he was determined to fulfill it with the hope of eventually returning home.

However, the mountain dwellers were completely unaware of the impending threat. A new conqueror was making a move to invade all areas of the archipelago. The one thing that was certain was the effectiveness of their attacks.

A man named Michael journeyed to the high mountains with his horse, sporting a hat resembling a mushroom and shoes with pointed tips. He reached the village where Jose had been rescued in the past. Initially, some of the warriors raised their weapons in preparation for a battle, but Michael surprised them by offering a variety of unfamiliar foods. These edibles were stored in metal containers, fizzy drinks came in glass bottles, and the foods were unlike anything found in the forest.

"Please! I am not here with bad intentions!" Michael pleaded.

The warriors ignored his words and hurled several spears and rocks from the entrance.

"Heha! Run!" Michael urged his horse to flee. With skillful agility, he twisted his body to face the attackers while riding backward. Drawing his magnum six-cylinder gun, he shattered the rocks in mid-air and deftly dodged the spears, redirecting them away from himself. The warriors were astonished by Michael's swift and precise movements, dropping their weapons as they focused intently on him.

Michael, a determined man, waited in the wooded area. His shooting skills provided him with roasted mountain native chicken, smaller in size that a domesticated one but packed with flavor. His horse grazed on fresh green grass on the tree bed while they waited for nightfall. When it was time to return to the village, Michael walked alongside his horse, guiding it with a rope around its head. As they approached the closed entrance, Michael shouted, "I am here bearing gifts!"

A guard opened the gate and saw the same man with mushroom headwear and pointed footwear holding a small fire. "I give you the gift of fire!" Michael declared as he lit a match. The warriors watched in awe, whispering among themselves about the mythical creature that Michael seemed to be, perhaps sent by the good god, perhaps Kabunian himself.

The leader observed from his window as events unfolded. "Let him in! I am intrigued!" he commanded the guards. Stepping outside to meet the man, the leader closely examined the matches the man kept lighting. He scrutinised the man's appearance, even touching the buttons on his shirt, without the man speaking a word. Finally, the man spoke, "I come from a distant land. I bring a message for you and your people."

The leader, with a look of disbelief, asked, "What message?"

The man declared, "God, through the powerful Jesus, offers a place called Heaven to all who believe in him."

"I am Michael, the messenger of God," the man added.

Michael distributed sealed canned food to the villagers and showed them how to open the cans with a dagger. The villagers gathered around him to inspect the food. He assured them that he would return with more canned food in the future. The villagers smiled and, with the blessing of the mambunong, allowed Michael to leave and come back another day.

Michael traveled through the forest with his loyal horse, which the villagers fed during his stay. As they journeyed along the familiar trail, a loud noise caught their attention, sounding like boulders being thrown. The horse slowed its pace as it caught sight of a towering creature, the Burika. This massive being resembled a fat man with fangs protruding from its mouth, dressed in a loincloth similar to the villagers. Its body was covered in hair, though not enough to be mistaken for animal fur. The horse panicked and fled running with a high-pitched whinny, while the Burika pursued, attempting to capture Michael and his horse. The giant's hand hovered near Michael's mouth, as if preparing to consume him. Fortunately, they managed to escape the Burika, who could not venture beyond the forest without risking suffocation. The trees provided the necessary air for the Burika to breathe.

The horse continued running until it came to a clean body of water that was safe to drink. Michael filled his water canister while the horse drank. The clear water was full of fish, and Michael caught several with his hands. He cleaned the fish, cooked them with butter in a cast iron skillet, and ate them. The horse found some cherry-like fruits by the body of water and ate as many as it could. After resting briefly, they resumed their journey.

They arrived in the capital city and met with General Steve Smith, the leader of the 43rd Asia-Pacific regiment, at the presidential palace, formerly known as the Edifice Del Gobierno Central. General Smith discussed the indigenous mountain dwellers and proposed a plan to colonise them through education. A formal order was issued for a group of educators, known as Thomasites, to be accompanied by soldiers to explore the mountains and teach the native population. Michael, who had some knowledge of the mountain geography, served as the navigator for the expedition.

They were ascending a hill, with women riding horses and men walking alongside. The men were leading the horses ridden by the women, and they didn't realise when the women vanished. It was only when those at the back of the group noticed the women in front disappearing without a trace that an alarm was raised.

"What's going on with our women? They're vanishing into nowhere, with no visible explanation or abductors," one of the soldiers exclaimed.

The men were on high alert, scanning their surroundings as they moved cautiously along the grassy path. They allowed the women on horses to lead the way, with the men flanking them, ensuring every step was taken with care.

One of the culprits behind the women's disappearance made a grave mistake. In his mind, he was invisible, but the travelers could see him. He was a Tamawo, a pale elf-like creature with menacing fangs. A soldier attempted to grab him, but he slipped away. Bullets seemed ineffective against the Tamawo, as they couldn't penetrate its skin. The loud gunshots startled the Tamawo colony, revealing their locations each time the vibrations disturbed them. The women travelers silently prayed as the events unfolded. The men identified the Tamawo's vulnerability and continued firing their guns into the air until the kidnapped women reappeared.

"We need to leave this place quickly," one soldier urged, and they all mounted their horses, galloping away from the Tamawo territory as fast as they could.

The group of hunters that Daniel was with suddenly came to a halt as dashing horses with men on their backs raced past them, as if they were fleeing from something terrifying. The hunters had not intended to interact with anyone, but circumstances brought them together. One of the hunters tried to throw a spear, but it missed its mark and flew close to Michael. Another hunter prepared to use a sling shot, but Daniel intervened, urging them to give the outsiders a chance. Daniel noticed that the travelers were dressed similarly to cowboys he had seen on television, like those in the show 'The Lone Ranger.' The hunters paused in their aggressive stance, though they remained ready to defend themselves if necessary.

The hunters led the way, with the women separated from the men. The hunters were on foot, as is typical in the mountains when hunting, to avoid slowing down during their outsiders. The women were ordered to ride the horses, while the men walked. From the top of a cliff, wild boars could be seen grazing in the wide grasslands below.

"Stay here and don't make any sudden moves," the hunter who seemed to be in command told the women. He assigned several hunters to look after the women, instructing them not to take their eyes off them. The rest of the hunters and the male outsiders went down to catch some of the wild boar. The native men swiftly ran and killed one with their spears, while the outsiders shot and killed more with their guns. After the hunt, the natives had only killed one boar, while the outsiders had killed four. The natives then pointed their spears and daggers at the outsiders. "You are no different from the conquistadors, those who attempted to invade us," one of the warriors said.

Other warriors intervened to prevent him from harming or killing the outsiders. One of them suggested that it would be more beneficial to imprison the travelers for potential future use. The outsiders, still bound together, prayed once more. The guns were not enough to eliminate all of the natives, as they could only kill a few of the many of their massive number.

The captured animals were loaded onto horses, and the group continued on foot. The travelers offered the natives canned food, which helped to build a rapport between them.

Daniel thought to himself, "I need to befriend these new outsiders. They might hold the key to my return home."

Pointing to the canned food, Daniel remarked to the native, "This type of food is beneficial for us. These outsiders are not here to harm us, but to introduce us to a new way of life."

The natives appeared to be open to Daniel's words as they approached, but he couldn't be sure if his message had truly connected with them. They reached Kafaguay village and introduced the outsiders to Kalag. All eyes were on them. The villagers had never seen such attire before. The women wore beautiful clothes adorned with flowers and intricate designs that captivated onlookers. The men sported mushroom-like hats and pointed shoes. Women wore skirts and blouses with leather gloves.

Michael and the other men attempted to impress the natives with various items, such as lighting matches, canned food, and pocket watches, that also served as bibles for reading. The outsiders observed that Daniel was just as eager to inspect the items as the others. However, Daniel's actions were not questioned by any of the foreigners.

The natives continued to be curious, watching the travelers closely. The women approached the children and offered them treats with artificial fruit flavours, which they had taken from hidden pockets in their clothing. It was the first time the native children had ever tasted something so pleasurable on their taste buds that it made them jump and laugh with more energy than they had ever had before.

At that moment, the outsiders gained the trust of the natives and were allowed to go free and do as they pleased. The locals started learning how to read from the outsiders, who also taught them about the Bible and how to tell time. They also brought in new crops from their native land that were grown in the mountains. New breeds of dogs, cats and other domesticated animals were also introduced.

Eventually, a Christian church was built in the village, and gradually, God, the saints and the teachings of the bible became integrated into the lives of the natives.

As time passed, more members of their community were able to spread the Christian teachings to other villages in the mountains, focusing on concepts such as loving thy neighbor, peace, and forgiveness. Pastor Robert Plan led the church delegates, and Daniel visited him regularly seeking guidance on how to return home. However, as days went by without a concrete solution on how he could return home and only hearing the same messages of love and forgiveness, Daniel became disheartened.

"Pastor, I believe that your group may be influencing the natives in a way that could lead to their exploitation and the taking of their lands and resources," Daniel expressed his concerns after observing that their teachings clashed with their actions.

"My child, you have misunderstood. Come to church and I can make you understand," Pastor Robert responded.

Although hesitant, Daniel not being religious himself, followed Pastor Robert into the church. There, Pastor Robert had Daniel read a passage from the Bible, Romans 12:10, which talks about being devoted to one another in love and honouring others above oneself. However, Pastor Robert seemed to interpret the passage in a way that portrayed their group as the heroes of love, with the natives needing to be transformed.

Daniel left the church with a look of disappointment on his face. He expressed his concerns to Kalag, who brushed them off. "Why do the natives trust these new conquerors so blindly?" Daniel muttered to himself. The thought of returning home weighed heavily on his mind, as he felt out of place in a world that was passing him by.

It's Sunday, a day for worshiping the Lord. The conquerors and locals came together at the church for another service. Pastor Robert emphasised the importance of loving your neighbour as yourself with authority in his voice. Both the conqueror members and the native converts listened attentively to his words. The church provided a meal with food from the conqueror's homeland, as they often did. Some indigenous people attended the service for the first time, brought by the indigenous converts as encouraged by the church.

"I notice we have some new faces here today," Pastor Robert remarked as he conversed with the congregation.

Pastor Robert and his church assistants arranged a river trip for baptism with some of the Thomasites after the gathering. The church made sure to reach out to as many natives as possible to share their faith.

"I baptise you in the name of the Father, the Son, and the Holy Ghost." This final sentence was spoken as the candidates for baptism were immersed in the water, symbolising their cleansing from sin. The crowd at the baptism responded with "Amen" and applause each time someone was submerged.

A group of muscular men on horseback, adorned with intricate tattoos representing the Busol, attacked the group. They were against the conquerors trying to assimilate the natives, in line with the Busol's beliefs. Daniel, who had not been present at the baptism, fought back with some Kafaguay warriors. The baptism attendees fled to the village, with some falling victim to the Busol's powerful gamans and others being stabbed with spears. Some of the conqueror men were able to shoot and kill some Busol with their guns. Daniel and the Kafaguay warriors engaged in close combat using their weapons.

Daniel's sword glowed gold, a sight that had not been seen by the conquerors before. With one swift motion, he cut five Busol in half, leaving the onlookers mesmerised.

A conqueror man attempted to shoot a Busol warrior who was charging towards him, but the bullet hit the warrior's gaman instead of the warrior himself. The bullet then ricocheted and struck Daniel in the left arm, causing him to cry out in pain as his arm hung limp. Despite his injury, he used his right arm to wield his sword and kill another Busol. The Busol retreated at the sound of the gunfire.

"Where is Pastor Robert?" inquired a member of the congregation.

The scene was terrifying, with the water turning red from the blood of the deceased. Despite this, the focus was on locating the pastor. Some searched in the water, diving in, while others ventured into the nearby forest, but he was nowhere to be found. A female member of the Thomasites led a prayer for the pastor's safety.

The Busol survivors, along with Pastor Robert and a Thomasite woman as hostages, were making their way back to the Dutab kingdom. The pastor had fallen due to a combination of injury and fatigue, prompting the Thomasite woman to go to his aid. A Busol warrior pointed his spear at the pastor, who was lying on the grassland they were passing through. The Thomasite lady begged, "Please! The pastor is injured! Let us rest and attend to his wounds!"

The Busol group provided treatment for the Pastor, including applying healing herbs from the surrounding area. They set up a temporary camp not only for the Pastor but also for themselves. A Busol warrior used his dagger to create a spark and start a fire, then used the dagger to expose it to the flames. He approached the Pastor, appearing as though he was going to stab the injured man.

"Please spare him! He is a man of God! Let him live!" The Thomasite woman pleaded with the Busol warrior holding the dagger.

"Move aside!" The Busol warrior retorted, nudging the Thomasite woman to the side.

He cut a bulge on the pastor's forehead and allowed the blood to flow from it. Using the endmost handle of his dagger, he crushed herbs and applied them. The Thomasite lady expressed her gratitude and apologised to the Busol warrior for her action.

The Thomasite lady was extremely determined. She asked the Busol warriors to join her in a prayer she was about to say. The Busol warriors stared at her intensely, almost as if they were trying to pierce her soul. The pastor, fully alert, quietly advised the Thomasite lady not to push the prayer on the Busol warriors out of concern for potential backlash. He suggested that she say the prayer silently instead and allow the Busol warriors to continue caring for their fellow Busols.

Chapter XXV

Daniel left without the Kafaguay villager's awareness. He recalled the route to the training ground of the Kapangan village. If the senior trainers and mentors were still there, perhaps he could persuade them to help him remove the Busol from power in the Dutab Kingdom once and for all. Daniel's exceptional attributes included his keen memory and steadfast determination despite his cognitive challenges and advancing age. Moreover, he was eager to go back to his own world.

Xiaoxian, who was taller and more muscular, stood guard at the entrance of the cave as a familiar man approached. He recognised the man's movements as Daniel's.

"What do you need?" Xiaoxian inquired as Daniel drew nearer.

"I need to speak with your leader," Daniel replied.

"Why?" Xiaoxian questioned.

"I just need to speak with your leader."

"What do you mean? You can talk to me."

Cheng happened to witness the exchange as he was heading to the communal restroom.

"Is that Daniel you're speaking with?" Cheng called out.

"Yes, Leader! What should I do?"

"Let him in and wait for me. I'll be right there. I need to go first."

Daniel had a heartfelt conversation with Xiaoxian that went on longer than most of the warriors had anticipated. Xiaoxian accepted Daniel's proposal with so much sympathy, pointing out that they, too, were outsiders who had been able to establish their society in the mountains without facing opposition. The warriors fell silent outside their leader's quarters as this reminder was delivered with intense emotion.

"Formation!" Xiaoxian ordered.

The warriors stood in a line formation, ready for Xiaoxian's next command.

"Conserve your energy for tonight! We are going to launch an attack on the Busols at Dutab Kingdom! Their tyranny has gone on for too long and it must be stopped now!"

Xiaoxian instructed three of the fastest warriors to head in different directions to seek support from allies.

The villages of Kapangan, Kafaguay, and Batan came together at dawn to strengthen their bonds by performing a traditional peace ritual. A mambunong sacrificed a native chicken, sprinkling its blood on the men to signify their unity. After reading the signs from the chicken, which indicated positive outcomes, several pigs were also sacrificed by burning. The spiritual leader communicated with the spirits through prayers, entering a trance-like state to receive guidance on the timing of their planned attack. The pigs were then butchered and consumed along with sweet potatoes, wild fruits, and ceremonial rice wine to fortify themselves for the upcoming battle.

With a surge of energy, they launched a sudden attack that caught the Busols off guard, leaving them no time to call for reinforcements. The unsuspecting Busol guards were quickly overpowered by the divine sword of Daniel and the powerful weapons crafted from the finest metallic compounds found deep beneath the earth in the towering mountains. The clash of weapons resulted in Daniel's group emerging victorious, their superior weapons easily besting the inferior ones wielded by the Busol. The combined efforts of the hundreds of allied villagers outnumbered and overwhelmed the dwindling Busol forces, leading to the downfall of their empire and plunging them into obscurity.

In a tragic turn of events, Pastor Robert tragically lost his life due to a combination of infection and his inability to escape the deadly grip of a Busol warrior who decapitated him. The only survivor among them was the Thomasite lady. Some Kafaguay prisoners also managed to survive the ordeal. The Dutab Kingdom was littered with human remains, emitting a strong odor of death. The allies searched the area, either stabbing survivors found among the casualties or decapitating those who were hiding.

"Oh my God!" exclaimed the Thomasite lady in shock.

"We must ensure that the deceased receive a proper burial, regardless of which side they were on," she added.

Daniel, who appeared to be communicating clearly with the conqueror, explained to the Thomasite lady that they would not have enough time to bury the large number of dead. The Thomasite lady insisted on a Christian burial ceremony, but Daniel ignored her and deferred to the leaders to make the decision. Pastor Robert's body was handed over to the conquerors, who were given free rein to do as they pleased.

"The Busols have been defeated! Victory is ours!" Sendong declared. They were now working towards restoring Dutab Kingdom to its former glory, and to achieve that, a worthy leader must guide the Kingdom towards a prosperous future for its people.

"Daniel is the chosen one!" a woman exclaimed, highlighting Daniel as the new leader.

"He is not a true mountain native! I cannot accept this! I believe I am better suited for the leadership role!" Nugal declared.

Leaders and warrior chiefs present in Dutab Kingdom were all aspiring for the position of ruler, each convinced that they were the most qualified. As tensions rose, the warriors and their leaders began to argue over who should hold the important position. Weapons were drawn, and a fight seemed imminent. Daniel stepped in to mediate and urged them to find a peaceful solution, but some saw his actions as an attempt to assert his authority as the Dutab leader.

"Please! Help us dispose of the bodies and maybe, just maybe, all of you can discuss your issues!" shouted the Dutab mambunong.

Most of the leaders and warrior chiefs were reluctant to serve the Dutab Kingdom in this way. They saw it as a symbol of their acknowledgment of Daniel's leadership. However, they were afraid of the consequences if they disobeyed the mambunong's order. They feared a curse that could last a lifetime and potentially harm their villagers or even their families. So, they began carrying the dead to a cave, stacking them on top of each other for burial purposes. The important individuals, or baknangs, were separated and placed in wooden coffins adorned with intricate carvings on the lids and sides.

The dispute made the mountains and its inhabitants disorganised. They were each buying the leadership role to feed each ego that possessed their entire characters.

The gods observed from their realm. In the vicinity of Dutab Kingdom, close to the waters, Kabunian materialised, and Napuagan trailed behind.

"Is this the outcome you desire? People filled with animosity towards one another?" Kabunian questioned Napuagan, asserting his authority as the supreme god.

"Hey! A simple greeting would have been nice!" Napuagan retorted loudly, his tone tinged with sarcasm.

"Enough with the nonsense! Can't you see what is happening to humans?"

"Leave them be! We won't exist someday! They will forget about us! I've cautioned you about this already!"

"No! I will step in and help them unite! Whatever happens, happens!"

They both vanished into thin air. Kabunian reappeared to Hogohog, the fireheart deity in her domain, the eternal flame of the vast burning expanse of the earth, Mainit. Her hair and extremities blazed even more fiercely upon seeing Kabunian's image.

"What do you require of me, Almighty Kabunian?"

"Travel to the realm of the humans! Use the power of your passionate fire heart to warm the hearts of the human race, encouraging them to replace hate with love."

Hogohog journeyed to the Dutab Kingdom and kindled the warmth in every heart.

"What is this warmth I feel in my chest?" Nugal exclaimed as he collapsed.

The others also felt the sensation in their chests, causing them discomfort. However, they recognised the importance of showing love and unity towards each other. Eventually, they rose to their feet and collectively proclaimed Daniel as the rightful leader.

Daniel was not enamored of being a leader. All he could think about was how he could return home. He tried to undermine his position in the hope of being disliked by the people. However, he still did his best to lead, as he saw that the conquerors were exploiting them. A nearby village was attacked by the conquerors, who were using their advanced weaponry to try to take over the gold-rich land. The reinforcements of these conquerors, with their superior technology in warfare, were no match for the combined forces of the villagers. Additionally, some of the villagers had been influenced by religion, believing that it was God's will for the conquerors to take over the gold.

A group composed of men, children, and women arrived at the gate of Dutab Kingdom.

"Please let us in! We have been traveling for a long time and haven't had much to eat!" one of the older men said to the guard.

"Wait here for a moment while I consult our leader," the guard replied.

He hurried to Daniel's quarters, waking him from his afternoon nap. "Your leadership, there is a group outside the gate requesting entry."

"What? Who are they and why are they here?" Daniel asked.

"I haven't asked yet, but they appear to be a group from a village with elders, women, children, and men. They seem to be in need and hungry," the guard explained.

"Allow them to enter, and I will meet with them," Daniel instructed.

The guard directed the group to enter just beyond the gate, where they were stopped until Daniel arrived.

"Why have you come here?" Daniel asked.

"Your leadership, we are survivors from Lomboy village in the western forest. Our village was destroyed by foreigners who were cutting down trees that fell on our homes. We tried to resist, but their weapons were too powerful for us to fight back," the older man explained.

Daniel asked for some servants to prepare a meal for the group. The group were stuffing food and chugging it down with drinks. After their meal, the women, elders, and children were taken to houses to rest. Daniel spoke with the elder to learn more about their experiences.

"No! This is unacceptable! We need to come together and stand up against this injustice!" Daniel shouted after hearing the elder's story.

"Please, let's not resort to violence. It would be wiser to try and have a conversation with them," advised an elderly woman who had also converted to Christianity who was also eavesdropping on the conversation.

Daniel was familiar with the old lady and her intentions, but he shunned her and her ideals. Instead, he instructed multiple messengers to reach out to their allies and other villages who were interested in a plan to remove the conqueror from their midst.

The elderly woman and other Christian converts continued to oppose Daniel's plan, urging him to consider forgiveness and unity in reaching a compromise with the conquerors. Despite their efforts, Daniel eventually stood up and declared, "I am focused on my role as a leader and will do everything in my power to protect the native residents and their homes!" He then left the Christian gathering, allowing them to continue their service without interference, as long as it did not disrupt the village's living conditions.

The time had arrived. A delegate from the Bokodians arrived, followed by the Kapangan representative and representatives from other villages. Their numbers were greater than expected, and Daniel's quarters was not large enough to accommodate them all. The meeting took place outdoors, with the majority of attendees agreeing with the plan while the few Christian converts voiced their disagreement.

The Dutab mambunong performed a ceremony with prayers to the gods coupled with buttering some pigs, which the Christian converts viewed as devilish. Disappointed, they eventually left the canao and returned to their respective villages. Some representatives observed the spread of Christianity in Dutab, sparking protests and suggestions of exile or even elimination of the converts as if they were enemies.

"No! We must not discriminate as long as no harm comes to us, as I mentioned earlier!" Daniel emphasised.

The representatives regarded him with suspicion, as if he was against them all. A person familiar with him noted his background, highlighting that he is a foreigner. The only representative who appeared to back his proposal of not eliminating the Christian converts was the one from Kapangan. The meeting was chaotic, with most members opposed to Daniel and his beliefs. This also led to animosity towards the Kapangan village. However, the hatred was momentarily halted by various factors, with the suggestion to focus on the current task.

Several of the allies agreed with the idea with a majority being forced into it. They only have one common enemy to target. One common problem for the benefit of the native mountain dwellers.

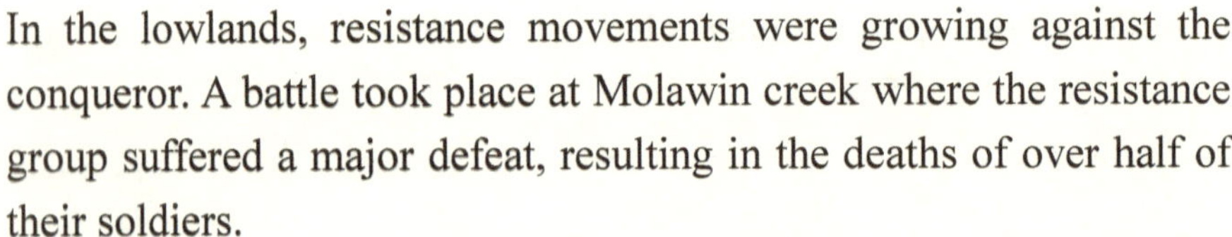

In the lowlands, resistance movements were growing against the conqueror. A battle took place at Molawin creek where the resistance group suffered a major defeat, resulting in the deaths of over half of their soldiers.

The conflict began when the native islanders' children were playing near the creek on the outskirts of the capital. Conqueror soldiers prevented them from swimming even imprisoning some of the children, sparking the revolt. A member of the resistance witnessed the incident and quickly informed their camp. With minimal preparation, the resistance fighters launched an attack on the conqueror's post using basic weapons like knives, bulos, bamboo spears, and a few rifles. The conqueror soldiers, armed with cannons and rapid-firing weapons, easily repelled the attack, killing the resistance fighters before they could reach their target.

A similar fate led to the fall of another resistance group, resulting in the defeat of the fight against the conquerors. The lack of communication among the resistance groups also hindered their unity and ability to launch coordinated attacks, with small groups targeting the much larger conqueror forces.

A christianised native from the mountains named Peter Langdon, who embraced Christianity and lived according to the teachings of God, encountered a group of lost conquerors in the mountains. While gathering firewood for his family, Peter, dressed in pants provided by missionaries and without a shirt, came across the soldiers. Instead of attacking him, the soldiers asked for directions to the center of the mountain villages. Peter guided them to Tirad Pass, leading them to Kafaguay Village where many conquerors had settled with the natives.

Daniel's attack was launched with high hopes of success, despite the primitive weapons of his warriors. Their numbers were enough to challenge the conqueror's forces. Upon reaching the logging area, the warriors wasted no time in attacking, throwing their spears and killing workers. The conqueror's soldiers managed to kill a few warriors with their guns, but they were outnumbered.

The warriors celebrated their victory by shouting and raising the decapitated heads of their enemies. They made sure to inspect the bodies and decapitate them to ensure no survivors. As they prepared to return to Dutab village, Peter's group arrived and caught them off guard, shooting the unprepared warriors. Despite some warriors managing to decapitate a few of the conqueror's soldiers, the tide turned against them. The warriors, though greater in number, were no match for the enemy's advanced weaponry and the element of surprise in the second battle, leading to their defeat.

Daniel was wielding his sword with a golden glow to the cowboy with his revolver guns. Daniel always deflected the bullets from hitting him with his sword. However, as he jumped over the cowboy to deliver a fatal strike, a stray bullet managed to hit him straight in the chest, penetrating his heart.

Everything became white, the ceiling, the walls and even the people's outfits. The room blazed with the sound of laughter, and smiles flared as he opened his eyes.

"May I asked everybody to please wait in the hall to give us space for checking him," the doctor requested.

A man with white coat and a woman with similar fair outfit behind him glared into his eyes.

"Take his vital signs," the man in white coat ordered his female companion.

He observed wires and what looked like a monitor beside him. It was then that he realised he was in the hospital, on a hospital bed.

"Where am I? What am I doing here?" he asked.

"I am Doctor Cruz and you have been in a vehicular accident. The jeepney you have ridden crashed into a concrete barrier. You are now in Santa Elena Hospital."

The native survivors fled from the brutal massacres carried out by the conquerors. The conquerors were cautious and finished off any fallen survivors by shooting or stabbing them, showing no regard for their lives. The escaped survivors aimed to regroup at a safe distance to avoid any more casualties. It was only after they had distanced themselves from the massacre that they took stock of their situation.

"Has anyone seen Daniel?" a warrior asked on their way back on Dutab Kingdom.

With no reply, they proceeded on their journey back to their starting point. Upon reaching the entrance, no one could confirm Daniel's whereabouts, assuming he had perished.

"I had advised him not to join us, but he was adamant," the Kapangan representative remarked, nodding solemnly.

Daniel tried to shift his body in his hospital bed, but it was as rigid as a log. He was unattended, with no one keeping watch over him except for the nurses on duty and visits from the doctor. The only time he glimpsed his colleagues was when he first woke up in the hospital. Apart from that, he was alone.

As the days went by, he regained movement in his upper body in a slow progressive pace, then his lower body. His progress in walking amazed the medical team, who had predicted that he would never walk again.

A nurse came into Daniel's room to check on him and informed him that he had a visitor named Kuchep. Daniel's eyes widened as he allowed the lady to enter.

"You must be wondering who I am and why I'm here," Kuchep said.

"No, you look exactly like Kuchep...Yes, Kuchep," Daniel replied, clearly surprised.

"You know me? Anyway, I only heard about you in the news and wasn't sure if it was you. I'm here to see if you might be my long-lost cousin, as grandpa mentioned before he passed away," She handed an old faded photo of him.

Daniel was amazed on how the lady was able to find him only by the way of the news and a photo. "I can vaguely remember but this kid on the picture, I believe is me. I was about six or seven."

Kuchep stayed for a bit, and during their conversation, they discovered that they were second cousins. It turned out that Kuchep's grandfather on her paternal side was the older sibling of Daniel's grandmother on his maternal side. When the nurse announced that visiting hours were over, Kuchep had to leave. Daniel felt a wave of sorrow surge into his awareness as he grasped the significance of family, something he had never truly appreciated before.

When it was the day of his discharge, the medical staff on his floor cheered him on and applauded him as he was wheeled out of the hospital exit.

"There you go, Daniel!" a nurse exclaimed.

"I am happy for you!" another employee added.

Daniel found himself smiling and feeling joy from the well-wishes of strangers. A taxi arrived in front of the hospital, and the guard smiled at him. "Glad to see you out," the guard said. Daniel returned the smile and even waved at the two, surprising himself.

The taxi driver had a cheerful demeanor and smiled as he asked, "Where are we heading, sir?" Daniel provided his address, and they rode in silence, humming along to the music the driver played in a cheerful manner. When they arrived at Daniel's place, he generously tipped the driver with the cash that the hospital staff had returned and thanked him. An elderly man named Russel saw him and greeted him with a smile. Daniel entered his apartment feeling light-hearted for the first time.

He climbed straight into bed and gazed up at the ceiling. His thoughts were swirling like a gymnast's ribbon. Delicate yet dizzying, mesmerising yet confusing. His mind struggled to make sense of it all. Were these thoughts real or just the fanciful musings of his mind?

Chapter XXVI

He still managed to make time for a trip, despite his busy schedule. It felt like he was gearing up for a journey around the world, as it was his first time venturing outside his familiar surroundings. He struggled to locate a bus station that offered service to his father's hometown. When he arrived at the first bus station, he saw many people waiting for buses.

"Have you booked a ticket?" was the question asked at every ticket counter, a step he had overlooked in order to guarantee a seat. He was told that there was no direct trip to his father's hometown. He would have to travel to the Highland City first that was a popular tourist destination then take another bus ride or any available public transport to his father's hometown. He was also informed about being a standby passenger without a confirmed seat was difficult, especially during the busy summer vacation season.

After checking four bus stations, he eventually managed to secure a last-minute seat in the middle at the back. This was a preferable option to looking for another available seat or enduring a long wait.

"Final boarding announcement for air-conditioned bus 385 bound for the highland city!"

He rushed towards the bus without a ticket and informed the conductor that he was a chance passenger. The conductor told him that he was lucky, as a passenger had canceled at the last minute. He could take their seat in the middle, right by the window corner, even though it was closed for the air conditioning to work. This was different from the regular buses where the windows could be opened, since there was no air conditioning. While the bus was moving, the conductor went to each chance passenger's seat to ask about their destination. He had a ticket booklet with fare prices and dates, using a puncher to punch holes for the corresponding prices and dates, tearing a piece for each passenger.

His impressive height of almost 6 feet barely touched the ceiling, especially with the air conditioning controls close by. Sitting beside him was an older man holding a briefcase, wearing a purple polo shirt, black tie, and slacks. Daniel, curious, guessed that he could be a salesman or an insurance provider or something. The elderly man, with his aged face and receding hairline, smiled and nodded towards him.

The conductor made a second round, asking for the passengers' fare.

"Sir, your fare, please," the conductor requested.

"Fare? How much do I owe you?" Daniel asked.

"Sir, I gave you your ticket a while ago. Haven't you read it?"

"Sir, show me your ticket."

Daniel took the ticket from his front jean pocket and handed it to the conductor.

"That would be 280."

Daniel felt embarrassed when he was unable to read a bus ticket, even though he had no intention of socialising with anyone on the bus. The awkward moment was exacerbated by the presence of an elderly man who observed the situation. Despite being on the verge of saying something, the old man could tell that Daniel was uncomfortable. He simply placed his attaché case in the overhead compartment, took a seat, and pretended to look in the opposite direction.

Daniel and the elderly man dozed off during the journey. They were roused from their sleep by the conductor's announcement. "We have arrived at the first stop. You have 15 minutes to use the restroom and grab some snacks."

Most passengers either went to the restroom or the convenience store. Daniel decided to use the restroom, while the elderly man preferred to spend more time in the facilities. Afterward, Daniel went to the convenience store and bought a pack of large spicy peanuts with dried anchovies and a 500 ml bottle of mineral water. As he left the store, the elderly man entered and attempted to greet Daniel, who ignored him and kept walking.

The elderly man, with a frown on his face and audible heavy breathing due to his large size, took a pack of soda crackers and a 500 ml bottle of mineral water to the counter. He presented his senior citizen ID which entitled him some small discount which happens to be the price of the soda cracker. He moved back to the bus in a manner resembling the speed of a snail.

"Has everyone arrived?" inquired the conductor.

"Since nobody is responding, I'm assuming that everyone is ready to go," he mentioned while taking a seat on the adjustable chair by the bus entrance.

The old man looked at Daniel with concern. "You're not used to people, are you?"

"I apologise. I'm feeling a bit anxious because this is my first time traveling far whilst alone," Daniel said with a nervous smile to the old man.

Daniel gazed at the elderly man with droopy eyes.

"I apologise for the interruption."

"No problem at all."

"I understand that life can be tough. Trust me, I've been through a lot in my years. You need to adapt, or you'll miss out on so much."

Daniel struggled to hold back his tears, not wanting to appear vulnerable. The elderly man, however, could see right through him.

He sensed the sorrow in Daniel's gaze and offered him a tissue to wipe away his tears.

"It's just... thinking about my grandmother, who raised me. I lost her when I was young and had to fend for myself."

"Well, it's okay. Everything will be fine at some point. I... I was a guerrilla fighter against the Japanese and continued my military service in the South against the terrorists. While I was there, I lost my... my wife. I didn't know she died alone."

"Why didn't you have any relatives or close friends?"

"I have a brother that... that I didn't see for 19 years as I continued being a soldier. That's where I'm heading, to visit him or at least spend my last days with him. I'm already 77, and he is about 68 or 69."

"I'm sorry to hear that. I'm sure you'll be reunited with your loved one soon. On my end, I recently discovered that my father has relatives in his hometown, so I'm reaching out to connect with them. That's why I decided to embark on this journey."

"Good luck to the two us."

The two chuckled, relaxed in their seats, and remained quiet until the bus arrived at the next stop. The restaurant they went into was spacious enough to accommodate 80-100 individuals. Daniel guided the elderly gentleman to the restroom at the back of the restaurant, then to the food counter. Daniel asked the old man about his meal choice and seated him at a wooden table with plastic chairs. Daniel then queued up, pointed out the dish he desired from the glass display case, and paid for it at the cash register.

"Here is your meal."

"How much is the bill?"

"I was touched by your story, so there's no charge."

"Thank you. By the way, I forgot to ask your name."

"Alright, I didn't plan on asking yours either, hoping it wouldn't come up. I'm Daniel, and you?"

"My name is Changkulap. It's a traditional name from the highlands, but I can't remember its meaning."

After having lunch together, they returned to the bus and engaged in lively conversations, showing genuine interest in each other's stories for the remainder of the trip.

The bus ascended a winding road through red mountains and pine woods. Daniel is focused and smiling, feeling a lightness within him.

"Ah! The mountains. It's been so long since the last time I experienced the mountains," Changkulap said. Daniel looked at him like a heavy weight had been lifted from him.

"Really? When was the last time you visited?"

"It was about the 60s… Maybe… maybe the 70s."

"That long, huh!"

The bus came to a halt in the middle of the highway. Ahead, there was a line of vehicles ranging from large trucks bigger than the bus to small 4x4 pickup trucks and even two-wheeled motorbikes. The conductor disembarked and walked ahead to see what was causing the delay. He came back a couple of minutes later.

"Guys, please be patient. A bus and a truck crashed into each other. It may take a while before we could pass."

Changkulap reclined once more and shut his eyes. Meanwhile, Daniel disembarked from the bus and stood on the side of the road along with the other male passengers. A police officer and men from various vehicles approached to assist with the accident. They worked together to maneuver the bus into a position that would allow the other vehicle to pass through.

A group of women arrived at the accident scene and recognised the need for more help. Daniel was impressed by their willingness to assist. More support came from the nearby village. The bus driver got on the bus to start it, while two men positioned themselves on either side to help push. Soon after, a dump truck arrived, and the men attached a rope from the dump truck to the front of the bus.

The bus inched forward along the side of the mountain, navigating the sharp curves carefully. It had to be repositioned a few meters to accommodate the mountain's steep incline. The rope holding the bus was straining as it neared its breaking point, but the bus finally came to a stop in a wider section of the road. Applause and cheers erupted from the passengers before they returned to their vehicles as the line of traffic began to move. The bus accelerated and started moving swiftly, prompting him to start running to catch it.

"Wait, we're missing a passenger!" someone yelled.

The bus was unable to come to an immediate stop while climbing the steep road. It paused briefly upon reaching a more level part of the road. The bus conductor promptly exited the bus and rushed back to the accident site. He gestured to Daniel, who was sprinting towards them. Daniel stopped near the bus conductor to catch his breath.

"Sorry about that, but we need to go now," the bus conductor said.

The passengers greeted him with applause as they boarded the bus, relieved to see him.

"Is everything okay now? Is everyone accounted for?" the driver asked.

The passengers all responded together with a yes. There were minimal stops on the journey, and passengers would indicate they wanted to stop by saying "para" (which means stop in Filipino) before getting off. The bus conductor would then help unload the passengers' luggage from the compartment under the bus until they arrived at a city or the final destination at the bus station.

The station looked like a motel, providing rooms for passengers with delayed travel plans or those wanting to stay at the bus company's lodgings. It had a designated baggage storage area and several ticketing booths. The front of the building could be confused for an airport. Daniel hoped to talk to Changkulap before they parted ways, but he couldn't find him in the crowd of passengers getting on and off the buses.

Sitting on the benches near the ticketing booths, he noticed a sign that said "Waiting area." Taking a moment to survey his surroundings, he saw a strong-looking man in uniform with a baton and mace on his belt glancing in his direction. Not making eye contact, he assumed the man was a police officer. Wiping sweat off his forehead, he observed as the police officer walked over when the lines at the ticketing booths briefly cleared.

"Sir, may I help you?" the guard asked.

"I… I… don't know. I don't know where to go."

"Sir, is there anyone who will come and fetch you?"

"None, I am alone and my first time here."

"So, you're not acquainted with this place, right?"

"Yes sir."

The guard flagged down a taxi and directed them to a nearby hotel. Daniel couldn't help but wonder what he was thinking, venturing out into the world without a clear sense of direction. At least he had a general idea of where the highlands was situated.

"Welcome to Igoy County," the taxi driver greeted as he turned on the taxi meter. Daniel returned the smile. "The folks in Igoy County are known for their kindness and honesty, so you're in good hands."

Again, Daniel smiled without saying a word.

After a few minutes of silence, Daniel mentioned, "This is my first time coming to this place."

"Yes sir, the guard told me." "Visiting family? Friends?"

"I am here to discover my heritage. I got a single clue that pointed me towards the highlands during my research."

"Really, I wish you the best, sir. I really do."

Their conversation passed like a feather blown in the wind.

"Here we are, sir. The exact address," the driver said, interrupting the flow of their conversation.

Daniel took his wallet from his right front pocket. The meter indicated the amount of 115.50 Php.

"Here you go. The exact amount."

The taxi driver grabbed a pen and a scrap of paper from the glove compartment. He quickly wrote down his name and phone number. "Sir, here's the deal. Keep this. It's my contact info. Just give me a hundred pesos. Consider the rest as your discount. You are Mr?"

"Thanks, I am Daniel, and what is this paper for?"

"Sir, you can contact me anytime you need a ride, and I will gladly be of service to you."

Daniel handed him the hundred pesos as he was unloading the hiking backpack from the second seat. He nodded and smiled, then took off after receiving the fare.

Daniel stood in front of a maroon gate, a simple rectangular iron structure blocking the view of the main house. He stood there for several minutes, gazing blankly at the gate with his hiking backpack on one side and a man purse slung over his shoulder. The area seemed deserted, with a bungalow house a few blocks away showing no signs of life. The neighbourhood was filled with half-constructed or abandoned buildings, adding to the eerie atmosphere.

"Hotel? Really?'

Dusk was falling. His breath turned misty, resembling that of a smoker, even though he didn't smoke. The cold air seeped into his bones, amplified by his lack of warm clothing. In the distance, a shadowy figure emerged, navigating the shifting light and darkness. As it drew closer, it revealed itself to be a frail human moving slowly, resembling a snail. It was evident what it was.

"Who the hell are you?" an old lady asked from a distance.

"I am Daniel."

"Daniel?"

"The taxi brought me here and I assume this is a hotel."

"Seldom have I got visitors. The only interactions I've got are with that lonely neighbour of mine and when I go to town to buy whatever I need that could not be provided by the land."

Daniel could not answer. His teeth were chattering, and his body was shaking like a mild earthquake.

"Come inside. I think I still have some cowhide jackets of my late husband. You look like you need some warmth so badly."

His legs were almost immobile, paralysed by the icy mist in the air. Seated on the wooden bench in the living room, he was stiff and incapable of any movement. The elderly woman fetched a blanket and a cowhide jacket, assisting him in putting on the jacket and draping the blanket over his chilled body. She then returned from the kitchen with a steaming mug of ginger tea, known as 'salabath.'

"Thank you. I expect to meet my father here but it's obvious that you live alone. I didn't even catch who you are and why I was led to this address."

"Ah… I am Miyek. Your father's town is about an 11–12-hour drive from here. They even have limited communication with only one telegram office."

"Okay, but who are you?"

"Drink your tea to warm your body and have some rest for tomorrow. As I said, I haven't had many visitors. So, you can sleep on the sofa. The restroom is over there whenever you need to go."

Daniel finished his tea. Miyek never offered him dinner or something solid to eat. Anyway, Daniel was too cold to even stand and do something at that point. He pulled the wooden table present to rest his legs and fell asleep.

Daniel was trekking up a huge mountain, surrounded by pine trees and damp moss. He marveled at how easily he could navigate the steep terrain. His legs were sturdy like tree trunks, and his upper body was as powerful as a bull's. A monkey swung from the tree branches, reaching out towards Daniel.

Suddenly, he felt a sharp pain and burning sensation on his neck. The monkey was striking him with its hand like a tennis racket. "Daniel, Daniel," Miyek called from the kitchen. The pain in his neck persisted, and when he reached to touch it, he discovered a large bug which he promptly threw to the floor in disgust.

"Daniel, please come and have your breakfast. You're running late for the first trip to your destination. I need to take you to the jeepney station. You'll need to catch the jeepney with the sign "Igoy County-Dutab" on the windshield. Dutab is the town where your father is located."

"You have to move quickly so that you will not arrive very late."

A taxi with a single passenger was traveling in the direction they were going.

"Flag that taxi. I am too slow, too old for the driver to notice."

"But it has a passenger."

"Just do it."

Daniel had forgotten the taxi he had taken before, which had the contact number. He attempted to hail a taxi, but it didn't stop. He ran after it and banged on the back window.

The taxi finally stopped, and the driver got off the vehicle.

"Are you crazy? Can't you see I have a passenger?"

"Please, back it up a little to that old lady."

The passenger stuck her head through the window and noticed how frail Miyek was.

"It's fine with me. They can ride along."

"Thank you, madam," Daniel rode beside the lady.

They let Miyek sit in the front passenger seat. "Thank you, "anak" (my child). You must know that taxis or rides barely pass on this side of town."

"You are welcome. There's nothing to it," the lady said.

"I'm Daniel, by the way, and she is Miyek. Hope you are not in a hurry."

"Sandra here, and it's okay. Don't worry about it. No rush. My boss just ordered me to buy him some stuff from the town center."

The three shared smiles and stayed quiet until they reached their destinations. Sandra got out of the taxi first and tried to pay, but Daniel refused. When traffic got in their way, Sandra took Daniel's offer and left quickly. Maybe Daniel was starting to become more willing to be open with others.

Daniel did not accept the change when it was their turn to exit the taxi. He viewed the change as the driver's tip without needing to request it. Miyek pointed out the line of jeepneys on the side of the road that were headed to Dutab. As Daniel stepped out of the taxi, he looked back for Miyek but she had disappeared. Puzzled, he asked the vendor selling boiled bananas and fried peanuts, who was next to the first parked jeepney, if he had seen an old lady. The vendor replied that he had no idea who Daniel was referring to.

His senses were heightened, and the feeling that he couldn't explain crawled all over him. He sat on one of the jeepneys, which nobody minded, not even the owner of the vehicle. He rested for a minute or two before a guy who was the dispatcher; a person responsible for calling and guiding passengers shouted, "Dutab! Dutab! Dutab!… Mapan (heading for)…Dutab!"

"Sir, are you going to Dutab?" he asked Daniel, who was lying in the jeepney.

"Ah… Yes!"

"This is the next stop. Please remain seated, as there are other passengers boarding. If you wish, you can sit next to the driver."

"Thank you, I think I will take the front seat."

"Hand me your backpack, sir, and I will put it on the top load."

"Sir, the fare is 180 pesos," the dispatcher said, with his arm stretched towards Daniel.

"Oh, I have to pay the fare right now?"

The dispatcher nodded, and Daniel handed over the exact amount.

The sun was shining bright, and the temperature was gradually increasing to a pleasant warmth. The journey was going smoothly with plenty of twists, turns, and sudden changes in elevation, reminiscent of the winding highway lined with pine trees. The rhythmic motion of the road caused Daniel to doze off. However, the journey soon became rough as the jeepney hit a bump, jolting Daniel awake as his cheek collided with the dashboard. With a sudden alertness, he could feel every bump and dip in the road as the vehicle shook and rattled. This was a stark contrast to his previous trip from the capital to Igoy Country.

The driver giggled a little upon seeing what's happened to Daniel. "You are not used to rough roads, are you?"

"I didn't realise how bumpy and dangerous the roads to Dutab are, especially on your side. A single mistake could send us plunging down the ravine."

"Yeah, you have to be used to it when traveling in these parts of the world."

"It is… my… first time," Daniel responded with an embarrassed demeanor. "Anyway, when is the stop?"

The driver looked at him with a weird, unexplained expression, as if asking such a question was ridiculous.

"You really did not travel in this area. There is no stop."

"What if you need to go to the urinate or are hungry and need to eat?"

"Just let me know, and I will search for a wider part of the road to do your business."

"And the food?"

"Every passenger has their baon (packed meals and drinks)."

"I need to urinate then."

The driver looked for a wider area on the road. Unfortunately, it took them around 20 minutes to find the spot. Daniel hurried to the back of the jeepney and relieved himself on a bush. The force even caused some leaves to fall off. He dashed on his returned to the vehicle, and they continued with their journey.

"I see a worm….. a worm…" one of the lady passengers teased.

Daniel did not get what the lady said at first because he thought she was talking about something he didn't know about. Everybody laughed so intensely the mountains could hear.

"Hey, your bird. Your bat," the driver said with a smirk on his face.

"My bat?... hey!" Daniel shouted, but he knew everybody was joking.

An old lady handed Daniel a boiled banana. "Here, I thought you might be hungry since you don't have a baon yourself."

Daniel, feeling embarrassed, took the banana from the back with gratitude.

"Wash it with some of my water," the driver handed his water canteen.

"Thanks," Daniel said, attempting to avoid the canteen lid touching his lip. The roughness of the road caused him to spill some of the water.

The trip led them to a two-storey concrete retro building with peeling paint. The frontage said Dutab Municipal Hall. Everybody got off the jeepney except the driver and two elder passengers.

"Do you know where you're heading?" the driver asked.

"No, actually," Daniel answered, looking around.

The driver pointed him towards a municipal employee who had been there during their discussion. He then drove the two elderly individuals to their homes and later parked his jeepney in the municipal parking lot before walking home.

"Hi, do you know anyone here?" the employee asked.

"I am not actually sure but according to my research, this is the hometown of the Kibara and my father is named Julio."

"Oh, you are a Kibara."

"Do you know where the house is?"

"Of course. Let me just inform my office that I will be out for a while."

The employee led Daniel on a 10-13-minute walk to meet the Kibaras. They talked and got to know each other. The employee was familiar with Daniel's story, which the town assumed was just a made-up story.

They knocked on the door of an old house that resembled a log cabin. The galvanised iron had turned a rusty colour from age. The door was crafted from a discarded old tire that had been flattened into the shape of an entrance. The employee knocked on the wooden part of the door. It was opened by a young fair-skinned lady with striking beauty, giving the impression that she may have had some Caucasian ancestry.

"Yes?"

"I just accompanied Daniel here who claimed to be your relative."

"Alright, I'll need to check with my uncle."

The woman allowed Daniel and the employee to enter while she went to find her uncle.

"Are you Julio's son?" the uncle asked, his eyes widening at the striking resemblance to Julio.

"Yes, that's correct. I'm just trying to learn more about my heritage."

"Who is your mother?"

"I'm not certain, but my grandmother was Petara. She passed away when I was nine years old."

"Why didn't you mention that earlier? I'm Paklit, your uncle. Your father, Julio, was my cousin."

"This is Christina, your second cousin."

"Nice to meet you," he said, shaking her hand eagerly.

After the employee returned to work, Daniel, Christina, and Paklit stayed behind to chat. Paklit shared the story of how Daniel's parents first met and the events that led to their separation.

According to Paklit, Martha, who was Daniel's mother, came from a wealthy family with numerous businesses in the city. Martha's parents disapproved of Julio because he was not as affluent as their family. The deaths of both parents were also marked by tragedy. They tried to run away to elope while Martha was pregnant, but they were caught in a lightning storm during heavy rain. Julio died immediately, and Martha was taken to the hospital but passed away later. An emergency c-section was performed to save Daniel, whom Martha's parents did not want to be involved with, so he ended up with Julio's parents. Paklit accompanied Daniel as they visited his father's grave, a simple mound of stones with a metal cross in the family cemetery.

The following day, a wedding was being organised just a kilometer from Julio's house. Every home was busy with preparations. Neighbours, relatives, and friends from the unfamiliar town, where Daniel was a stranger, were all participating. He watched the mix of traditional and Christian rituals planned for the wedding, which brought back memories of his time living in the mountains, especially during the second invasion when the conquerors introduced the mountain residents to the Christian religion.

Daniel was enthusiastic about helping out in any capacity. However, the townspeople, especially the men, questioned his skills when it came to tasks like chopping firewood, butchering pigs, and other wedding preparations typically done by men. They recommended that he stay at his uncle's house and only attend the wedding reception for lunch, where he could witness some pre-wedding customs led by the town's mambunong.

Expressing his willingness to help, Daniel told his uncle Paklit who was busy butchering a pig. Despite Paklit's doubts about his ability to handle heavy labor, Daniel insisted that he could manage. Paklit eventually allowed Daniel to gather firewood from the woods. The townspeople watched in amazement as Daniel excelled in the tasks assigned to him, chopping trees without effort and carrying logs as if he had been doing it his whole life. His body seemed to remember his past experiences from the ancient world, making him a *natural* at the chores.

Chapter XXVII

The wedding took place at the only church in town, which happened to be the Catholic church. While there was a Protestant fellowship in the area, it was not as well-established as the Catholic church. The traditional Catholic wedding ceremony was conducted by a priest officiating the event.

As a foreigner, Daniel was given the honour of sitting in the front rows near the stage. Throughout the ceremony, people glanced at him and whispered to each other. They didn't even mind his towering height that almost overshadowed everybody at the back. One of the bridesmaids seemed particularly interested in him, but he chose to focus on the wedding and not engage with her advances, out of respect for the couple and their families.

At the reception, Daniel was given a seat at the principal sponsors' table. He was introduced to the sponsors, who graciously accepted him and welcomed him as a guest.

"How are you finding the wedding?" one sponsor asked.

"I am quite enjoying the wedding," Daniel responded.

"Don't hold back, just enjoy the food," another sponsor said.

After the meal, a program followed as the second part of the event. Singing intermissions were performed with great emotion for the newlyweds. Sponsors shared heartfelt pieces of advice, and Daniel, who had only crashed the wedding, was unexpectedly given the opportunity to speak in front of everyone.

"I wasn't supposed to speak here because I am not familiar with the newlyweds. I feel like a wedding crasher. Besides, I am not in the position to share advice for a newlywed as I am single myself. I only came on stage with the newlywed's request. For those who don't know me, I am Daniel, the son of Julio Sungkian and a woman from the capital city. I came here to find my relatives based on my own research. All I can say is to wish the two of you a happy wedding and I hope that you will always support each other through the good and bad times in your marriage. Once again, congratulations on your wedding and may God bless you both."

The audience applauded with smiles and lot of positivity vibes at his speech. The elder men were getting the instruments ready for the tayaw dance. The newlyweds were tasked with performing the first tayaw, followed by Daniel dancing with a partner as requested. His partner was the bridesmaid who had been glancing and smiling at him in church. The crowd cheered as they watched Daniel confidently execute the steps, accompanied by the gangsa, solibao, and tikitik. His partner, who played the lady's role, winked at him and flashed a sweet smile as she was executing her dance movement.

After his turn as the tayaw was finished, many people approached him to show their appreciation for his excellent performance. Some shook his hand, others expressed their gratitude verbally, and some simply nodded in approval. His partner kept glancing at him throughout the entire wedding celebration. When the crowd thinned out a bit, she finally took the opportunity to chat with him.

"Hello, I'm Xi Yan," she said with a smile as he greeted Daniel.

"I'm Daniel."

"I know. I've heard your name before."

"Xi Yan, you must have Chinese heritage. Your eyes are slanted and your fair skin is unique," Daniel observed.

"Yes, my father was Chinese, but I've never met him since birth. My mom is Kuling and is now married to Bula-es," Xi Yan explained.

"Nice to meet you," Daniel said.

They chatted like they were friends for a long time at the back of the reception venue, discussing their interests and Daniel inquiring about Dutab municipality and life there.

Magic and destiny must be true. There was a certain sparkle in Daniel and Xi Yan's smiles that seemed to indicate something significant in their hearts.

"Come on. Grab your wat-wat and let's head home. Unless you'd rather stay," Christina interrupted.

"Okay, I'll come with you," Daniel said with last glance at Xi Yan. They returned to the house missing the dance for all at the after wedding party. Daniel quickly went to the toilet to relieve himself. The food must have caused a sudden urge to go. It wasn't a complete disaster in the bathroom, but there were large chunks of smelly waste that filled the house leaving an unpleasant trail in the air.

"Wow! The house smells so bad, you must have had a bad case of diarrhea!" Christina exclaimed as she opened all the windows.

Daniel emerged with a cherry face. Christina instructed him to go outside to let the air dissipate the smell. Daniel stood near the main entrance, where others with wat-wat in hands from the wedding were standing. They greeted Daniel as he waved back. A passing couple asked him why he was outside, to which he responded with a wave and a smile.

"Sorry, the smell has dissipated. You can come in now." Daniel settled on the couch while Christine took a seat in a chair next to it. As the day turned into night, they both drifted off. Meanwhile, Paklit was still at the wedding, indulging in alcohol and enjoying the company of friends and fellow townspeople.

Paklit sat near the wooden fire where they did the cooking. Another man Mayma was having conversations with him. Their heads were full of alcohol. Other men passed and took shots of the alcohol in front of the two, the San Miguel Gin, and returned to their positions. Paklit separated a hind leg of the butchered pig to take home but Mayma took it from the hiding place and gave it to his nephew to take home. Suddenly, a groggy Paklit went where he had hidden the pig leg expecting to find it there but nothing.

"Where the hell is my leg!" he shouted, attempting to provoke the man next to the hiding spot.

"I have nothing to do with your damn leg!" the man replied, annoyed by Paklit's alcohol-laden breath near his face.

The man then pushed Paklit, causing him to fall onto the 'ebey,' the wild grass serving as a makeshift chopping board. Another man helped Paklit to his feet.

"We saw Ba-ay take the leg," a bystander chimed in.

Paklit approached Mayma with a wide grin on his face, looking as though he might explode. Their faces were so close, it seemed like one might bite the other while the other was ready to throw a punch. The onlookers held them back as they both yelled.

"You stole my share! I had the right to that leg for helping with the butchering and cooking!" Paklit yelled, attempting to scratch Mayma.

"No way! I claimed it fair and square. You're out of luck!" Mayma retorted.

Their drunken state made it easy for the crowd to subdue them. They were eventually escorted out of the wedding venue, with Paklit being guided home. Mayma was left lying on the ground, disliked by the townspeople for his troublemaking ways. His nephew eventually came to take him home.

Paklit slept on the cold cement floor at home and woke up early in the morning. He took a refreshing cold bath in the spring without the cleaning powers of shampoo and soap, then changed into fresh underwear and clothes. This revitalised him and gave him a new burst of energy. Later, he was seen boiling water in an aluminum kettle at the outdoor cooking area behind the house, using wood to start the fire.

"Have some coffee," he said as he poured some into the two porcelain cups, handing one to Daniel and one to Christine.

"What happened yesterday, Uncle?" Christine inquired.

"I have no memory of how I got home. I woke up this morning and found myself lying on the floor," he replied.

"You two stay here, I need to go feed the chickens," Christine said.

"What do people do for fun around here besides attending weddings?" Daniel asked.

"We have the Agno River at the base of the mountain, Mt. Timbac where the cave with mummified remains of our ancestors is located, and various forests and nature to explore," he explained.

"I have to go to my garden now. Those carrots won't take care of themselves," he added.

Daniel offered to help with the garden, demonstrating his readiness to roll up his sleeves and get to work. He had shed his inhibitions and was prepared to do whatever was necessary to lend a hand. Paklit paused, deep in thought, with his index finger and thumb on his chin in a contemplative pose. Daniel watched him with anticipations. "Alright," Paklit finally said, "You can come and immerse yourself in the Dutab way of life."

Paklit picked up the hoe and urged Daniel to do the same. They hiked a few kilometers on the mountainside towards the east. Despite his previous night's drinking, Paklit showed no signs of being hungover. He didn't faint, experience shortness of breath, or show any other symptoms. What was even more impressive was his endurance while using the hoe to weed the carrot garden with precision. Daniel kept up with him, but he needed to take occasional sips of water from the nearby spring, unlike Paklit who only drank water after completing his task.

The work was completed in just half a day, with tasks including weeding, watering the vegetables, and applying a small amount of organic fertiliser from the decomposed food scraps and animal droppings pile. They sat at a simple structure resembling a kubo house without walls, resting and gazing at the gardens on the mountainside that looked like a stairway.

Paklit asked Daniel if he had plans to meet the rest of the family while he was visiting, against the backdrop of the breathtaking scenery. Daniel admitted that he hadn't considered it before, as his life had been focused on work and making a living without taking any risks in life. However, he expressed a desire to discover his identity and understand the meaning of having a family.

In the mountain community, it was rare for people to share intimate feelings or engage in heart-to-heart conversations as it was not a common practice within the culture. Paklit seemed to empathise with Daniel's sentiments, lighting a cigarette with a match and exhaling smoke like a dragon.

"I've never seen a cigarette like that before. A green cigarette?" Daniel asked, looking at the smoke with curiosity.

"Well, this is made with ped-ped (wild leaves used as a cigarette paper substitute) for the outer covering and filled with five fingers," Paklit explained.

"Five fingers?" Daniel asked staring at it with much amazement.

"Yes, it's marijuana, maryjane."

"Is that even legal?"

"Not technically, but the authorities usually turn a blind eye."

"Besides, it has been part of the mountain natives usage as medicine or recreation."

Daniel continued to watch his uncle smoke the marijuana like a regular cigarette. His uncle even offered him some, but he politely declined.

Paklit suggested that it was almost time for lunch and recommended that they go home. He then stood up and began walking.

Chapter XXVIII

The lunch consisted of stew made from recycled water, cabbage, and giant onions. Daniel noticed a strong smell coming from the 'bungsos,' a preserved intestine soaked in salt brine for days or even weeks.

"I was ready for anything except that foul-smelling intestine," Daniel said, covering his nose and mouth.

"This is tasty, smelly but tasty. It's cooked, after all," Christine remarked.

"Give it a try, even just a small bite," Paklit urged.

Upon tasting the bungsos, Daniel reacted with distaste at first, but developed a liking for the dish later on, which was reserved for special rituals.

A new telegram service in town had been operating for several months without any clients. The only message they received was for Daniel from his job.

The message read: "Daniel... Return to work... Supervisor..."

Daniel and Christine had planned to visit the Timbac Cave to see the mummies, including their ancestor Apo Kibara. However, the telegram indicated that Daniel was needed back at work soonest. He promised Christine and his Uncle Paklit that he would return soon and provided his address and telephone numbers for both his apartment and workplace in the capital city.

His return to work was smooth. He was the first person to arrive at the office, aside from the janitor who unlocked the door. His desk was piled high with papers. He felt frustrated, as he couldn't believe that no one had been able to take over his work while he was away.

"This is going to be a long day. I need to get started right away."

His primary task was to manage the inventory of sales for the company's core business of selling kitchen utensils, including pots, pans, plates, forks, spoons, mugs, and various other kitchen and dining items. He found that additional responsibilities from different departments within the company were also added to his workload. These individuals often neglected their duties and depended on his intelligence and efficiency to finish their tasks.

The employees entered one by one after a few minutes. Many passed Daniel as if he had been working continuously at his job. They didn't notice his absence or presence, and they didn't even have the audacity to greet him with good morning or to say hi, especially those for whom he had done work for a long time.

Daniel didn't react but continued with the task at hand. He didn't complain directly to those ungrateful workers. Unbeknownst to the employees whose work Daniel had completed, he took pictures and made written accounts of the workload he had done for others. He used to provide details to those who were supposed to do the work, but things had changed. He had the courage to stand up for himself and took a passive approach to seek revenge.

Brandon, one of the employees, found out about Daniel's actions. He was reprimanded for the incident and warned that further behavior like that would result in termination. During a lunch break in the company's canteen, he confronted Daniel like a raging wolf.

"Daniel! You ratted me out which I don't like! You'll see!" Brandon got up close to Daniel's face.

Despite Daniel being taller, Brandon's muscular build made him a formidable opponent.

"Go ahead! Take a swing! I dare you! Come on! So that everybody could witness the true you!" Daniel responded with newfound confidence.

Brandon was detained by his colleagues in the office, causing the rest of the day to proceed as usual. Daniel was engrossed with his work when his supervisor summoned him to his office. "What could this be about? What does the boss need from me?" Daniel wondered, anxiety was building up. He walked into the office in a calm, cool demeanor, hiding his inner turmoil.

"You call for me, sir?"

"Ah, yes, Mr. Daniel."

"The incident of you making those reports, even the reports that you shouldn't have done came to my attention."

"Yes, sir. That is true."

"Do you want to take any action on it? I am willing to support you."

"I appreciate your gesture, sir, but I have already addressed it."

"Are you certain?"

"Yes, sir, and thank you again."

"Alright then. If you need anything related to your work, feel free to approach me."

"Yes, sir."

"I don't want any chaos in the workplace; you can now return to work."

Daniel felt a weight lifted off his shoulders. Knowing that someone cared about his seemingly insignificant life gave him a newfound sense of purpose. He approached his work with a fresh perspective, valuing even the smallest details as much as major events. This pride in his work boosted his productivity.

At the end of the day, when it was time to go home, Daniel remained full of energy and enthusiasm to complete his work as if there was no other opportunity to do so. Brandon also stayed behind, pretending to do some extra work. He was accompanied by three of his close buddies and co-workers, who seemed to be under some sort of hypnotic or mind control influence from Brandon. They always obeyed everything that Brandon commanded them to do.

Around 11 pm, Daniel finished the task at hand and prepared to head home. He tried to flag down a taxi, but nobody was stopping. Brandon and his friends ambushed him with a sudden attack.

"Keep moving! He's not getting in your taxi!" Brandon yelled as the taxi was pulling up to Daniel.

Daniel was held back by the three individuals as he struggled to break free. Brandon swiftly punched him in the stomach, causing Daniel to collapse, memories of the past accident and some episode of his mountain experiences flooded his mind.

"You think you're better than me!" Brandon yelled in Daniel's face.

In response, Daniel delivered an uppercut, initiating a physical altercation. He fought back fiercely, overpowering his attackers. He slammed one to the ground and delivered kicks to the others. With swift movements, he seemed to wield his invisible sword similar to when he was fighting in the mountains, his long arms striking Brandon and his friends, causing them to fall to the ground.

"Hey! Stop right there!" a security guard rushed to them, armed with a flashlight, baton, and a 38-caliber firearm.

The guard requested additional assistance, and two more guards pursued Brandon and his friends, while Daniel was restrained on the ground. Brandon managed to escape, but the other two were apprehended. They were brought to a windowless room with only a few plastic chairs. The police and company supervisor were informed about the incident.

Brandon and his friends were terminated, and Daniel received a one-month suspension without pay following the company's internal investigation. The police inquired if Daniel intended to report and take legal action against Brandon and his friends, but Daniel declined, deeming it not worth the effort. He decided to return to Dutab to resume his journey of self-discovery.

He had everything planned out, from packing his clothes to checking his supplies and booking his bus ticket in advance. He didn't inform his work because he wasn't sure if he would return to his ancestral domain on a permanent basis. All he knew was that he was eager to experience more of Dutab.

At the bus station, he boarded the bus that matched the number on his ticket and took his seat by the aisle. Soon after, a woman who resembled Xi Yan sat across from him, also by the aisle. Daniel's eyes lit up and he smiled, but the woman looked at him as if he was out of his mind.

"Why are you looking at me like that?" she asked.

"It's me, Daniel!" he said, still smiling at her.

"Daniel? I don't know you at all."

"Yes, you do! We met at the wedding! You were a bridesmaid and we had a conversation!"

"Please stop talking to me like that! It's strange and I'm certain we've never met before!"

The lady turned away as the bus started to move.

After a few minutes of the bus ride, Daniel caught the lady's attention once again. She was still puzzled by Daniel's behavior. Despite his efforts to explain himself, the lady couldn't understand why he was so insistent on talking to her. It wasn't until Daniel referred to her as Xi Yan that she realised he was mistaking her for her twin sister. She clarified that she was actually Yichen, the twin sister. They both laughed about the mix-up, and Daniel apologised, which Yichen graciously accepted. They chatted once and a while during the journey and even shared a table during a lunch break.

The bus driver warned the passengers, "Get ready. There's a police checkpoint up ahead." As predicted, a group of police officers armed with long barrel guns and short backup weapons on their waists stopped the bus at a temporary barrier marked "Police Checkpoint." The passengers were asked to disembark while the officers conducted a thorough search of the bus. After giving a thumbs-up signal, one of the officers signaled for the passengers to reboard the bus and continue their journey.

"What was that all about?" a curious passenger asked.

"There were killings on this road just the other day. They were mandated to do a checkpoint for every vehicle passing," the bus conductor answered.

They reached their destination. Daniel asked Yichen to pass on his regards to her twin sister. They both chuckled at the mix-up. Yichen agreed to fulfill his request and they said their goodbyes.

Daniel arrived at his uncle's house where there was a larger group than previously. An older man wearing glasses greeted him at the door. Although he didn't recognise Daniel, he assumed he might be a relative due to his blurred vision.

"Who are you just barging in like that?" a teenage boy demanded.

"I'm Daniel Kibara," he replied, emphasising his family name.

"I've never seen you before. Are you an uncle, cousin, or some unknown brother?" the teenage boy inquired.

"Is Uncle Paklit here? He can clarify," Daniel suggested.

A young lady appeared from the kitchen. "Who's this handsome stranger?" she asked.

"Hey, that's your relative! He's a Kibara!" Paklit announced as he came out of his room.

"All of you! Come! Let's gather!" Paklit exclaimed.

"He then proceeded to introduce Daniel to everyone. Daniel recognised many of his relatives' names, such as his second cousin Kuchep, a nephew from a cousin named Tampulak, an aunt named Kitan, and others.

Daniel felt a sense of comfort as he was welcomed with open arms by them, yet he couldn't ignore the nagging sensation that their names held a strange familiarity. Despite this, he engaged in conversation with everyone present, uncovering hidden family histories and stories of the elders that only intensified his sense of connection. It was as if he had known them and shared a past life with their ancestors, a notion that seemed far-fetched but resonated deeply within him.

"I almost forgot! Dinner is at Grandma Kuling's house," Paklit mentioned.

They all prepared for a mountain hike because Grandma Kuling's house was located on Akey, the mountain visible from Paklit's backyard.

"How old is Grandma Kuling?" Daniel asked as they made their way to her.

"She's around 89, 90, or maybe even 91. It's just an estimate because during her youth, they didn't have birth certificates. She was only registered and given a birth date when the colonisers arrived," Stumbalik, Daniel's late father's cousin, explained.

"She's so stubborn. She refuses to leave her house, her vegetable garden, and her animals even when some of us offered to take care of her in town proper or even in the city," another relative named Albert added.

The family reached Grandma Kuling's house. Daniel was amazed at how the elderly lady was able to prepare such a delicious meal. On the table, there were boiled sweet potatoes, stir-fried wild greens, boiled etag with black beans, and steamed red rice. The meal was plentiful, and it seemed like Grandma Kuling had prepared just the right amount for everyone, almost as if she had planned it in advance. Even more surprising is that Grandma Kuling interacts with them as if she were as young as a robust flower.

The walls of her house were constructed from thick, sturdy logs, and the roof appeared to be made of a tightly woven material. The interior was adorned with carvings inspired by the local mountain people and their environment. Once again, Daniel was impressed by the craftsmanship.

"Who is this guy?" Grandma Kuling asked.

"That's Daniel, Julio's son," Paklit replied.

"I had no idea Julio had a son."

"Well, apparently he does, and he's right here," Kitan added.

"Hello, Grandma Kuling," Daniel greeted.

Grandma Kuling invited him to sit close and talk with her. They talked about Julio, Dutab, and exchanged life stories. Daniel found Grandma Kuling's stories very familiar, as he was well-versed in his culture and its history. He just needed to recall them accurately. Grandma Kuling gave him palata, ancient coins believed to bring good luck. Some relatives noticed her action, and while Christine and Paklit were unfazed, others seemed puzzled by it.

"Out of all the grandchildren, Grandma Kuling chose you to give the palata," Albert whispered from the kitchen table in amazement.

Albert was always on the lookout for opportunities that would benefit him. At his age of the 50's, he had a clear understanding of his own identity. Everyone also had a clear perception of his true identity. While he appeared sweet and friendly on the surface, he was often described as a "wolf in sheep's clothing." Despite his family's love and patience, he continued to take advantage of their love and generosity. That was simply who he was.

After the gathering, it was time to head home. Christina gathered two pieces of firewood and lit them to create wooden torches. She gave one to Kitan and kept the other for herself. The group exited together but split up, with Albert accompanying Kitan's group to the west and Daniel going with the group moving to the opposite direction.

"What's up with Albert?" Daniel asked as they walked away from the other group.

"Don't worry about him. He's always been like that. We don't fully trust him, but he is still family. We just need to be cautious around him and watch what we say or do," Paklit explained.

"Yah! Don't pay attention to him. Just be extremely cautious around him!" Christine exclaimed.

"By the way, I don't have any harvest for tomorrow and I have a day to spare. If you're interested, I can join you and some of our family members to visit Timbac cave to visit the mummies," Paklit said.

They all went to rest the night off to live another day.

Despite numerous attempts to locate Daniel, particularly by those who believed he was the true chosen one or saviour, he remained elusive. Skilled trackers and searchers did their best, but as time passed without his presence, his memory faded. It was concluded that he had likely perished during the initial confrontation with the conqueror.

The conquerors continued their logging and mining activities, establishing large industries around extracting natural resources. The native dwellers of the mountains formed pacts among the villages through peace-pacts in an effort to drive the conquerors away and maintain their connection with nature, which they deeply respected.

Unfortunately, they were unable to overthrow the conqueror's power, and the activities persisted. The situation was further complicated by the increasing number of native Christian converts who had adopted the conqueror's way of life. Over time, Daniel became a figure of folklore and uncertainty arose among the natives about his existence, questioning whether he was a real person or just a character in a fantastical tale.

The conqueror's progress in the mountains continued. They introduced schools, commercial buildings, advanced agriculture, and industries without causing any obvious harm to the natives. A period of peace ensued.

However, it became clear that the conquerors' true intentions differed from their teachings, which had been temporarily masked by their seemingly benevolent activities. Large gold mining corporations were established, electricity was generated through the construction of dams that flooded rivers and nearby resources, and the Kafaguay village was transformed into the first industrial city. The Dutab Kingdom became the government center for the conqueror, who implemented English as the mode of communication for everyone.

The memory of the chosen one, gods, and mythical creatures had become obscure, only appearing in legendary tales. The natives had embraced Christian beliefs and Western culture and traditions, leading to a decline in the practice of old traditions among the natives. In fact, many traditional practices were considered evil, leading the indigenous people to abandon customs such as the mambunong, tattoos, headhunting, and other cultural traditions that became socially unacceptable. Country music was embraced by the natives more than their traditional musical styles. They admired iconic country artists like Johnny Cash, Merle Haggard, Hank Williams, and many others. Often emulating their cowboy boots, hats, acoustic guitars, and twangy vocals. "Country roads, take me home, to the place I belong..."

The family visit to Grandma Kuling left a lasting impression on Daniel, even though he couldn't recall the specifics or why it had resonated with him. What he did know for sure was that it had given him a strong sense of his identity and heritage. This newfound awareness motivated him to explore and embrace this aspect of himself that had been hidden for so long. He was excited to delve into his roots and understand the connection he had to the indigenous people of the mountain.

That evening, Albert absentmindedly twirled his mustache as he pondered. He had a restless night, consumed by Grandma Kuling's choice to bestow the palata upon Daniel, a newcomer to her knowledge. Albert worried that Grandma Kuling might be contemplating Daniel as a potential inheritor of her estate, which encompassed the house, a 487-square-meter vegetable garden, and an entire mountain. It was possible that Daniel was being considered as the sole heir, with the palata acting as an initial sign.

The day in town was typical, with people busy tending to their vegetable gardens and rice fields. The professionals, including politicians, government employees, teachers, and a lone midwife, were also going about their day. Daniel, Paklit, Christine, and three other relatives enjoyed a breakfast of stewed pesing (taro leaves and stems) with kintoman (red rice) and chili oil for dipping sauce.

"Remember, we're hiking to Timbac cave today. Make sure to bring water and snacks, as there won't be any stores along the way," Paklit reminded them during breakfast.

Paklit stuck with his original outfit for the hike, opting for jean shorts, flip flops, an old wrinkled t-shirt, and a faded cap. In contrast, Daniel and the rest of the group wore jogging pants, sneakers, and appropriate jackets and headgear for protection. Christine, however, wore old jeans, flip-flops, and just a t-shirt. The contrast between the two groups was stark: those accustomed to hiking versus those who only did so when necessary.

Chapter XXIX

The hike progressed slowly, resembling a slithering snake. The mothers, children, and visiting men were causing the pace to slow down. Paklit and Christine were impressed by Daniel's ability to endure the high-altitude hike. Paklit, Christine, and Daniel were the only ones who took sips of water, unlike the others who had finished their snacks and water bottles along the way. They were also catching their breath with a sense of despair after climbing the mountain to reach the top where the cave was situated.

"Where did you learn to hike? Or better yet, how did you manage to survive the hike?" Kuchep asked, leaning against the entrance of the cave. Daniel stood in front of the entrance.

"I'm not sure, to be honest. The longer I stay here, the more it feels like I belong. Like I've been here and lived this life before," Daniel replied.

"What does that mean? It's a bit strange."

"I'm not sure. It's just..."

Paklit silently departed from the group without saying anything. His absence went unnoticed until they reached the cave. They were confused by the iron gate secured with a padlock, unsure of how to gain entry. Eventually, Paklit reappeared with a woman holding a set of keys.

"I went to the caretaker's house to get the key for the gate," he explained.

"Hello, I'm Sharon, the caretaker of Mt. Timbac. I work for the government to ensure that tourists and visitors do not harm the mummies or the cave," she introduced herself.

Sharon explained that only one visitor at a time, including herself, was allowed to enter. Visitors were not permitted to touch anything, including the cave walls, wooden coffins, and mummies, and vandalism was strictly prohibited. They were also instructed to follow all of Sharon's guidelines.

Each person felt the eerie presence of death in the cave. Their hair stood on end, as if anticipating a horrifying demise. The reason for this sensation was unclear. It was thought that the mummified bodies belonged to important figures in society, like the leaders, wealthy individuals and powerful warriors. It was believed that the desecration of the burial site would bring misfortune not only to the individual but also to their descendants. It was crucial to follow all the caretaker's instructions.

"I almost forgot. You are the Kibaras. One of the mummies was the old man Kibara but nobody knows specifically. If you want you can come to the office where I also live and have some freshly brewed coffee and left over rice cake," Sharon offered.

They all visited the caretaker's office, a wooden house with a galvanised iron roof. Inside, the living room was adorned with historical photos of Dutab, artifacts, and people, each with detailed descriptions. Actual artifacts like old baskets, bolos, clothes, and more were also on display. A shelf held books about various mountain tribes and historical events, creating a mini museum and library for all to enjoy.

Sharon guided them to a room that resembled a kitchen, equipped with a dining table for one and wooden chairs placed around it. The room also featured a fireplace that doubled as a cooking area, as well as a cabinet with a glass door displaying kitchen utensils. She brought out two thermoses and a generous portion of rice cakes. "Here are the snacks. You can find forks and cups in the cabinet. Enjoy," Sharon informed them.

They conversed, with Sharon sharing the history of Kibara and highlighting the importance of some of their ancestors. Some had been World War II heroes who fought against the Japanese, while others had held leadership positions in the ancient Dutab Kingdom and played various other significant historical roles. Daniel was one of the keen listeners, asking Sharon more questions than the others in the group, especially the younger ones who seemed disinterested. Albert remained mostly silent, shooting glances at Daniel as if his gaze could be lethal.

When it was time to head back home, the group expressed their gratitude to Sharon, who in turn mentioned that they were always welcome to visit again. Albert continued to sneak glances at Daniel on the way back.

"Hey, could you please stop that?" Paklit scolded Albert, with everyone else agreeing.

"Yes, we're here to enjoy Dutab and each other as a family," Kitan added, noticing Albert's behavior towards Daniel.

Albert was not pleased with the comments made about him. He distanced himself from the group, muttering, "This is ridiculous... Daniel shouldn't have been given the palata! I'm not even sure if he's a Kibara..." as he walked away.

He has not been seen since, and they were wondering where he could have gone. The group he was with searched Paklit's residence first and then the neighboring areas. Despite the few recognisable houses, they did not find him. They noticed that Albert's belongings were missing, leading them to believe that he had left for the city.

They allowed it to go unnoticed and carried on with their activities. Paklit had to take care of his garden, and to his surprise, many of his older relatives came to help, with Christine and Daniel leading them. Meanwhile, the children and teenagers left were debating with their parents, guardians, and elders about leaving for the city, just like their Uncle Bert did. They were unhappy because there were no ice cream, burgers, or video games, and they were missing their friends from the city.

After completing their tasks, everyone decided to visit Asapa Falls, the largest waterfall in town. Although it was relatively close to the town, the only challenge was the slightly steep climb required to reach it. While the adults had no issue with the ascent, the children and teenagers were hesitant to hike again after their challenging experience at Timbac cave.

"Kids, want to have some fun?" Tampulak asked as they entered the house.

"Definitely!" the teens replied, while the children cheered, "Yay!"

"What kind of fun?" one of the teens asked.

"We're going to swim at Asapa Falls. Let's go, you can see it from here."

The teens and children were excited about swimming, but when they saw the falls, they started complaining about its height and the difficulty of getting there. The adults on the team tried to persuade them that it would be a great experience. Eventually, they were all forced to go, despite their initial protests.

They were amazed by the height of the waterfall, which was surrounded by trees and greenery on both sides. The rocks on either side were smoothed by the flowing water. Even the catch basin had smooth rocks and greenery all around. People swimming and doing laundry were present when they arrived.

They all had a great time swimming. Paklit brought a dozen boiled brown eggs from his chicken coop. They also had cooked rice and ingredients for the main dish such as tomatoes, tamarind, onions, salt and ginger. Paklit trained Daniel and the others who were interested on how to catch bunog or river fish, which they later cooked into a sinigang dish, a sour fish soup.

"I can see ripe bananas over there! Does anyone know if they are wild or if someone owns them?" Paklit called out to the others swimming.

"I'm not sure, but we think they are wild," a group of boys replied.

Paklit then asked the boys if they could help him pick some bananas to share as dessert, and they were also invited to enjoy some of the leftovers. Suddenly, a loud splash interrupted everyone.

"What was that?" Daniel asked.

It appeared that no one had seen who or what caused the splash. A few minutes later, a large man emerged from the waters. It was Bryan, a local resident near the falls.

"I was wondering what caused the big splash. It was you all along," Paklit said, recognising the diver.

"Maybe those bananas belong to you. We picked some of the fruit," he added.

Bryan smiled and said, "It's okay. Those bananas were actually planted by an old man a long time ago, but no one has claimed them since."

Paklit invited Bryan to join the boys in eating, and he accepted the invitation.

"Hey, this is Bryan, by the way," Paklit introduced him to the family.

"Hello, by the way. Bring some of the boys to my house. I have some guavas and honey that I can't finish on my own. I want to give them to you," Bryan said.

They went to Bryan's house, which had a hay roof, log walls, and a door made from galvanised iron scraps. The guavas were on a tree to the right of the house. Bryan pointed at the guavas and gave them a plastic bag to put them in. He then went into his house and came out with two 1-liter coke bottles filled with honey. "Here is the honey," he handed them to Paklit. Paklit and his companions thanked Bryan and they all left.

They returned to the falls and shared the fruit, honey, and leftovers with everyone present. Daniel bit into a guava that had a red interior and the greenest peel he had ever seen. He observed the people enjoying life without any apparent problems chewing on the fruit. He sat on the right side of the falls, feeling the water splashing on him. Despite not having much as evident by their simple demeanor, the people seemed content and happy with their uncomplicated lives. Daniel was unaware that he was smiling as he watched them.

A stranger, a muscular man with a beard, offered him a bottle of beer. "Pal, have some beer," he said loudly. When Daniel didn't respond, the man tapped him on the shoulder and repeated his offer in a louder tone.

"Oh! Sorry! I didn't hear you!" Daniel exclaimed, feeling startled.

"It's okay, Mayma anyway," the man introduced himself.

"I'm Daniel," he said, gazing at the man as if he recognised him.

Mayma joined Daniel and they engaged in conversation. Mayma shared stories from the past that his grandfather used to recount. He revealed that his grandfather was once a renowned head hunter, but the practice had ceased because it became illegal in the eyes of the law. As they sipped on their beers, Mayma invited Daniel to join a group of men at the end of the catch basin, where a large boulder was situated. He introduced Daniel to everyone and everybody introduced themselves to Daniel. Daniel spotted his Uncle Paklit among the group, enjoying a case of beer and some deep-fried bunog with chili and soy sauce for added flavor.

The men were enjoying beers and pulutan, a type of food that pairs well with alcoholic drinks. Among the group were Baltazar and Pindang engaged in a heated conversation. They were answering each other's questions and responding to each other's comments. Baltazar's voice suddenly grew louder, and Pindang became argumentative. Both men were determined not to back down in their argument, although neither could remember the original cause of the disagreement.

The exchange was fueled by alcohol-induced words. Paklit and others near Pindang intervened and restrained him, while Baltazar was also held back. Both men were making gestures as if they were about to fight. Daniel, wanting to avoid the conflict, moved away from the chaos. Before the situation could escalate further, the group decided to leave and escorted Baltazar and Pindang to their respective homes.

"What was that about?" some of the people asked.

"I'm not sure. Just two intoxicated men having a disagreement," Daniel replied.

They simply chuckled at the situation and continued to enjoy the waters.

"I think we should leave too," Christine proposed.

They all left, while the arriving group stayed behind. Four beers were left by the men, and Daniel chose to bring them to his Uncle Paklit. The family made small talk, observing that going down the falls was simpler than hiking up, a conclusion evident from the terrain's incline.

Later that afternoon, the bus conductor gave Christine a letter addressed to them from an unfamiliar address. Excited, she opened in the presence of Daniel and Paklit, thinking it was important. It turned out to be a letter from a lawyer hired by Albert, along with the transfer papers for Grandma Kuling from The Land Title Bureau.

Paklit was furious, exclaiming, "I can't believe Albert would do this!"

Daniel and Christine remained quiet, providing support to their uncle. Daniel suggested that a family gathering was necessary. Upon examining the title transfer document, it was evident that Grandma Kuling's signature had been forged, as she was known to be a 'no read, no write individual' in short, an illiterate person.

The situation quickly turned into animosity towards Albert. Each family member felt that his actions were selfish and unacceptable. They began meeting at Paklit's house whenever they had free time, discussing plans to take legal action against Albert or even resort to extreme measures like hunting him down, similar to some mountain tribes' practices of headhunting during tribal conflicts. However, the most reasonable solution was to have a conversation with him, and even Daniel was prepared to give the money back to Albert without hesitation.

A family gathering was arranged where several relatives expressed their concerns about Albert. Those living nearby his address were urged to have a conversation with him to resolve issues within the family. Additionally, they were reminded about the upcoming family reunion in a month and a half, and Daniel was strongly encouraged to attend without fail.

Daniel reassured, "Don't worry, I haven't heard anything from work yet. I'll stay until they need me to come back."

After a day or two of the family meeting, some of the original relatives returned to their respective homes with the commitment to attend the family reunion. Daniel remained behind while he helped his Uncle Paklit with gardening and occasionally helped Christine with household tasks.

During his visit to Grandma Kuling, Daniel gained valuable insights into his heritage and mountain culture. He noticed that certain aspects of mountain culture were not embraced by the townspeople. Some devout Christians even viewed these traditions as satanic and condemned those who continued to uphold them.

A small gathering of the Banangan Family was taking place in their residence just below the elevated municipal hall. The event was open to everyone in town, as it was a tradition that once an occasion became public, no formal invitation was needed. Pigs were squealing, and the only remaining elder who practiced as the mambunong was invited to perform some rituals. According to the belief, one of the Banangan children had dreamed about their grandmother, which required the butchering of pigs.

Roy, the eldest sibling among seven, was present in their gathering with his wife Rose, son Takidang, and daughter Badasang, who had the dream. The mambunong required Roy's siblings to be present as well for it was Roy's side of the family who initiated it. Hilda, Roy's youngest sister and a devoted member of a Christian fellowship, chose not to attend, believing the ritual to be unchristian. Despite her family's wishes, she did not attend. Their parents had passed away years ago, and it was believed that the mother's spirit appeared in the granddaughter's dreams.

Hilda's strong Christian faith created a rift in her relationship with her siblings. She chose not to participate in family gatherings, like birthdays, because they were not mentioned in the Bible. She also refrained from singing secular songs and adhered to other religious restrictions as dictated by her Christian fellowship group.

The situation was widely known in town, with Daniel being a silent observer. Dangla, who resided a few blocks away from Paklit's house, paid a visit one day. Upon arrival, she encountered only Daniel. She attempted to discuss Bible studies with him and persuade him to join her fellowship, but Daniel consistently declined. Christine noticed Dangla departing her uncle's residence as she was on her way back from purchasing potatoes at the small store next to the municipal hall, which functioned as the town's market.

"Daniel! I saw Dangla leaving the house! Be cautious about getting involved with her group!" Christine cautioned Daniel.

"Don't worry. I'm aware of what her group is all about, as it's the same group that one of our colleagues belongs to and tried to recruit me into," Daniel replied with a smile.

"Okay I am relieved to hear that. I don't want to deal with another person who claims to know all about the Bible and criticising everything else as the work of the devil," Christina said with a sigh of relief.

The family reunion was finally here, taking place at the Elementary school grounds. The day before, clan members came together to prepare, with even police officers and other townspeople joining in. Strong men set up makeshift tents using a parachute borrowed from the municipal government. Pigs, carabaos, and even dogs were donated for the butchering. A mambunong, though not part of the clan, was invited to perform a spiritual ceremony.

Some clan members objected to the mambunong's presence, expressing their concerns during the reunion. Instead of getting to know their family, they departed from the venue with sudden heavy hearts. The others begged them to stay, but they were determined not to compromise.

Daniel observed the situation and thought to himself, "If they don't want to attend the family reunion, it's their loss. Those of us who are attending will not be ashamed."

The event began with a prayer from the mambunong, followed by a Christian prayer. Various songs were played and sung, including native, Christian, and secular tunes. The elders of the clan shared stories about Kibara and the olden days, which sparked memories in Daniel's mind. This feeling was intensified when family members were introduced on stage according to their grandparents. Daniel recognised many relatives by their names, such as Betot, his gay uncle, Mayangao, his granduncle, Kitan, his aunt, Dulagan, his uncle, and others.

The mambunong looked at Daniel with a perplexed expression, seeing him as a visitor from a bygone era in the mountain civilisation.

"What are you talking about?" Daniel asked with fear in his eyes.

"Don't worry. It is nothing bad. But do you recall something like you have lived in the past or something to that effect?"

Daniel was looking at the clouds, not paying any attention to the elder giving his speech on stage. "I had an accident and I had this long dream, but I can't remember it all."

"That was not a dream. Your soul was transported to the past."

Daniel was about to answer, but his sub-clan under his grandfather was called, and Christine called him out to be on stage.

A municipal employee approached him at the side of the stage and handed him a telegram from his workplace. The message stated that he was required to return to work as soon as possible. Uncertain of what to do, Daniel found himself being pulled into the bendiyan dance. Most of the younger family members did not join in, leaving mostly elders and some adults to participate. Daniel moved gracefully to the music of the gangsa, solibao, and tikitik. His enthusiasm was evident in his dance moves, and after the performance, he received applause from everyone.

"Look at Daniel! He may not have grown up in the mountains, but he dances like a pro! Isn't that embarrassing for us mountain dwellers?" the host joked.

Daniel took the stage and announced that he needed to return to the capital city for work and he was required to report the next day. His relatives begged him to stay a bit longer for the reunion, but he explained that he had to catch the last trip back and make it in time for work. He apologised for the situation and went to Grandma Kuling's house to say goodbye and apologise for leaving abruptly. He quickly packed his belongings, including his wet clothes from the clothesline, which he separated into a plastic bag and placed in his backpack.

He was thinking about Xi Yan but didn't have time to bid his farewell. Fortunately, he found a seat on the bus, avoiding having to stand in the aisle. The driver, Pangtal, was known for cramming the bus full of passengers, picking up anyone who flagged it down without concern for safety. He felt sympathy for those who needed to flag down the bus as trips were not readily available.

Daniel was frustrated by the slow driving as he needed to reach the city quickly for another trip to the Capital City. The bus was packed with passengers and luggage, with some even on the roof, called the top load, causing it to sway on the bumpy road. Daniel was seated on the left side, near the ravine, and was vigilant of the bus's movements. Suddenly, the driver shouted, "White Lady!" referring to a female spirit believed to be a victim of abuse by her husband, whose presence was said to bring misfortune to those who saw her.

The bus driver lost control of the vehicle, causing it to fall into the ravine and catch fire. Due to the lack of a rescue team and phone service, the accident went unnoticed for several hours. A passing elf truck, loaded with vegetables, spotted the burning bus. The driver and his helper quickly got out of the truck to help. They checked for survivors but found no response, so they traveled to the nearest town, Bokodian Municipality, for help. The town's men quickly organised a rescue operation, using a jeepney and their own tools and rope. Upon reaching the accident site, they shifted from rescue to retrieval efforts for there was no sign of life.

The clan received news of the accident a few hours after the retrieval operation. Everyone was shocked, and a prayer was offered. All able-bodied individuals traveled in a municipal-owned jeepney, a vehicle based on the G.I. wheelies commonly used for public transportation. They arrived at a cleared section of the road where remnants of the bus were still visible. The townspeople had erected a large wooden cross near the accident site by the ravine, not obstructing the road. The atmosphere was filled with sorrow and mourning. A pastor led a prayer for the victims, followed by a ritual performed by the mambunong.

Back at home, Grandma Kuling was inconsolable, crying uncontrollably to the point of almost having a heart attack. She was held and comforted by others. The Catholic church held a vigil, offering prayers for the victims and their families, seeking peace and comfort. Meanwhile, the Christian fellowship also prayed during their usual Sunday service, but they condemned the accident and criticised the victims, suggesting that they were being punished by God because most of them were Catholic, a faith they disapproved of and believed God would not save due to the church's practices.

"I am devastated by what happened to Daniel and the others on the bus. It's especially heartbreaking for Daniel, who was so passionate about learning about his heritage, unlike others who didn't seem to care," Kuling said, tears of sorrow streaming down his face.

The End

Acknowledgements

I am Lester Laoagan. A native Igorot from the Mountainous region of the Cordillera, Philippines. I have been reading many stories in my lifetime. However, I discovered writing when the world was hit with the COVID-19 Pandemic. When I am not writing, I do online work on the side. I also take care of my autistic brother together with my mother due to his dependence on us with his activities of daily living.

I would like to thank our almighty Lord because without him, all of this wouldn't be possible. I would also like to thank my loved ones, friends and those who supported me throughout my writing journey.

Thank you, First Nations Writers Festival.